KT-152-698

Lynda Page was born and brought up in Leicester. The eldest of four daughters, she left home at seventeen and has had a wide variety of office jobs. She has tried her hand at window dressing and overlocking and is presently Operations Liaison Officer at Land Rover Parts Ltd.

Lynda Page lives in a village near Leicester with her two teenage daughters.

Evie

Lynda Page

HEADLINE

First published in 1992
by HEADLINE BOOK PUBLISHING

First published in paperback in 1993
by HEADLINE BOOK PUBLISHING

20 19 18 17 16 15 14 13 12

ISBN 0 7472 3994 0

Printed and bound in Great Britain by
Clays Ltd, St Ives plc

HEADLINE BOOK PUBLISHING
A division of Hodder Headline PLC
338 Euston Road
London NW1 3BH

For Lynsey and Laura

I fully support a Government Health Warning against children – you have aged me beyond repair, but nevertheless, daughters don't come any better. To you both, with all my love, Mum.

ACKNOWLEDGEMENTS

Thank you to my friends and colleagues for all your help and support, and special thanks to Darley Anderson.

With love to Jenny Pullen, my 'bestest' friend.

Chapter One

'You thieving devil, Evie Grayson! You're no better than a common crook. I knew if I waited long enough I'd catch you at it!'

Florence Grayson stopped abruptly to catch her breath, her steel grey eyes staring piercingly across the room towards the girl she was addressing. She watched intently as the figure of her younger sister froze in horror, and she smiled – a sly smile of satisfaction which played on her thin lips. Her outburst had achieved just the result she had intended; her patience had finally paid off. She folded her bony arms under her flat bosom and took several steps into her bedroom.

'Thought you could fool me, didn't you? Thought I'd gone out. Well, I knew all along what your little game was.'

Evie stared open-mouthed at her reflection in the mirror. The appearance of Florrie was the last thing she expected. She quickly gathered her wits, took a deep breath and turned to face her sister.

'Florrie, let me explain . . .'

'Explain? There's nothing to explain!' spat Florrie.

Before Evie could say another word, Florrie lunged forward, swung back her arm and hit her forcefully across

1

the face. The blow sent Evie reeling backwards and she fell against the wall, knocking the breath out of her body. Florrie leapt after her, grabbed her by the hair and swung her around.

'What else have you stolen besides my blouse?' she demanded.

'Nothing, Florrie. Nothing, honest. I was only trying on your old blouse to see if the colour matched my new skirt. Now let me go, you're hurting me.'

'Hurting! Is that all? Try this!'

Florrie gave Evie's hair an almighty tug.

Evie screamed in pain and her anger boiled over. In retaliation she swung back her leg and kicked Florrie hard on the shins. Florrie yelped loudly and released her grip.

'You . . . you little brat!' she hissed.

She made a grab for Evie's hair again, missed and caught hold of the blouse, ripping a large hole in the sleeve. At the sound of tearing, Florence pushed Evie forcefully away.

'Now look what you've done. I bought that blouse with my first wage packet. You little bitch!' She stepped forward and went to attack Evie again, but this time her sister was too quick for her and blocked her arm.

'You hit me again, Florrie, and you'll regret it.'

The tone of Evie's voice left Florrie in no doubt that she meant business. She stared in amazement. This was the first time that Evie had ever stood up to her wrath and the shock had stunned her. She quickly regained her composure and scowled ferociously.

'You'll buy me a new blouse,' she demanded.

Evie's mouth opened wide in disbelief. 'You must be joking!'

'I said, you'll buy me a new one, or . . .'

'Or what?'

Florrie threw back her head and her eyes glinted wickedly. 'I'll tell Mam you took the day off work last Tuesday and were seen down the town.' She gave a sly smile as she watched the look of surprise spread across Evie's face.

'I did no such thing, Florrie Grayson!'

'I know that, but will Mother believe you? Especially since she found out you never went to Mavis's the other night, but to the pictures with Peter Maydown.'

A look of confused horror crossed Evie's face. 'It was you! It was you who told her! You've been spying on me.'

'You shouldn't lie, Evie, then your lies won't catch you out.'

'I wasn't lying! I was on my way to Mavis's when I bumped into Peter. His date had let him down and I felt sorry for him, so I agreed to go to the pictures to cheer him up.'

'That's not the way Mother saw it,' Florrie responded smugly.

'No! And you made sure of that, didn't you, Florrie?' Evie narrowed her eyes. 'Just what were you doing in town on Friday night – apart from spying on me, that is? You said you were going to help the Vicar clean out the hall. If anyone lied to Mother, it was you. If you saw me going into the pictures you couldn't have been anywhere near the church hall.'

'That's no concern of yours, Evie Grayson. I'm twenty-three years old and what I do on a Friday night is my business.'

Florrie patted her fine, mousey hair and felt the customary

stab of jealousy in the pit of her stomach as she looked at her younger sister.

At eighteen, Evie was blossoming into a beautiful young woman. Her copper red hair, thick and lustrous, flowed down to rest gently on her shoulders. Her creamy smooth skin had been spared the redhead's customary freckles, and large emerald green eyes stared watchfully from under her long, dark golden lashes as she waited with bated breath for her elder sister's next move.

Florence stared back at Evie with distaste. She felt neither love nor compassion for the young woman who stood before her. The fact was she detested the two people she lived with. They were the cause of all her pain and suffering and one day she would make them pay for it. She heard the sound of the back door shutting and knew their mother had returned.

Sharply she said, 'You'll give me the money for my ruined blouse. I want five shillings.'

'Five shillings!' Evie laughed. 'That old thing isn't worth tuppence.'

'You'll give me what it's worth, and I want it now!'

'Oh, you do, do you? Right!'

Evie pushed past Florrie and marched to her bedroom. She grabbed hold of her purse and turned to face her sister who had followed her.

'Here!' shouted Evie. 'Here's what it's worth.'

She slapped two pennies into Florrie's outstretched hand, gave her an almighty shove out on to the landing, slammed the door shut and threw across the bolt.

'Damn you, Florrie!' she hissed under her breath.

Pulling off the offending blouse, she hurled it disgustedly into the corner of her bedroom. Then, sighing deeply, she walked over to her bed and threw herself down on it. She gazed around the room, her expression lightening as she remembered the fun she and her mother had had as they had traipsed all over town looking for materials to redecorate it.

They had chosen a rose-patterned wallpaper and pink candlewick bedspread to match. Newly fitted shelves spanned the wide recess by the side of the chimney-breast and were crammed to overflowing with well-thumbed popular romance books, toiletries, and odds and ends that Evie had collected over her eighteen years. The large pine wardrobe was bursting with clothes and accessories and by the Lloyd Loom chair sat Evie's pride and joy: a record player surrounded by an assortment of seventy-eight r.p.m. records.

Jumping up, she ran over to the record player, selected a popular jive and turned up the volume. She swayed to the rhythm of the music as her thoughts dwelt longingly on the dress she had seen in Lena's Modes. It was a dream of a dress. The colour matched her emerald green eyes exactly; its full skirt and five net underskirts would enhance her figure to perfection. The dress had surely been created with her in mind and she was going to have it at all costs.

She wrapped her arms around her body and hugged herself as she thought of what she would look like wearing the dress. She would look wonderful; handsome young men would be falling at her feet, fighting for her attention. She threw herself on her bed and folded her hands behind her head. Another few weeks and she would have enough money to buy it, just in time for the annual church ball. A broad grin crossed her face. Janice Moran would be beside herself with jealousy. 'That will teach her to try and out-dress me,' Evie thought mischievously.

* * *

The Graysons, Edith and her daughters Florence and Evelyn, lived in a comfortable, three-bedroomed semi on the north side of Leicester. Henley Road was a pleasant, grass-verged, tree-lined street, served by a good bus service and in easy walking distance of a parade of shops. The residents were all respectable, hard-working people who tended their well-kept gardens and kept their children and animals under control.

Evie, like most young girls of her time, took the city she lived in for granted. Her mind was too fully occupied with the latest fashions, boys, film stars, and other teenage trivia to notice the fine Victorian buildings that lined the streets and housed the assortment of stores she visited regularly in the centre of town. What she did notice was the range of clothes and accessories they stocked. It never crossed her mind that many of her purchases were manufactured in the various factories dotted in and around the city. She thought only of the increased variety of styles and colours since the war finished over five years ago.

As she hurried to and from work it never occurred to her that not only was Leicester in the forefront of the hosiery trade but also in engineering and shoe manufacturing. What interested her was the variety of jobs that were on offer to women as she scanned the *Leicester Mercury*, just in case she decided to change her occupation.

The years of hostilities had left their mark on the old Roman town. Men returned full of energy and hope to find only a dreary, miserable environment in which to live. Their town, which had fared better than some in the great depression of the 1930s, was badly in need of a face lift. Gradually, improvements had taken place. Old building sites were cleared to make way for new factories, and housing estates sprang up to cope with the ever increasing number of people moving to the city in the hope of finding work.

Leicester, in 1951, was classed a woman's town. Liberated by the war, they were no longer content to stay at home, and contributed greatly to the workforce. Young women of Evie's age had no problem in finding work in the hosiery trade, even if the pay was low and the conditions antiquated. Work for men was more scarce and the dole queues stretched endlessly. The war had changed things: it was now their wives who were the breadwinners.

The rationing of luxury items was still in force and women, fed up with the drabness of the war years, were taking a great interest in fashion again. To be the best in the business was paramount, and designers, factory owners and traders wanted their clothes to be the ones most sought after, and would go to any lengths to achieve this.

Factories of all sizes produced everything from knickers to suits, ballgowns to bathing costumes. Goods from Leicester were sold everywhere in the world.

The more affluent members of society had money to burn, gained mostly by a nose for business or, in some cases, on the thriving black market during the war. These people flaunted their wealth. They wanted to look good and be admired. They bought cars, television sets and telephones, and were held in awe by their less fortunate neighbours. The working-class people of Leicester, as in the rest of the country, wanted to enjoy themselves. They revelled in broadcasts of 'The Goons' and 'The Archers' on the radio, and on Friday nights packed dance halls would ring with the sounds of the big bands belting out all the latest hits, such as 'Magic Moments' and 'Singing in the Rain'.

Evie spent her leisure time dancing at church socials, going to the pictures and dreaming of boys – in complete contrast to her older sister, who apart from work seemed interested only in church matters.

Twenty minutes after her confrontation with Florrie, Evie gingerly poked her head around the door of the comfortably furnished living room. Her mother was sitting by the fire knitting; the standard lamp behind her armchair cast a soft glow over her fine features. At forty-three, Edith Grayson was still a very attractive woman. Her chestnut brown hair had only the odd strand of grey and the only signs of aging were the fine crow's feet around her tawny eyes. At five foot seven, Evie was an inch taller than her mother and still had a long way to go before she acquired Edith's social graces, but for all the age difference, at a distance strangers would have mistaken them for sisters.

Edith raised her head as her daughter entered.

'Is she out?' Evie asked tentatively.

'If you mean your sister, yes, she is.'

'Good.'

Evie entered the room and threw herself on the settee, her long legs hanging over the arm. Edith watched as Evie plumped up a cushion behind her back and settled herself.

'What was that commotion I heard when I came in?'

'Oh, nothing, Mam.'

'Evie, were you two fighting again?'

'It wasn't me, it was her,' sulked Evie. 'I borrowed her old blouse just to see if the colour matched the new skirt you made me, and she hit the roof.'

'And did you ask her permission to go into her bedroom to try it on?'

''Course I did.'

'Evie!'

'Well, no, not exactly.' She hung her head. 'I thought she was out.'

'Oh, Evie.' Edith dropped her knitting in her lap and sighed. 'I get sick to death of these silly, petty arguments. When are you two going to learn to live together?'

'You should be asking her that question, not me. She starts as soon as I walk into the room. She'd try the patience of a saint.'

'And you're no saint, are you, Evie? You're just as bad. How would you feel if she went into your room and tried on your clothes, eh?'

Evie looked at her mother and shrugged her shoulders.

'See, you wouldn't like it.' Edith picked up her knitting and slipped a needle through a loop of wool. She gave another sigh and her face softened. 'I know Florrie can be difficult, my dear. But it doesn't help when you provoke her.'

'I don't have to provoke her. The slightest thing starts her off.'

'Well, next time she starts, just take a deep breath and walk away. Then she'll get fed up and stop doing it. Please, Evie.'

'What?' she retorted, lowering her long legs to the carpet and sitting forward. 'Why should I?'

Edith slapped down her knitting again and stared crossly at her daughter. 'Because I ask you to, that's why.'

'You mean, you want me to let her do the rotten things

9

she does, and not say anything? Is that what you mean, Mam?'

'Yes.'

'Well, I won't! She treats me and you like dirt and I'm not going to let her get away with it any more.' Evie felt her hackles rise. 'She's not even in this room and she's got us at it. I hate it when we fight, Mam, especially over her. She's a nasty, spiteful piece of work. I sometimes wonder if she *is* my sister.' Evie paused and frowned. 'She isn't like you and me. She's always picking fault and being hurtful.'

'Well, maybe that's not her fault,' Edith said softly.

'Well, whose fault is it if it's not hers? She's your daughter, Mam. Who does she take after? Dad?'

'No, she doesn't take after him,' Edith replied sharply. 'I've told you before, your father was a kind, loving man.' Her voice softened to a whisper. 'It's just a great pity he died so young.'

'Yes, I know, Mam,' said Evie, ashamed. 'I didn't mean to say that, I'm sorry.' She paused thoughtfully for a moment. 'Who does Florrie take after, then? You never talk about the rest of the family. You told me they were all dead. Were they like Florrie – nasty and wicked?'

'She's not all nasty and wicked, Evie. She can be quite kind sometimes. Look how she nursed old Mrs Bayliff back to health when she broke her hip.'

'Yes, she did. But that was only because she was hoping the old lady would mention her in her will.'

'Evie!'

'Sorry, Mam.' She tightened her lips. 'There's one thing I do know – that our Florrie doesn't take after either of us, in looks or manner.' She stopped abruptly and stared at her mother. 'Are my relatives all dead, the whole lot of them?'

'Yes,' Edith snapped.

'Well, what were they like? Please tell me, Mam.'

'There's nothing to tell,' Edith said abruptly. She looked up at the clock on the mantle. 'Evie, switch on the television, there's a good show on . . .'

'Oh, come on, Mam, stop changing the subject. There must be something you can tell me. Everyone has a mother and father . . .'

'I've told you before, Evie. There are some things that don't concern you.'

The girl sighed loudly. 'Don't concern me! Surely my own family history concerns me?'

'Go and make another cup of tea, Evie.'

'What?'

'I said, go and make a cup of tea. Please.'

She stared in defiance at her mother, then slowly stood up, picked up the tea tray and headed towards the small kitchen. Once again her mother had avoided answering any of her questions. Evie frowned. Why? Just what was it she was afraid of? The kettle began to boil and Evie picked up a tea towel to dry the cups. She knew she would have to carry on wondering, because apart from her mother there was no one else to ask. She picked up the kettle and poured boiling water into the teapot.

As Evie busied herself in the kitchen, Edith sat deep in thought. She had watched her daughter intently as she left the room. Now a worried expression crossed her face. Evie was practically an adult. She was bright and inquisitive, and avoiding her questions was getting more and more difficult.

She shuddered. Evie would have to be told the truth about her past. She knew her daughter would weather the shock, but was she herself strong enough to withstand the inevitable backlash and repercussions? Edith picked up her knitting as she heard footsteps in the hall. Yes, sooner or later she would have to be told. But for her own part, Edith would prefer it to be later. Much later.

As Evie placed the tray on the coffee table, Edith noticed she had brought in only one cup.

'Are you not having a cup of tea?'

'No. I thought I'd pop over to Maureen Green's house for a while. Her brother managed to get hold of a pile of American movie magazines from his pal at the American Air Force base at Cottingham. He says we can look through them.'

'Oh!' Edith tried to hide her dismay. 'I don't know about you mixing with Americans . . .'

'Mam, I'm not. It's only the magazines we're looking at.'

Edith looked relieved. 'Oh, well, in that case I don't mind. But you won't be late, will you? Only you know how I worry when you're out in the dark. You never know who's lurking about.'

'Stop fussing, Mam. I'm eighteen now, I can take care of myself.'

'What do you mean, stop fussing? You might be eighteen but you're still under my care, Evie, and don't you forget it.'

'Mam, I'm not a little girl any more. You don't have to check on everything I do. I'm quite capable of making up my own mind about things.'

'Yes, I do realise that, Evie. But all the same, I'll decide when you're grown up enough for me to stop worrying about you. Now, you'd better go or it won't be worth it.'

Evie relented. 'Okay, I'll catch the last bus and be in by eleven.'

'All right, love. I'll have your Ovaltine ready. And you'd better wrap up well and take your umbrella in case it rains.'

Evie leaned over and kissed her mother on the cheek. 'You don't have to wait up, Mam, I'll be perfectly all right.'

'I don't mind, Evie, I like to see you home safe. I wouldn't sleep knowing you were still out.'

'Okay, Mam.' Evie walked out of the room and donned her warm winter coat and thick knitted scarf. She picked up her umbrella, looked at it for a moment, and smiled to herself as she put it back into the umbrella stand and walked out of the front door into the damp January night.

Alice Trimble walked slowly down the long aisle of overlocking machines. A thin bony woman, she eyed her charges like a bird of prey, ready to claw with red-painted talons anyone stepping out of line. She stopped abruptly in front of Evie and folded her arms under her flat bosom. The girl stopped her machine and looked up at her supervisor.

Mrs Trimble was wearing a scarf turban-style, in the fashion popularised in the war. A curler had lodged between the edge of the turban and her ear and Evie stifled a smile. The wearing of turbans had been generally abandoned after the war, but Alice Trimble still wore hers. Most of the factory women swore, but the supervisor's language was dreadful. She was very clever, acting the lady in front of the management, but when they weren't around, the girls under her charge watched their backs.

Most of her charges knew that Alice Trimble stole finished garments and lengths of cloth. She would hide the purloined articles in the big waste baskets, ready to be picked up on her way out at night. Alice's husband had a stall on the market and Evie often saw him selling bargains that had previously been sewn up by her and her fellow workers.

None of the girls liked Alice Trimble. Now, as she stood menacingly in front of Evie, the girl shuddered, wondering what was in store for her.

'You're wanted in the office,' Alice said harshly.

Evie strained her ears to hear what the supervisor was saying over the drone of the machines. She felt a feeling of foreboding creep over her.

'But what have I done?'

Alice Trimble's face spread into a broad grin. 'Well, gel, I ain't sure. But it must be bad 'cos the Personnel bloke's come down. Now get off your arse and get up there.'

Evie switched off her machine, and with trembling legs scurried down the aisle towards the Factory Manager's office.

Alice Trimble stared after her, beady little eyes glinting in anticipation, hoping the girl was about to be sacked. There was something fishy about Evie, something she could not put her finger on. She tightened her arms under her bust. Well, she would soon know.

She turned towards Maureen Green who sat behind Evie.

'What yer staring at, yer gormless idiot? Get back to work. We don't pay yer tuppence a dozen for nothin'.'

She stalked off, and Maureen stuck out her tongue and motioned with two fingers at her back.

Evie's heart raced as she tapped gently on the glass door of the office and entered. The small room was crammed with filing cabinets, piles of sample garments and rolls of cloth. Jack Pollock, a small, rotund, bald-headed man in his fifties, sat behind a large desk. This, like the office, was cluttered, and as Evie opened the door the draught sent a sheaf of papers flying on to the floor. Jack ignored the papers, smiled up at Evie and motioned her to sit down.

'This is Mr Williams, the Personnel Manager,' he said kindly.

Evie looked across at the distinguished-looking man seated to the left of Mr Pollock. Mr Williams nodded his head in acknowledgement and waited while she settled herself in a chair placed before Jack Pollock's desk.

'You've been here, let me see ... .' Mr Williams was opening a brown file '. . . over four years, and you've been in several departments on the factory floor since you started.'

'Yes, I have, sir. I feel like a yo-yo sometimes.' Evie wanted to bite back the observation and quickly placed her hand over her mouth.

Mr Williams's lips twitched into a brief smile. 'I can imagine. But this is 1951 and we like our girls at Dawson's to be flexible.' He closed the brown file and looked straight at her. 'We've a vacancy in the General Office, to learn the switchboard, typing, etcetera. Your name's been put forward.'

'Oh!' was all Evie could say.

'The pay's lower than in the factory, but we'll make it up and send you to College to learn typing and office procedures. It's a good opportunity, I hope you will consider it.' Mr Williams stood up and smiled at her. 'Think on it and let Mr Pollock know your decision tomorrow.'

Evie nodded as Mr Williams picked his way over the littered floor and departed. She turned to Jack Pollock.

'Why me, Mr Pollock? None of the other girls has been around the factory like I have, and now this.'

'It's not your place to ask questions, Miss Grayson. Just be grateful you're getting the opportunity. If you've any sense you'll jump at it.' Jack Pollock looked at his watch. 'Now back to your machine, time is money.' He stood up. 'Come and see me in the morning. And if you have any sense, you won't say anything to Mrs Trimble or the other girls about this.'

She nodded and left the office deep in thought, walking slowly back to her work station.

The girls sat in long rows, heads bent over their machines, not daring to look up in case the supervisor caught them, or even worse they lost time, which meant money.

Dawson's had been in production since the 1850s and the present Mr Dawson was the grandson of the founder. The factory was situated on St Margaret's Way, about half a mile from the town centre and handy for the shops and adjacent main bus station. Dawson's consisted of several Victorian buildings all huddled together around a central courtyard. The buildings were antiquated and badly in need of repair. The old water troughs catering for the horses of bygone days had been removed. In their place stood flowerbeds and a large lawned area where, during the summer months, workers would lounge and eat their pack ups.

Dawson's made garments from scratch. They knitted their own fabric, dyed it, cut it into shape, and then passed it to girls like Evie for overlocking, sewing and finishing, ready to be sold to outlets worldwide. The range of clothes and undergarments Dawson's produced was wide and the Dawson trade mark was well respected throughout the trade.

Evie had worked here since leaving school at fourteen. She had had no intention of working in the hosiery trade, much preferring a more glamorous occupation, but had somehow found herself, one April morning, walking through the large iron gates of Dawson's with the rest of the four thousand workforce. She had started off in the laundry and progressed to the machining and overlocking departments, mastering several trades on the way. Now she could turn out a good garment quickly and neatly.

She arrived back at her machine just as the hooter sounded. She sighed with relief to have been spared Alice Trimble's cross examination until next morning.

Later that night, she related the day's events to her mother and Florrie as they sat around the kitchen table eating their evening meal. Apart from her own bedroom Evie loved this room the most. It faced south, and during the summer the sun's rays filled every corner of the room from early morning until late into the evening. Edith had painted it yellow and white, and to Evie it always felt warm and inviting whenever she ventured in. As a young child, she had often hidden in the large pantry and crammed her mouth full of home made biscuits, or better still small Welsh cakes filled with juicy currants, not for one minute feeling guilty for her greediness.

On this cold dark night, the yellow and white gingham curtains were tightly drawn and the room radiated warmth as Evie hungrily ate her delicious meal of faggots and mushy peas.

'It's a grand opportunity, Evie. You are going to accept, I hope?' Edith asked.

'Oh, I don't know what to do yet, Mam. If I do take it none of the girls is going to speak to me again.'

'That doesn't matter. You've got a chance to improve yourself and you'll soon get to know the other office girls. They're a better class . . .'

'Oh, yes?' Florrie piped up, unable to control her jealousy any longer. 'The girls on the factory floor aren't good enough for our precious Evelyn, is that it?'

'Don't be silly, Florrie,' Edith snapped. 'I only meant that the office girls are a bit more refined, that's all. Why do you have to take everything I say the wrong way? You work in the Accounts Department. You should know well enough what I mean.'

Florrie's small eyes hardened. 'I got there by sheer hard work. What's she ever done to earn this promotion? Why, she can't even sew straight. That's why she's overlocking knickers . . .'

'I can sew straight, Florrie, that's unfair,' shouted Evie. 'And the knickers I happen to be working on at the moment are an exclusive line . . .'

'Girls, stop this.' Edith tried to interrupt the heated exchange.

'Well, I think it's fishy,' Florrie continued, ignoring her. 'The management doesn't just pick someone from the factory floor to work in the office. There must be three hundred girls in the overlocking department, and they pick Evie? No, something's not right.' She paused for a moment and the corners of her mouth twitched. 'What have you been doing, spreading your favours around?'

Without thinking, Evie picked up her glass of milk and threw it over Florrie who gasped for breath. She scraped back her chair and stood up, the milk dripping from the ends of her hair down on to her clothes.

'You little . . .' she hissed.

'That's enough. The pair of you get upstairs.' Edith pushed her chair back and jumped up. 'I'll have none of this in my house,' she shouted angrily.

'My father's money paid for this house!' Florrie spat, glaring intently at her.

'Your father was my husband. That makes it *my* house. Now get upstairs the both of you and don't come down again tonight.'

'But I'm starving, Mam, I want to finish my dinner,' Evie cried.

'I said, get up the stairs!'

Edith stood resting her clenched fists on the table as she watched the two girls depart. Several moments later she took a deep breath, stormed up the stairs and banged loudly on Florrie's bedroom door. When there was no response, she banged even louder.

'Open this door now, Florrie!' she bellowed.

She heard the bolt slip back and watched impatiently as the door slowly opened.

'What do you want?'

Edith pushed past her and marched into the room. It felt cold. Florrie had not bothered to light her gas fire. The room was very sparsely furnished. The brown, almost threadbare carpet and slate grey quilt lying neatly on the single bed accentuated the icy atmosphere. Florrie had flatly refused to let Edith decorate the room for her, insisting that she liked it just the way it was.

Florrie stood with her back against the closed door. Her black straight skirt and grey blouse hung limply on her small thin body. The old-fashioned bobbed hairstyle did nothing but accentuate her sharp, plain features. Edith itched to take her in hand and show her how much more attractive she could make herself, but as always with any kind offer, Florrie had flatly refused. Now her small grey eyes hardened as she looked at her mother with distaste.

'Well, what d'you want?'

Edith's face paled. 'Will you stop speaking to me like I'm a lump of dirt? I'm your mother, and while you're in my house you will treat me as such. I told Evie the other night and now I'm telling you – I want both of you to stop this feuding. I will not put up with it any more. Is that understood?'

'You're telling me to get out, is that it?'

'I'm saying nothing of the sort. Stop twisting things, Florrie. This is your home for as long as you want, but you will live here under my rules.'

'You mean, I can stay here under sufferance?'

'Under sufferance!' Edith hissed. 'Anyone would think you lived in a hovel. I keep the house spotless. It's got all the latest facilities. You come and go as you please, and there's always a hot meal waiting for you. You call that sufferance? It's about time you sorted yourself out, Florence, and counted your blessings.'

Florrie walked over to her dressing table and picked up a packet of cigarettes. She selected one, lit it and slowly exhaled the smoke. She stared at Edith, a slight smile playing on her lips.

'Just answer me one question, Mother – was it sufferance for you when my dad died and you were left with me on your hands?' Florrie watched as Edith's face turned even paler.

'What d'you mean?'

'You know perfectly well what I mean.'

Edith sank slowly down on to the bed and stared at her intently.

'You know, don't you?'

'Know? Of course I know! How stupid do you think I am?'

Edith sighed deeply. 'How long have you known I wasn't your real mother?'

'Does that matter?'

'Yes, it does!'

Florrie took a long draw on her cigarette and eyed Edith mockingly. 'My grandmother told me the day of my father's funeral.'

'Your grandmother! I don't understand. . .'

'Yes, my grandmother. My real mother's mother.'

'But you never knew her . . .'

'Oh, but I did. I saw quite a lot of her before she died. She was very informative, was my grandmother. Told me lots of things about you.' Florrie raised her head, a smug expression on her face. 'Anyway, to confirm what she said I went through your drawers and found my birth certificate.'

'You did what!'

'Well, it was obvious that *you* were never going to tell me.'

'Florrie, I never told you because I didn't want to hurt you any more than was necessary. What would you have done if I had told you? Left home? To go where? Live with your drunken old granny in a rat-infested tumbledown back-to-back?'

'My grandmother did not drink!' Florrie cried.

'Oh, but she did, Florence. Enough to fill a dustbin with bottles every week. I certainly wasn't going to let you go there.'

'Why not? I'd have been better off with my grandmother. She loved me. She was my own family. You and that daughter of yours are no relation to me.'

Edith's stomach churned from the impact of these words. 'You do love to hurt people don't you, Florrie? You get a great deal of satisfaction out of hurting people close to you. I can't understand you.' She paused for a moment and ran her hand over her forehead. 'For your information, your grandmother didn't want you.'

'She did!' Florrie shouted. 'She told me. She begged you to let me go to her. She even offered you money . . .'

'No, Florrie. Your grandmother lied to you. She took money from me to stay out of your life.'

'You liar! My grandmother was right. You're a devious liar. She told me not to believe a word you said. Anyway, what did it matter to you where I lived?'

'It mattered a great deal, and still does. Whether you like it or not, Florence, I care about you.'

'What a load of rot!' she sneered. 'All you've ever cared about is your precious Evie.'

'That's not true and you know it.' Edith ran her fingers through her hair. 'Why didn't you say something? Why didn't you tell me you knew? At least I could have explained.'

'You've had plenty of opportunity to explain, but you just kept up the pretence.' Florrie stubbed her cigarette out in an overflowing ashtray and attacked Edith head on.

'I've hated you for what you've done to me. You killed

my dad then took my share of his money and used it to keep yourself and that daughter of yours in luxury . . .'

'Now just a minute,' Edith cut in savagely. 'I did not kill your dad. He . . . he . . .'

'Hanged himself,' Florrie snarled. 'Yes, I know that as well. It was because of you he took his own life and left me all on my own, and don't you deny it.'

'I am denying it, Florrie, and you have no right to be saying things like this. Your dad was under a lot of pressure . . .'

'Under a lot of pressure! Why was he? I'll tell you why. Because of your carryings on!'

'My carryings on?'

'Yes, with that bloke. The one you're still carrying on with.'

Edith sighed. 'Oh, that bloke. Florrie, you don't understand . . .'

'No, and I don't want to hear your lies about it. But I do want my share of Dad's money.'

Edith rose from the bed. 'Your father left no money. He never even had an insurance policy.'

Florrie clenched her fists. 'Don't lie. We live like lords and you say he left no money? You must think I'm really thick or something. Even I can work out that the money me and Evie give you plus the money from your job at the wool shop doesn't keep us in this luxury.'

'No, it doesn't,' Edith said quietly. 'But how I keep this house up is none of your business.'

'None of my business . . .'

'No, it's not.' Edith straightened her back and glared at Florrie. 'Sit down. You're going to hear some home truths, whether you like them or not.' She saw Florrie open her mouth to speak. 'I said, sit down.'

Florrie's mouth snapped shut as she lowered herself on to her bed.

Edith walked across to the window and leaned against the sill.

'I'm sorry you found out the way you did. I'm also sorry you felt you couldn't come to me about it.' She clasped her hands together. 'I don't know what else your grandmother told you and I don't want to, but you'll hear my side.' She raised her head and stared at Florrie. 'I loved your father very much, and when your mother died we married and I took you on as a daughter. When Evelyn came along, we treated you the same. If you had a new dress so did Evie, and that's the way it has continued. Life was hard, your dad's wage at Dawson's wasn't all that great, but we managed.' She paused and took a deep breath. 'No one was more heartbroken than I was when Freddy died, but I had two children to support so I went out to work and brought you up the best way I could. I treat you as a daughter. It's not my fault that you decided to shun me and block everything I've tried to do for you. But I will carry on regardless until the day you decide to leave.'

'And the sooner the better, eh?' Florrie cut in. 'But you still haven't explained how you managed to buy this house?'

'No, and I don't intend to. That is none of your business. But I can assure you, it was my money and not your dad's. And when I die, everything I own is split between you and Evie.'

'Nice,' Florrie said sarcastically. 'Well, you can take my name out of your will. I won't need it.'

'Oh, won't you?'

'No, I won't, and I don't intend to tell you why not either.'

'That's your prerogative.'

'Yes, it is.' Florrie took a deep breath and tightened her lips. 'I don't believe a word you've said. I don't believe you've ever cared a damn for me, and I don't believe you loved my father or that he left no money.'

Edith narrowed her eyes. 'Again that's up to you, and to be honest, when you're in this mood, I don't really care. But what I do care about is Evie. She doesn't know you are only her half sister, and if you breathe a word, your feet won't touch the floor.'

'Are you threatening me?'

'Yes, I am,' Edith said coldly. 'Things are bad enough between you both as it is, without dropping this on her.' She paused for a moment and looked hard at Florrie. 'It wouldn't hurt you to smile a little and enjoy life. It's much more pleasant to be civil, it makes life a lot happier.'

'Does it? For whom? You?'

'Yes, and you. Now, I'm asking you to stop your spitefulness, and maybe we can have a bit of harmony in this house for a change.'

Edith walked towards the door and opened it. She turned and addressed Florrie once more. 'And in future, if you're going to work late, I would appreciate a telephone call, because I am fed up with throwing good food in the dustbin.' She left the room and shut the door.

Florrie watched Edith depart then walked over to her bed and threw herself down. Lying with her back against the headboard, she crossed her thin arms behind her head and stared up at the ceiling. Her thoughts drifted back over the years. She was ten years old and it was the day of her father's funeral.

It had been horrible. Her safe happy world had crumbled around her. Never again would she look up into the handsome face of her father and see his clear blue eyes twinkling down at her as he tucked her into bed; hear his merry laugh when he was happy or his scolding when he was angry. She would never feel his comforting arms encircle her small thin body, making her feel safe and secure. Her heart had broken into pieces as she had watched them lower her beloved father's coffin into the sodden wet earth. She had looked up to see her mother's beautiful face all ashen and drawn as she stood grief-stricken by the graveside holding Evie's hand. Florrie had desperately wanted to run and hold her, to comfort her, to grieve with her for the wonderful man they had all lost. Instead, before anyone could stop her, she had turned, fled through the cemetery, thrown herself on a bench and wept.

'Well, yer on yer own now, gel.'

The voice, harsh and rasping, made her jump and she uncovered her face to see a gnarled old figure standing before her. The woman was dressed in shabby, dirty clothes. The black shapeless coat was tied around the middle by an old piece of string and Florrie cringed as the woman shuffled forward and sat down next to her.

'She killed 'im, yer know. As sure as I'm sitting 'ere, she killed 'im. I've come to warn yer, gel, you'll 'ave to watch 'er now. Make sure you get what's coming to yer, or she'll 'ave the lot.'

Florrie sniffed loudly and wiped her face with the back of her hand. She rose hesitantly and sidled away, desperate to escape from the frightening old woman.

'Don't mind me, me duck. I'm only yer granny,' the woman said haughtily as she put her hand in her pocket and pulled out a dirty ragged handkerchief. She placed it to her nose and blew loudly, inspected it, then thrust it back. 'Don't need to be frightened of me, gel. I'm the only family you got left. 'Course you wouldn't know that. She'll 'ave kept that from yer.' She nodded her head towards Florrie. 'Dangerous, see.' She paused and sniffed loudly. 'Wouldn't do for you to know, that would really put paid to 'er plans. Wouldn't surprise me if she put the noose round 'is neck 'erself. She's devious that one, spiteful and devious, and you'll 'ave to watch 'er.' The woman patted the bench. 'Sit down. It's about time yer learned the truth, 'cos you won't 'ear it from anyone else.'

'I have to go,' Florrie stuttered, eyes wide in alarm. 'My mother will be looking for me.'

The woman raised her head sharply. 'Yer mother! She ain't yer mother and she's no right to say she is. Your mother was my daughter. I should know, I watched yer come into the world. Scraggy little brat yer were. We didn't think you'd live. But yer did. Then she comes along and takes 'im away. Me poor daughter died wi' shame and you were left to 'er mercies.'

Florrie, frightened and shaking, stared agog at the woman. 'I think you've got me mixed up with somebody else, Mrs . . . er . . . Mrs . . .'

'Badcock. Mrs Badcock. Your mother was me daughter Edna, and if yer want proof, just ask that woman for yer birth certificate. That should tell yer all yer need to know. Anyway, I've only to look at yer. You're the spit of our Edna. I'd 'ave known yer anywhere.'

Florrie stared at the ugly dirty creature and felt a shiver

27

of fear pass over her. How could she be related to this awful woman? Her mother was Edith Grayson. She was! Florrie could never remember a time when her mother had not been there. Her mother loved her. She was always saying so. Her mind raced. This woman was wrong, she was mixing her up with someone else. She had to be; there was no other explanation. She suddenly froze. Maybe the woman had escaped from the loony bin? Oh, her mother would go daft if she knew she had been talking to strangers.

'I have to go.'

'Please yerself. Only you get 'old of yer birth certificate.' The woman rose and wagged a swollen finger in Florrie's direction. 'Yer can find me at 13 Forest Street. Remember, 13 Forest Street. Ask for yer Granny Badcock.' She laughed harshly and shuffled away.

Florrie watched the figure waddling and coughing its way down the narrow path until it disappeared, then she ran as quick as her little legs would carry her back to her mother and safety.

The encounter preyed on her mind though, until finally she just had to find out for herself. It had been fairly easy to slip into her mother's room and rummage through her drawers. Edith had taken to sitting by the fire for long periods just staring into the flames and didn't notice her slip away.

Florrie finally found what she was looking for and as she unfolded the document an icy fear gripped her heart. The woman had spoken the truth. The name of her real mother, written in black spidery handwriting, leapt from the sheet: Edna Badcock.

From that moment Florrie changed. The happy carefree child became an aloof, ill-mannered stranger. She felt alienated from her family, gripped by an overwhelming feeling of desolation. Not only had she lost her father, but the people she had always thought were her mother and sister, and as time went by bitterness worked its way into her very soul.

Edith was bewildered and confused by the sudden change in her. At first she put it down to grief for the loss of her father, but as time went by and Florrie's attitude worsened, no excuses could be made. She fought long and hard to return the child to her former self, but everything she did or said had no effect. Florrie sank further and further into her own isolated world.

Eventually, she plucked up the courage to visit her grandmother. She had been disgusted by what she found. The stench and the filth repelled her. Empty bottles and stale food littered the two small rooms she occupied; piles of dirty clothes and newspapers blocked the corners and spilled out over the worn linoleum. But still she returned, driven by an obsession to discover her origins. Her grandmother wasted no time in spilling out her venom on the unsuspecting girl, fuelling her more and more with hatred and contempt for the woman who had cared and loved her for nearly all her young life. Florrie vowed on her grandmother's deathbed to devote her life to wreaking revenge on the woman who had not only been responsible for her father's death but also caused her real mother and grandmother so much pain.

Florrie unfolded her arms and sat up. A smile played around her mouth. The time for getting even was drawing closer. It had taken cunning and planning to achieve her aims and in the process she had been fortunate enough to come across a man who loved her – loved her for herself as she loved him – and who was only too willing to help. He had his own reasons for wanting to be party to her plans, but that didn't matter. The only thing that mattered was satisfying her own hatred, and that was about to be done.

Edith meanwhile sat at the kitchen table, tears of grief cascading down her cheeks. She wrung her hands in despair as she lifted her swollen eyes towards the ceiling. 'Oh, Florrie. Poor, poor Florrie. What did I do to make you hate me so much?'

Chapter Two

It was Saturday afternoon and Evie was doing what she liked most of all: meandering around the shops in the town centre. Lewis's Department Store, with its four floors of quality merchandise, held an irresistible fascination for her and her pace quickened as she dodged through the crowd of people towards the Helena Rubenstein perfume counter. Several perfume testers later, she looked in her purse and frowned. The blouse she had bought to go with her new chocolate brown skirt had cost more than she had anticipated and if she wanted to buy her weekly supply of stockings and a new pair of earrings, the delectable fragrance she had fallen for would have to wait for another week.

Reluctantly she left the perfume behind and found her way out of the store. She glanced up at the time as she passed by the clock tower standing proudly at the bottom of Gallowtree Gate. 'Blimey,' she muttered under her breath. The time had flown by and if she didn't hurry and get the rest of the shopping she would be late for her meeting with Mavis.

She quickly scurried around the maze of green-canvas-topped, wooden trestle market stalls, amid the cries of the stallholders shouting their wares. The market was packed with shoppers pushing and shoving to get the best buys and as she dodged through them, she glanced at the list her mother had given her. Quickly, she sussed out the stalls with the best bargains and made her purchases, keeping an eye on the stall holder, just in case he tried to fob her off with mouldy fruit and vegetables taken from the back of the pile.

As usual, her own purchases caused her the biggest headache as she stood faced with the problem of wanting to buy three pairs of earrings and only having enough money for two. She finally chose a pair of imitation pearl clip-ons that were dearer than the other three pairs put together, deciding to make do with one pair of stockings for the week. If she laddered them, she could always beg a pair from her mother.

She arrived at Brucciani's coffee house with two minutes to spare. Brucciani's was situated on Horsefair Street and was the favourite meeting place for hundreds of exhausted shoppers. Evie breathed deeply as a tantalising aroma wafted towards her. She was ravenous and her mouth watered at the thought of the delicious freshly made cups of coffee, lavishly filled sandwiches and assortment of cakes waiting for her on the counter.

She put her shopping bags down on the pavement and rubbed her hands together. It was turning bitterly cold as the late January afternoon began to draw in. Trust Mavis to be late, she fumed. She turned to look in the window. The place was bulging at the seams and Evie hoped that when Mavis finally arrived they would not have their usual scramble to procure a seat. As she waited, her impatience mounted. Mavis had said on the telephone that morning, that she had some important news and Evie could not wait to find out what it was. To her relief she spotted Mavis coming towards her, and smiled. It was a comical sight watching the tiny figure of her friend dodging her way through the crowds.

'Where have you been?' she scolded. 'It's nearly half three. I told my mother I'd be home before five. You really are the limit, Mave.' Evie stopped her ravings and looked at her friend closely. 'You all right? You look a bit peaky.'

'Yes, I'm okay. Look, I'm sorry I'm late. I missed the bus.'

'Come on, let's get a coffee. I'm frozen.'

'Er . . .' Mavis paused.

Evie's eyes narrowed as she looked at her friend. 'Mavis Humphreys, you're not going to tell me you've no money again? You were broke last Saturday. What are you doing with it all?'

Mavis lowered her head and bit her bottom lip.

Too cold to wait for an explanation, Evie grabbed her shopping bags and elbowed Mavis towards the door. 'Oh, come on. I'll treat you, again. Take these bags and get a seat, I'll bring the coffee over.'

She bought two coffees and two tea cakes, laden with butter. Once seated, the pair sipped their coffee and proceeded to demolish their food.

'Well?' asked Evie, her mouth full. 'You haven't said a word since we got here and I've loads to tell you.'

Mavis swallowed and took a deep breath. 'I'm getting married, Evie.'

Evie gawped. 'What! Getting married?' This was the last thing she had expected to hear.

'Yes.'

'But I thought you and Stephen were just friends? I

didn't realise it had gone this far. You never breathed a word.'

'Oh! It's not Stephen,' Mavis said, staring intently into her coffee cup.

'Not Stephen? Who is it then?'

'Paul Jenkins,' Mavis whispered, slowly raising her head.

'Paul Jenkins!' Evie's first instinct was to laugh in disbelief. But the look on Mavis's face told her she was anything but joking about Paul Jenkins. 'Not that bloke I saw you with when you were waiting for me one night? The girls are always talking about him. I know at least three women he's been out with in the factory and they haven't a good word to say about him.' She frowned fiercely. 'And why haven't you told me before?'

'Because I knew what you'd say. You don't know him, Evie. He's not like they say he is, honest.'

Evie looked at her friend in exasperation. 'Mavis, that man is at least ten years older than you!'

'I know all that, Evie, and I've heard of his reputation,' Mavis replied quietly. 'But we're in love and he's changed, honest he has. He's never looked at another woman since he met me.'

'Love!' Evie groaned. 'You can't survive on love. As far as I know, Paul Jenkins hasn't even got a job.'

'He'll get a job. It's just that nothing in his line has come up yet, but he's looking,' Mavis said, trying to sound enthusiastic.

'What line is he in then?'

'He's a speedway rider. Only he hasn't got a bike at the moment. He had an accident on his last one and smashed it up.'

'A speedway rider! Mavis, what are your mam and dad saying about all this?'

'They don't know yet,' she whispered.

Evie rubbed the back of her hand across her forehead and exhaled loudly. 'That's why you've no money. You've been giving it to him, haven't you?'

Mavis bent her head. 'Well, I can't see him short.'

Evie opened her mouth to say something, but quickly stopped herself. She took a deep breath. 'I wouldn't like to be in your shoes when you do tell your parents. Can't you put off getting married until he's got a job? Your mam and dad might not take it so bad then?'

'We can't, Evie.'

'Can't! Why not?'

Mavis looked at her hesitantly. ''Cos . . .' She sighed. 'I'm expecting.' Slowly she raised her head and waited for her friend's response.

Evie puckered her lips in bewilderment. 'Expecting! Expecting what?' Her mouth gaped open for the second time that afternoon as the truth dawned on her. 'Oh, Mave. You're not having a baby?' she blurted.

Mavis slowly nodded.

Evie stared at her in horror. She finally lowered her gaze and with shaking hands picked up her cup and saucer, which rattled loudly as she drank the dregs. 'I need another.' She jumped up and went over to the counter and bought two more cups of coffee.

Seated once more, facing her friend, she said, 'I don't know what to say, I'm flabbergasted! Why on earth didn't you tell me?'

''Cos I was scared out of my wits, Evie. You don't know what a relief it was when Paul said he'd marry me.'

Mavis leant over and grabbed hold of her friend's hand. 'Can't you be pleased for me?'

Evie's body sagged. She felt deeply distressed at the devastating news her friend had divulged, but Mavis's pleading eyes got the better of her.

'Yes, of course. Of course I'm pleased for you,' she lied. 'And I'll do anything to help.' She took a deep breath and tried hard to smile. 'I'm going to be your bridesmaid, I hope?'

Mavis's eyes lit up in relief. 'That goes without saying, only I don't think I'll be having a white wedding, do you?'

Evie half smiled then frowned as a thought came into her head.

'Just a minute . . . a few weeks ago we were sitting in my bedroom looking through the dictionary on all the words to do with sex. We were both in hysterics 'cos we'd never learned anything. You must have . . . you know . . . done it then and you never said a word.'

Mavis looked sheepishly at Evie. 'Oh, I couldn't. I couldn't tell you.' She grimaced. 'Anyway, it's not all it's cracked up to be.'

Evie leaned forward in case anyone could hear their conversation. 'What? You mean, you don't hear music and bells ringing?'

'No. I can assure you, you don't!'

'Oh.' Evie frowned. 'Well, do you feel any different? Like a woman? You know, sort of glowing.'

'No, I don't,' Mavis said. 'It was all over before I knew what was happening. My knickers were off, a few grunts and groans, and that was it. I was lying on the canal bank in all my glory, wondering what all the fuss was about.'

'No?' Evie said.

'Yes!' Mavis laughed. 'You remember Pamela Kendrick at school: fourteen and she'd been with most of the lads, and we tortured ourselves wondering what it was all about? Well, you're not missing anything, Evie. You keep your legs crossed. I wouldn't like to see you in the mess I'm in, all for a few minutes of passion.'

'Oh, it is passion then?' she probed.

'Not on the canal bank, it isn't. Just bloody cold.'

Evie sighed. 'Oh, Mavis, but at least you know now what you've been missing. I don't. I'll still lie in bed wondering.' She shrugged her shoulders. 'I think I'll end up an old spinster, just like our Florrie.'

The two friends burst into fits of giggles.

'I can't really see that happening, you silly ha'porth. You were the best looking girl in our class,' said Mavis.

'Well, why is it I haven't got a boyfriend?' Evie asked seriously.

'Because you're too damned choosey and you know it,' Mavis answered sharply. 'Look at Ronald Wormaleighton. I think he's a corker. But you, just because he works for Ginns and Gutteridge . . .'

'Mavis, come on. Could you go out with someone who was an apprentice undertaker?'

Mavis hid a smile. 'No, I suppose not. But he is nice-looking, and as long as he didn't call for me in the hearse . . .'

Both girls collapsed into fits of laughter again. Mavis's turned to tears.

'Oh, Evie, I'm dreading telling my dad, he'll blow a gasket. Him being a director of his company and so well known in town. It'll be the death of him.'

It was Evie's turn to grab her friend's hand. 'Look, he

might not take it so bad. ' She tried to sound sympathetic. 'At least Paul is going to marry you.'

Mavis sniffed. 'Yes.' She smiled wanly. 'But I'm worried, 'cos he wants me to ask my dad for some money so he can buy a new bike. He reckons there's big winnings to be had in the speedway competitions. But I don't really want to, Evie. Dad's been good to me and I just feel it's bad enough telling him I'm pregnant without asking for money.'

'You're right,' she retorted. 'Paul's got a nerve asking you to do that.' She paused. 'But you'll have to speak to them soon, you won't keep the baby hidden for long.' She peered over the table and frowned. 'How far gone are you?'

'Nearly four months,' Mavis whispered.

'Nearly four months! Bloody hell, Mavis, you're going to have to tell your parents – and quick.' She looked at her friend closely. 'You can't tell,' she said in surprise.

'No, thank goodness. But my clothes are starting to get really tight now.' Mavis hung her head. 'I suppose I was hoping that it was all in my imagination and that I would wake up one morning and everything would be all right.'

'That only happens in books, Mavis. Anyway, tell your mother, and the sooner the better. She'll break the news to your dad and you'll just have to keep your fingers crossed that they don't disown you.' Evie sighed deeply and her eyes softened. 'Your mother's a lovely woman, Mavis. She'll be understanding, you'll see.'

Mavis smiled wanly. 'The gossips are going to have a grand time with this one. I'll be the talk of the town, branded forever as a fallen woman. How am I going to cope with that?'

Evie exhaled loudly. 'Well, you're going to have to

ignore them. Just make sure you tell your mother before she gets wind from somewhere else – that really would make matters worse. If it's possible,' she added under her breath.

Mavis nodded.

'I will, Evie. It's not going to be easy though.'

'You should have thought of that before you let Paul have his way,' she blurted before she could stop herself.

Mavis glared at her friend for a second, before her shoulders sagged. 'Yes, I should have. But you don't think of the consequences at the time, do you?' She paused for a moment. 'I'll try and do it on Monday night when Dad goes to his snooker club. It will give me time this weekend to sort out what I'm going to say.'

'Well, it's got to be done, Mavis, you can't get out of this one.'

Mavis shuddered at the thought, then leaned forward. 'Remember when we were at school? Our big ambition in life was to have a husband, two kids and a perm – all by the age of twenty. It looks like I'll achieve that, doesn't it? Anyway,' she smiled wanly at her friend, 'enough of me. What's your big news?'

Evie related the events at work. 'So you see, from Monday I shall be working in the office.'

'Oh, Evie, I'm so proud of you.'

'Yes, until I get everyone mixed up on the telephone! Have you ever seen a switchboard? The only one I've seen was in a film. It had plugs and cords and holes and things, and I haven't got a clue where you put everything.' She laughed. 'I shall be out on my ear in a week, you'll see.'

'You'll be fine,' Mavis said with conviction. 'I can see you running the whole factory before long.'

Evie giggled. 'That'll be the day. Come on, you, I've got to get home, it's my mam's night out tonight. I've got the tea in these bags, and you know what our Florrie's like if the meal's not ready when she gets in from her church duties.'

Mavis clicked her tongue. 'Don't know how you put up with her!'

'Oh, she's not all bad. Sometimes she acts quite human.' Evie smiled.

Mavis looked at her friend thoughtfully. 'Evie, where does your mother go on her Saturday night jaunts?'

Evie frowned. 'I don't really know.' She thought for a moment. 'It's funny, she's been going out once a month for years and I've no idea where she goes.'

'Have you ever asked her?'

'You of all people should know that you don't ask my mother questions like that,' Evie replied. 'She tells me off enough as it is for prying into her affairs.'

'Well, what d'you think she does?'

'I've told you, I don't know! I suppose I've always thought she's meeting an old friend or something.'

Mavis's eyes opened wide. 'D'you think she's got a secret lover?'

'Mavis!'

'Well, why not? You mother is a lovely-looking woman. For her age, that is.'

'Yes, she is,' Evie agreed, and looked quizzically at her friend. 'D'you think it could be a lover, then? I never thought of that. I mean you don't with your parents, do you? Seems disgusting somehow.'

'Yes, it does.' Mavis pulled a face. 'I can't imagine my parents doing it.' She shuddered. 'Doesn't bear thinking about. I wonder how old you are when you stop.'

'Oh, about thirty, I would say.' Evie nodded knowingly. 'No. It's not a lover, she's too old. Must be an old school friend.' She looked at her watch. 'Oh, my god, Mave, it's half-past four. I'm really going to get it in the neck now.' She thought for a second. 'Look, why don't you come home with me? We can have some tea, Mam won't mind. When she's gone out, we could have a proper talk. What do you say?'

Mavis lowered her eyes. 'I can't. Not tonight, Evie.'

'Why?' She looked disappointed.

'I'm seeing Paul.'

'Oh, I see,' Evie said haughtily. 'Well, I'd better be going. I'll walk with you to the bottom of Churchgate.' She tilted her head to one side and raised an eyebrow. 'D'you want to telephone me when you're free sometime?'

Mavis ignored the sarcastic remark and helped her pick up her shopping.

Evie was angry with Mavis. She really wanted to grab her friend by the shoulders and shake some sense into her. But it was too late for that. Mavis was pregnant and about to be married, and the shock had hit Evie badly.

Their friendship went very deep. They had met at infants school, joined the Brownies then the Girl Guides, attended their first dance, met their first boyfriends, and shared all their secrets together. Evie felt very protective towards her friend and this catastrophic episode in Mavis's life worried her deeply.

Evie joined the queue and boarded the bus. She sat staring out of the window as the bus ploughed through the dark, icy Leicester streets. She was worried. She could not for the life of her see Mavis married with a baby. Not the

Mavis she knew. The Mavis who had been pampered and petted all her life, given every comfort her parents could afford.

She shuddered and moved up in her seat as an unkempt elderly man plonked himself down beside her. An extremely unpleasant smell reached her nostrils and she pulled a face. She turned to look out of the window again.

She pictured her mother. Just where was it she went to on her Saturday night jaunts? Evie was momentarily annoyed with Mavis for bringing up the subject. It was none of her friend's business what her mother did.

She sighed with relief as the man got up and moved down the bus. She inched up her bags and made herself more comfortable. It started to rain and Evie watched a trickle of water weave its way down the window. She sighed. Her conscience troubled her deeply. Should she have told Mavis that only that afternoon as she had been waiting outside Brucciani's she had spotted Paul?

He had had his arm around a gaudily dressed woman. They had been laughing intimately together as they pushed open the door of the Eclipse public house and disappeared inside.

Chapter Three

Evie woke early for her first morning in the office. A feeling of apprehension mixed with excitement settled over her. She dressed very carefully in a dark navy suit, one of her mother's that had been quickly altered over the weekend. 'Can't have you looking a mess,' Edith had fussed, accidentally sticking a pin into Evie's leg. She had stifled a howl of protest and silently suffered while her mother finished the alterations.

The starched white blouse scratched her skin and the roll-on she had borrowed to hold up her stockings nipped her thighs. She shut her mind to her uncomfortable state and at eight o'clock sharp pushed open the half glass door marked GENERAL OFFICE.

She was greeted by thirty stony faces, staring up at her from behind rows of desks. The General Office was large and forbidding. It was painted in cream and brown, which over the years had darkened, creating a dreary, dull environment. The desks were placed in rows and several housed large grey machines which seemed to have hundreds of numbered buttons on the front of them. Evie learned later that these machines were called comptometers and were used for adding large columns of figures.

At the far end of the room sat a large, middle-aged

woman. She rose and walked towards Evie. The first thing that struck her was the size of the woman's bosom. It was enormous and swayed dangerously as she lumbered forward. As she came closer, the woman smoothed her hands over her dark mud green woollen dress. Her dull grey hair was scraped tightly back into a small bun at the base of her neck, accentuating her bulbous nose. She was the ugliest woman Evie had ever seen. The woman stopped abruptly and leaned forward, her large nose only inches away from Evie's face.

'We start work at eight, not five past. You'll be docked five minutes' pay.' She frowned fiercely and her chins increased from two to three.

Normally, Evie would have been unable to control her laughter. Now she felt her legs shaking as the woman continued: 'Mr Stimpson, the Office Manager, has been waiting for you. Not a very good start, is it? Best get in there, and report to me on the way out.' She nodded towards a large wooden door.

Evie walked past the desks, conscious of all the staring eyes upon her. She took a deep breath and tapped on the door. A loud voice boomed, bidding her to enter.

Mr Stimpson looked at his watch. 'Not good to be late on your first day.' He scowled at Evie. 'We start at eight prompt, so best to be here at a quarter to.' His voice was low and menacing and Evie shook.

Mr Stimpson had been with the company for forty years and was very old-fashioned in his approach. He did not like women: to his mind they belonged at home not in an office environment. He ruled his staff with a rod of iron and woe betide anyone who made a mistake.

He studied Evie intently from behind thick-lensed glasses.

He had deeply resented Mr Williams entering his domain and ordering him to take her through all the aspects of his office. Mr Stimpson did not like being told how to appoint his staff, especially a young chit out of the factory. He firmly believed that all the girls in the factory were brainless and doubted this one would be any different. Still, orders were orders and would have to be obeyed.

'You'll start with the switchboard and we'll see how you get on. Report to Miss Sargent: she's your supervisor and will keep a close eye on you and report back to me.' Mr Stimpson picked up a piece of paper and started to read.

Evie realised she was being dismissed. The interview had finished and she had not uttered a word. She whispered a thank you and quickly left the office.

Miss Sargent met her at the door. 'This way.'

She marched down the office and Evie followed. The switchboard was situated behind the entrance door at the bottom of the large room. Evie looked at it forlornly. It was nothing like the ones portrayed in the American films she had seen. This switchboard was just a wooden box with metal doll's eyes that flicked down to signal which extension was calling.

Under each eye was a switch which was flicked up to answer, and down to connect a call. A handle on the side was turned to ring the extension bell. To the right of the switchboard was an old Imperial 80 typewriter which looked as though it weighed a ton. She realised Miss Sargent was speaking and quickly turned her attention to what was being said.

'There's a list here of all the extensions. Speak clearly and precisely at all times. Get the proper name of the

caller and announce them before you put them through,'
she barked. She then turned to the typewriter. 'You're to
be enrolled at the Charles Keene College to learn shorthand
and typing. It's a night class and held once a week.'

One of the doll's eyes on the switchboard flickered
down and a loud buzzing noise made Evie jump.

'Well, don't just stand there, girl. Answer it.'

Evie's mouth dropped open as she threw her handbag
on the floor by the desk, grabbed the telephone receiver
and stared blankly at it.

'Oh, for goodness' sake, girl! Didn't you listen to a
word I said?' Miss Sargent grabbed the receiver off her
and flicked up the key directly under the buzzing eye.
Having satisfied the caller, Miss Sargent replaced the receiver
in its holder and turned to Evie.

'Don't ever act like that again. You're not on the factory
floor now.'

She pushed Evie on the shoulder with the flat of her
hand. 'Sit down and I'll go over it once more.'

Two minutes later, Miss Sargent left Evie on her own
and marched back to her desk. Two doll's eyes dropped
down at the same time, and the buzzer rang long and loud.
Evie took a deep breath and picked up the receiver.

Lunchtime finally arrived and Evie walked quickly up
Churchgate, through the market place towards Town Hall
Square. She found a vacant seat, sat down and unwrapped
the egg sandwiches her mother had carefully made up for
her. She took a small bite and chewed slowly as she watched
the fountain in the middle of the square spew out its icy
cold water. The square to the front of the large imposing
Victorian Town Hall was thronged with people who were

using it either as a short cut to the town centre or as a meeting place for a quick gossip with friends.

Evie felt desolate. The morning had crawled by, hour upon endless hour. No one had spoken to her and she had had to struggle alone with the switchboard, desperately trying to remember names and extension numbers, conscious that Miss Sargent's bulging eyes were watching her every move from the other end of the office.

She put the sandwich back into the brown paper bag and screwed down the corner, sniffing quietly as she did so. She couldn't go back. Nothing would induce her to return to that dreadful place. Why, oh why, had she agreed to leave the comfortable haven of the factory for this hell? She jumped as she felt a light touch on her shoulder and quickly looked up to see a girl of about her own age standing before her.

She was one of the prettiest girls Evie had ever seen. Her blonde hair was piled up in a French pleat and Evie noticed that several grips holding it in place were beginning to work loose. Her black skirt was slightly creased and the cardigan of her pale yellow twin set had a small hole which the girl was fiddling with.

'Miss Grayson?'

Evie nodded apprehensively.

The girl smiled and sat down beside her.

'I'm Miss Jones, Jennifer Jones, from the office. Me friends call me Jenny.' She paused for a moment. 'I 'ope you don't mind but I followed you up 'ere. The Sergeant Major was really 'orrible to you this morning. So I thought I'd come and tell you we're not all like that. Well, I'm not, anyway.' She gave Evie a broad smile and opened a paper bag she was holding. 'Wanna sandwich? Potted meat today. My favourite.' She offered the opened bag to Evie who shook her head.

'No thanks. I don't feel much like food.'

'Doesn't surprise me,' Jenny said. 'But you 'ave to eat. Won't do no good starvin' yerself. Me mother makes us clear our plates. Says we should eat what we're given and be grateful. She even makes me eat dark cabbage when she knows I 'ate the stuff. It's somethin' to do with the war, I think. She's always going on about the stuff they couldn't get, what with the rations and all that. Is your mam the same? Me dad now, 'e's never been the same since 'e came back.' She frowned. 'I'm not supposed to know this, but me mam 'ad an affair wi' an American from the Airforce base and me dad found out. 'Course, there were a terrible row. 'E beat the bloke up and nearly killed 'im. 'E wa' sent back to America real sharpish.'

Evie looked at Jenny in amazement.

'Don't look like that. Lots of women went off wi' other blokes while their 'usbands were away. Me mam were a good-lookin' woman.' Jenny sniffed loudly. 'Anyway, Dad threatened to take us kids away if she didn't behave 'erself. Said she'd find 'erself on the streets. Poor old Mam gave in. Dad's never let 'er forget what she did. Treats 'er like a slave. If yer ask me, I think she'd 'ave bin better off wi' the American bloke. She's aged years since me dad came 'ome. All 'e does is snarl and growl at 'er.' She looked at Evie quizzically. 'What did your dad do in the war?'

'Oh . . . er, he didn't go.'

'Didn't 'e? Was 'e one of those con . . . con . . . one of those men that didn't believe in it then?'

'No!' Evie retorted sharply. 'He wasn't a conscientious

objector, if that's what you mean. He died before the war even started.'

'Oh, I see . . . I'm sorry,' Jenny said with remorse. 'Must 'ave bin 'ard on your mam then? Bet she found it tough to manage.'

Evie looked thoughtfully at Jenny. 'I suppose it was. Only it didn't seem to be.' She stared out across the square. 'I've never really thought about it before, but from what I can remember, we always had food on the table and good clothes to wear.'

'Did you? Must 'ave bin black market stuff, then.'

'No, it wasn't!'

'It must 'ave bin. 'Ow else did she manage, 'er bein' on 'er own?'

'I don't know. But I do know it wasn't thanks to the black market.' Evie narrowed her eyes and scowled at Jenny. 'My mother is just a good manager.'

'She must 'ave bin a bloody miracle worker to manage durin' the war wi'out the black market.' Jenny patted Evie's knee. 'It's nothin' to be ashamed of. We'd 'ave all died of starvation if it 'adn't of bin for my mam's connections . . .' She saw the expression on Evie's face and quickly changed the subject. 'What kinda sandwiches you got?'

Evie looked down at her lunch bag. 'Egg.'

'I love egg sandwiches. Swop yer one.' Jenny took the sandwich that Evie offered her as she continued talking. 'They never had eggs in the war, you could only get powdered ones. Mam says you couldn't make a decent cake or anythin', except if yer were lucky enough to get some on the side like.' She gave an infectious giggle. 'Me mam makes rotten cakes anyway, so I dread to think what her war ones were like!' She paused again and looked

Evie up and down. 'I like your suit. When you walked in the office, I thought to meself, "God, she's smart." I wouldn't mind a suit like that. I'm savin' like mad, but I give Mam a good wack out me wages 'cos Dad's pay's not all that good and most of what 'e gets goes behind the bar of the Navigation Arms.' She shrugged her shoulders. 'Not that I'm bothered. Mam couldn't manage without the bit I give 'er. Look, if you don't mind me sayin', I'm freezin'. I forgot to put me coat on. Let's walk back.'

Jenny rose and Evie found herself unwittingly following suit, bemused by the constant chatter.

'Where d'you live?' Jenny asked. 'We live in the prefabs, up the New Parks Estate. It's a little community on its own. We've even got our own Co-op.' She stopped abruptly. 'That reminds me – Mam's divvy's due soon. 'Ope I get some of it.' She sniffed and ran the back of her hand under her nose. 'Where was I? Oh, yes. The prefabs were built just after the war – only for the time bein', or so the Council said. But we're still in 'em. They're quite nice really and you get a fridge and cooker.' She laughed again and nudged Evie's arm. 'Sounds as if I'm trying to rent you one, don't it?' She looked serious for a second. 'You don't say much, do you?'

It was Evie's turn to laugh.

''Ere, that's better.' Jenny nudged Evie's arm again. 'You don't 'ave to tell me – I know. I talk too much! Well, let's face it, we can't breathe in the office, let alone talk, so I 'ave to make up for it some'ow. Where do you live?'

'Henley Road . . .' Evie started.

'Oh, that's not far from me. We can catch the bus 'ome together. 'Ere, we're nearly there.' Jenny grimaced as they turned the corner of St Margaret's Way. 'I'd better tell yer a few things before we go in.'

'I'd appreciate that,' Evie said eagerly.

'Well, you've met our Miss Sargent. You'll 'ave to watch 'er. I ain't surprised she's not married. With a face like 'ers, she'd frighten any man to death,' Jenny said unkindly. 'She sees everythin'. And if she misses somethin', which ain't often, Doreen Hardwood snitches to 'er. Hardnose Hardwood, that's 'er nickname. She's a right old cow. She tells Miss Sargent everythin'.' She started to giggle. 'Actually, Miss Sargent's got a mother and *she's* a right old dragon. She's about ninety-four and rules the 'ouse wi' a fist of iron. Woe betide if our Sally steps outta line.'

Evie's face lit up in amusement. 'Honestly? Sally!'

'Yeah, it's true. Sally Sargent. A big lump of a thing like 'er wi' a pretty name like that. Funny, ain't it?'

'Certainly is. I'll never be able to look her in the eye again.' Evie smiled. 'Mind you, it explains why she's so obnoxious at work.'

'Ob . . . what?'

'Obnoxious. Horrible and nasty. It's because of her mother. She has to do what she's told at home, so she plays the high and mighty at work.'

'Oh, does she?' Jenny looked at Evie in awe, then grimaced. 'That's not what I think. I think she'd be a nasty piece of work, mother or no mother!' She sniffed and bent down to straighten the seam in her stocking. 'That's better. Now who else is there? Oh, yes, Burt Digby. Poor little sod! 'E's another one who's nagged somethin' rotten at 'ome and 'e only talks about his train sets, so 'e's no bother, bless 'im.' She pulled a wry face. 'But Mira Grindley . . .' She grimaced and blew out her cheeks. 'She's a rum

51

customer. She's after Miss Sargent's job and Miss Sargent knows it, so sometimes the sparks fly. I just keeps me 'ead down and gets on wi' me work. Then there's Mr Stimpson – I call him Stingy Stimpson. That man's 'orrible and yer 'ave to mind your P's and Q's when 'e's about. Just get on wi' yer work, and you'll get on fine, but for God's sake, don't be late again or they'll dock yer pay and make you feel like a criminal.'

'I won't.' Evie grimaced. 'I can't afford to get my pay docked. I'm saving for a new dress.'

Jenny grinned and placed her hand on Evie's arm. 'It ain't such a bad place to work, and when you've been 'ere five years, yer gerra chicken at Christmas. Ten years, a turkey, and after twenty, guess what?'

'What?' asked Evie, bemused.

'An 'amper full of stuff they couldn't sell in the canteen,' Jenny answered sarcastically.

They entered the gates and Evie saw Florrie walking across the yard.

'She's a stuck up so and so, that one,' Jenny whispered, nudging Evie in the ribs. 'Just 'cos she works for the Chief Accountant. Right cosy set up it is. Thinks she's Lady Muck. Doesn't speak to the likes of us in the General Office. Her sister works in the factory.'

'I know.' Evie let a smile spread across her face.

Jenny turned to Evie. 'You know Florence Grayson then?'

'Yes.' Evie smiled. 'I'm her sister.'

For the first time in nearly an hour, Jenny was speechless.

Evie burst out laughing. 'It's okay. I think the same as you. Only I have to live with her.' She grabbed hold of Jenny's arm. 'Come on, I daren't be late again today. I'll meet you at the gates at five-thirty. You can tell me more on the bus home.'

Evie pushed open the door to the office that afternoon in a more optimistic frame of mind. She liked Jenny: the girl had been like a breath of fresh air. Evie could see them becoming good friends. She winked at her before she turned her back and sat down at the switchboard.

Two hours later, Miss Sargent marched down the office. She grabbed hold of Evie and hauled her to her feet.

'I've had a complaint about you, Miss Grayson.' Her voice was loud and it echoed round the room.

Evie bowed her head as she saw that everyone had stopped working and was staring over at her. Doreen Hardwood had a smirk on her face and was nudging the woman next to her in amusement.

'Look at me when I'm speaking,' ordered Miss Sargent. She half turned as though addressing an audience. 'I won't name names, but one of the managers has complained you were rude to him – told him to wait while you connected his call then took ages about it. Well?'

Evie's hackles rose at the nastiness in Miss Sargent's voice.

'I'm sure I didn't, Miss Sargent. He must have been mistaken . . .'

'How dare you back-answer me?' Miss Sargent's face turned purple. 'Are you saying he's a liar?' Without waiting for Evie to answer, she continued, 'You factory girls are all the same. You'll never make office material. I don't know what possessed the Personnel Department to send you up here in the first place. One more complaint, girl, and I shall tell Mr Stimpson.' She bent her head closer to Evie. 'And you know what that means. Out!' She turned on her heels. 'Now get back to your work, and be warned.'

She marched up the office. Evie willed herself not to cry as, apart from Jenny's, all she could see was a sea of grinning faces. She turned her back and sat slowly down on her chair.

Two weeks later Evie was deep in conversation with her mother and tempers were rising.

'I tell you, Mam, I hate it. Miss Sargent has it in for me, she's on at me all the time. It's all lies, but she just wants me out. If it wasn't for Jenny I'd go daft.' She sniffed loudly and took a deep breath. 'I want to go back in the factory. I'm going to tell Miss Sargent tomorrow.'

Edith nearly dropped the saucepan she was holding as she swung round to face her daughter.

'That you will not, my girl.' She banged the saucepan down and walked over to the table. 'You'll show that Miss Sargent what you're made of, and leaving is not the answer. Just ignore her, and don't give her any excuse to get at you. And if she does, just smile sweetly and say you'll try harder.'

'I can't, Mam. I hate the woman.' Evie sniffed again.

'You can and you will.' Edith placed her hands on the table and leant forward. 'Knuckle down and you'll soon be moved to a better position,' she said with conviction.

'What makes you so sure?' Evie eyed her mother with suspicion.

Edith paused for a moment. 'Well . . . they moved you out of the factory, so you never know what might happen in the future. You must be prepared.'

'Oh, Mam. Some people have been in the same department for donkey's years, why should I be so different?'

'Because you're my daughter,' Edith said, raising her voice.

'What's being your daughter got to do with anything, Mam?'

Edith ran her fingers through her hair in exasperation and glared at Evie. 'I've had enough of this conversation. If I hear another word about leaving, I'll box your ears. Now, eat your dinner and get ready for night school.'

'But Mam, you don't understand . . .'

'Oh, I understand all right, our Evie. This learning business is too much trouble. Am I right?' Edith pulled a chair out from under the table and sat down facing her daughter. 'Now listen, Evie, and listen good.' She lowered her voice and spoke firmly to her daughter. 'You'll get stuck in and learn as much as you can. Do you understand what I'm saying?'

Evie nodded her head sullenly.

'You can do this office lark standing on your head. But I know you, Evie. Your head is too full of films and boys.' She folded her arms across her chest. 'So understand this, girl. You'll go in to work tomorrow and do your very best, and I won't listen to another word about your leaving. There's no telling where this job will lead to. For a start you could be more enthusiastic about your typing lessons.'

As Edith spoke, Evie stared at her open-mouthed.

'Are you listening to me, Evie?'

'Yes, Mam,' she said forlornly. 'Only I hate going to College nearly as much as the office. I can't get the hang of this typing business. They stick you in front of a typewriter with a blank keyboard. How the hell do I know what keys are what?'

'You learn, Evie. And I've told you before, I will not

tolerate swearing in this house.'

She frowned. 'Hell's not swearing.'

'It is in my book.' She pushed Evie's dinner before her. 'Now eat this all up and go and get ready for College or else you'll be late.'

'But, Mam, it's not just the typing, it's the shorthand as well. It's driving me mad. I can't get to grips with all the different signs. You have to use a thick stroke for this sound and a thin stroke for that sound – and that's only the start. There's hundreds of different squiggles to learn. It's all like Chinese to me. What that Pitman chap was thinking about when he came up with the idea is beyond me. I think he was mental . . .'

'Evie! That's enough.'

'But you don't understand, Mam. None of the other girls likes me.'

'What makes you say that?'

'Well, as soon as I told them I used to work as a machinist, they all stuck their noses in the air and now they avoid me.'

'Oh, Evie!' Edith sighed. 'Well, I'm afraid that's something you'll have to come to terms with. Before you're finished, girl, you'll have a lot harsher things to face than that. And if you want to better yourself . . .'

'*Me* want to better myself?' Evie cut in. 'It's *you* that's pushing me to do that. I was quite happy in the factory.'

'Were you, Evie? Would you really be content sewing knickers for the next forty years?'

'You sound like our Florrie.'

'You know what I mean,' Edith said coldly.

Evie stared at her mother for a moment. 'No. I suppose I do want to get on.' She sighed. 'But it's such hard work.'

'Of course it's hard work. Nothing comes easy.'

'I'm beginning to see that,' Evie said sharply. She shrugged her shoulders. 'All right, you win. I'll give it one more try.'

'Good girl.' Edith sighed with relief. 'Now eat your dinner.' Ten minutes later she looked up at the clock and frowned. 'I told our Florrie to telephone if she was going to be late again. Her dinner will be dried up.'

'Serves her right,' Evie muttered under her breath as she pushed her plate away. 'I'd better be going or I'll be late.'

Edith watched in silence as her daughter left the room.

Evie lay in bed that night, watching the shadows moving across the ceiling. She mulled over and over the conversation with her mother. She sighed deeply, pulled the covers further up under her chin and rubbed her feet over her hot water bottle. Why was her mother so adamant that she stick at that dreadful job? What would it matter if she left? She could get another job: they were crying out for factory workers. What was so important about learning office duties, when she could earn enough money in the factory?

Her mind went blank for a while until a thought struck her. Maybe her mother wanted her to have a better life than she had: a career even. She smiled to herself. Career indeed! What was she thinking of! She thought of her mother's job. She supposed working in a wool shop wasn't that well paid or fulfilling, and maybe her mother wanted more than that for her. Her thoughts drifted back to earlier in the evening. After the row with her mother, she had attacked her typing lessons with gusto and had actually enjoyed what she had learned. 'Yes, I did,' she said aloud in astonishment. 'I really did enjoy my lessons.'

Maybe she could do it, if she put her mind to it. She took a deep breath and stretched her body under the bedclothes, feeling new life and warmth creep through her.

She would do it. She'd prove to her mother and Miss Sargent that she had the makings of a good worker. It was all up to her. She'd show them. She'd start tomorrow.

'"Tomorrow is another day",' she quoted out loud, picturing herself as Scarlett O'Hara, draped on the stairs in the last scene of *Gone With The Wind*.

She giggled to herself as she turned over and settled down to sleep.

Edith noticed the change in her daughter the following morning as she heard Evie singing in the bathroom as she got ready for work. Relief swept over her. She rubbed eyes that were sore from lack of sleep. It would have been disastrous if Evie had carried out her threat and left her job. All the years of planning and sacrifice would have been in vain. She went to the bottom of the stairs and called Florrie for breakfast.

She banged her bedroom door shut and plodded down the stairs.

'What's up with her this morning? She won the pools or something?' she snapped sarcastically as she pulled out a chair and sat down.

Edith ignored the remark and placed a plate of bacon and eggs in front of her. Florrie picked up her knife and fork and stabbed her egg yolk. She watched as it spilled over her plate.

'I'll be late tonight so don't make me any dinner,' she said tonelessly.

'How late?' Edith queried.

Florrie looked up sharply. 'How should I know? When my work's finished.'

'Working late again? I didn't realise the firm was that busy.'

Florrie put her head down and tackled her bacon. 'Well, our department is.'

'I'll put your dinner in the over then,' Edith offered.

'You needn't bother. I'll grab some fish and chips on the way home.'

Edith was annoyed at Florrie's attitude, but was saved a further confrontation by Evie's bouncing through the door.

'Morning,' she sang as she kissed her mother on the cheek.

Florrie completely ignored Evie's presence as she sat down opposite her at the table.

'Morning, Florrie.'

Still Florrie ignored her. Evie looked at her mother and winked.

'We're going to the pictures tonight, Florrie. *Rebecca* is on at the Roxy, with Laurence Olivier and Joan Fontaine.' Evie's eyes glazed over as she placed her elbow on the table and rested her chin in her hand. 'Oh, I think Laurence Olivier is dreamy.' She pictured herself in his arms for a moment, then brought herself back to reality. 'Anyway, want to come?'

Florrie stopped eating and glared at Evie. 'Since when have you ever invited me to the pictures?'

'Why not? You're my sister.' Evie took a bite of toast. 'Thought it might make a change for you, that's all.'

'I've got to work late,' Florrie said, realising that Edith was watching her intently.

'Work late? Why?' asked Evie in surprise.

'Why? 'Cos we're busy!' Florrie stood up. 'I can't sit around here, I have a living to earn.' She stormed out and banged the door shut behind her.

Evie frowned as she looked at her mother. 'That's odd.'

Edith picked up her cup of tea and sat down opposite her daughter. 'What's odd, dear?'

Evie pushed her empty plate away and wiped her mouth.

'Well, it's just that I overheard Mr Stimpson say that times are bad just now because the price of wool has shot up. It's affecting all trade at the moment. They're on short time in the factory.' She grimaced. 'We've to use our spare time getting all the files and what nots sorted out.' She paused thoughtfully and took a sip of tea. 'Mind you, Florrie wouldn't lie about working late, would she?' She shrugged her shoulders and looked at the clock. 'Is that the time? I must dash. Can't be late, can I?' She grinned at her mother before rushing out of the door.

From that morning, Evie threw herself into her work. She quickly became a wizard on the switchboard, being complimented over and over again on her polite manner and quick response, making doubly sure that Miss Sargent found no excuse to find the slightest fault. She passed her first shorthand and typing exams with honours and found herself actually looking forward to her next ones.

Mr Stimpson and Miss Sargent were still the bane of her life, but she learned to smile sweetly and do a better job than they had originally asked of her, which irritated them enormously but delighted Evie.

Unbeknown to Mr Stimpson, Miss Sargent would give her letters to type, always making sure that her initials were on them and therefore taking the credit. Inside, Evie was seething, but she knew that the extra practice it gave her would only enhance her own speed and efficiency. She learned, in her own time, how to operate the comptometer machines. Compared to these, typing was easy. But after many long and painful lunch hours, she mastered the art and could add up a four-foot tally roll nearly as quickly as the more experienced operators.

She was really beginning to enjoy her job, especially since she and Jenny had become good friends. As her nineteenth birthday approached, Evie felt the world was hers.

Evie awoke with a feeling of apprehension on the morning of Mavis's wedding day. The last few weeks had not been easy for her friend and as the wedding preparations had got under way, Evie felt more and more that Mavis was making a terrible mistake.

Her parents had been greatly shocked by the news and had done their best to persuade their only child not to go ahead with the marriage. Nothing they said would change Mavis's mind, so the family had relented. Mavis's father had found rooms for the couple, and paid the first six months' rent. Aunties, uncles, cousins and grandparents had rallied round with the furniture. Much to Paul's annoyance, Mavis had not approached her father for any money, but under pressure had promised she would do so after the wedding.

Evie dressed herself in a blue wool two-piece costume she had bought especially for the occasion. The wedding was to be held in church at Mr Humphreys' insistence. No daughter of his was going to be married in a register office, pregnant or not. The blue costume was just right. It was just a pity it was being worn in such circumstances.

She walked slowly down Imperial Avenue towards the church. The oak trees in the churchyard loomed majestically over the rows of ancient tombstones, their leaves glistening with thick frost that refused to melt in the watery March sun. Evie shivered, wishing she had put aside her vanity and worn her thick coat over her suit. As she entered the gates, she could see Mavis and her father deep in conversation on the church steps. Mavis was wearing a loose-fitting silver grey silk suit and Evie's first thought was that her friend must surely feel frozen with the cold. Mavis looked small and frail against the magnificent church, and not at all over five months pregnant.

Evie thought sadly of the times they had both imagined their weddings. Wonderful flowing white dresses had been visualised, with bridesmaids in powder blue. She quickly changed her thoughts, put a smile on her face and quickened her pace. She hesitantly joined Mavis and her father, not wanting to disturb their conversation. Harold Humphreys turned to her. Evie noticed how he had aged since the last time she had seen him. His face looked grey and deeply lined and his heavy-lidded eyes pleaded with Evie as he caught hold of her arm.

'You tell her, Evie. You're her best friend. Tell her she doesn't have to marry him. We'll help her and look after the baby.'

Evie took a deep breath and half smiled at her friend. Before she could say anything, Mavis spoke.

'I've told you, Dad. We love each other. Please, please

don't spoil my big day,' she pleaded.

Evie saw the colour drain out of Harold Humphreys' face and his broad shoulders sagged. His arms fell limply to his sides and he slowly turned and walked up the steps into the church.

Mavis turned to Evie. 'You ready?'

She nodded.

The pair joined Harold at the church doors. Mavis linked her arm with her father's, and with Evie behind, they walked slowly down the aisle.

The wedding reception was in full swing. Harold Humphreys had hired the Co-operative Hall to accommodate all the family and friends. Evie stood by a pillar at the edge of the dance floor and smiled as she spotted Mavis gazing adoringly up into Paul's eyes as they danced a waltz played by Melvin and his Playboys. She could hear snatches of conversation as she stood sipping her glass of ice cold lemonade. 'It won't last. Shotgun weddings never do . . .' Evie's anger rose. Harold and Grace Humphreys had stood by their daughter and had not tried to hide the fact that she was pregnant. Yet still people had to be nasty.

She felt the presence of someone at her side. She turned her head and found Paul leering at her. He put his arm round her shoulders.

'Has the delectable Evie not found anyone to dance with? Come on, I'll dance with you.'

She shook his arm free. 'No, thanks.'

Paul looked at her and his mood turned ugly. 'What d'you mean, no!'

'I mean, I don't want to dance, thank you.'

He seemed undeterred. 'Well, I'll claim my kiss then.'

Evie's stomach churned. 'What kiss?'

'Oh, Evie,' Paul said mockingly. 'I thought even you would know that it's tradition for the bridegroom to kiss the bridesmaid.'

'What would you know about tradition?' She looked at him in disgust.

Paul studied her for a moment, a sly smile playing round his thin lips. 'Don't like me much, do you?'

'And should I?'

'Oh, I get it. Jealous 'cos I never made a play for you, eh?'

She looked at him in contempt. 'I don't like you because you've ruined my friend's life.'

He laughed. 'Ruined her life! But she loves me, Evie,' he said sarcastically.

'Yes, poor soul, and of course she has a father with a bit of money.'

'All helps, Evie.' He smirked. 'I'll still have that kiss.'

'You lay one finger on me, Paul Jenkins, and I'll . . .'

'You'll what?'

'I'll tell Mavis I saw you with another woman going into the Eclipse on the day she told me you were getting married.'

Paul looked stunned for a moment, then shrugged his shoulders.

'That was my sister.'

'You liar . . .'

'Hi, you two. Getting to know each other better? I'm glad.'

Evie and Paul turned sharply as a beaming Mavis approached them.

'Er . . . yes.' Evie smiled quickly. 'Excuse me, I need a

breath of air.' She turned and left abruptly.

Mavis watched her friend go, perplexed by her sudden departure. She turned back to Paul.

'Come on.' She linked her arm through her husband's and looked adoringly up into his eyes. 'My Auntie Mabel wants to meet you.'

Mavis caught up with Evie about an hour later. She smiled up at her friend, an enquiring expression in her eyes.

'Are you all right, Evie? Only there seemed to be some tension between you and Paul earlier on.'

'I'm fine,' Evie said quickly. She took a sip of her lemonade and put the glass down on a table. 'I suppose I'm jealous of you and Paul.' She looked at Mavis and smiled wanly. 'I've lost my best friend, haven't I?'

Mavis grinned broadly and stuck her arm through Evie's. 'Don't be daft. You and I will always be friends. Being married changes nothing. Anyway, if anyone should be jealous, it's me. You and Jenny spend a lot of time together now. It's me who feels pushed out.'

Evie turned and hugged her friend tightly. 'Oh, Mavis, nobody will take your place. We go back too far.'

'Same here. Now come on, let's enjoy the rest of my day. It's been grand so far, hasn't it? The weather's been perfect. All the relatives have got on, and Paul . . .' Mavis looked around the room in search of her husband. A slight frown crossed her face as she spied him propping up the bar deep in conversation with a blonde-haired girl one of her cousins had brought along. She turned quickly back to Evie. 'And Paul's the most wonderful man in the world, and I'm so happy.'

Evie forced a smile. 'I'm glad for you. I wish you and

Paul all the happiness in the world.' She kissed Mavis on the cheek. 'Now I'm going to go and have a dance with your dad.'

'Oh, he'll like that,' Mavis said, her eyes twinkling. 'And I'm going to rescue Paul. He seems to be stuck with that woman at the bar.'

Evie turned her head and looked across the room. 'Yes, he does, doesn't he?'

Chapter Four

'Yer seen the notice on the board in the canteen, Evie? The works are gettin' a bus trip up to Blackpool for the day. I ain't ever bin to the seaside. Shall we go?' Jenny said excitedly as they walked out of the factory gates one hot July lunch time. 'It'll only cost three bob and we could take a pack up for lunch. What d'you say? It's not till the beginnin' of September. Gives us bags a' time to save.'

Evie grinned enthusiastically. 'Yes, it does sound fun.'

'You ever bin to the seaside?' Jenny asked.

'Yes. Several times.'

'Oh! What's it like? I've only seen the sea in pictures.'

'It's all right.' Evie shrugged her shoulders. 'We used to go for holidays to Unstanton before the war. It's only a little place but the beach was smashing. There was no fair or anything, just a few swings and a round-about. But I can remember enjoying myself.'

'Oh!' Jenny exclaimed in awe. 'Unstanton, eh! Most people I know go to Skegness and that's usually only for the day.' She scratched her chin thoughtfully. 'The furthest I've ever got outta' Leicester wa' to Bradgate Park. It were during the war, while me dad wa' away. 'Course, we had to walk the ten miles, 'cos we couldn't afford the bus fare. But it wa' a smashin' day. We saw all the deer and the rabbits. Mam made a picnic and we sat on top of Old John. You could see all the countryside for miles. On the way back we stopped at a farm and the farmer's wife gave us some fresh milk straight from the cows. Our June wa' really sick the next day. Mam blamed the milk: said it hadn't bin steri'whatsited like the stuff we get from the Co-op.' Jenny grabbed hold of Evie's arm and pulled her to a halt. 'Let's go, Evie! I'd love to see the sea and 'ave some fun.'

'Yes, why not?' Evie grinned as they started to walk again. 'Although I'll have to ask my mam first. She's a right fusspot when it comes to something like this. I'm sure she thinks someone is going to kidnap me.' She frowned. 'I've been trying for ages to pluck up the courage to ask if I can go to the Palais one Friday night.' She looked at Jenny enquiringly. 'Have you ever been down the Palais?'

Jenny clasped her hands together with delight. 'Yeah. Only once, mind. It wa' fabulous. The dance floor's massive; it's got a fountain in the middle and gets packed with the most wonderful lads. I went wi' Edna Greenbaum from the corner shop. She told 'er mam she wa' goin' to the synagogue and I told mine I wa' goin' to the dance at the church 'all, and off we went.'

'You never! Blimey, Jenny, you've got a nerve.'

'Yeah, and it were worth all the trouble.'

'Did anyone ask you to dance?'

''Course! I don't know 'ow you dare ask such a thing!' Jenny retorted haughtily, before bursting into gales of laughter. ''E wa' a soldier, doin' his National Service, and wa' covered in spots. We started to jive and I fell over.'

'You fell over?' Evie gasped. They both paused by the kerb and waited while a bus thundered past.

'You 'eard. I fell over,' continued Jenny, wiping her eyes as tears of laughter fell down her cheeks.

'How did that happen?' Evie asked as they crossed the road.

'Simple – I can't jive! Well, I can't jive doin' the girl's bit, I can only do the boy's. I felt a right idiot. It wa' that Marilyn Williams's fault.'

'How was it her fault?' Evie frowned. 'Was she at the dance with you?'

'No, you silly ha'porth. Me and 'er used to practise at the church dances and she would only dance wi' me if I did the boy. So that's all I can do. I tell yer, I felt really stupid, sprawled on the floor with me legs in the air, showing next week's washin'.'

'So would I. What happened next?' Evie giggled.

'The sod walked off and left me,' Jenny sulked. 'Everyone wa' lookin' at me. Good job I didn't fancy 'im.' Her face lit up and she giggled. 'Oh, but I tell yer, Evie, the Palais is great. The Big Band plays all the latest music, and 'alfway through the evenin' they play the Gay Gordons and the '''Okey Cokey''. That bit's really funny, 'cos I can't do them proper either.' She paused thoughtfully for a moment. 'We could learn to jive together – we could practise in your bedroom. You've got a record player, ain't yer? We could take it in turns to do the boy and girl, couldn't we? What'd you say, eh?'

'Oh, yes, Jenny, let's,' Evie agreed enthusiastically.

'When we get really good, we could go down the Palais one Friday night and show 'em all 'ow brilliant we are.'

'I'd love to. It sounds heavenly. But you know how old-fashioned my mother is about these things.'

Jenny grimaced. 'My mam's only too glad to 'ave us

from under 'er feet. I can't understand your mam. Doesn't she trust you or somethin'?' She sighed. 'Oh, well. We'll start practisin' our dancin' and I'll put our names down on the list for the trip, in case they run outta seats. You pick the right moment to make sure the answer's yes.'

'I'll do my best. I want to go as much as you,' Evie sighed.

Jenny nudged her arm. 'Arnold from the dye 'ouse is goin' on the trip. I've fancied 'im since the Christmas do.'

Evie laughed. 'Jennifer Jones, all you ever think about is lads!'

'And you, Evelyn Grayson. I've seen the way you eye Michael Whatsisname in Accounts. I'll see if 'is name's on the list, then we can make a foursome.'

'Don't you dare!' Evie retorted, nudging her friend in the ribs.

Both girls collapsed into giggles as they arrived at the Town Hall Square. All the benches were taken, so they sat on the grass and began to eat their sandwiches. Jenny finished her lunch and blew into the brown paper bag, then smacked it between her hands, making Evie jump.

'C & A 'ave gorra sale on,' she piped up, unaware that Evie was annoyed at the fright she had just given her. 'They've some smashin' swagger coats on offer, only thirty-nine and eleven. D'you reckon I could save enough to get one before the sale finishes? Be just the job for Blackpool. Real swanky, I'll be.'

Evie shook her head. 'You'll never have any money. You spend everything you get.'

'That's what money's for, ain't it?'

Evie shrugged her shoulders. 'Well, yes . . . I suppose so. But my mam makes me save half a crown a week and it's built up nicely over the years.' Evie looked thoughtfully into the distance. 'I quite fancy a car, you know. You can get a nice little secondhand Austin A40 for about four hundred pounds . . .'

'Four 'undred pounds! Evie Grayson, 'ave you really got four 'undred pounds?'

Evie's mind came back from her dream. 'What? Oh, I don't know how much I've got, my mam keeps the book. Anyway, if I did know I wouldn't tell you, Jenny Jones. You'd have it all spent before I could blink my eyes. Oh, but wouldn't it be nice to have a car? No more queuing for buses and sitting next to smelly people, and we could go out for runs on a Sunday into the country.'

'Mm,' Jenny agreed thoughtfully. 'And we could eye up the lads. Mind you, we can do that on a bus, and a bus is good enough for the likes of me. I could think of better things to do wi' four 'undred pounds than buying a car.'

'Oh, yes. Such as?' Evie asked sarcastically.

Jenny frowned as she thought. 'Well, for a start I'd get a whole new loada clothes. Think what I could buy wi' all that money.' Jenny stopped for a moment trying to do calculations in her head. She quickly gave up. 'Well, I'd get a 'ell of a lot, anyway. Then I'd take me mam and dad away for the week. Somewhere exotic . . . like Bournemouth. All the best people go to Bournemouth. It's the air, you know.'

Evie laughed at Jenny's mimicry. 'Yes, and what else?'

'I'd get a television set for me dad. 'E'd love that, might stop 'im grumblin' so much, and a new gas cooker for me mam.' She clasped her hands together. 'Oh, Evie, there's lots of things I'd do wi' that kinda money.'

'Yes. But we can both dream as much as we like, my

mother won't let me touch it. I have to save it and that's that.'

'Oh, yes? And yer could be dead tomorrow, so what's the point?' Jenny frowned. 'I 'ope you've made a will and left it all to me.' She giggled.

Evie shook her head. 'Jenny Jones, I give up on you.' She stood up and threw her empty sandwich bag into the rubbish bin. 'Come on, let's get back and we'll get our names on that list. I'll speak to Mam over the weekend about the trip. And if she won't let me go to the Palais, I'll sneak out, like you did.'

Jenny laughed loudly. 'Yer learnin', gel. You stick wi' me, I'll show yer.'

'Yes, that's what worries me. Anyway, come round on Friday night and we'll start our dancing practice.'

'Yeah, okay,' Jenny agreed enthusiastically.

'Keep your fingers crossed Mam agrees to the trip.'

'I'll cross everythin' if it means you'll be able to go.' Jenny jumped up from the grass and grabbed her friend's arm, pulling her to her feet. The pair ran through the town back towards their workplace.

Persuading Edith to let her go on the Blackpool trip had been much easier than Evie had dreamed, even though she did tell her mother one white lie. Edith merely listened and nodded.

'Okay. As Miss Sargent will be there keeping an eye on you, I don't see why not.' She frowned. 'Although I'm not so sure about this Jenny. She's a bit rough, Evie.'

'Mam! Jenny's been a good friend to me. If it hadn't have been for her, I wouldn't still be in the offices at Dawson's. I'd have walked out by now.'

'Yes, I realise that, Evie. I know it was hard for you and still is, and she's stood by you. It's just that . . .'

'What, Mam?'

'Well, she swears and . . .'

'Yes?' Evie interrupted sharply. 'She also comes from a council estate, spends what little money she has on clothes and enjoying herself. I know what you're thinking, Mother. You're thinking she's common and not good enough for me. Well, you're wrong. Jenny makes me laugh. She listens to my problems and makes me see things as they really are. She's good for me, Mam. She makes me realise how lucky I am, and I don't intend to stop being friends with her just because her family is poor.' Evie stopped for breath. 'I'm surprised at you, Mam. You told me how hard up we used to be when we lived in Tudor Road, and how during the war all the neighbours pulled together and shared what they had. For some people it's still like that. I thought you of all people would understand. You've always brought me up to be fair about things and tolerant of people's situations.'

Edith clapped her hand to her mouth. 'Oh, I'm sorry. I didn't mean . . .'

Evie rushed to her mother and put her arms around her. 'It's all right, Mam, I know you worry about me, but finding Jenny was the best thing that could have happened.'

Edith sighed deeply, pulled away from her daughter and sat down in her chair. 'Bring her round for dinner one night, that'll give me the chance to get to know her better.'

'Honest, Mam? And you promise not to say anything if she swears or troughs her food?'

Edith smiled. 'I promise, and if you save for the fare,

I'll give you some spending money – enough for you to split with Jenny.'

'Thanks, Mam!' Evie clasped her hands together and rushed off to tell her friend. Jenny had talked of nothing else since they had decided to go. She was beside herself with joy at the news and the pair began to plan their outfits for the special day.

The week before the trip to Blackpool, Evie put on her lavender cotton duster coat over her matching gathered skirt and white blouse and walked into the kitchen where her mother was making a fruit cake.

'I'm off, Mam.'

Edith looked up from her baking. 'Off! Where?'

'Mam, I told you. I'm going to see Mave and the baby.'

'Oh, yes. Sorry, love, I forgot. Give her my regards, and don't forget the baby clothes I knitted. They're on the table in the living room.'

'No, they're not. I have them here in my bag.' Evie went over and kissed her mother on the cheek. 'I'll be home before six.'

'Okay. Have a nice time.'

Evie smiled at her mother as she left. She was looking forward to the visit. She had not seen much of Mavis since the birth of the baby, and there was so much to catch up on. Paul would not be around so Evie hurried to the bus stop, determined not to waste any of their precious time together.

Mavis and Paul had just moved from the rooms Harold Humphreys had found for them as they could not pay the rent. They had found cheaper ones in a dismal terraced street off the Fosse Road, a complete contrast to the large, comfortable house Mavis had lived in with her parents. Evie walked briskly down the street and knocked tentatively on the door. A sour-faced landlady eyed her suspiciously and reluctantly let her in.

Mavis embraced her friend warmly. Evie pulled back from the embrace and eyed her closely. She was shocked at how tired and drawn Mavis looked. Her hair and clothes were in dire need of a wash and the usual sparkle and zest for life had gone out of her eyes.

'You look tired,' Evie said in concern, taking off her duster coat and laying it on the back of a chair.

'Who wouldn't be with a new baby, and a husband that stays out half the night?' Mavis muttered under her breath.

'What was that?'

'Oh, nothing, Evie. Want some tea?'

'Yes, please.'

Evie walked over to the cot and peered inside. The baby stirred slightly and puckered its lips. 'Oh, she's beautiful. Just like a little red rose. Her name suits her perfectly – Rosie.' She gently put her hand into the pram and ran the side of her finger down the baby's face. 'Oh, Mave, her skin's so soft! I could just eat her.'

Mavis smiled as she poured the boiling water into the teapot. 'You wouldn't say that if she woke you in the middle of the night, screaming her head off!'

'No, I suppose not.' Evie smiled. 'Paul helps though, doesn't he?'

Mavis ignored the question as she walked over with Evie's cup of tea.

As she accepted it, Evie looked around the dismal room and shuddered. The accommodation consisted of a kitchen-cum-living room, small bedroom and shared toilet. Baths were taken weekly at Mavis's parents' house or at the Vestry Street Slipper Baths. The room filled Evie with gloom which she tried to shake off as they settled themselves on chairs at the table by the large bay window. She realised that Mavis was speaking to her.

'It's a devil getting the pram up and down the stairs. The landlady won't let us keep it downstairs. Miserable old devil, she is.'

'Well, when Paul gets a job you can move to a better place.' Evie spoke, trying to sound optimistic.

Mavis sighed loudly. 'I'm beginning to wonder if he ever will.'

Before she could say any more she started to cough. She jumped up and rushed over to the sink. Evie looked on aghast. Mavis straightened up and ran the tap.

'Sorry about that, Evie. It's just a chest cold.' She turned towards her friend. 'Can I ask a favour?'

'Yes, sure.'

'Will you watch Rosie while I run up the town? I hate to ask, only I haven't been since she was born.'

Evie felt dismayed and tried to hide her annoyance. 'Yes, 'course I will. I suppose we can chat when you come back.'

'Thanks, Evie.' Mavis grabbed her coat and bag before her friend could change her mind. 'There's a bottle over near the sink if Rosie wakes, and there's some bread in the bin if you fancy some toast. I won't be long.'

'But . . . what if Paul comes back?'

'He won't.' Mavis shook her head. 'He's gone . . .' she paused, 'up the Speedway.'

Evie gave a long sigh as she watched her friend rush out of the door. She turned and gazed out of the window,

deep in thought. Several children were playing on the paved
street below. A group of young boys were playing marbles
in the gutter, a group of girls were skipping and another
lot playing hopscotch. Evie smiled as memories of herself
and Mavis came to mind, playing the same games in another
street not far away, only their street had been tree-lined
and grass-verged not paved and starved of greenery like
this one.

She turned from the window and stared round the room
again. Things were far from well in this household. She
got up and walked over to the kitchen area and poured
herself another cup of tea. Instinctively she picked up a
cloth and wiped the work surface, cringing slightly as the
grease and dirt attached itself to the already grey-stained
material. Her worst fears were materialising. It was obvious
that Mavis was no housekeeper. She turned and leaned
back against the grimy cooker, looking round the rest of
the room. The good furniture, hastily put together by Mavis's
loving relatives, was badly in need of a dust, and behind
the armchair Evie could see a dirty nappy. She felt her
anger mounting.

How could Mavis have let herself go like this, and what
kind of man was Paul to let her live in this hovel? Her
thoughts were interrupted by a loud knock on the door.
Rosie started to howl.

Hell! thought Evie, not quite sure whether to answer
the door first or pick up the screaming baby. The door was
pounded again and Rosie howled even louder. Evie clumsily
picked her up then gingerly walked over to the door and
opened it.

Before her stood a small, pretty woman. She wore a
bright red low-cut blouse, revealing a lot of cleavage, and

a powder blue skirt that was just a little too short. Her lips were painted bright pink and her permed hair dyed peroxide blonde.

Evie frowned as she tried hard to rock Rosie gently in her arms and keep her balance. The baby's screams grew even louder as Evie stared at the woman.

'Yes?' she said.

The woman hesitated and looked past her into the room. She turned her gaze back to Evie, a puzzled look on her face.

'What can I do for you?' Evie asked.

The woman took a breath. 'I've bin told Paul Jenkins lives 'ere.'

'Yes, he does, but he's not in. Why?'

Evie's eyes were drawn from the woman's face by a slight movement at her side. She looked down and saw a small child on leading reins.

'Keep still, Johnnie.' The woman tugged at the reins sharply and the child jerked upwards and started to cry. 'And for Christ's sake, stop yer bawlin'.'

Evie looked down again at the child and noticed a puddle on the floor. 'He's wet himself,' she said.

'Oh, bloody 'ell, Johnnie! Damn' kid. Can't tek 'im anywhere. Can I use yer lavvy?'

'Er . . . yes. It's out the back.' Evie motioned with her head towards the stairs.

'Huh. Thought these places 'ad indoor lavvies,' the woman moaned as she jerked the reins again. 'Come on, Johnnie. I'll be back,' she addressed Evie, then pulled the child and disappeared down the stairs.

Evie walked slowly into the room, perturbed by the woman's intrusion. Rosie's howls turned to a whimper as she sucked her lips together in hunger. Evie went over and picked up the bottle of milk that Mavis had left and stuck it into the baby's mouth. Rosie took one suck, spat out the teat and started to howl again. Evie frustratedly pushed the bottle in again and got the same result.

The woman came back into the room slamming the door shut behind her. She dragged Johnnie across the floor and held out the reins.

''Ere. You cop 'old of 'im and give the baby to me.' She grabbed Rosie out of Evie's arms and snatched the bottle.

'No wonder she won't tek it. The bottle's bloody cold! Don't you know nothin' about babies?'

Evie sat dumbstruck as the woman plonked Rosie unceremoniously back into the pram and put the bottle into the hot kettle.

Johnnie started to cry again. Thick green mucus ran from his nose which he wiped on the back of his sleeve. The woman went over and smacked him round the head. Evie sat with her mouth open in astonishment.

'Don't do that, yer mucky bugger!' the woman shouted at the small boy. He cried even louder. 'Gorra bit of bread or somethin' for 'im?'

'There's a loaf over there.' Evie nodded towards the large white enamel bread bin. The woman helped herself to a crust and gave it to Johnnie. She then tested the bottle and handed it to Evie.

''Ere, try it now.'

Evie took the bottle and went over to pick up the whimpering Rosie. Settled with the baby sucking happily on the teat, she addressed the woman once more.

'Look, who are you and what do you want?'

The woman opened her bag and took out a cigarette. She lit it and drew deeply. She walked towards Evie and sat down opposite her.

'I told yer, me duck. Paul Jenkins. Well, not 'im. I don't care if I never sees 'im again, but I want me money.' She looked hard at the bewildered Evie and sighed. ''E's done it to you as well, ain't 'e? Well, you ain't the first and you won't be the last. The bastard stole fifty quid off me. Just took it and scarpered. Me granny left me that money. Saved all her life, she did. It were all in tanners and threepenny bits. That didn't matter to 'im, or the fact that I needed it.'

'What!' Evie groaned disbelievingly. 'He did what?' She pulled the empty bottle from Rosie's mouth, stood up and walked over to the pram, placing the baby gently inside.

'You ain't winded 'er. You 'ave to wind babies or they scream the 'ouse down . . .'

Evie swung round. 'Look, just shut up a minute!' she said angrily as she walked back to the table and sat down. 'I don't know you and I certainly don't know what you're talking about . . .'

The woman leaned forward and placed her hand on Evie's.

'It's all right, dear, I know.' She looked sympathetic. 'I know what 'e's done. You don't need to be shy wi' me. The bleeder's got you in the family way, stole yer money and left. See, I know. 'E did it to me, and I've found out since to two others. Nothin' but a dirty, thieving liar! You're well shot of 'im.' She withdrew her hand and took another draw of her cigarette, dropping ash on to the linoleum. 'I'm surprised at the likes of you falling for 'im, though. 'E's certainly movin' up in the world.' She gave a superior smile. 'But I tell yer this, me duck, 'e ain't gettin' away wi' it. I want me money. I need it for the kid 'ere, so where is 'e?'

Evie wiped her hand across her face. 'Are you telling me Paul's been married before and has other children?' she asked, horrified.

'Married! Who said anythin' about marriage!' The woman fell back in her chair, her face contorted in anger. 'Did that bastard marry you?'

The two woman stared at one another, each trying to take in the facts that were emerging.

'Not me,' Evie spoke sharply. 'My friend.'

The woman leant forward and stubbed her cigarette out in an ashtray that sat in the centre of the table. 'Oh! You're just watchin' the kid then?'

Evie nodded.

The woman laughed. 'Thought yer didn't know much about babies. Will she be long, this friend?' She leant back in her chair and folded her arms.

'No. And I'd prefer it if you weren't here when she does come back.'

'Why? Bit soft, is she?'

'No, she isn't,' retorted Evie sharply.

'Must be if she's bin took in by the likes of 'im.' The woman narrowed her eyes at Evie. 'I'm stayin'. I want me money and I ain't leavin' till I get it. Understand, lady? I know I won't get anythin' out of 'im, so it might as well be 'er. And bein's I'm staying for a bit, I might as well introduce meself. I'm Ruby. Ruby Gittings.' She reached for her bag and lit another cigarette. 'Might be 'ere for a while so what's for tea? The kid'll be starvin' soon.'

Evie's anger mounted as she scraped her chair back and stood up. 'Look . . . Ruby, my friend has no money. Paul hasn't done a day's work since before he met Mavis, so you're wasting your time. All this is going to be a hell of a shock to her . . .'

'What will be a shock, Evie?'

She turned her head sharply to see Mavis framed in the doorway.

'Oh!' She clapped her hand over her mouth. 'I didn't hear you come in.'

Mavis placed her bags on the floor and shut the door behind her. She bit her bottom lip and looked hesitantly at Ruby.

'What's going on, Evie, and who's this woman?'

Mavis sat huddled in her chair. Her hysterical sobs had quietened, but her thin body still shook. She blew loudly into a sodden handkerchief and looked up at Evie through watery eyes. Ruby had long since gone. Evie had shown her the door and told her never to return. Bread crumbs were scattered over the linoleum and the smell of urine still lingered. Evie felt worn out and drained, her emotions caught between anger and heartbreak for her friend.

'She could be lying,' Evie whispered, trying hard to comfort Mavis.

Mavis shook her head. 'She's not lying, Evie.'

'She's not?'

'No.' Mavis blew her nose again. She twisted the handkerchief round her fingers. The silence in the room was deafening. At last, Mavis spoke again.

'I've known something wasn't right for a while. Soon after we married really.' She paused again, finding the words difficult to say. 'Paul started to be secretive about things: where he'd been when he went out and so on, and I was too afraid to tackle him. He'd keep asking for money. Money I needed for food and the electric. I'd give it to him and me and Rosie went without. He started to get on to me about asking Dad for money.' She bent her head. 'He smacked me hard when I told him I wasn't going to. I couldn't. I just couldn't ask Dad for money, not after all he's done for me. I began to suspect Paul. Don't know why. Just instinct, I suppose.'

All the time Mavis was speaking, Evie sat in stony silence staring at her friend, her face portraying none of the turmoil she was experiencing.

Mavis continued, sniffing loudly between words.

'He'd say he was going to the Labour Exchange or round the factories to make enquiries about a job. I just knew he'd never been but I was frightened to know the truth. If I asked too many questions he'd get nasty and start hitting me.'

'Hitting you! Mavis, why didn't you tell me?'

'I couldn't.' She stopped abruptly and paused for a moment. 'About three weeks ago, I had a visitor.' She hesitated again.

'Well, who?' prompted Evie.

'Paul's sister.'

'Sister!' Evie queried in astonishment. 'I didn't know he had any family, let alone a sister.'

'Well, he has. And he comes from quite a wealthy family at that.'

'Wealthy! I don't understand. If Paul comes from a wealthy family, why is he always so broke?' Evie shook her head in bewilderment.

'Because he spent all his money, Evie, on gambling and women. And because of his bad ways his family has disowned him.'

'Don't you think you'd better tell me the whole story, Mavis?' Evie said firmly.

She could see the tears welling up in her friend's eyes again. Mavis tried hard to fight them and lowered her head as one escaped and raced down her cheek. She wiped it with the back of her hand as she made to rise from the chair.

'I'll just check the baby.'

'The baby's fine, Mave. Just tell me: I am your best friend.' Evie pushed her unceremoniously back into the chair.

Mavis shuddered and took a deep breath. 'Paul comes from Lancashire. His family own property and land, and from what I can gather are loaded with money. Paul apparently had money of his own, left to him by his grandmother.' She sighed deeply. 'Barbara, his sister, told me he gambled it all away. His father found out what he had done with his inheritance and was furious and wouldn't give him another penny, so he stole from the family business . . . forging cheques, something like that. When his father discovered this, he threatened to call in the police but the rest of the family persuaded him not to. They didn't want to blacken the family name. So his father cut Paul off, told him he never wanted to see him again.'

'Oh, Mavis.'

'That's not all,' she continued. 'Barbara was very fond of her young brother so she kept her eye on him, hoping that the big wide world would straighten him out. Paul went from bad to worse.' She sniffed loudly. 'He's . . .

he's been in prison for stealing.' She blew her nose again. 'Barbara was very nice, but upset to find Paul had not changed. I found myself telling her about him wanting to borrow money off my father. She was really angry and told me not to ask my father under any circumstances. She said Paul would only gamble it away.' She looked up at Evie and smiled wanly. 'She took a shine to Rosie but said there was no point in telling the family about her or myself as they would not want to know. They've wiped their hands of Paul and that's that. She gave me twenty pounds, wished me the best and left.'

'I don't know what to say.' Evie's voice was strained with emotion.

'What is there to say? Paul's a rotter. He's bad to the core and these other women are the final straw.' Mavis's body sagged. 'I'm worn out, Evie. Tired and exhausted and don't know what to do.' She burst into floods of tears again. 'I still love him, you see. As much as I try to hate him, I can't. The pain's terrible. It's more than I can bear. I bet he's with one of his floozies now.' She looked up at Evie through watery eyes. 'How can I tell my family about all this, after they begged me not to marry him?'

Evie could not contain her anger any longer. 'Mavis, you'll have to face him when he comes home . . .'

'He isn't coming home, Evie.' Mavis's voice rose hysterically. 'He's left me. He found out his sister had been. You should have seen him. He went berserk. Smashed half my dinner service, and when Rosie began to cry, he threatened to throw her out of the window. Evie, I was so scared! He took the twenty pounds out of my purse and left. I haven't seen him since.'

Evie froze. 'Get your clothes and the baby. Now, Mavis!'

She looked bewildered. 'Why?'

'I'm taking you back to your mam. You're not staying a moment longer in this house.'

Mavis shrank back into her chair. 'I can't, Evie. I can't face them.'

'You can and you will. Now if you don't come with me, I'll fetch them here,' Evie exploded. 'Look at you, Mavis! Look at the state you're in!' She stormed over to the middle of the room. 'Look at this flat. It's a pigsty. Paul's brought you down to this. Think of the home you came from. You had your whole future in front of you. You worked in your dad's office, your mam did everything for you, and look at you now. You've got nothing. You're an utter mess, and if you think I'm going to go away and do nothing about it, then you have another think coming.' She stopped her flow abruptly and stared at Mavis sitting pathetically in the chair.

Her body shook as she started to have a coughing fit.

'You're not well, either. What's wrong, Mave? That's more than a cold. Have you been to the doctor's?'

She slowly nodded.

'And what did he say?'

Evie had to strain her ears as Mavis whispered, 'The doctor thinks I've got TB. I have to go to hospital next Wednesday. That's why I needed to go into town and get things to take in with me.'

Evie clasped her hand to her mouth. 'Oh, God, Mave. Oh, you poor love. That settles it. Get your things now. I'm taking you home.'

Later that night, Evie related her tale to her mother as she sat huddled on the settee. Edith was astounded. 'That poor girl,' was all she could say, over and over again. When Evie had finished, Edith sighed loudly.

'What about her parents?' she asked.

'They were marvellous, Mam. Shocked to hell, but marvellous. Mr Humphreys has threatened to kill Paul if he should set eyes on him again. I just wish I could take some of the pain away from Mave, especially with this TB hanging over her head.' Evie looked at her mother, a worried frown crossing her face. 'Do you think I did the right thing, Mam?'

Edith rose and sat next to her distraught daughter, gently placing an arm around her shoulders.

'You did the right thing,' she said softly. 'I would have done the same in your position. You and Mavis have been friends a long time and there's no way you could have left her in that flat. The poor girl is at rock bottom and you've taken her back to where she belongs.' Edith sighed. 'I don't think you've heard the last of Paul, though.'

Evie's mouth dropped open. 'What d'you mean?'

'Well, he's bound to want to know where his wife is. After all, she's his meal ticket, and when his money runs out . . .' Edith tightened her lips.

'Oh, I see what you mean.' Evie clasped her hands. 'Oh God!'

'We'll not worry about that now, Evie. She's in the best place and her dad is certainly no pushover. So, if Paul does make trouble, he'll not get away with it.'

'No. I just hope he keeps away. If he's got any sense he will.'

'Men like him haven't got any sense, Evie.' Edith hugged her daughter tightly. 'Now come on. You need to go to bed. Just remember, Mavis is one of the lucky ones. She has a decent family and you as a friend. She'll come through all right. It'll take time though.' She smiled at her daughter. 'You handled it well, Evie. I'm proud of you.'

She felt instantly better.

Edith thought for a moment. 'If Mavis has got TB, she'll be in Groby Road Hospital for at least a year – that's if they've caught the disease in time. I hear the treatment is just plenty of rest and fresh air.' She took a breath. 'While she's away, will her parents look after Rosie?'

'Oh, yes. Mavis's mother dotes on her. I think they're waiting to hear what the test results are first, before they make any plans. Oh, what a mess! That Paul wants shooting. Can you believe he married Mave and he already had those other women and children?'

'When you've seen as much as I have, Evie, you can believe anything.' Edith spoke sternly. 'Now you're exhausted. Come on, up to bed and I'll bring you some hot milk.'

'Not hot milk. I hate it!' Evie grimaced.

'I don't care, it'll settle your stomach. And I'll stay until you drink it all.'

'There's nothing wrong with my stomach ...'

'Evie!'

She was too tired and drained to argue with her mother, so she kissed her on the cheek and crept up the stairs, heeding Edith's warning to be quiet so as not to wake Florrie.

Even the hot milk could not stop her thoughts churning round and round in her head. When sleep did finally steal over her, the milkman had already made his deliveries.

Chapter Five

The day of the Blackpool trip dawned bright and sunny. Evie walked slowly down the stairs and into the kitchen. She hugged her dressing gown tightly round her as she watched her mother poking bacon and eggs in the frying pan. Edith sensed her presence and turned round.

'There you are. Come and sit down. There's fresh tea in the pot, your breakfast won't be a moment.'

Evie smiled and sat down slowly. 'You shouldn't have got up, Mam. It's far too early. I could have seen myself off,' she said, yawning loudly.

'It's no bother to me, love. I wanted to make sure you went out with a decent breakfast inside you, and I've made up a few sandwiches for you and Jenny.' Edith placed the steaming food in front of her daughter. 'My, you don't look very happy. Not feeling well?'

'I'm all right, Mam. I just feel guilty, that's all. I really don't feel in the mood for this trip.'

'Guilty. Oh, I see.' Edith picked up her cup of tea and sat down opposite her daughter. 'Look, Evie. You can't feel guilty for having some enjoyment. Mavis is in the best place. She's being well looked after and hopefully she'll be out of the sanatorium before you know it. You told me her mother is delighted to look after Rosie and

89

that the child is thriving and getting as fat as a pudding. Now come on, cheer up, and eat your breakfast before it gets cold. I don't want you missing the bus, not after all the trouble you went to to persuade me to let you go.' Edith patted her daughter warmly on the arm. 'Pity you couldn't have persuaded Florrie to go with you.'

'Oh, Mam.' Evie pulled a wry face. 'Can you see our Florrie with a "Kiss Me Quick" hat on, eating fish and chips out of a newspaper? She'd turn the vinegar with her face!'

'Evie! That's enough of that kind of talk. You're most unkind.'

'Unkind or not, it's true. I don't think our Florrie sees any joy in life. Look what she said about Mave. Said it served her right for being such a fool. If anyone is unkind, it's her.'

'Evie, you've made your point. Now remember to take your coat in case it gets cold,' her mother said sternly.

'Mam, we're in the middle of a heat wave! It's that hot the tarmac is melting on the roads and you want me to take my coat?'

'That may be so, but it can get mighty chilly on the sea front and I don't want you going down with a cold.'

'Oh, Mam,' Evie muttered under her breath.

The early morning sun was already beating down as Evie waited for Jenny at the bus station. She was feeling very chic in her floral waspie waist skirt and a white cropped cotton top. She had compromised with her mother and had a thick cardigan tucked right down into the bottom of her bag. The drab surroundings of the bus station came alive with colour as women of all ages, excited at the prospect of a day out, descended dressed in their best clothes. Evie raised her hand and patted her neatly tied pony tail, confident that she could compete with the best of them.

'Ain't it excitin'?' Jenny said as she bounded up to Evie, her bag bulging at the seams. 'And you look nice,' she said as she gave Evie the once over.

'So do you.' Evie smiled, scanning Jenny's skintight bright green Capri pants and halter neck top. 'Did you make that outfit yourself?'

'Yeah. D'you like it?' Jenny said, putting her bag down and giving a twirl. 'I didn't get the pants finished 'til after eleven last night, then I couldn't get to sleep wi' excitement. Oh, look! There's Arnold and 'is mates.' She nudged Evie's elbow, making her drop her bag, its contents clattering all over the tarmac.

'Jenny!' Evie groaned loudly as she bent down and started to pick up her bits and pieces.

'Plasters, barley sugar, aspirin . . . Christ, Evie, you're a walkin' chemist! What else yer got in there?'

'Nothing,' she snapped. 'Just help me before anyone sees.'

'Okay, keep yer 'air on.' Jenny bent down to help her friend. 'Don't we both look great? I bet we turn a few 'eads today. Pity I never got me swagger coat, but I suppose it would 'ave bin too warm to wear it anyway.' She straightened herself up. 'There, all done.' She looked around the bus station. 'Blimey, look at all these people. Looks as if there's more than our crowd goin' to Blackpool today.'

The bus station was becoming congested as even more people poured inside. Buses started their engines and the smell of diesel fumes filled the air.

Evie and Jenny soon spotted friends from their own

factory and went over to join them. Shouts of 'Where's our bus?' 'Hang on, Hilda's not here yet', and 'I need a window seat, else I'll be sick', were drowned out, as loaded buses started to leave for their destinations.

Evie and Jenny jostled with their group to get a good seat. Jenny finally sat down next to Evie and plonked her bag unceremoniously on her knees.

'Damned ironic, ain't it?' she fumed.

'What is?' Evie asked, glad at last to rest her legs.

'That Sandra Bates from the Personnel Department, pushin' everyone out the way so she can grab the whole back seat for 'er cronies. Mind you, wi' a backside like 'ers, what chance 'ave the likes of us got to get past?'

'Jenny, calm down. We've a good seat . . .'

'I know,' she interrupted, 'but I wanted to sit at the back. We could 'ave knelt on the seat and waved at the cars goin' past.' She turned round and gave Sandra Bates a dirty look then nudged Evie. 'Look now. She's made Arnold sit next to 'er. Thieving cow! I knew she wa' after 'im.'

Evie carefully turned her head and looked over.

'He may be sitting with Sandra, but his eyes are on you,' she said with laughter in her voice.

'Are they? Are they really, Evie?' Jenny patted her hair. 'What's 'e doin' now? Is 'e still lookin'?' she demanded.

Evie slowly turned her head again. 'Yes, he's still looking. Sandra has her hands all over him, but his eyes are on you. I reckon he's trying to make you jealous.'

'Yer reckon?' Jenny patted her hair again. 'Well, 'e'll 'ave to try harder 'cos it ain't workin'.' She fumbled in her bag and pulled out a mangled sandwich. ''Ere. 'Ave 'alf a fried egg sandwich. I don't know about you, but I'm starvin'.'

Evie collapsed with laughter as the bus pulled out of the station and the jollifications began.

As long as she lived, Evie would never forget that journey. The whole bus came alive with the shouting of rude jokes, the passing round of beer bottles and the continual exchanging of seats. Between the never ending toilet stops, the loud singing of popular wartime hits echoed in unison. Evie's ribs ached with laughter as the bus finally rounded a corner and a loud cheer erupted at the first sight of the sea.

Jenny stood up and stared out of the window.

'Oh! Oh, Evie. Look 'ow blue it is!' She took a deep breath. 'I can smell it. I can!' She sat down again, then stood, then sat, wriggling excitedly in her seat. 'I need the lavvy. I 'ope we get there soon.'

Another cheer rose as the bus pulled to a stop opposite the sea front. A great surge of people desperate to alight caused mayhem as the harassed bus driver tried in vain to shout over the throng: 'If you're not back by six, I'll be gone.' He was pushed aside roughly in the scramble to get off.

Evie and Jenny joined several more friends from the office. Most of the morning was spent going in and out of the parade of arcades and the hot, airless shops that lined the sea front. Several purchases were made of cheap souvenirs, assorted hats and sticks of rock.

Jenny was particularly proud of the tasteless toilet-shaped ashtray she had bought for her father and insisted to an harassed assistant that she wrap it really well, so it would not get broken.

A ride in the lift to the top of the Blackpool Tower caused great merriment, because to Evie's dismay she found she could not stand heights and was goaded and teased mercilessly by her friends, Jenny included.

Tired out, the girls sat on a bench and demolished fish, chips and pickled onions, laced with salt and vinegar.

'Right, what are we gonna do now?' demanded Janet, a rotund, cheerful girl of seventeen. She screwed up her empty newspaper and threw it under the bench. 'I need a drink, let's go to a pub.'

Several voices agreed and Evie's face paled. She had never had an alcoholic drink before and did not know what to say. The other girls started to move away as Evie grabbed Jenny's arm.

'You're not going, are you?' she asked.

'Yeah, why not?' answered Jenny, shrugging her shoulders.

'But we're not old enough to drink.'

''Course we bloody are! We're over eighteen. For God's sake, Evie, stop makin' excuses and don't be such a misery guts. We're on 'oliday. Besides, I ain't never had a grown up drink before, so now's me chance.' Jenny leaned closer. 'Anyway, if that lot find out we'll be the talk of the office on Monday mornin'. Look, they're waitin' for us. Come on.'

Evie looked over to where the other girls were beckoning them to hurry. She hesitated, not wanting to be made a fool of again. 'Oh, well,' she relented, 'I suppose a glass of lemonade won't hurt.'

The Golden Galleon was bulging at the seams. The bar was completely hidden by a sea of faces and foaming glasses. People were shouting at each other, hoping to be heard above the piano being pounded with gusto by an elderly woman at the far end of the room.

Evie looked round in astonishment – not that she could

see much. The view consisted mostly of people's backs as she was pushed further inside. She gulped with trepidation as a gin and orange was thrust upon her amid calls of 'Drink up, we've time for another before we go to the fair'. She gingerly tasted the liquid, not knowing what to expect, and was surprised to find she quite liked the taste. Before she knew it, the glass was empty and another was shoved into her hand.

Jenny spotted Arnold and his mates among the crowd and to her delight they made their way over to join them. To Evie's dismay it soon appeared that she was being paired off with a tall, spotty youth with nothing at all about him to attract her. She tried to catch Jenny's attention, but she was too busy gazing into the eyes of Arnold to notice Evie. One hour and three drinks later, the now larger crowd left the pub, laughing and singing.

If my mam could see me now, Evie thought, with my Kiss-Me-Quick hat on, my arm round a strange man, dancing the Can-Can on the sea front! She giggled to herself and cheered as loud as the others as they ran into the fair-ground.

Her fourth ride on the dodgem cars proved too much for Evie and she went off in search of a seat. She was genuinely delighted when Bernard, the spotty youth, ambled up and presented her with a giant teddy bear he had won on the rifle range. He sat down beside her and she felt his arm slide around her shoulders. She froze and quickly looked around.

'Where's the others?' she demanded.

Bernard shrugged. 'How should I know?' He pulled her close. 'Come on. Let's find a quiet spot.'

Evie grabbed his arm and removed it from her shoulder.

'Where's Jenny? I must find her.' She jumped up and started to walk away.

'What's with you, frigid or somethin'?' Bernard jumped up and pulled at her arm.

'Don't!' Evie retorted. 'I need to find my friend.'

'Oh, Christ, I've lumbered meself with a mammy's gel. And 'ere's me thinkin' me luck 'ad changed. Yer seemed a cut above the rest of 'em and you're certainly the prettiest. Still I ain't stayin' round 'ere to be made a mug of.'

Bernard looked at her in disgust as he straightened his jacket and stalked off, quickly to be swallowed up in the thronging crowds of holidaymakers.

Evie looked round in dismay. It didn't take her long to realise she was alone. She straightened her back and barged her way through to the fairground entrance, trying to get her bearings. She knew that Jenny would not have deliberately left her, but that still did not quell the rising panic that rose up in her. She had lost her friends and was all alone in a strange town.

She made her way across the road and descended the steps on to the beach. The sand found its way into her shoes, so she took them off and wriggled her toes in the golden grains. The beach was as crowded as the streets and she lost herself for several minutes watching the sunbathers. In the far distance she could just make out the bathers frolicking in the warm sea, and fought back a compulsion to race along the beach, strip off and join them.

A toddler caught her eye, weaving his way through the games of cricket and rounders. His mother, holding her skirt around her thighs, chased him relentlessly and Evie laughed aloud at their antics. Row upon row of striped deck chairs were occupied by old men wearing knotted handkerchiefs and ladies with large hats and even larger handbags – depicting exactly the scene popularised in the cartoon postcards displayed outside every store on the sea front.

Evie gave a deep sigh as her loneliness mounted, then gave herself a good mental shake. Right, so my friends have abandoned me. So what? It doesn't mean I have to sit here all day. She jumped up and grabbed her bag and the teddy bear. The next thing she knew she had hit a solid object. She fell back, landing on the sand with a thud, her bag and the bear flying across the beach.

'Oh!' she groaned loudly as a pair of strong arms pulled her to her feet.

'Are you all right?' a deep voice asked.

Evie nodded as she brushed the sand off her clothes.

'Well, look where you're going the next time!'

At this remark Evie looked up and found herself gazing into the deepest blue eyes she had ever seen. Her gaze travelled over the rest of the face and she held her breath. Standing before her was her dream, all her film star heroes rolled into one, and she felt a tremble go through her body. Before she could say a word, the man had walked off.

Evie stared after him, her pride and her backside bruised. She brushed the rest of the sand off her clothes, collected her belongings and made her way up the steps and on to the street. She ambled slowly down the Golden Mile, past the shops, cafeterias and the arcades filled with penny slot machines. She paused at one of the penny arcades to watch a young lad collect his winnings. She smiled as he proceeded to put them back into another machine. His face dropped as he lost the lot. Evie walked on through the crowds. The bear and the bag felt cumbersome in the overpowering heat and she longed to park them somewhere. She hitched the bear back under her arm and stopped in front of an ice cream parlour.

She scanned the board in front of the parlour and her mouth watered. Two minutes later, armed with the largest ice cream cone they had to offer, topped with strawberry sauce, Evie continued her stroll, stopping here and there to look at a trinket that caught her eye in a gift shop window. Her heart leaped as she spotted a brooch in the shape of a heart: it was studded with red stones and she knew she had to have it. She took a large lick of her cone, turned abruptly to walk into the shop – and for the second time that afternoon bounced off an unexpected obstacle. Her belongings dropped to the ground, the half-finished ice cream spattered over her blouse and she gave a shriek as the strawberry sauce dripped on to her skirt.

'Do you make a habit of this?' a voice said harshly. 'Just look at my shirt!'

Evie dragged her eyes away from her own ruined outfit, and gasped. Standing before her was the man from the beach, and his face bore a thunderous glare.

'Your shirt!' she exploded. 'Just look what you've done to me. My clothes are ruined.'

'It was you who came charging round the corner.'

'I did not!' Evie retorted as she fumbled in her handbag for her handkerchief.

'Here, use this.'

She looked up at the man and hesitated before she took the proffered handkerchief. 'Thank you,' she said grudgingly.

She wiped her clothes and grimaced at the stains that

were left. She gave the man his handkerchief back and looked at his shirt. It was pale cream and matched the light flannel trousers that covered his long muscular legs. She slowly raised her eyes and looked at his face. His large blue eyes, fringed with long black lashes, were looking at her intently and Evie felt herself blush.

Feeling embarrassment steal over her, she quickly gathered her belongings and made to walk off.

'Er, just a minute, where do I send the cleaning bill to?' he demanded.

The tone of his voice made Evie's temper rise and she turned abruptly back to face him. 'Wash them,' she said icily. 'Or is that beneath you?'

The man ran his fingers through his dark brown hair and grinned broadly, his lips parting to reveal strong even white teeth. He raised his hands in mock surrender.

'I think we'd better call a truce before we have a war on our hands. You've obviously gone to a lot of trouble to catch my attention. Well, you've succeeded. I'm all yours.'

Evie gaped. 'Well, of all the cheek . . .'

Before she could say any more the man grabbed her arm and guided her out of the shop doorway and down the street.

'Where are we going?' she asked.

'Where would you like to go?'

'Well . . . er . . .'

He stopped abruptly and looked at her. 'Oh, God. I hope you're not one of those empty-headed females who can't make a decision?'

Evie glared. 'How dare you . . .' she began.

He grinned again, eyes twinkling in amusement. 'Come on, we'll go for a drink.' Without waiting for an answer, he guided her towards a pub and pushed open the door. 'You grab a seat while I get the drinks, and for God's sake hide that silly bear.' He turned from her and marched away towards the bar.

Evie found a vacant table in a quiet corner and parked her bag and the teddy bear. The lunchtime trade had slackened considerably and she was able to study the man as he stood at the bar. He carried his six-foot frame with confidence, and as he strode back towards her carrying two halves of bitter, she felt herself blush for the second time that afternoon, and it wasn't because of the heat.

He sat down opposite her and she gazed up at him through her lashes. She found him more attractive each time she looked at him. She judged him to be about twenty-three, and his clothes were very smart and expensive. He smiled at Evie as he placed her glass in front of her.

'I haven't introduced myself.' He held out his hand. 'My name's Edward.'

She accepted the proffered hand. 'Evie Grayson.'

'Pleased to meet you, Evie Grayson.' He grinned broadly. 'Do you often go into pubs with strange men?'

For the third time that afternoon, she turned scarlet.

'No, I don't,' she retorted. 'I'm not a tart if that's what you think. I just happen to have mislaid my friends.' Her face turned white as she jumped up, picked up her bag and the bear and made to leave.

'Hold on, hold on.' Edward spoke sharply, then lowered his voice. 'I'm sorry, that remark was out of order. It didn't come out the way I intended. I think we'd better start again.'

Evie took a deep breath and felt her anger quickly evaporate. She smiled and put down her belongings.

'Okay,' she agreed.

'Phew! Some temper you've got there, girl,' he said as he picked up his glass and took a sip of the foaming liquid. 'Are you here on holiday?'

'No. Just for the day, on the works' outing.'

Edward smiled. 'So am I, of sorts. What town are you from?'

'Leicester,' she answered proudly.

'Are you?' He grinned. 'So am I. I knew we had to have something in common. And don't get mad,' he said quickly. 'That was meant as a joke.'

Evie smiled as she picked up her glass and took a sip of her drink. She grimaced as the alien taste hit the back of her throat.

'How did you lose your friends?'

'Oh, at the fair. Somehow we all got separated. I've looked all over for them, but no luck.'

'That's another thing we have in common. I've lost both my friends too. The last time I saw them, they were chatting up two blondes.' Edward frowned and picked up his drink.

They both lapsed into silence. Evie desperately searched her mind for something intelligent to say. Anything would be a godsend. She'd never before had any problem making conversation. Why now? She suddenly had visions of him making a polite excuse and leaving her. Her heartbeat quickened. Her brain had dried up and she felt helpless.

'Tell you what, let's drink up and get out of here. It's a shame to miss all this sunshine.'

Evie sighed with relief and quickly agreed and they were soon outside walking along the front. She held her head high, finding herself proud to be alongside this tall, handsome man, desperately hoping she would not bump into Jenny or any of the other girls, so cutting short their association.

Out of the pub she found Edward easy to talk to and very quickly had told him most of her life story. He listened as she chatted, adding a comment or a question here and there as the afternoon slipped pleasantly away. They walked for miles right past the edge of town and Edward bought meat pies from a little café nestled between the sand dunes. They sat outside as they ate. Edward told Evie he worked for his father in the family business and liked nothing more than to spend his Saturday afternoons going to watch a football or cricket match with friends. Eventually he glanced at his watch.

'What time did you say your bus left?'

'Oh, not 'til six,' she answered casually.

'I hate to tell you this, but you have ten minutes to catch it,' said Edward, a frown forming between his brows. He held up his arms in an apologetic gesture. 'I suppose you're going to blame me?'

'Well, you're the one with the watch,' she scolded.

'Okay, you win. I should have checked the time earlier, but I was enchanted by your chatter.'

Evie ignored his remark and looked around her. 'I must catch that bus, Edward. Can't we get a taxi or something?'

He looked around. 'We're in the back of beyond. I don't suppose there's a taxi within a mile of here.'

'Oh, God!' she groaned. 'If I miss that bus, there'll be hell to pay from my mother.'

'Look, don't worry. I'll get you home,' he said.

'How?'

'In my car.'

'A car! You have a car?'

'Yes, don't look so surprised. If we're lucky, we'll get you home before the bus.' He stood up and helped her to her feet.

They walked quickly back towards the town.

'What about your friends?' she asked breathlessly.

'Oh, lord knows where they've got to. Still, I'm glad I lost them or I wouldn't have met you, would I?'

Evie felt a warm glow of pleasure.

'But how will they get home?' she asked.

'If they're stupid enough to get lost, then that's their fault. Besides, they have plenty of money on them. They can catch a train. Come on,' he ordered.

Edward led her through the streets towards his car. She gasped as he opened the door of a brand new Ford Zephyr.

'Is this really yours?' she asked in awe.

Edward just nodded and opened the door for her.

Evie climbed in and relaxed against the leather seat as he drove the car expertly out of Blackpool and pointed it in the direction of home. She felt her eyelids droop as the car purred along the country roads. Twilight was beginning to fall and her thoughts were running wild. Would he ask to see her again? Was she attractive enough for him, intelligent enough even? After all, a man with a car, and who dressed and talked as smartly as he did, wouldn't want a dumb redhead for a girl friend. Her worried thoughts were interrupted as the car unexpectedly slowed to a halt.

'Damn!' he said, thumping his fist against the steering wheel.

Evie pulled herself up in her seat. 'What's wrong?'

'Petrol. I've run out of damned petrol!'

'Oh!'

He turned abruptly to face her. 'Look, Evie. I didn't do this on purpose. If it's any consolation, I'm always running out of the damned stuff.' He paused and turned his head to look out of the back window. 'I noticed a sign a short while ago. There should be a village not far away. You stay here . . .'

'No, no. I'll come with you. I must telephone my mother. She'll be worried if I'm not back at the time I said I would be. I'll have to explain about missing the bus.'

He rested his head against the steering wheel a moment. 'Will she be angry?'

'Oh, she'll be angry all right. But I'll tell her the bus broke down, then she might have calmed down a bit before I get home.' Evie smiled bravely, dreading the forthcoming conversation.

The village was further than Edward thought. During the three-mile walk, not one car passed them but they spent the time chatting contentedly. Nevertheless Evie's feet throbbed as they rounded the corner and the village came into view.

'Thank God for that!' She sighed with relief. 'I don't think I could have walked another step.'

'Me neither,' he agreed. 'Look, there's a telephone box over there. I'll leave you and go and find a garage. Need any change?'

'No, thanks. I have some.'

'I'll meet you back here then, in about fifteen minutes.'

They parted and Evie made her way to the box. She felt light-headed and her heart sang as she picked up the receiver and asked the operator to connect her call. As it went through her heart plummeted. Please, Mam, please don't be angry, she thought worriedly.

'That you, Mam?'

'No,' came the retort. 'Do I sound that old?'

'Oh, it's you, Florrie. Is Mam there?'

'No. It's her night out.'

'Oh, I forgot. Er . . . look, Florrie, I can't explain now but I'll be home later than I thought. The . . . bus broke down. I'll explain when I get home. Can you tell Mam? Please, Florrie,' Evie shouted down the telephone. 'If I'm late she'll worry and imagine all sorts of things. Florrie? Florrie, are you still there?'

'Yes. There's no need to shout, I'm not deaf,' she snapped.

'Will you tell Mam, Florrie? Tell her not to worry. I'll be home in a few hours. Please?'

'I will if I see her.'

The receiver went dead. Evie stared into it for several seconds until she realised someone was tapping on the window. It was Edward and as she turned he held up a petrol can and grinned. She replaced the receiver and went out to join him.

'Everything all right?' he asked in concern, noticing the worried expression on her face.

'Yes, I think so. My mother wasn't in. I spoke to my sister.'

'Florrie, the one you told me about? She'll tell your mother, don't worry. Come on, the sooner we get this in the car, the sooner we can get you home.' He took hold of her hand and they started to walk back to the car.

'I had to get the garage to open up for me. The bloke wasn't pleased, but soon cheered up when I slipped him two bob.' Edward laughed. 'Don't look so glum, Evie. I'll have you back home before you know it.'

She beamed up at him. She could not wait to see Jenny's face when she told her her tale.

By the time they arrived back at the car, Evie was exhausted. She watched as Edward emptied the can into the tank and climbed gratefully into her seat. He started the engine and they proceeded on their journey. The events of the day had taken their toll and Evie was soon fast asleep. Edward's worried eyes searched the roadside for another garage. The Ford Zephyr did only fourteen miles to the gallon and they would soon run out of petrol again. He sighed with relief as a transport café came into view. He pulled the car to a halt and looked over at Evie. Should he wake her or leave her to sleep?

His eyes lingered on the girl slumped in the bench seat beside him and his lips curved into a smile. Tendrils of red hair had escaped from her pony tail and fell softly over her ears. Her long golden lashes rested gently on her cheeks. She shifted position and her floral skirt rode up, exposing long slender legs. He stared at her, transfixed. That lovely vision would stay with him for the rest of his life. He breathed deeply as he forced his eyes away from her. Reluctantly, he slipped out of the car and proceeded to fill the tank.

They arrived back in Leicester in the early hours of the morning. Evie, now fully awake, guided Edward towards her house. Switching off the engine, he turned to face her, staring silently at her for a moment.

'I'd like to see you again, Evie.'

'Would you?' Her heart thumped so loud she thought he would hear it. 'I'd like that.'

'What about Tuesday then? We could go to the pictures. Bob Hope and Bing Crosby are on at the Regency in "The Road to something or other". Have you seen it?'

Evie quickly made some calculations. Tuesday was College night and she had already seen that particular picture and hadn't really enjoyed it.

'No, I haven't,' she lied. 'I would like to.'

She felt herself blush and was glad it was dark.

'Seven-thirty, then. Outside the Regency.'

Before Evie could answer the door of the car was yanked open. Her mouth dropped open at the sight of her mother standing on the grass verge, dressed in her quilted dressing gown and slippers.

'Evie, get into the house this minute,' she ordered.

'Mam . . .'

'Don't "Mam" me. Do you realise, I've been frantic? Now get into the house, and you'd better have a good explanation.' She totally ignored the presence of Edward as she folded her arms and waited for her daughter to move.

Evie felt embarrassment steal over her. She turned to Edward but words failed her. She slid out of the car and ran towards the house.

Clutching her handbag, she threw herself down on the settee. The front door banged shut and Edith stood framed in the doorway.

'Well?' she demanded. 'It's one o'clock in the morning. Where have you been?'

'Mam, I telephoned. Didn't you get my message?'

'What message? Don't try to fool me. Now what have you been up to?' Edith sat down on the edge of the armchair, her face contorted in anger, and Evie shook.

She stuttered and stammered as she poured out her tale under Edith's stony stare. When she had finished she looked into her mother's eyes.

'It's the truth, Mam, honest,' she pleaded.

Edith rose, folded her arms under her bosom and paced backwards and forwards.

'True or not, Evie, I trusted you. Against my better judgement, I let you go on the works outing and now you've let me down. Losing your friends was bad enough. But coming home in a strange man's car! Well, I thought you had more in you than that. He could have done anything. An innocent girl like you.'

'But he didn't and what else was I supposed to do? I couldn't walk home.' Evie sniffed as tears pricked the back of her eyes.

'You shouldn't have missed the bus in the first place,' Edith snapped. 'And just look at the state of your clothes. I dread to think what you got up to.' She paused. 'I'm surprised at Miss Sargent for letting you go off like that. I've a good mind to go and see her and give her a piece of my mind . . .'

'Oh no, Mam,' Evie shouted in horror. 'It wasn't her fault, honest.'

Edith stared at her daughter. 'No, I suppose not, you probably gave her the slip when she wasn't looking. I bet the poor woman's frantic with worry. Is she on the telephone? I'd better give her a call and put her mind at rest, and apologise for your behaviour.'

Evie's face turned white and her mind raced. 'She's not on the telephone. In fact, she's not at home, she's staying with a sick friend . . .'

Edith stared at her daughter. She walked over and stood

with her back to the fireplace. 'I think there's something you haven't told me, Evie.'

She looked at her mother. 'What d'you mean?' she said innocently.

'Evie!'

She bent her head and took a deep breath. 'Miss Sargent never went on the trip,' she whispered.

'Pardon? Speak up, girl!'

Evie raised her head. 'I said, Miss Sargent never went on the trip.'

'I thought as much,' Edith said icily. 'And I don't think she ever was going, was she?'

Evie shook her head. 'No.'

Edith rested her hands on the fire surround. 'I think you'd better go to bed. And, Evie, you'll not see that man again.'

'But why? Why, Mam?' she shouted as she jumped up out of her seat.

'Because if he were decent, he would not have let you miss that bus. Now I'll not say another word on the subject, except that you're not to go out of this house unless it's to go to work or College, until further notice.'

Evie's stomach dropped and her heart missed a beat.

'Mam,' she pleaded.

'Go to bed. I have spoken my last words on the subject.'

Evie jumped up and ran upstairs. As she passed Florrie's door it opened and her sister's laughing eyes looked into hers. Florrie's whole face was wreathed in satisfaction. Evie stopped in her tracks and stared at her sister in total disbelief. Florrie slowly closed the door, leaving Evie staring open-mouthed. Slowly the truth dawned on her. She walked into her bedroom, threw herself on the bed and wept.

Several minutes later she rolled over, stared up at the ceiling and sniffed loudly. How could Florrie have been so mean? It had been an act of pure spite. Some day, I'll get even with you, Florence Grayson, she pledged.

She switched her thoughts to Edward. Meeting him had been the most exciting thing that had ever happened to her. Everything else paled into insignificance. She sat bolt upright and wiped her face on her sheet. Tuesday was College. Well, she wouldn't go, she would meet Edward instead. Her mother would never find out. I don't care if she does, I'm going, Evie vowed. She hugged herself, feeling the cold of the night, then pulled off her clothes and climbed wearily into bed.

Edward walked through the back door and into the kitchen. He stopped for a moment and blinked his eyes.

'Oh! It's you, Gerry. You gave me a turn.' He pulled out a chair from beneath the table and sat down opposite his sister.

'Hi, big brother. Have a good time in Blackpool?'

'Yes, thanks. Not bad at all. Anyway, what are you doing up at this hour?'

'Oh, I couldn't sleep. I've just made a cuppa, want one?'

'Please.'

Geraldine Bradshaw scraped her chair back from the large pine kitchen table and walked over to the fitted units that covered three-quarters of the massive kitchen. Reproduction wooden beams covered the ceiling and suspended from them, on large metal hooks, hung copper saucepans and brass ornamental jugs. She picked up the tea pot, pulled a large china breakfast cup before her and poured her elder brother a cup of tea. She walked back to the table and rejoined him.

'I've given you a big cup. You look as though you could do with a good drink. Why don't you help yourself to Father's whisky?'

Edward smiled warmly. 'This'll do fine.' He looked at Geraldine for a second and his eyes twinkled. 'What's his name?'

'Who?'

'The man who's stopping you from getting your beauty sleep.'

'Oh, you! It's not a man. I'm just not tired, that's all.'

Edward took a long drink of his tea. 'That's better. Fancy something to eat?' He stood up, made his way to the pantry and, selecting cheese and bread, began to make a sandwich.

'No thanks, not one of your giant creations. I have to watch my weight.'

Edward laughed and turned towards her as he waved the carving knife in the air. 'There's nothing wrong with your weight. One of my doorsteps would do you good.'

Geraldine giggled as she placed an elbow on the table and rested her chin in her hand. She looked fondly at her brother.

'Well, what's her name then?'

'Eh?'

'The woman who's kept you out so late.'

'What makes you think it's a woman?'

'Because I know you. What's she like?'

Edward stopped making his sandwich. 'She's okay. About your age, very attractive, and like you, very inquisitive. You'd get on very well together.'

'And?'

'And what?' he replied as he went back to making his sandwich.

'Stop playing games, Edward. Are you seeing her again?'

He stopped what he was doing and turned round. 'Yes. On Tuesday. Now stop asking questions.'

'Tuesday. Oh! Aren't you going with Father, then? Have you changed your plans?'

Edward dropped the carving knife and clasped his hand to his forehead. 'Oh, God, I forgot! I have to go to London on Monday and we won't be back until Wednesday night. Damn!'

Geraldine grimaced. 'You'll have to contact her and make other arrangements.'

'Yes, only . . . I don't know her address. I dropped her off, but I'm not sure where. She directed me. I was too tired to take much notice.' He paused. 'I can't remember her last name either. Now what was it . . . Green, no. Greyland . . . Grey something . . . or was it Brown? Oh, blast!'

Geraldine stood up and walked over to her brother, placing her hand on his arm.

'Another poor lovesick soul to be left waiting and wondering . . .'

'Gerry, shut up. It can't be helped.' Edward pulled a wry face and stared into space. Shame really, I quite liked her, he thought ruefully. The memory of Evie asleep in the car rose before him and he grimaced. The girl had a lot more going for her than most of the others he met, and what a temper! He smiled to himself. Quite refreshing to have someone stand up to him for a change. Usually girls hung on his every word. Still, she probably wouldn't give him another thought. He shrugged his shoulders as he picked up his sandwich and took a large bite. 'I'm going to bed.' He addressed his sister through a mouthful of food. 'You'd do the same if you had any sense. Samuel Gold will be over tomorrow to see Father and I want to be up and out before he comes.'

Geraldine sighed. 'What are you going to do about Sophie, Edward?'

'Do?' He looked at Geraldine in surprise. 'Nothing.'

She watched thoughtfully as her brother left the room. She collected the cups, cleared up the mess he had made and followed him.

By the time Evie got up the next morning, Florrie had already left the house and did not come back until after her sister had gone to bed.

Edith was very curt towards Evie who spent a most uncomfortable day doing chores her mother set her. She was filled with hatred for Florrie for the way she had treated her, and banged and crashed around the house until finally her mother banished her to her bedroom for the rest of the day. She spent the rest of the time playing records and thinking of Edward, and wishing Tuesday would arrive.

Chapter Six

Evie stared stonily out of the bus window. She spotted Jenny at the bus stop and ignored her wave. Jenny bounded on to the bus and plonked herself down beside her just as it pulled away, jerking all the passengers forward.

'Phew! It's a bit crowded today,' she said, nudging Evie's elbow. 'Didn't yer see me wave?'

Evie turned and faced her. 'Yes, I did see you, and I don't know how you've got the nerve to talk to me,' she snapped angrily.

'Why? What 'ave I done?'

'What have you done! You bloody left me in Blackpool.'

'I never left yer! Yer went missing! We looked all over the place, then thought you must be wi' Bernard. It wasn't till 'e got on the bus wi' Brenda Chapman that I really started to worry. It were too late then, 'cos the bus pulled out. Anyway, you got 'ome all right.'

'How did you know?'

'Your Florrie told me yesterday when I telephoned,' Jenny said sulkily. 'I couldn't sleep a wink on Saturday night for worryin'. So first thing Sunday mornin' I walked to the telephone box. Before I'd even 'ad me breakfast.'

'You telephoned yesterday?' Evie queried, frowning deeply.

'Yes. I've already told yer. Florrie said you were in bed and she'd pass the message on.'

Evie took a deep breath and exhaled loudly.

'Didn't she tell you then?' Jenny said angrily. 'No wonder you're mad wi' me. The rotten sod!'

'No, she didn't tell me. Anyway, it still doesn't excuse the way you left me. Anything could have happened.' It was Evie's turn to sulk. The bus jerked to a halt and both girls were thrown forward. Several more people piled on and a woman stood at the side of Jenny. She stared at her and Jenny stared back. She wasn't going to give up her seat for anybody. She turned back to Evie and continued their conversation.

'Well, nothin' did 'appen, did it?'

Evie pressed her lips together and ignored Jenny's question. She wanted to keep her secret to herself for the moment.

'Florrie said some bloke brought you 'ome,' Jenny said casually.

'Florrie said that?' Evie stared out of the window. 'What if some bloke did? I bet you weren't caring how I got home. Too busy with Arnold.' She tried to keep her voice calm.

'That's unfair, Evie. I was worried, and so were the other gels. But what could we do? We thought you'd go to the coppers or somethin'. Anyway,' she grinned, completely changing the subject, 'talking of Arnold . . . 'E took me dancing last night. Oh, Evie, 'e's wonderful.' Jenny looked into the distance starry eyed. In her mind's eye she saw herself and Arnold dancing to the Dallas Boys at the Trocadero.

'Dancing? You went dancing on a Sunday night! Didn't

116

your mother mind?' Evie turned back to face her.

'I didn't tell 'er. I told 'er I was comin' over to your 'ouse.'

'You did what?'

'Well, what she don't know, don't 'urt. She's not as strict as your mam, but she'd draw the line at me goin' dancin' on a Sunday night. She'd say it was unseemly.'

Evie was intrigued.

'How did you get out all dressed up if she thought you were only coming to my house?'

'Oh, that were easy. I 'ung me dress in the outside lavvy.'

'Jenny Jones, you'll be the death of me,' Evie laughed.

'It were worth all the trouble. Arnold's a wonderful dancer – and kiss! Oh, Evie, can 'e kiss! I felt me legs buckle. I'm seeing 'im again on Wednesday. This is it, Evie. I'm in love.' She sighed deeply. 'If you need me as an alibi any time, let me know.'

Evie was silent for a moment.

'I just might, Jenny. I just might at that.'

Jenny looked at Evie and a broad smile spread over her face.

'Oh, yeah? So you can see this bloke?'

'What bloke would that be?'

'Don't play games with me, Evie Grayson. The bloke that brought you 'ome on Saturday night.'

Evie looked at Jenny in silence and smiled sweetly. Jenny frowned, realising she was not going to get any information. It annoyed her intensely. She stood up abruptly.

'Come on, it's our stop.'

The two girls walked into their workplace in silence.

They arrived to a flurry of activity from the staff who

had got there before them. Jenny walked to her desk and sat down. As Evie placed her bag at the side of her desk Miss Sargent marched up to her.

'Get this area tidied up. Mr Dawson Senior is visiting tomorrow and we don't want him to think we work in a pigsty.' She marched away, barking orders at the rest of the staff.

Evie looked round at her work area. It was spotless. Stupid woman, she thought as she picked up a sheet of headed paper ready to type a letter.

Evie walked slowly into the kitchen, threw her bag on the floor and sank down on a chair at the table.

'God, what a day.' She smiled gratefully as her mother placed a steaming hot cup of tea in front of her.

'Dinner won't be long. Drink that up, you'll feel better.' Edith went back to mashing the potatoes. 'Been busy then?'

'No more than usual.' Evie sighed. 'But everyone is running round like crazy 'cos of this visit.'

'What visit's that? The King?' Edith laughed as she cut a knob of butter and added it to the potatoes.

'Might as well be for all the fuss and palaver they're all making. Mr Dawson Senior is doing us the honour. He's coming to do a presentation to a bloke in the factory who's retiring after fifty-odd years, and he also wants to have a look round. I must admit, I'm quite looking forward to seeing the old boy, I've heard so many stories about him. I can't imagine them all being true, though.'

Edith swung round and as she did so the potatoes on the spoon she was holding slipped to the floor.

'Mr Dawson Senior? Evie, are you sure?' Edith's voice rose sharply.

She raised her head and looked intently at her mother. 'Yes. Why?'

Edith noticed the potatoes on the floor and bent down to wipe them up. She straightened and turned back towards the cooker.

'Oh, nothing. I just wondered,' she replied quickly. She placed a plate of sausage and mash in front of Evie and wiped her hands on her apron. 'I have to go out.'

Evie gulped on a piece of sausage. 'But you never go out on a Monday. I thought you were going to finish sewing my skirt?'

'It will have to wait, I must go out,' Edith snapped. 'Now eat your dinner. And tell Florrie, when she bothers to come home, that hers is in the oven.' She took off her apron, folded it up and walked out of the kitchen.

Several minutes later, Evie heard the front door slam. I wonder what's got into her? she thought. She scraped her chair back and walked over to the oven, where she took a sausage off Florrie's plate.

Five minutes after that, she heard the front door slam again and Florrie strode in.

'Your dinner's in the oven,' Evie said through clenched teeth.

'Where's *she* gone? I saw her catching the number fourteen,' Florrie asked flatly as she removed her plate from the oven.

'I don't know. Anyway, I want to talk to you.'

Florrie looked critically at her plate. 'Are we on rations or something? She put the hot plate down on the table, threw the tea towel on the work surface and sat down.

'I said, I want to talk to you,' Evie repeated.

'Oh? What about?' Florrie asked nonchalantly as she tucked into her dinner.

'You know damned well, Florence Grayson,' Evie fumed. 'Why didn't you pass the message on?'

'And what message would that be?'

'The one I gave you on Saturday night? You know damned well which message I mean!' Evie shouted.

'Oh, that message.' Florrie took another mouthful of food. 'I forgot.'

'Forgot? Forgot! You never forgot. You did it on purpose.'

'What if I did?' Florrie smirked.

'You're hateful, you are. Just you wait, Florrie Grayson, you'll need me one day, you'll see.'

'And what would I need you for?' She smirked again. 'Seems to me, Evie, that you've got above yourself since you went into the office. But you'll soon get your comeuppance when they send you back to the factory.'

'Send me back to the factory! What do you mean?' Evie asked, bewildered.

Florrie sat back in her chair. 'Well, after all the complaints about your work, I just thought . . .'

'Complaints! What complaints? I haven't had any complaints,' Evie shouted, her face turning red as she remembered her first day in the office.

'Maybe you haven't heard them, but I have. I'd pull your socks up if I were you.' Florrie scraped her chair back and looked smugly at Evie who glared back.

'You've got a nerve criticising my work! What about you and all those late nights you've been doing? If Mr Stimpson knew . . .' Evie stopped in mid-sentence, leaned forward and waited for an answer.

'I don't work for Mr Stimpson and my late nights are nothing to do with you,' came the sarcastic reply.

'They are when the rest of the factory is slack and you seem to be doing more hours than ever. What are you up to, Florrie? I know you're up to something.'

'Up to something? What are you implying?' Her sister spoke menacingly. 'I'd watch your mouth if I were you. You can get into a lot of trouble making unsubstantiated accusations.' Her eyes narrowed and her mouth hardened. She stood up slowly and placed her hands on the table. Speaking slow and softly, she addressed Evie. 'Now do the pots, like a good girl. I'm going upstairs for a bath.' She left Evie staring angrily after her as she walked out of the kitchen.

Evie stared for an age at her empty dinner plate. Hatred for her sister mounted. She was now certain that Florrie had deliberately not given her mother the telephone message. She was also certain that she was up to something after hours at Dawson's. But what could it be? she wondered. Evie picked up her plate and threw it over to the sink, where it fell and smashed.

'Damn!' She clenched her fists. 'Damn the woman!'

A troubled Evie walked into work the next morning. She had spent a restless night worrying about her job, and with a growing determination to find out just what her sister did after everyone went home at night. She awoke feeling jaded and her reflection in the bathroom mirror showed it. She had applied a layer of panstick in the hope it would hide the dark circles under her eyes. If her mother noticed she was wearing makeup for work, it was too bad: without it she looked awful.

As soon as she opened the office door, Miss Sargent marched up to her.

'Don't bother taking your coat off. You're coming with me.'

Evie stared at her open-mouthed but judging by the look on Miss Sargent's face, thought it better not to ask where they were going. She followed her supervisor out of the office, down the stairs towards the basement.

Finally Evie could contain herself no longer. 'Why are we coming down here, Miss Sargent?'

Still marching in front of Evie, she answered brusquely, 'There's some archive material that needs sorting out. I'll show you exactly what needs doing.'

'But why today? I thought old Mr Dawson was visiting? Who'll look after the switchboard and the rest of my work?'

Miss Sargent stopped abruptly. 'It's not your place to ask questions. You'll do as you are told.'

She marched forward again and led Evie down into a dark, dingy passage. At the end of the passage was a door.

'Right, here we are.' Miss Sargent prised open the door and switched on the light. The basement room had no window and was filled from floor to ceiling with boxes of old files. The strong smell of damp was overwhelming and dust and grime lay thickly all about. Evie shuddered as she spotted an enormous spider hanging from its web where several small insects had been trapped.

Miss Sargent turned to Evie, a slight smile playing on her lips.

'Mr Stimpson wants all this lot putting into date order.'

Evie scratched her head and stared round at the hundreds of boxes full of old invoices and other documents. Her heart sank.

'Right, get to it,' Miss Sargent barked. 'I'll send someone down with a cup of tea at teabreak and you might as well have your lunch while you work, because Mr Stimpson wants the job finished today.'

She departed, leaving Evie staring after her.

The girl put her bag down on the floor and felt the tears well up in her eyes. Florrie's words suddenly sprang to mind. She ran her hands through her hair and thought in horror that her sister was right. She was no good at her job and this was the start of them trying to get rid of her.

She stared around the room and felt her temper rise. If they wanted rid of her, they would not find it easy. She rolled up her sleeves and picked up her first box file.

Two hours later, Jenny poked her head around the basement door and laughed loudly at the sight that greeted her.

'Bloody, 'ell, Evie. You're filthy,' she giggled.

Evie straightened up and brushed a cobweb from the end of her nose.

'It's okay for you to laugh. Just look at me! Look at my good suit. I hate that Mr Stimpson.' She walked over and grabbed the cup from Jenny's hand and drank greedily. 'Boy, I needed that,' she said as she smacked the cup back into its saucer and handed it back.

'Just what are yer supposed to be doin'?' Jenny queried.

'Don't ask me. I'm too mad even to think about it.'

Jenny pulled a face. 'I'd better get back. Are yer comin' up for dinner?'

'No. The old so and so says I've got to stay down here. She says I've got to be finished today. You tell me, Jenny. How can I sort this lot by myself in one day?'

She shrugged her shoulders. 'Search me. Anyway, I'd

better get back. If I know Miss Sargent, she'll be timin' me.'

'Okay, I'll see you later,' Evie said sullenly. 'Oh, has the visit been made yet?'

'Yes. I couldn't get over the old man. 'E's all wrinkled and crippled with arthur-eye-tist.'

Evie screwed up her face. 'Arthur . . . what!'

'Yer know, that disease that sends your bones all funny.'

'Oh.' Evie hid a smile.

'Anyway, they've laid a big buffet on in the board room. Mildred Carpenter wa' tellin' me in the canteen, when I went to fetch the mornin' tea. The amount of food would feed us for months. Bloody waste, if yer ask me.' Jenny shook her head. 'See yer later.' She wagged her finger at Evie. 'Now get back to work or I'll dock yer wages.'

She ducked as Evie threw a box at her, and laughingly shut the door as it split open and spilled its contents all over the dusty floor.

Evie worked hard throughout the day. Her back and arms ached from the lifting of the heavy boxes, her good suit was ripped having caught on an old rusty nail sticking out from the wall, and she was covered in dust. She straightened up and looked round. She had hardly scratched the surface of the task and gave a deep sigh. I'll be down here for years tackling this lot, she thought forlornly. She jumped as the door was thrust open and Miss Sargent strode in.

'It's home time, Miss Grayson. Have you finished?' she asked curtly as she looked Evie up and down, grimacing in disgust at the state she was in.

Evie held her breath and quickly checked herself before she spoke.

'No, I'm sorry,' she apologised.

'Well, never mind. Come along. We'll leave it for now.' She motioned Evie to get her bag and led her out of the room. Miss Sargent switched off the light and closed the door behind them. Evie silently followed her through the maze of corridors and up the stairs into the daylight.

'Do I go back tomorrow, Miss Sargent?' she ventured to ask.

'What?' Miss Sargent stopped and turned to her. 'No, I'll let you know when. You're to go back to your own job tomorrow.'

'Oh?' Evie frowned. 'But, Miss Sargent . . .'

The supervisor swung on her heel. 'I've told you before, Miss Grayson, about back-answering. Go and get yourself cleaned up and then you can go home.'

'Yes, Miss Sargent. Thank you, Miss Sargent,' Evie said, managing to keep the sarcasm out of her voice.

She walked into the ladies' toilet and soaked her hands in hot, soapy water. She looked up into the mirror and grimaced at her reflection. 'Don't ask, Evie,' she said aloud, unable to understand the need for today's charade.

She dried her hands and looked at her watch. Her heart leaped. She'd better hurry or she would miss the bus. She was meeting Edward tonight and would have to appear calm and collected when she arrived home. She hurried out of the factory, her mind full of thoughts about what to wear. She realised that she just might need Jenny's help and hoped that her friend would still be at the bus stop.

As luck would have it, she was.

'Look at the state of you,' Jenny laughed. 'Don't stand wi' me, I'm ashamed to know yer.'

'Never mind that. I need your help.' Evie grabbed Jenny's arm and took a deep breath. 'I'm supposed to be at College tonight, only I'm not going.'

'Oh?' Jenny frowned. 'Where yer goin' then?'

Evie paused for a moment, unsure whether to take Jenny into her confidence. She quickly decided that her friend would not be satisfied unless she heard the whole story and time was short, so she quickly divulged her tale.

'You crafty devil!' Jenny sniggered, smacking Evie playfully on her arm. 'You could 'ave told me sooner.'

'There's not been the chance. Anyway, are you going to help me or not?'

''Course I am,' Jenny replied, pretending her feelings were hurt. 'What are friends for?'

'Thanks, Jenny,' Evie sighed with relief.

She related her plan while Jenny listened intently.

'Let me get this right.' Jenny frowned. 'You're goin' to stuff yer trews and jumper into your bag, pretend yer goin' to College and then catch the bus to my 'ouse. I've to 'ave the iron on ready to press yer clothes and you want to borrow me makeup.' She paused. 'What time yer meetin' this bloke?'

'His name's Edward!'

'Well, Edward then.'

'Seven-thirty, outside the Regency.'

'You're cuttin' it fine.' Jenny looked seriously at her friend, then relaxed and smiled warmly. 'But we'll manage. For the cause of true love.'

Evie turned and hugged her friend. 'Thanks.'

'Yer can thank me when we've pulled this caper off.

From what you've told me, though, 'e sounds worth it. Fancy goin' out wi' a bloke that's gorra car.' She raised herself on tiptoes as she peered over the crowds. 'Where's that ruddy bus? Trust it to be late tonight.'

Evie alighted at her stop and raced to the front gate. She slowed her pace and tried to calm herself down, taking deep breaths as she walked round to the back door. She walked slowly into the kitchen and placed her bag on the floor. Her mother was serving up the dinner.

'You're late tonight,' Edith said.

'Yes, I thought the bus was never going to come,' Evie said casually.

Edith turned and faced her daughter and her face clouded over. 'Just look at the state of you! What on earth have you been doing?'

'You may well ask!' Evie retorted. 'I've been down the cellar all day sorting out all the old files.'

'Oh,' Edith sniffed. She walked over to Evie and fingered her suit. 'Well, this is ruined. There's no way I can repair that hole. You really should learn to be more careful.' She spoke sharply as she walked back towards the stove, picked up a plate of food and placed it on the table. 'Well, you'd better eat while it's hot. I don't want this ruined as well.'

Evie looked at the food and her stomach turned over. Eating was the last thing she wanted to do. She sat down and picked up her knife and fork. She looked at the clock on the wall through her lashes. The time was two minutes to six. She would have to catch the half-past six bus if she was going to meet Edward on time.

She forced the food down. Normally she would have savoured the tasty meat pie her mother had cooked, but tonight it tasted like cardboard.

Edith noticed her daughter's mood.

'You all right?'

'What?' Evie looked up sharply. 'Oh, yes. I'm not very hungry, that's all.'

'Oh, that's a shame, I've made a nice bread pudding for afters.'

'Sorry, Mam, but can we have it tomorrow?'

'Okay, but it's never the same when it's heated up.' Edith looked at her daughter in concern. 'I hope you're not sickening for something, it's not like you to be off your food.'

'Mam, there's nothing wrong with me. I'm just not hungry, that's all,' Evie muttered as she looked up at the clock again. 'I'd better get a move on, I'll be late for College.' She pushed her plate away and prepared to leave the table, taking care not to appear over-keen.

Edith tutted. 'I knew I had something to tell you. The College secretary telephoned. Your teacher's ill, so there won't be any classes tonight.'

'Oh!' Evie's stomach dropped as she gazed at her mother in horror.

'Don't look so alarmed, young lady,' Edith said in surprise at Evie's reaction to her news. 'You won't miss anything. They've asked me to dictate some pages out of a book for you to take down in shorthand. You have to take it with you next week.' Edith smiled. 'I'm very pleased with you, Evie. I didn't realise you were so keen.' She stood up and picked up the plates. 'I thought we could read from *Little Women*. You've always liked that book.' She turned her back and walked towards the sink, unaware that Evie's world had shattered into tiny pieces.

The girl's mind raced. She had to find a way to get out of the house.

'Could . . . er . . . could we do it tomorrow, Mam? I'd like to go and see Jenny. She's got a few problems and needs to talk them over.' The words tumbled out of her mouth and she waited apprehensively for her mother's response.

'No, I'm sorry, Evie,' Edith answered firmly. 'You're not going anywhere, problems or no problems. After the episode on Saturday night, you're confined to the house until further notice. I'm only allowing you out for College.' She saw Evie's mouth open to speak and raised her hand to stop her. 'I'll hear no more on the subject. Now help me with these dishes, please, and then we'll start on your homework.' She turned her back and busied herself at the sink. 'Florrie's dinner will have to go in the oven again. I'm getting a little tired of her coming and going as she pleases. She's starting to treat this house as a hotel . . .'

Edith rattled on, unaware that Evie was not listening to a word she was saying. All Evie could see was Edward waiting outside the Regency. How long would he wait before he realised she was not coming?

She felt a tear trickle down her cheek and quickly wiped it away with the back of her hand. She knew her mother meant business and nothing she said would change her mind. Resigned to defeat, she slowly stood up and dragged herself over to the sink where she picked up a tea towel and started to dry the dishes. Her eyes kept darting to the clock and she watched helplessly as the minutes ticked by.

Suddenly a feeling of determination surged through her. She rushed out of the kitchen and up the stairs, where she pulled off her clothes, threw on her trews and jumper, grabbed her coat and ran back down. She was met at the door by her mother.

'Evie!'

'Don't try and stop me, Mam. I'm going to meet him. I don't care what you say.'

A forbidding look crossed Edith's face. 'If you defy me, Evie . . .' But her words were lost. Evie had already rushed out of the door and had slammed it shut behind her.

The bus was late and she arrived at her destination breathless. The time was twenty minutes to eight so she was ten minutes late. There was no sign of Edward and she paced nervously up and down the pavement. At half-past eight she resigned herself. She had missed him and it was her mother's fault.

She made her way home and stormed into the living room. Edith raised her eyes and looked coldly at her daughter.

'I missed him. He must have thought I wasn't coming, and it's all your fault. I hope you're happy now, Mother!' She rushed from the room and up the stairs. Bolting her bedroom door, she threw herself on her bed and wept.

Chapter Seven

Evie's heart was broken. The laughter and light had gone out of her eyes and life felt meaningless and empty. All her waking hours were spent wondering what Edward was doing and picturing what might have been. She began to spend many hours in her bedroom, shut away from the world, playing sad, soulful ballads on her record player. Jenny tried desperately to bring her friend back to normal, but after nearly six weeks was beginning to give up.

Edith was distraught. She had agonised for hours, knowing that the depression that had settled over her beloved daughter was mostly her fault. She knew she should have listened to Evie's explanation about that fateful day. Evie's reaction to the whole situation confused and worried Edith to such an extent that she quickly changed tactics and did all she could to encourage her daughter to socialise. Unfortunately, this did not happen. All it did achieve was to push Evie further and further away from her.

Evie went to work, came home, went to her bedroom and played her records. She passed no more than the time of day with Edith, speaking only when she had to. Edith was still totally unaware of the part Florrie had played in the incident. Evie was convinced that her mother's knowledge of Florrie's behaviour would not have changed her mind, so she had not even bothered to explain.

The only person unconcerned was Florrie. She had quickly sussed out the situation and homed in on it, dropping troublemaking remarks whenever possible and feeling generally happy about the whole situation. So from that fateful night the Grayson household was filled with a strained and icy atmosphere.

Evie had been seconded for a short period to the invoicing section and hated every moment of the day as she produced endless invoices on the heavy typewriter. To make matters worse, the invoicing section was in the Accounts Office, meaning that Evie spent her working days under the spiteful eye of Florrie.

The Chief Accountant Mr Grady, or Greedy Grady as Jenny called him, spoke to none of his staff, feeling they were beneath him and not worth his breath. The General Office was paradise compared to this department and Evie could not wait to get back to her own job.

She picked up the twentieth invoice of that morning and stared at the consignee's address. It was for Edward & Company, Clothes Wholesalers, and her heart plummeted. She typed the invoice with her usual care and attention but when she got to the amount, to her horror made a mistake. Instead of typing £2300.11s.6d, she typed £2301.16s.1d. She corrected her error as neatly as possible and laid the invoice on top of the pile and proceeded with the next.

The day ground slowly to a halt. She tidied her desk and walked quickly out of the office. Getting away from the factory was her main priority. As she walked past the General Office door, it opened and Miss Sargent came out.

'Ah, Miss Grayson. Enjoying your holiday in the Accounts Office, I trust?' She fished in her handbag for her gloves, pulled them out and clicked the bag shut. 'Well, you needn't get too settled, you'll be back under my wing shortly. I wasn't pleased about your helping out there in the first place. My department's short-staffed now. How am I supposed to cope? The powers that be don't think of that, do they?'

All the time she was speaking, she was looking at Evie as though it was her fault she had been moved. Miss Sargent started to pull on her gloves.

'Well, I have to get home, can't stand gossiping to you.' She walked away, leaving Evie staring blankly after her.

She waited for a moment before she made her way out of the factory; she wanted to make sure Miss Sargent had gone. As she came out of the factory gates, she stopped abruptly and held her breath. Before her, leaning against a wall, was Paul Jenkins.

She lowered her head and started to walk quickly, but it was too late – Paul had seen her. He took a final draw on his cigarette and threw it to the ground, grinding it out with his foot. He caught up with her and grabbed her arm, pulling her to a halt.

'Not so fast. I've things to ask you,' he snarled.

Evie shook her arm free and turned to face him. She quickly took in his dishevelled appearance. He was badly in need of a shave, his clothes were unwashed and, judging by the smell that reached her nostrils, so was he.

'Where's my wife?' he demanded angrily.

'Where's your wife?' Evie repeated, disbelief showing on her face and in her voice. 'You haven't seen her for three months and you've the nerve to ask me where she is?'

She gave Paul an icy stare and made to walk away, feeling totally disgusted in his presence. He grabbed her arm again and yanked her back towards him.

'Don't walk away from me. I've asked you a question and I want an answer. Where's my wife?' he demanded again. 'I've been to the flat and the landlady told me she'd gone. Now, where is she?'

Evie was conscious that people leaving the factory were looking at them and whispering as they walked past. She stared at Paul as her anger mounted.

'You disgust me,' she said, through clenched teeth. 'You haven't attempted to see Mavis for months, and now, when it suits you, you come back and demand to know where she is. What's wrong, Paul? Short of money, or has your latest floozie chucked you out?' She looked at him for a second and took a deep breath. 'See,' she said smugly, 'I know all about you, and so does Mavis, *and* we know about your being in prison. So if I were you, I'd get away from here and thank God for a lucky escape.'

She stared at him and waited for a response. She felt panic rise within her and tried hard to stop her legs from trembling.

Paul stared back. He fumbled in his pocket and pulled out another cigarette.

'You know nothing, you little bitch,' he hissed. 'This is all your fault. She was happy. I only had to go away for a while and you put your nose in, didn't you? You never wanted her to marry me in the first place. I always reckoned you were jealous and now I know I'm right. What's up, Evie? Can't get a man of your own so you take it out on

your friend?' He grabbed hold of her shoulders and started
to shake her. 'You tell me where she is, or I'll . . . I'll . . .'

Suddenly, Paul was wrenched away. He lost his balance
and fell to the ground. Evie stumbled back and stared
round bewilderedly as she became aware of another presence.

'Or you'll what?' a deep voice asked harshly.

Evie turned her head quickly and found herself looking
into Edward's face. She held her breath and desperately
tried to control her confused emotions. Edward bent down
and wrenched Paul to his feet. He held him by the shoulder
with one hand, his other clenched ready to punch him.
Edward stared stonily at Paul's sneering grin.

'If you know what's good for you, you'll get as far
away from here as possible. And make sure you don't
come back,' Edward said icily.

Paul pulled himself away from Edward's grip and brushed
himself down. 'Who the hell are you to be telling me what
to do, eh?'

'Someone who can make life very difficult. Now if you
know what's good for you . . .' Edward continued.

'I came to find out where me wife is and I won't leave
till she tells me.' Paul looked at Evie defiantly and waited
for a response.

She took a deep breath and set her mouth grimly.

'Mavis is in hospital with tuberculosis, and she's divorcing
you.'

Alarm spread over Paul's face. 'Tuberculosis!' He looked
from Evie to Edward in horror. 'That's catching, isn't it?'
He wiped the back of his hand across his mouth.

Evie noticed the beads of sweat that had formed on his
brow. She felt her blood boil as she clenched and unclenched
her fists.

'You miserable little toad,' she hissed. 'All you care about is yourself.' She stepped forward and jabbed him with her finger. 'If I were you I'd get out of here, and quick. Mavis's father has a contract out on you, and I tell you, you won't be a pretty sight when they've finished. If there's anything left of you, that is. They'll probably fish you out of the canal with concrete boots on.' She stopped talking abruptly and stared coldly at him.

Edward let go of Paul and looked at Evie bemused. He turned back to Paul and raised his eyebrows. 'Like the lady says, best get out of Leicester as quick as you can.' He leaned forward, looking Paul straight in the eyes. 'And I'd forget about Mavis. If you know what's good for you, that is.'

Paul took a step away and looked back and forth between Evie and Edward. He wagged his nicotine-stained finger at Evie.

'Think you're clever, don't you? Well, I'm going but don't think it's because of you.' He turned on his heel and strode hurriedly down the street.

Evie and Edward stared after him in silence until he disappeared. Finally, Evie turned to Edward and smiled shyly.

'Thank you,' she whispered.

'It was my pleasure. Couldn't leave a lady in distress, could I?'

She lowered her eyes, studying her shoes intently. There was an awkward silence. Finally she raised her head and looked straight at him.

'I'd better be going then.'

'Yes, me too.'

They stood staring at each other, then Evie made a

move, walking several steps away from him.

'Well, thanks again, Edward.' She turned and started to walk again. She stopped, hesitated and turned around. Edward had started to walk in the opposite direction and she felt him once again slipping away from her. Do something. Do something, her thoughts screamed.

'Edward?' she called. He stopped and turned to face her. 'Look, I'm sorry about the night we arranged to meet. I didn't stand you up, I arrived late and must have missed you.'

He looked at her blankly for a moment, then exhaled loudly. 'Oh, that night!' He shrugged his shoulders and smiled. 'Can't be helped. These things happen.'

Evie looked at him quizzically. 'Edward, you did come to meet me that night?'

'Er . . . yes, 'course I did. Why?'

Evie shook her head as the truth dawned on her. 'Oh, nothing.' She frowned, took a deep breath and spoke sharply. 'By the way, what happened to my teddy bear?'

'Teddy bear?'

'The one I left in the back of your car.'

'Oh, that thing. I gave it to my sister.'

'You did what? But it was mine.'

'Yes, but I never thought I'd see you again, so I didn't think it mattered.'

'Oh.' Evie's face fell. The next words tumbled out before she had time to think. 'Weren't you waiting for me tonight, then? I thought . . .'

'Well, no,' he cut in. 'I've just come from a meeting with someone in the factory. Actually, I forgot you worked here.'

'Oh, I see.' She blushed with embarrassment.

Edward looked at his watch. 'Look, I have an hour or so to kill, would you like to go for a drink?'

Evie felt nauseous. All the weeks she had been in the depths of despair over this man, and he had never given her a second thought! Her pride hurt terribly and she felt anger rise up in her. 'No, thank you.'

'Okay.' He shrugged his shoulders. 'Some other time then.' He turned to walk away, then stopped abruptly. 'I tell you what, meet me on Saturday and I'll take you for a meal.'

'Oh, I don't want to put you to any trouble.'

'It's no trouble, Evie. I've no plans for Saturday.'

'I'll give it a miss, thank you.'

Edward looked shocked. 'You're really turning me down?'

'Yes, why not? Has it never happened to you before?'

'Well, no. Actually it hasn't.' Edward looked at her for a moment. 'Look, I really would like to take you out.'

'Would you? Well, why does it sound as though you're doing me a favour?'

'Does it?' Edward raised his eyebrows in surprise. 'I didn't mean it to.' He paused for a moment and frowned. 'Will you meet me or not?'

Evie stared at him, her stomach turning somersaults. 'Okay,' she said slowly.

'Good.' He smiled. 'I'll see you Saturday then. Eight o'clock at Lea's Corner, and don't be late.'

'I won't. Just make sure you turn up this time.'

'What d'you mean by that remark?'

'Nothing. Just let's say you're lucky to be getting a second chance.'

He looked quizzically at her and then smiled. 'I shan't underestimate you again, Evie.'

'No. You'd better not.'

Edward grinned as she turned to leave. 'Oh, just answer me one question?'

'Depends what it is.'

'Has your friend's father really got a contract out on that Paul fella?'

Evie choked as she stifled a laugh.

'No.'

'Well, what made you say that then?'

'I saw a gangster film once with Humphrey Bogart and it worked for him.'

Edward threw back his head and laughed long and loud. 'I'm glad I bumped into you tonight.' Unexpectedly, he grabbed her shoulders and pulled her towards him, kissing her full on the mouth. 'Until Saturday.'

'Saturday,' she said breathlessly, reeling from the kiss.

Evie sat staring out of the bus window, not seeing the streets and shops that passed before her. Her mind was fully occupied. The feelings she was experiencing were new to her. They worried her, excited her, but she knew if this was what they called love, then she never wanted these feelings to stop. All the trauma she had been through in the past couple of months had been worth it. She spied her bus stop, jumped off and ran home.

Her mother greeted her with apprehension, fussing round her as she took the dried-up dinner out of the oven and heated the gravy. Evie explained her encounter with Paul, but left out Edward's involvement. Edith was not surprised.

'I knew he'd come back,' she said, her chin resting in her hands as she sat with her daughter while she ate her dinner. 'It was just a matter of time. I like what you said, Evie. That was a good ploy.' She grimaced as she envisaged

Evie and her encounter. 'Wish I'd been there, or better still Mavis's father.' She paused. 'Will you write and tell her?'

'No. I don't think that would be a good idea. She'll be in the sanatorium for ages yet and I don't want her to be worried that Paul could turn up at any time.'

'You're right, love,' Edith agreed.

'I will write to her, though.' Evie found herself chatting away to her mother, temporarily forgetting their long estrangement. 'I owe her a letter. What I would really like to do would be to go and see her. I miss her badly.' She sighed, pushing her empty plate away. 'I know I can't though.' She sighed.

'She'll be better before you know it, you'll see.' Edith tried to sound comforting. 'In the meantime you have Jenny. She seems like a nice girl. Bit rough and ready, but a nice girl.'

Evie laughed. 'Yes, I have Jenny. Her and Mavis are like chalk and cheese, and I love them both dearly. But Mavis . . . well, we have roots. I can tell her anything and she understands. She never questions me or makes me feel daft. I can be myself with her and she with me. Do you know what I mean, Mam?'

'Yes, I do. You're lucky to have a friend you feel so much for. Friendship like that is hard earned,' Edith said fondly.

'Yes, I am lucky. I'll write to her tonight, and I'll go and take Rosie out on Saturday morning for an hour or so to give Mr and Mrs Humphreys a break. I'll telephone them later and make the arrangements.'

'That's a good idea,' Edith agreed. 'I have to work in the morning and then I shall go straight into town. I don't want to be too late as it's my evening out.'

Evie picked up her cup and drank her tea slowly, all the time looking at her mother. She placed the cup back in its saucer and took a breath. 'I'm . . . I'm going out on Saturday night,' she said quietly.

'Are you, dear? Anywhere nice?' Edith asked in surprise.

'No. Just out. We're not quite sure where yet,' Evie said coyly.

'Oh, that's nice. You and Jenny have a good time.'

'Thanks.' Evie sighed with relief, glad her mother had not probed further. She looked at the clock. 'It's gone nine. Is our Florrie not home yet?'

'Florrie's in bed, she's not feeling at all well.'

'Florrie's not well?' Evie questioned. 'I've never known her take to her bed before.'

'No. She's not often sick, but she is now. Really flushed and definitely running a temperature. I wanted to get the doctor, but she protested so loudly I gave up. If she's not any better tomorrow, I shall get him in regardless.'

'I hope she's got something really serious and is in bed for months. No, better stiil, that she has to go away like Mavis,' Evie said unkindly.

'That's enough, Evie. Now, if you're going to have a bath, you'd better go while the water's hot,' Edith said, changing the subject, not wanting an argument now she and Evie were on speaking terms again.

Evie pushed back her chair and stood up. 'I'm sorry, Mam. I didn't mean that.'

Edith smiled. 'Go and have your bath. And, Evie?'

'Yes.'

'Are we friends?' Edith asked tentatively.

Evie stood still for a moment, then quickly walked towards

her mother. She placed her arms round her and hugged her tightly.

'Oh, yes, Mam. Yes, please.'

Evie tossed and turned that night in her snug bed. Not that she was desperate for sleep: she wanted to think of Edward, to remember his kiss, his arm round her shoulders, his protectiveness towards her during her encounter with Paul. She lay awake long into the night, willing Saturday to come.

Saturday morning finally dawned. By the time Evie rose, Edith had already left the house. She had left a note asking Evie to take Florrie a cup of tea before she went out, which she grudgingly did.

Florrie lay against the sheets, pale and drawn, and accepted the tea without a word of thanks. The doctor had been, much against her wishes. His diagnosis had been vague, he wasn't sure what was ailing her, but nevertheless, despite Florrie's protests, had confined her to bed for at least a week, saying he would monitor her condition. It worsened over the next few days and an attempt to get up and go to work was thwarted as her legs collapsed beneath her.

Before she left the room, Evie remembered a piece of information she had forgotten to give Florrie. She turned and addressed her sister, her voice flat and unemotional.

'By the way, Mr Grady is off sick. He had to be taken home yesterday. I suppose that means I'll have to stay in your department for a while longer. There's hardly any staff left at the moment.'

Evie noticed the look of horror that passed briefly over Florrie's face. Her eyes widened as she stared at Evie. She tried to raise herself, but failed.

'Are you sure?' Florrie croaked.

Evie frowned. 'I'm not likely to make it up, am I?' she retorted, staring quizzically for a moment at Florrie's frozen expression before she turned and left the room, banging the door shut behind her.

Typical Midlands weather of fine drizzle and thick fog surrounded Leicester that cold November morning. This small matter did not deter Evie in the slightest. She wrapped up warmly and with a jaunty air set off to Mavis's parents to pick up Rosie as previously arranged.

As always she was received warmly and made to sit down with a cup of tea and a slice of rich dark fruit cake. Evie was slightly alarmed to find that Mrs Humphreys was not very well.

'It's just a cold,' her friend's mother told her. She had been delighted with Evie's offer to take Rosie off her hands for a couple of hours and had wrapped the baby up nice and warm. Evie asked the older woman if she would like any errands doing while they were out and she had gratefully accepted the offer.

'You could get some wool for me,' Mrs Humphreys croaked. 'I usually get my wool in town, but any local shop will do. While I sit here, I might as well make myself useful and knit something for the baby.'

Evie said she would be delighted, accepted the shopping list from Mrs Humphreys, put Rosie in the pram and set off.

They walked through Braunstone Park and down Imperial Avenue, to the Narborough Road. The pavements were filled to overflowing with Saturday morning shoppers. Items of all descriptions could be bought from the hundreds of assorted shops that lined the busy thoroughfare.

Evie guided the heavy green perambulator through the throng of people, stopping now and then to gaze into a shop window at something that caught her eye. After making several small purchases, she pulled the pram to a halt at The Knitting Pin and looked in the window at the display of knitting wools and hand-knitted garments. She looked up at the name of the shop and it dawned on her that this was where her mother worked. Her mother had always instilled in her daughters never to come into the shop or approach her while she was working. The manageress was a tartar and it was not the done thing to stand and gossip while you were being paid for serving.

She hesitated and looked up and down the road. She was sure there was not another wool shop within a couple of miles. She squared her shoulders, made sure Rosie was wrapped up safe and warm, and entered the shop. After all, she was a potential customer.

The shop was small. Every inch of space was utilised to the fullest with assorted types of wools in all colours and other knitting accessories. A movement to her left signalled the presence of someone and Evie jumped. A stout shop assistant of about middle age addressed her.

'Hello, madam. Can I 'elp you?' The woman smiled invitingly.

Evie stepped forward. 'Please. I'd like some baby wool for a cardigan.'

'Well, you've come to the right place for that, me duck.' The woman looked slightly embarrassed at using the well-worn local expression. 'Any particular colour, madam, and d'you need a pattern?'

Not knowing whether Mrs Humphreys already had a pattern, Evie decided to choose one just in case and also settled for four balls of pale yellow wool. She checked outside to see that Rosie was all right and waited while the woman wrapped her purchases. Evie noticed a door slightly ajar between two rows of shelves and looked intently at it, hoping her mother would not appear.

'Anythin' the matter?' the woman asked, noticing Evie's worried frown.

She quickly turned her head back to face the woman. 'Er . . . no. I was just wondering what was through there?'

The woman looked to where Evie had been staring. 'Oh, that. That's just the stockroom and where we 'ave our tea. I was just about to make one when you came in. I'm on my own this mornin'. I thought Mrs Grayson would be back by now, it's obviously takin' longer to interview the new staff than she thought,' she said as she added up the bill.

Evie frowned. 'Interviewing staff?'

'Yes. For the new shop further down the road. Mrs Grayson felt she was losing trade from people at the bottom of Narborough Road going into town for their wool. So when the old bicycle shop came up for sale, she bought it. It's been all done out. It's much bigger than this one. I'd like to have worked there meself, but this shop is handy for 'ome. I can pop back at lunchtime to feed the kids and check on Grandad. You know 'ow it is.' She looked at Evie in concern. 'You look worried, me duck. Anythin' the matter?'

Evie was stunned and silently pressed her money into the assistant's outstretched hand.

'No. There's nothing the matter,' she began hesitantly. 'But I always thought Mrs Grayson was just an assistant?'

'Oh, no, Miss. Mrs Grayson is the proprietor. She's had

this shop for at least fifteen years, and the one on Fosse Road for the last five.' She clapped her hand over her mouth in alarm. 'Oh, I'm not supposed to tell anyone she owns the shops. You won't say anythin', will you? Only I'll get the sack.'

Evie shook her head in bewilderment. 'Why is it such a secret?' she asked, trying to keep her voice even.

'Oh, I don't know that, Miss. I just know that if anyone asks we're to say Mrs Grayson is just the manager. That was really drummed into all of us when we took the jobs.' The woman looked intently at Evie. 'You won't tell anyone, will you?' she pleaded again.

Evie shook her head.

The woman sighed with relief and gave her a smile. 'Thanks, Miss. Only I've never told another livin' soul until now.' She stepped sideways to face the large iron till and pressed several keys, jumping backwards as the money drawer shot open. 'Smashing to work for, is Mrs Grayson,' she continued. 'Always a Christmas box, and she pays decent wages. Very fond of 'er, I am. You don't know Mrs Grayson, do you?' she asked hesitantly, slamming the till drawer shut and handing Evie her change.

Evie looked startled. 'Er . . . no. Just vaguely through a friend, that's all,' she said, quickly accepting the change and slipping it into her coat pocket.

'Oh, that's a relief.' She looked at Evie intently, 'It's strange, you look ever so much like 'er. I could have sworn you were related.'

'I'm sure I would know if we were,' Evie answered sharply. She gathered her purchases and made for the door. The woman stared after her.

Evie puzzled over the conversation all the way back to

the Humphreys'. Surely the woman must be mistaken? Her mother did not own the shops. She would have said so, not made out all these years that she just worked there. Buying shops took money and she felt certain her mother did not have the amount needed for anything on that scale.

She shook her head in bewilderment. The woman had spoken so positively. Well, there was only one thing to do: she would tackle her mother at the earliest possible opportunity and clear the matter up. She handed Rosie back to her doting grandparents. Mrs Humphreys was delighted with Evie's purchases and they sat talking for a while, about Mavis's progress and the baby. Mrs Humphreys noticed Evie's distracted air and asked her if she was all right.

'I'm fine.' She smiled. 'Just a bit tired, that's all.'

Evie said her goodbyes, telling Mrs Humphreys that she would be writing to Mavis and promising to call again soon. Evie kissed Rosie and was seen to the door by her friend's mother. She caught the bus home deep in thought.

But concern about her mother was soon overtaken by the frenzy of getting ready for her date with Edward. She searched her entire wardrobe for something suitable to wear that would both impress and delight him.

She threw the last item on the bed in disgust. She had nothing to wear and was in a state of despair when she heard the front doorbell chime. She sighed and made her way slowly down the stairs to open the door. Before her stood a grinning Jenny.

'Hi,' she said as she pushed past Evie and walked into the hall. 'Christ, it's bloody freezin' out there! Make us a cup of somethin'. 'Ave yer got any Camp coffee 'andy?'

Evie glared at her. 'Make your own, there's a bottle in

the pantry. I'm trying to find something to wear for tonight.'

'I thought you'd be havin' trouble. So little me has come to 'elp.' Jenny smiled and rubbed her gloved hands together. 'Now make that coffee and we'll 'ave a fashion parade. Can't 'ave me friend goin' out looking like a rag bag, can we?'

'Oh, Jenny, what would I do without you?' Evie relaxed and took her friend's coat.

'You'd be lost, that's what. I've bin as excited as you since yer told me about this date, and I want to make sure you look right.'

Evie stifled a laugh. Her friend's dress sense was not quite the same as hers, but she was delighted to see her and glad of the company.

'I tell you what, Jenny, fancy having a go at my hair? I'd rather like to see what I'd look like with a French pleat, something like yours. I'd love to look sophisticated.'

Jenny smoothed her hair with the flat of her hand. 'Thanks, Evie. Nobody's ever said I look soffistimicated before. Suppose I am really.' She looked so delighted that Evie hadn't the heart to dispel her pleasure by correcting her.

Both girls walked into the kitchen and Evie placed the kettle on the stove.

''Ow's madam? Still in bed?'

'Yes.' Evie nodded. 'I feel quite sorry for her really, she's ever so poorly.'

'Well, yer wastin' yer breath wi' that one. I wouldn't feel sorry for 'er.'

'I'm sure you would have done if you had seen her trying to get up for work. She was yelling like a banshee, determined she would get there, but her legs gave way and she fell on the floor. It wasn't the least bit funny.'

'No, suppose not.' Jenny hid a smile. 'Can't see why she wa' so determined to get to work though. I'd give anything to 'ave a good excuse to stay off.'

'And at times, so would I,' Evie agreed. 'Here, pass the cups, the kettle's boiling.'

Jenny did as she was told and the girls made their way up to Evie's bedroom, armed with their cups of coffee, a plate of biscuits and two slices of cherry slab cake.

An hour later, Jenny stood back and admired her handiwork.

Evie swung her legs round on her stool and faced her dressing table. She stared long and hard at her reflection and gasped in delight. Jenny had piled her hair high, she had two small kiss curls at the sides of her ears and the back was fastened tightly into a French pleat.

'Why, Jenny, it's wonderful! I've been transformed.'

'Well, don't move. I need to spray it.'

'Spray it?' Evie queried, looking alarmed.

'Yes, you clot, wi' sugar and water. It stiffens yer 'air and stops it falling down. Ain't yer ever used it before?'

'Well, no. I've never needed to, not with my hair style. I've heard the girls in the factory talk about doing it, though. One girl says a hairdresser friend of hers found a bluebottle nest in a woman's head once. Apparently, she just used to flick a comb through her hair every morning and add more of that spray and it attracted the flies.'

'Phew, that's 'orrible.' Jenny pulled a face.

'Yes, it is. So I don't want any on, thank you,' Evie said firmly.

'Don't be daft. It's fine as long as you keep yerself clean. That woman probably never washed 'er 'air for months on end, dirty bugger. Now come on, 'old still

149

while I spray.' Jenny produced an old glass perfume spray bottle out of her bottomless handbag and before Evie could stop her, had sprayed long and hard all over her hair. 'There, all you 'ave to do now is give it a good brush when you get 'ome and wash it in the mornin'.'

Evie blinked her eyes as the liquid sprayed all over her face. She admired herself once more in the mirror.

'Jenny, you're a genius, thank you. I feel great.' She hugged her friend and turned to her bed. 'Now all I have to do is find something to wear.'

Jenny frowned at the pile of clothes. 'For goodness' sake, Evie. You've got more clothes 'ere than Marshall and Snelgrove's. Try this on.'

She held up a delicate blue dress. It had a wide princess neckline, gathered waist, and flowed in folds to just below the knee.

'I don't like that.' Evie shook her head.

Jenny rummaged through and picked up a black skirt and red-patterned jumper. ''Ow about this, then?' she demanded.

'Oh, no.' Evie shook her head again. 'Not for a Saturday night.'

Jenny picked up several more garments and was greeted with the same response.

'See, I told you.' Evie sighed. 'I've nothing to wear.' She sniffed and looked ready to burst into tears.

Jenny felt exasperated. 'Don't sit there like a stuffed dummy. You're meetin' the love of yer life tonight. Now get lookin', there's got to be somethin' 'ere. Mind you, 'e probably won't give a damn what you wear as long as you turn up. Why not go in the nude?' She looked at Evie seriously.

'Jenny!'

She collapsed into laughter then picked up the first outfit that Evie had taken out of her wardrobe earlier that afternoon.

'What about this? The colour's just right for you.'

She handed Evie an emerald green two-piece of thick satin. The skirt was straight, and sat smoothly against Evie's slender hips. The jacket was round-necked, cut lower than she normally wore, but not enough to show any of her cleavage. The neck was edged with a collar of fur that sat perfectly across her shoulders. Jenny admired her friend.

'It's perfect, Evie. 'Specially wi' that new 'air do.'

Evie agree. 'Yes, it is, isn't it?' She slipped off the suit and hung it up carefully. 'I'm all excited now,' she declared, clasping her hands together. 'I've got a nice pair of black shoes and handbag to go with it.'

'Good, that's you all set then. Come on, let's tidy up this mess. Then, can we watch your television, please?'

Evie smiled. 'Yes, of course. I forgot you haven't got one, have you?'

'No need to rub it in. We can't 'elp being poor,' Jenny said haughtily.

'I never meant it like that and you know it.' Evie grabbed her friend's arm. 'We'll leave this mess. I'll tidy up later. What time is it?'

'About five I should think. I broke me watch yesterday. Dropped it in the sink while I wa' cleaning me teeth.'

'Oh, Jenny.' Evie laughingly shook her head. 'I'd better make Florrie a cuppa, she'll be gasping by now.'

The friends made their way down the stairs and while Jenny sat glued in front of the flickering black and white pictures on the television set, Evie mashed a pot of tea and willed the time to pass quickly so she could see Edward.

As she poured the tea she heard the telephone ringing and rushed to answer its beckoning call. It was her mother. She would not be coming home until quite late and Evie would probably be in bed by the time she got back. She told her daughter to have an enjoyable evening and rang off.

Evie stared into the receiver for a second. She had wanted to see her mother, but it would obviously have to wait until the morning.

Edward was waiting for her when she arrived and his admiring eyes told her everything she needed to know. She herself scanned his expensive navy blue suit, white shirt and boldly patterned tie. Proudly she placed her arm through his and held her head high as they walked down the road together.

He guided her towards the Bell Hotel where they were greeted in the luxurious dining room by the head waiter.

'Your usual table, sir?'

They followed the waiter as he led them through the tables to a secluded corner, where a chair was pulled out for Evie and she sat sedately down. She looked around admiringly.

'It's very nice here,' she said, shaking out her snow white napkin and placing it over her knees. 'D'you come here often, Edward?'

'Quite a bit. Why?'

'They seem to know you well, that's all, and it must be terribly expensive.'

'You can always pay half if you're worried,' he said in amusement.

Evie laughed. 'You asked me out, you can pay.' She accepted the menu from the waiter and studied it intently. She closed the menu, placed it on the table and leaned forward. 'D'you bring a lot of girls here?' she said casually.

'One or two, in the past.' He looked at her and his eyes twinkled. 'You don't happen to be jealous by any chance?'

'No!' she retorted as she blew out her cheeks. 'Just interested, that's all.'

The waiter arrived to take their order and they both settled down to enjoy a delicious meal.

Later Evie sat back, her coffee cup in her hand. 'That was lovely, Edward. Thank you.'

'My pleasure. Would you like anything else?'

'Oh, no. My skirt's straining as it is.' She smiled over at him. 'The other night, after the trouble with Paul, you said you often came to Dawson's. Who did you have your meeting with?'

Edward took a sip of his coffee. 'Richard Dawson.'

'Oh! I am impressed. You must be something in business to have an audience with him. I've never even set eyes on the great man, or his father come to that.' She looked at him quizzically. 'Does your father's company supply Dawson's with materials or something?'

'Not exactly. I suppose you could say we're rivals. But I've always got on with Richard and we get together now and again to catch up on things.'

'Oh! Just who is your father, Edward?'

He looked at her for a moment and tilted his head to one side. 'Charles Bradshaw,' he answered.

Evie gaped. 'Not *the* Charles Bradshaw?'

'That's the one.'

'I don't believe it! You're Edward Bradshaw. Well,

I've heard a lot about you. My God! With your reputation, I wouldn't have thought the likes of me would be good enough for you.'

'And what do you mean by that remark?'

'Oh, nothing. I've heard you like the ladies, that's all. "Love 'em and leave 'em", that's what the gossips say.'

'Never listen to gossip myself, and if you had a brain neither would you,' he said sternly. 'So I've had a few girlfriends. There's nothing in the rules to say you have to marry the first girl you meet, is there?'

Evie looked at him, ashamed. 'No, I'm sorry. I suppose if I'm honest, I've had one or two boyfriends. But then, I'm not in the public eye like you.'

'No. It can be a pain sometimes.' He summoned the waiter, who hurried over to them. 'We'll have more coffee, please.'

They sat in silence while he re-filled their cups.

'Phew!' Evie sighed. 'I seem to be hearing a lot of revelations today.'

Edward fingered his chin thoughtfully. 'What d'you mean?'

'Well, it's strange, really. Through a chance conversation, I learned that my mother owns three shops.'

'Well, what did you think she did?'

'She always told me she just worked in one, as an assistant.'

'Well, whoever told you must have been mistaken then.'

'No,' Evie said flatly. 'The woman was so positive. Anyway, she said she worked for my mother, and you wouldn't mistake a thing like that, would you?'

Edward leaned across the table, his face full of interest. 'Now why would your mother lie about a thing like that?'

'That's what I keep asking myself. It doesn't make sense.' Evie stopped for a moment and frowned. 'I shouldn't be telling you my family secrets.'

'Why not? It makes life more interesting. Besides, it's nice to know other people have problems.'

'I bet your parents have never lied to you.'

'All the time, Evie, and over the past couple of years it's got worse. I'm often catching them out, especially my father.'

'Really! What does he tell lies about?'

Edward shrugged his shoulders. 'Mostly about work. He sometimes forgets that I'm in the business too. Then my mother gets on to him about the late hours he keeps and I know he usually leaves the office before I do.'

'Don't they get on?'

'They got on very well until about two years ago. Then things started to go wrong between them. Father would nag Mother about the amount of money she spent, and so on.' He paused for a moment. 'I put it down to the fact that my father married my mother on the rebound. He was in love with another woman who jilted him on the eve of their wedding, ran away and married some gardener or something; her family disowned her for what she did.' He shrugged his shoulders. 'My father was furious and to be honest I don't think he ever got over it. I don't know the full story, only bits and bobs mentioned when I was younger. I think it was his pride that was affected more than anything else. He's a very proud man, is my father.' Edward shook his head and paused thoughtfully. 'I suppose compared to other people my parents get on very well, but like I said, over the past couple of years they've seemed to be drifting apart. Father has become very crotchety and you can hardly speak to him these days without his losing his temper and going off in a huff. I sometimes wonder if it's because he's got another woman stashed away somewhere.' He stopped and looked at Evie for a moment. 'Am I shocking you?'

'Not at all,' she answered matter-of-factly. 'You might have done a few months ago but not after what I found out today.' She frowned deeply. 'At least you know your family history – I don't. My mother flatly refuses to talk about any of my relatives.'

Edward grinned. 'Families are peculiar if you ask me. I sometimes feel I'd be better off without mine. Except my sister, of course. Geraldine and I have always got on well.'

'Wish I could say the same about my sister. She can be a right bitch sometimes.' Evie frowned. 'But I would love a grandma or an auntie. I've always envied people with large families. All those big Christmas parties.' She sighed. 'There was only ever the three of us.'

'But think of all those presents you'd have to buy.'

Evie laughed. 'Yes, but I still reckon it would be nice. Just a granny would do.'

'As long as she wasn't like my grandfather.'

'What's wrong with your grandfather?'

'He was an old tyrant. He's dead now, passed away last year.' Edward smiled. 'It's funny, but I quite miss the old devil, even though he and Dad pushed me into the family business when really what I wanted to be was a car mechanic.'

'A car mechanic!'

'Yes, don't look so surprised. I'm a wizard with engines.'

'But not at filling your tank with petrol.'

'Okay, you win. But I'd love to own a garage one day.'

Edward paused and stared into space. 'I suppose it's all right for a woman. All you have to do is find a rich husband. Thereafter it's all coffee mornings and fund raising.'

'What? How dare you! Is that what you think of women, Edward? That they're all out for what they can get?'

'Well, aren't they?'

'No, not all of us. I happen to want to make something of myself. I don't want to be reliant on a man to take care of me for the rest of my life.' Evie stopped abruptly, shocked at her own outburst. She took a sip of coffee. 'At first, I admit, I just wanted to find the right man and get married. But as I've grown older, I've realised there's more to life than marriage and babies.' She paused and took a breath. 'When I pass all my exams at College, I shall certainly be looking for a more rewarding job, and any man that marries me will have to accept that I don't intend to become a little housewife waiting on him for the rest of my life!'

Edward looked hard at her. 'Very commendable. With your philosophy of life, I just hope you'll find a man dumb enough to take you on!'

'Don't be sarcastic.' She raised her head defiantly. 'I gather any woman you marry will have to have a degree in house management, look beautiful all the time, and jump to your every command?'

Edward raised his eyebrows and nodded. 'Would be nice. That's if I ever get married. I've not really given it much thought.'

'Doesn't seem like it,' Evie retorted. 'Seems to me you have it all worked out.' She smiled sarcastically. 'I suppose I'm not being fair. It's not your fault you were born into an affluent family and have servants to wait on you.'

'I shouldn't get carried away, Evie.' Edward spoke coldly. 'Yes, I admit, we live in a big comfortable house and have a couple of servants to help us. But my father is always entertaining for one reason or another and my mother couldn't possibly do all the work by herself. And I have to work for a living, and damned hard, I can tell you. The higher up the social scale you are the harder it is to stay there, Evie, and don't forget it.' He ran his fingers through his hair. 'I slogged at university for three years and got a degree. When I joined the company, my father made me start at the bottom and work my way up. Being his son meant nothing. I had to prove myself and it wasn't easy. He made sure I had a difficult time, which in the long run paid off. I could run that place single-handed, and will do when he steps down.' He leaned forward and looked Evie straight in the eye. 'Be assured, nothing has been handed to me on a plate. And as for my wife, should there ever be one, yes, I shall expect her to look after me. What man wouldn't?' He stopped abruptly and drew breath.

Evie sat back in her chair, uncomfortable. Edward's outburst had left her speechless. She was also surprised at her own words. She cast her eyes away from him in embarrassment and studied the small crystal vase of freshly cut flowers that sat to the side of the table. Edward was right. When a man had worked hard all day, he would want to come home to an attentive wife and be looked after. And what about her? Did she really want a career? Until her outburst she hadn't given it much thought and felt guilty for misleading Edward, letting him think she had her future all worked out when in truth she hadn't. And what about marriage? Wasn't it expected that when you married you stayed at home and looked after your husband?

Realisation swept coldly over her. No, that was not what she wanted. She wanted to make her mark on the world, to do something useful with her life and be fulfilled. She wasn't quite sure what, but she would find her slot in time. These new revelations shocked and surprised her but she smiled inwardly to herself. Yes, she wanted to marry, to feel loved and cared for and to have someone to care for in return, but it would have to be an equal marriage, one that was worked at from both sides. She shifted uncomfortably again as a thought sprang to mind. This was only their first date and she was already contemplating the future. She raised her head sharply as she realised Edward was speaking to her.

'I'm sorry, what did you say?'

'I said, I would like to see you again.'

'Would you? Oh!'

'You sound shocked. Don't you want to see me?'

Evie relaxed against the back of her chair and smiled warmly. 'Yes, I would. Only . . .'

'Only what?'

'We seem to have a great many differences of opinion.'

'I couldn't agree more, but I find that quite a challenge. I'll soon get you round to my way of thinking.'

'I shouldn't be too sure of that!'

'Well, it will be fun trying.' Edward looked up and caught the waiter's eye. 'I've enjoyed tonight, Miss Grayson. How about the pictures on Tuesday?'

She laughed. 'I seem to remember your asking me something like that before. Yes . . . er . . . no. Tuesday is my College night,' she said, feeling proud of the new determination which filled her. 'I have some exams to pass and need to attend every class from now on. I'm free on Monday or Wednesday this week.'

'Monday it is then.' Edward looked at his watch. 'Better get you home. I don't want your mother accusing me of keeping you out late again.'

Evie raised her eyebrows. 'She's not an ogre. She worries about me, that's all.'

'Yes, I suppose we did arrive home rather late from Blackpool. Was she really annoyed? She seemed in a bit of a state when I left you.'

'Just a little.' Evie smiled as she remembered the aftermath of the wonderful day they had met. She stood up and allowed Edward to help her on with her coat and watched intently as he went over to pay the bill. I could get very fond of you, she thought.

They sat in silence on the journey home, neither wanting the evening to draw to a close. They arrived at her front door and Evie was relieved to see the lights were out. Her mother had not arrived home yet. Edward switched off the engine and turned to face her, his arm sliding round her shoulders. He kissed her on the lips. Evie felt her body respond to his embrace. Edward withdrew his arm and smiled at her.

'Monday then. Lea's Corner.'

'Okay.'

Evie slipped out of the car and watched as Edward drove down the road and out of sight. She sighed contentedly as she walked towards the house, then stopped abruptly. She had to face her mother tomorrow. There was no way she could let the revelations of the morning go unchallenged and the thought filled her with misgivings.

* * *

Evie was up and dressed before nine o'clock the following morning. Her mother greeted her warmly.

'Nice to see you up so early. Are you coming to church with me?' Edith asked, well aware of what the answer would be.

'Mam, you know I haven't been to church since I was fifteen!' Evie answered scornfully.

'All right. I just thought it would be nice for my daughter to accompany me, that's all.' Edith sighed. 'Would you like some breakfast?'

'No, thanks. Just a cuppa will do. I'm not hungry this morning.'

Edith made to rise from the table.

'Finish your breakfast, I'll mash a fresh pot,' Evie said as she filled the kettle and put it on the stove. She turned and watched her mother thoughtfully.

Finally, Edith pushed away her plate. 'I enjoyed that. But it's unusual for you not to be hungry.' She looked at her daughter quizzically. 'You're not sickening for something, are you?'

'I'm fine, Mam. Stop fussing.' Evie paused. 'How's Florrie?' she asked.

'Not good,' Edith answered, a worried look crossing her face. 'She's covered in spots this morning. The doctor's due back tomorrow. I'll wait and see what he says. I personally think she's got measles, and a bad dose at that. It certainly hasn't done her temper any good. As soon as I mentioned she was still unfit for work, she started. It's a wonder you never heard her shouting.'

'Oh, so that's what woke me?' Evie frowned. 'I'll pop up later and see if there's anything she wants.'

Edith looked at her daughter in surprise. 'That's good of you, I'm sure she'll appreciate that.'

'We'll see,' Evie said, unconvinced.

The kettle started to boil and she poured the steaming water over the tea leaves. She picked up the pot and two clean cups, placed them on the table, pulled out a chair and sat down. As she waited for the tea to mash, she took a deep breath and decided it was time to tackle her mother.

'How was your day yesterday, Mam?' she asked casually.

'Good, thank you,' Edith answered lightly. 'Very busy. The shop was packed all morning, we hardly had time for our elevenses.' She looked at Evie keenly. 'I'm sorry, love. I never asked how you got on. How was your evening?'

'Fine,' she said flatly.

'And Rosie? Did you have a nice walk?'

'Yes. She's growing fast. Mavis still has a long way to go, but the signs are she'll come out as good as new. Mrs Humphreys has spoken to the doctors. They seem to think it will take at least a year before they can be absolutely sure the disease has gone.'

'It's a real killer, but at least the doctors are optimistic.'

Evie poured the tea and passed a cup over to her mother.

'Thanks, dear.'

'Mrs Humphreys isn't well,' Evie continued, 'so I got some shopping for her while I was out. She's knitting Rosie a cardi so I had to get some wool.' She watched her mother's face intently. 'I went into your shop.'

'Oh?' Edith looked up sharply. 'I thought I'd told you never to do that. You know I could get into trouble.'

'I don't see why, Mam. After all, I was a customer.' Evie paused and took a sip of her tea. 'I never saw you.'

Edith was silent for a second. 'Oh! I was probably in the back.'

'No, you weren't. You were at your new shop, interviewing staff,' Evie said coldly.

'What d'you mean, interviewing staff?' Edith said in alarm. 'I don't know what you're talking about. Now, I must get ready for church.' She made to rise, but was stopped by her daughter.

'Don't, Mam. Don't lie to me any more.'

'What d'you mean, lie? What are you accusing me of, Evie?'

'That wool shop is yours, so is the one on Fosse Road and the new one you have at the bottom of Narborough Road,' cried Evie.

Edith's eyes narrowed. 'How did you find out?'

'Does it matter?'

'Yes!' she shouted. 'It does matter. How did you find out?'

'Your assistant told me.'

'She'd no right . . .' Edith seethed.

'She told me by mistake, let it slip out before she realised what she was saying. She didn't know I was your daughter. She thought I was just another customer. Why, Mam? Why have you lied all these years? Not just to me, but to Florrie as well?' Evie leaned forward and stared at her mother intently. 'What are you hiding, Mam?'

'I'm not hiding anything,' Edith said quickly.

'I don't understand. Why make out you were just an assistant when all the time you were the owner? I can't see the point,' Evie said in bewilderment.

'Can't you? Evie, don't you realise some things just aren't any of your business?'

163

'Any of my business! You're my mother. Of course it's my business!' she shouted. 'Where did the money come from to set the shops up? That's what I want to know.'

Edith paled. 'Evie, since you were small you've never been content with a simple explanation for anything. You always want to dig further. "Why? Why? Why?" were the only words you ever used to say as a child. The whys and the wherefores are nothing to do with you. You now know that I own three shops. Be content with that and start minding your own business.'

'So, Florrie was right. You did spend Dad's insurance money!' Evie exploded.

Edith scraped back her chair, stood up and leaned over the table, her face contorted in anger. 'I have told you and I have told Florrie, time and time again – your father left no money. The money I set up the shops with was mine.'

Evie scraped her own chair back and stood up to face her mother. 'Yours! How could a factory girl have money like that?'

'There you go again, Evie, jumping to conclusions. I've never said I was just a factory girl.'

'But you implied as much.'

'I implied nothing. I said I met your dad in the factory. I never said what I was doing there.'

'Well, what were you doing if it wasn't working?' Evie said coldly.

'Why? Why? Why? You never learn, do you, Evie? This is none of your business.' Edith straightened up and untied her pinny. She screwed it into a ball and threw it on the chair. 'Now if you don't mind, I'm going to get ready for church.'

'I do mind, Mam. I still want to know why you've lied

and what other things you haven't told me. I feel I can't trust you any more.' Evie spoke icily, watching her mother's every move.

'Well, that's for you to decide. Sometimes lies are better than the truth. You have a lot of growing up to do, my girl. You have to realise that some lies are deliberate, and told from the best of intentions.'

'How can I decide that, Mam? You've told me hardly anything about your past. All I know is that you're my mother, someone I have loved and trusted all my life – until now.'

'Well, bear that in mind while you're hurling your accusations at me,' Edith snapped. 'Think of the times I have comforted you when you have been sick, given you a good home, welcomed your friends, dressed you and cared for you. I trust these things do count?'

Both women stared coldly at each other. Evie felt a sickening anguish rise up in her stomach, fear gripping her very soul. Just what was her mother hiding? These doubts were mingled with a desperate longing to put her arms around her and apologise for the horrible accusations she had thrown in her face. But pride stopped her. Her mother hadn't trusted her with her secrets and Evie wanted to hurt her as much as she herself was hurting. She stared defiantly at Edith and could not help but retaliate.

'While you're here, Mother, I've something to tell you,' she said nonchalantly.

'Oh! And what might that be?' Edith answered in the same tone as her daughter had used.

'I'm seeing Edward,' she divulged haughtily.

'Edward?'

'The man who brought me home from Blackpool.'

Edith moved towards her daughter. 'I thought I told you not to see him,' she snapped, forgetting her resolve of the last few weeks.

'I know what you said,' Evie began, 'but who I see is none of your business.'

'Oh, but it is. Until you are twenty-one you are still under my care and protection, and I know nothing about this boy.'

Evie raised her head defiantly. 'I'm beginning to wonder whether you're fit to be in control of an innocent young woman,' she said, her voice full of sarcasm.

Edith's mouth dropped open at her daughter's words and tears sprang to her eyes. 'How dare you!' She raised her hand and smacked Evie across the cheek.

Evie fell back against the chair and placed her hand to her smarting face. Her defiance rose even higher.

'Oh, I dare, Mother.' She regained her balance and straightened her back. 'If it's his standing in the community that worries you, then you needn't bother. His father owns Bradshaw's. So you see, you can still hold up your head in church,' she said harshly.

Evie's defiance turned to bewilderment as she saw her mother's expression change from anger to horror.

Edith sat down slowly on a chair and stared at her daughter, her mouth gaping. 'Bradshaw's?' she muttered.

'Yes, Bradshaw's!' Evie shouted. 'His grandfather founded the company, and one day Edward will take it over, and I won't stop seeing him, not for you or anyone!' Her smug words were lost on her mother. Evie stood clenching and unclenching her fists, waiting for a response. When none came, she bit her bottom lip, bewildered at her mother's unexpected silence.

'Edward Bradshaw . . . Are you sure?' Edith whispered.

''Course I'm sure. Why?' she asked.

Edith groaned and placed her head in her hands. 'Evie, you must stop seeing this boy,' she pleaded.

'Stop seeing him? Why, Mother? I can't, I love him.' Evie's shoulders sagged, all anger and defiance leaving her. She stared at Edith, waiting for an explanation.

'Edward Bradshaw, of all people . . . Evie, why him?' Edith raised her eyes in appeal. 'Look, you must not see this boy again. Please say you won't – for me, Evie. Please?' she begged.

She sank down on the chair facing her mother. 'I can't, Mam, I can't. Why are you asking me to do this?'

'Don't ask me to explain. I can't.' Tears formed in Edith's eyes and started to fall down her face.

The sight of her mother crying brought a lump to Evie's throat. She placed a hand on her arm. 'Why can't you explain? You ask me to stop seeing the man I love and you won't tell me why,' she said, trying to keep her voice even. 'I thought you wanted me to be happy. I am happy, Mam. Edward is everything I've ever dreamed about. You'd like him. He's smart and intelligent.' Her mind whirled. 'Look, let me bring him to meet you. You'll see for yourself then.'

'No! No!' Edith shouted. 'You mustn't bring him here. His parents must never find out . . .'

Evie withdrew her hand. 'What have they got to do with this?'

'Nothing! Nothing, Evie. Forget I said that,' Edith replied quickly. She jumped up from her chair. 'I'm sorry, I can't talk about this any more, not at the moment. It's been such a shock. Never in a million years did I expect this. I've got to go, I've got to get to the shop . . . no church, I must go to church. You do what you have to, Evie. See Edward if you must – but be prepared for the consequences.' Ashen-faced, she rushed from the room.

'Consequences? What consequences?' Evie shouted after her, but her words were lost: Edith had left.

Evie sat at the table for an age, staring into space. She went over and over the argument and nothing made sense. The only conclusion she could draw was that her mother had deliberately lied, and the thought upset her deeply. She rose and walked into the hall where she put on her coat and gloves and wound her thick knitted scarf around her neck. She would go and see Jenny. Maybe she would make some sense of it all.

She was greeted at the door by a tired faded woman of about thirty-five. Her clothes, worn and dirty, hung limply on her sagging body. On her feet were a pair of men's navy socks and her toes poked out of an old pair of slippers that were at least two sizes too big. Evie smiled warmly as Jenny's mother ran her hands through her greasy, grey-streaked hair.

'Hello, Mrs Jones. Is Jenny in?'

Mrs Jones's heavily lined eyes twinkled in recognition of her daughter's friend. 'Come in, gel. It's brass monkey weather out there, ain't it? Jenny's in 'er bedroom. She's gorra mardy on, 'cos I won't ask that lad of 'ers for tea. Well, yer can't give a visitor bread and lard, can yer?'

Evie smiled as she followed Jenny's mother down the passage towards the bedroom. It deeply saddened her to think that this woman had once been full of life and had lived it to the full, only to give up her chance of happiness and resign herself to a life of drudgery for the sake of her children.

'Who the bloody 'ell's that?' a voice boomed. 'Can't a man get any peace on a Sunday, wi'out 'alf of bloody Leicester knockin' on the door?'

'It's Evie, Jenny's friend,' her mother shouted back. She turned to face Evie and lowered her voice. 'Don't mind 'im, me duck. 'E's got the mardys as well, 'cos 'e lost all 'is money at the bookie's yesterday and can't go for a pint today. Serves 'im bloody right!' They arrived at Jenny's bedroom door and she opened it.

'Evie's 'ere. Trust you'll talk to 'er?' She flattened herself against the door to let Evie through and closed it behind her.

Jenny's bedroom was a mess. The old dressing table housed an assortment of odds and ends. Empty stocking packets, well-thumbed copies of the *Red Letter* and odd curlers were littered across the floor. An old chair in the corner of the room was piled high with clothes.

'Hi, Evie.' Jenny looked up from the magazine she was reading and gave her friend a smile. 'What brings you 'ere on a Sunday mornin'?'

'I've come to see you,' Evie answered. She picked her way over the debris to the bed Jenny shared with her sister June, and sat down. 'I don't know how you can live in this mess,' she said, looking round the room.

Jenny folded her magazine and narrowed her eyes. 'I happen to like it like this, and if you're in this kinda mood you can bloody well go 'ome!' She unfolded her magazine and began to read.

Evie sighed. 'I'm sorry, Jenny. What are these?' she asked, picking up a folder of drawings.

'Just some scribbles. Give them 'ere.' She went to grab the pad, but Evie was too quick for her.

'These are good,' she said, flicking over the pages of the pad as she admired various designs for women's clothes which Jenny had drawn. 'In fact, these are excellent. Does anyone know you have a talent like this?'

'Don't be daft! They're only my doodlings.' Jenny frowned, trying to snatch the pad back again.

Evie looked intently at one particular drawing. 'This dress is divine, I'd love one like that.' She looked at Jenny seriously. 'You really must do something with these.'

'Do what?' Jenny laughed. 'Now give me back me pad and tell me the real reason you're 'ere. You look the picture of misery. You and Edward fell out or somethin'?'

Evie flicked over the pages, shut the pad and handed it back to Jenny. 'No, Edward and I haven't had a fight. It's my mother.'

She proceeded to tell Jenny most of the events of that morning. Her friend listened intently, but seemed unconcerned.

'Well, what do you think then?' Evie asked.

'I think you're makin' too much of it all,' she said.

'Do you?' Evie frowned.

'Yeah. Stands to reason. Mams are always havin' a go at us. Maybe she's jealous of you and Edward. Doesn't like the thought of losing yer. Or she might be worried that Edward's parents won't think you're good enough for 'im – that's why she doesn't want 'em to find out. He sounds as though 'e comes from money. Does 'e?'

Evie shrugged her shoulders. 'I think his parents have a fair bit. His father's got a good job.'

'Well, there yer go then. Yer mam's trying to protect

yer against a showdown with 'em. You know what mothers are like wi' their sons. They probably have 'im betrothed to some pimply, rich "debbytant",' Jenny scoffed. 'But don't you worry, gel.' She bent over and patted Evie's hand. 'You're good enough for the likes of 'im. So if I were you, I'd carry on seein' 'im and keep yer gob shut.'

'D'you reckon I should?'

'Yeah, why not? You might end up marrying 'im, eh?'

'You're as bad as Mavis. You both read too many of those romance books.'

'Not as many as you do,' Jenny scolded.

'I suppose you're right.' Evie raised her head. 'Why should I stop seeing him?' She paused and looked at Jenny in concern. 'What d'you think of this business about the wool shops?'

'Not much. Jealousy of course!' Jenny raised her hands. 'I wish my mam had a secret like that, then maybe we wouldn't 'ave to 'ave bread and lard for tea tonight.'

'Are things that bad?' Evie asked.

'No!' she exclaimed. 'There's a pot of jam in the cupboard. Mam's always exaggeratin'.'

'Oh, Jenny,' Evie laughed.

'Maybe your mam is fiddling the taxman. That's why she wants no one to know she owns those shops.'

'No, it's more than that.' Evie shook her head. 'I just feel hurt that she hasn't trusted me.'

Jenny tutted. 'I still think you're makin' a big deal out of it all.' She thought for a moment, then grinned. 'Maybe she has a deep dark secret: she's robbed a bank or somethin' and the coppers are after 'er?'

'Don't be ridiculous, Jenny,' Evie snapped. 'But you

could be right about the deep dark secret.'

'Well, in that case, you're just gonna 'ave to find out, ain't yer?'

'But how?' Evie asked.

'I don't know.' Jenny shrugged her shoulders. 'You're the one wi' the brains, but if your mam was so upset at yer findin' out about the shops, why cause more trouble? Why don't yer leave well alone?'

'That would be the easy thing to do,' Evie answered.

'Might be the most sensible. You might just find out somethin' you don't want to 'ear.'

'D'you reckon?' Evie looked worriedly at Jenny.

'Yeah, I do. Yer mam obviously kept it a secret for some reason.'

'Mm. You could be right. Oh, God! What if it's something awful?' Evie looked at Jenny in horror.

She sucked in her cheeks. 'Stop being so melo . . . melo . . . stop overactin'. Yer mam probably never told yer because she didn't want to. My mam never tells me anythin'. I don't even know how much divvy she's got comin' from the Co-op.'

'Yes, you're right, Jenny. I'm probably blowing this up out of all proportion.'

'Good gel.' Jenny patted her friend's knee. 'Now, are you stayin' for dinner? You can 'ave the dog's share.'

Evie laughed. 'You are a card, Jenny. Thanks for the offer, but I'd like to have a walk in the park and clear my head before I go home.'

'Suit yerself.' Jenny yawned and clasped her hands behind her head.

'How are things with you and Arnold?' Evie asked.

'Okay.'

'Only okay? I thought you were head over heels for the bloke.'

'Oh, that was last week. 'E's started to talk about marriage and puttin' our names down for a council 'ouse. They're buildin' some new ones up Stocking Farm Estate and 'e thinks we'd 'ave a good chance of gettin' one.'

'You don't sound so keen?' Evie looked concerned.

'I ain't so sure I am. I'm not nineteen yet and the thought of bein' tied with bills and rent frightens me to death.'

'Well, the only thing I can say about that, Jenny, is you can't really love him enough.'

'You could be right. D'you know, I was so relieved when Mam said I couldn't bring him for tea this week. I shouldn't feel like that, should I?' Jenny looked at Evie for guidance.

'Not really,' she answered. 'If you truly loved him, you would live in a shed on bread and lard and not give a damn.'

'Yes, I know, and to be 'onest I don't think I could with 'im. I'm not saying he ain't bin fun to go out wi' . . . but marriage. No, I don't think I'm ready for that yet.'

'You'll know when you are.' Evie smiled.

'Like you do wi' Edward?' Jenny smirked knowingly.

'Mm.' She smiled and rose. 'Thanks, Jenny.'

'For what?'

'For listening and making me see sense. Now all I have to do is face my mother.'

'Talking of mothers . . .' Jenny jumped up and rushed over to her wardrobe. It was a monstrosity of a thing that filled an entire wall of the small bedroom. She wrenched open one of the doors and pulled out an article of clothing.

She held it up and watched her friend's face.

'Well, what d'you think?'

'It's a fur coat!' Evie said in amazement.

'I know it's a fur coat, yer daft sod. What d'you think?'

Evie walked over and fingered the object.

'It's good quality. Where did you get it from?'

'Me grandma got it from the church jumble for ten bob. A bargain, ain't it?'

'Certainly is. What are you going to do with it?'

'Wear it, of course. Ain't every day you gets given a fur coat. Well, stole really. Mam wanted it, but I got in first. She ain't 'alf mad. Don't you think I'll look smashin' in it?'

'Er . . . yes,' Evie fibbed, not having a particular liking for fur coats.

'I knew you'd say that. Trouble is, it's a bit long and baggy, so I thought I'd make it into a jacket. While you're 'ere you can 'elp me.'

'Me help? How?'

'I'll show yer.' Jenny cleared a space on the floor with her foot and laid the coat out. She produced a pair of scissors.

Evie's face paled. 'Are you really sure about this?' she asked nervously.

'Just grab 'old of that end and pull it straight, while I cut.'

With no more ado, Jenny knelt down and took a large snip into the coat. Evie guessed it was too late to stop her friend and grabbed hold of the opposite end and pulled it straight, enabling Jenny to cut right across the middle.

'There!' She grinned as she smiled at her handiwork. 'All we need to do now is glue up the bottom.'

'Glue up the bottom!' Evie groaned.

'Well, it's quicker than sewin'!' Jenny retorted as she produced a large pot of Bostik and unscrewed the lid.

'God, that stuff stinks!' Evie grimaced, wrinkling her nose as the force of the smell reached her nostrils.

'Stop moanin', Evie. I'm gonna spread the glue across the hem, then you fold it over and press it down, got that?'

'I don't like the sound of this, Jenny.' Evie saw the look her friend gave her. 'Okay, you stick, I'll press.'

The girls set about their task then sat back and admired their handiwork.

'See, I told yer. Not bad, eh?' Jenny said proudly. 'I'm goin' to wear it on Saturday night over me blue costume. Should look a treat.'

Before Evie could say anything, both girls noticed with horror that the drying glue was pulling the bottom of the coat in, gathering it up like a concertina.

'Oh, my God, Evie! What's happenin'? You get that end and we'll pull it out to straighten it. Quick, before it's too late.'

Both girls grabbed opposite ends of the coat and pulled. Nothing happened.

''Arder!' Jenny shouted.

They pulled their ends as hard as they could. Suddenly there was a horrendous ripping noise as the fur coat split straight down the middle, right up to the collar.

Evie looked at Jenny. Jenny looked at Evie. They both looked at the mutilated jacket. Jenny dropped to the floor and doubled over, tears of laughter spurting from her eyes. Evie clutched the wardrobe door in the hope it would support her legs as she too nearly collapsed in hysterical laugher. Both girls rocked backwards and forwards, trying to control themselves in case Jenny's family should hear and come to investigate. It took several long minutes for them to regain control.

'Jenny, Jenny . . . what on earth are we going to do?' Evie asked wiping her eyes.

'Search me,' she cried with mirth. 'I think it's too late to do anythin' now. God, Evie, that's the funniest thing I've ever seen.'

'I know,' she agreed. 'My ribs are killing me.'

''Elp me hide it in the bottom of the wardrobe. I'll just 'ave to 'ope Mam forgets all about it.'

Evie grabbed the jacket and Jenny the off-cut. Jenny found a large brown paper carrier bag and squashed what was left of the coat inside. She made a space at the bottom of the wardrobe, put the bag in and piled as much stuff as she could find on the top.

'There. Mam never goes in 'ere.' Jenny blew out her cheeks. ''Opefully it'll stay 'idden for ever. If she does ask for it, I shall say that you borrowed it for a do or somethin'. You know me, I always manage to think up some good excuse when I'm in a tight corner.' Jenny giggled, finding the whole incident extremely funny.

Evie nodded in agreement.

'I really must be going now.'

Jenny looked at her friend. 'Okay. I must say, though, you look better than when you arrived.'

'I feel it. I haven't laughed like that for ages. It's done me the world of good.'

'Yes, well, as long as you don't expect me to repeat the performance. Next time I'll try sewin' it. Don't look at me like that, as if to say I told you so,' Jenny chided her friend.

'As if I would.' Evie smiled as she buttoned up her coat and rewound her scarf.

Jenny rose to show her friend to the door. 'I'll see yer in the mornin' and don't be late.'

'As if I'd dare,' retorted Evie. She shouted her goodbyes to Jenny's parents and made her way out into the November sunshine.

She walked slowly down the road and turned into the park, avoiding a woman with a pushchair as she entered the gates. For a winter's day, the park was extremely crowded and Evie paused for a moment and watched the antics of several children playing football. The ball came thundering towards her and instinctively Evie raised her leg and kicked it back, to the loud cheers of the players. She smiled in pleasure, turned and carried on walking.

The talk with Jenny and the incident with the fur coat had done her the world of good and Evie felt suddenly glad to be alive. An overwhelming feeling of love for her mother flowed through her and she felt so proud. So what if she had kept the wool shops a secret? The main thing was that her mother had taken a gamble and succeeded; even if she had failed, at least she had tried. Evie hugged herself. She would take the initiative and apologise for all the hurtful things that had been said.

With a spring in her step she arrived at her front gate, took a deep breath and prepared herself.

Chapter Eight

Evie knew the house was empty as soon as she opened the back door. The wireless was silent and the usual appetising smell of roast beef and Yorkshire pudding was missing. She walked through the downstairs rooms wondering where on earth her mother had got to. It was well past the time for her return from the Sunday Morning Service and as she stood with her back to the stove, a sick feeling rose up in her stomach. Had something happened to her mother? Had she done something dreadful after their argument? She pondered several unpleasant possibilities and the sick feeling worsened.

Her eyes alighted on the table. In the centre, propped up against the empty teapot, was a folded piece of paper. She grabbed it and quickly read. Edith, on arriving home from church, had found that Florrie had taken a turn for the worse and had summoned the doctor. He had immediately called an ambulance and Florrie had been whisked into hospital. Her mother was there now and would be home as soon as possible.

Evie sat down and tried to calm herself. She re-read the note, folded it and placed it back on the table. The hatred she felt for her sister vanished; in its place came concern and pity. A tear trickled down her cheek which she quickly wiped away. She looked up in alarm as she sensed a presence and turned to see her mother standing by her side.

Evie scanned her face, but her mother's expression added greatly to her fears. She jumped up from her seat.

'Is she . . . is she going to be all right?' she blurted. 'What's wrong with our Florrie, Mam?'

Edith took the pin out of her hat and placed them both on the table. She sighed. 'She's holding her own. It's just a matter of waiting, I'm afraid.'

'Holding her own? I don't understand. I thought she just had the measles.'

Edith struggled to take off her coat and placed it over the back of the chair. 'That's what we all thought, but it appears she's got pneumonia and is allergic to the medicine the doctor gave her last week. That's what caused the spots.' Edith paused and stared unblinkingly at her daughter. 'Florrie's very ill, Evie. I'm really worried.'

She sat down on a chair at the kitchen table and placed her head in her hands. Evie stared at her mother until it dawned on her just how distraught she was. She rushed over and placed her hand on her mother's shoulder.

'Try not to worry, Mam. She'll pull through. You know what a fighter Florrie is.' She tried to stop her voice from quivering with emotion. 'Sit there, I'll make you a strong cuppa.'

'Thanks, love,' Edith muttered.

Evie filled the kettle with water and put it on the stove. She turned and looked at Edith and her heart softened. She felt tears sting her cheeks. 'Oh, Mam,' she sobbed. 'I'm sorry. I'm so sorry for all the trouble I've caused. I really didn't mean to pry and say all those terrible things.' She picked up a tea towel and sobbed quietly into it.

Edith turned and looked at her daughter. The sight of Evie brought a lump to her throat. She stood up and walked over to her. She placed her hands on her shoulders and pulled Evie gently towards her. 'Stop crying, Evie. It won't make Florrie any better.'

'It's not just that, Mam.' Evie sobbed louder, placing her head on her mother's shoulder. 'What if Florrie doesn't get better? I keep thinking of all the rotten things I said to her, and what I said to you this morning . . .'

'We both said a lot of things, Evie. I want to forget all that. I just want Florrie to be well and for us to be a family again.'

Edith sighed loudly as the kettle started to boil. She released Evie and walked over to the stove. Picking up the teapot, she put in two spoons of tea and poured on the boiling water. She placed the pot on the table, along with the cups and saucers.

'I must go and see her,' Evie whispered. 'Is there anything she needs?'

'You can't at the moment. She's in intensive care. But when she's out of there and in a normal ward, you can go. Let's just pray it won't be long. The hospital has promised to telephone if there's any change. In the meantime, we must try and carry on as normal. We can do that, can't we, Evie?' Edith asked, looking sternly at her daughter.

'Oh, yes, Mam. I'm sorry for what happened this morning, I really am.'

'Okay. Let's drop it now, please.' Edith turned and picked up the milk and sugar. 'I must think about getting the dinner.'

'I'm not hungry, Mam.'

'We'll carry on as normal and that means having our

Sunday dinner. I don't want you going down with anything. I couldn't cope with that just now.'

'Okay, Mam, dinner it is. I'll help.' Evie paused and looked at her mother and her eyes softened. 'Can I just say one thing?'

'What's that?' Edith asked.

'I'm proud of you.'

Edith patted Evie's hand.

'And so am I of you. Thanks, love.' She smiled warmly. 'Right, let's drink our tea whilst it's hot then you can peel the spuds.'

Edith telephoned the hospital later that evening. Florrie was still in intensive care, but was holding her own.

Evie groaned to herself as she entered the Accounts Office the following morning. 'Oh, Florrie, get better soon then I can go back to my own job,' she muttered under her breath.

The Accounts Office was even more depressing than the General Office. Still, at least Mr Grady wasn't in to cast his piggy little eyes in her direction, making her feel small and inadequate. As she took off her coat and sat at her temporary desk, Mrs Fanshaw rushed over. She was a petite, fussy woman, whose face always held a worried frown. A nervous tic in her left eye jumped vigorously as she pushed a large, heavy red book under Evie's nose, plus a pile of invoices.

'You'll have to tackle these this morning, Miss Grayson,' Mrs Fanshaw said apologetically as she looked nervously over her shoulder. 'With all this illness around we're ever so behind. The Wages Section is the only one that's fully staffed at the moment and they can't spare anyone, what with Christmas approaching and the bonuses still to be made up. Our section usually gives a hand, but that's impossible just now.' She pushed the book further in front of Evie. 'Miss Grayson, your sister,' she added quickly, 'is the only one who normally enters these invoices, but they're so far behind I can't leave them any longer. No, no, I just can't, can I?' She looked at Evie for justification of her actions. 'Well, I can't leave them, can I?' she said again.

'No, I suppose not.' Evie shrugged her shoulders nonchalantly.

'That's what I thought. I mean, I have to try and keep things going. It's the least I can do.'

'Yes, I suppose you must,' Evie repeated again, using the same nonchalant tone.

'Yes, right. I said as much to my Ernest last night.'

'What are these?' Evie grimaced, becoming thoroughly bored with Mrs Fanshaw's twitterings.

'They're carbon copies of invoices, dear. The top copy has been sent to the customer.'

Evie closed her eyes and inwardly groaned. 'I know that, Mrs Fanshaw, but what do you want me to do with them?'

'Oh, I see. Sorry, dear.' She gave a little giggle as she opened the large red book. 'This is the cash ledger and all these invoices have to be entered, so that when we get the cash or cheques in, we can enter the invoice as paid.'

'Oh, I see.' Evie smiled. She looked at the open ledger. 'I enter the invoice number here, and here what was sold, and here the amount, and here the purchase tax.'

Mrs Fanshaw looked at Evie, most impressed. 'Yes, that's right. You're a very bright girl, you know.'

She smiled broadly and Evie noted that for a split second the woman had relaxed. The action changed her whole face and for a moment she looked very pretty and younger than her fifty-three years.

'Please use your best handwriting, Miss Grayson, and don't, for goodness' sake, get any ink blots on the pages. There'll be hell to pay if you do.'

'I'll try my best, Mrs Fanshaw.'

Evie smiled warmly at the woman, pleased to do something different for a change. Mrs Fanshaw scuttled away and left her to start her job. She picked up her pen and the first invoice, then carefully entered the details and placed the invoice back on the desk in a separate pile from the rest.

Morning tea had been drunk and Evie was halfway through the pile when she picked up her next invoice. It was the one she had typed a couple of weeks previously for Edward & Co. She smiled at the memory, remembering her feelings of total desperation. How things change in a few weeks, she thought.

She started to enter the details, then stopped abruptly. Something stirred in her mind. She frowned. Something was wrong and she couldn't quite put her finger on it. She stared hard at the invoice. It seemed perfectly all right. All the columns added up and the total was correct. She placed it down and continued her work. She hesitated, picked up the invoice again, frowned and scratched her chin.

Mrs Fanshaw passed her desk and stopped.

'Are you all right, Miss Grayson? Only you look a little worried,' she asked in concern. 'This job's not too much for you, I hope?'

Evie shook herself. 'I'm fine, thank you,' she answered.

Mrs Fanshaw peered over her shoulder. 'You're doing a grand job, keep it up.'

Evie smiled. 'Thank you.'

What a change from Miss Sargent, she thought. In all the time she had been working for the woman, she had never heard one word of praise. But still she could not concentrate her mind on her work. What's wrong with me? she thought angrily. I've got piles of work to do and I sit wasting time like this.

Then it hit her. She suddenly realised what was wrong. The correction to the mistake she had made was not there and the amount was different. I'm sure it is, she thought. She racked her brains trying to remember what the amount had been. As much as she tried, she could not. Everything else on the invoice was the same as she had typed it, but she distinctly remembered making a mistake and although she had corrected it neatly, on the under copies she remembered the correction could be seen clearly.

She realised Mrs Fanshaw was looking at her again and quickly put down the offending paper and picked up another. As she carried out her work, she worried even more.

If she had been told the correct procedures, then something was wrong with that invoice. She looked at the clock on the wall on the far side of the room and saw it was nearly lunchtime. She quickly made up her mind. She would not go out with Jenny, she would stay and talk to Mrs Fanshaw.

At the sound of the dinner hooter, Evie jumped up and walked quickly to the General Office. She told a dismayed Jenny that she would not be joining her at lunchtime as she had to work through. She left her friend staring moodily after her.

Back in the Accounts Office, she took her sandwiches out of her bag and started to eat. She noted that Mrs Fanshaw was seated at her desk engrossed in a magazine.

It was not the done thing to approach an older member of staff and Evie sat deliberating on just how she could get her into conversation without appearing forward or breaking any rules. A thought struck her and she hoped it would work.

She rose and walked over to Mrs Fanshaw's desk.

'Excuse me, Mrs Fanshaw, would you like a cup of tea?' she asked pleasantly.

Mrs Fanshaw looked up in surprise and nearly choked on her sandwich.

'Yes, please, dear. I usually go down to the canteen and get one after I have finished eating, but if you're going I'd appreciate one very much. Thank you.' She handed Evie a couple of pennies.

Evie arrived back and placed the tea on Mrs Fanshaw's desk.

'You are a good girl, not a bit like your sister.' Mrs Fanshaw smiled. 'I just wish we could keep you in this department.'

'So do I,' Evie lied shamelessly. 'I must admit, I am enjoying the work I'm doing this morning. It's put all the pieces together.'

'What do you mean?' Mrs Fanshaw asked.

'Oh, it's just that I typed all those invoices a couple of weeks ago. I now know what happens to them afterwards.'

Mrs Fanshaw looked keenly at her as Evie continued.

'I know that companies buy goods from us. The Sales Section work out the cost and raise the invoice; it's then sent to us to work out the purchase tax and calculate the total amount. Mr Grady then has them for checking and entering into the ledger. He then passes them to us for typing and then the top copy goes to the customer and the other carbon copy is for our file. When the customer pays his account, we enter the amount he has paid, and the balance owing.' Evie gave a triumphant smile as she finished her account.

'Well done, Miss Grayson. I'm most impressed. Sit down a moment.'

Mrs Fanshaw indicated a chair at another desk and Evie pulled it over and sat down.

'It's really a pleasure to get a young girl showing so much interest in her work. Usually young heads are filled with boys and willing Friday night to come round.' She smiled. 'You seem to really like it in this department. How would you like me to ask Mr Grady to get you transferred?' She waited for Evie's response.

'Oh, I don't think Miss Sargent would be very pleased,' Evie said quickly, feeling totally horrified at the prospect.

Mrs Fanshaw looked downcast. 'Yes, I dare say you're right. Still, with a bit of luck, you might be transferred to us in due course.'

Evie tried to smile. 'Yes, I might, if I'm lucky.' She paused. 'Er . . . Mrs Fanshaw, can I ask a question, please?'

'Yes, of course, dear. Fire away.'

'What happens if you make a mistake on an invoice? I mean, a bad mistake, one that can't be put right. Does the invoice get ripped up and a new one typed?' Evie spoke lightly.

'Oh, no, my dear. To make a mistake as bad as that is practically a criminal offence.' Mrs Fanshaw spoke gravely. 'All invoices are uniquely numbered and if one was just ripped up there would be an investigation as to why it was missing, and also it would mess up the sales ledger.'

'Oh, I see. So it's not possible to have two invoices

with the same numbers, then? Not even for safeguard, if something should go wrong?' Evie asked innocently.

'Oh, my dear, no. That would be catastrophic. We don't make mistakes. We are not allowed to.' Mrs Fanshaw looked quizzical. 'Why do you ask?'

'I just wanted to get it all straight in my mind, Mrs Fanshaw. I hope you don't mind, but you are an expert at these things.'

Mrs Fanshaw smiled at the compliment Evie paid her. 'I don't mind, my dear. You have a lot to learn and I'm only too pleased to nurture an inquisitive mind.'

Evie started to go hot under her blouse, feeling guilty for misleading Mrs Fanshaw. Her misgivings regarding the invoice were proving to be correct and she felt more than ever determined to get to the bottom of the mystery. Why had the invoice been retyped. By whom? And how? She tackled Mrs Fanshaw again.

'Do we buy the invoices already printed?'

'Yes, they come in pads from the printers. They keep stocks for us already printed and we call for fresh supplies as and when we need them. They print new pads when they are running low. Wadham's do all our other printed matter as well. They get a lot of business from us.'

'Wadham's, you say? Mm.' An idea started to form in Evie's mind. 'Mrs Fanshaw, what would happen if they printed duplicates of anything by mistake?'

'I don't understand. What do you mean?' Mrs Fanshaw frowned.

'Well, say that they'd printed one lot of invoices with a certain set of numbers and then by mistake printed another lot with the same numbers?'

'Oh, they can't do that,' Mrs Fanshaw said, aghast.

'The second lot would have to be destroyed. To have two lots of invoices on the loose with the same numbers would cause terrible confusion. No, Wadham's would have to destroy the lot and absorb the cost. They're very careful, very careful indeed, to ensure mistakes like that never happen.' She looked at Evie very thoughtfully. 'I've never been asked these kind of questions before.'

'I'm sorry, Mrs Fanshaw, I didn't mean to be rude or too forward.' Evie spoke hurriedly.

Mrs Fanshaw relaxed. 'It's all right, my dear. I used to be like you until I had the stuffing knocked out of me by a terribly old-fashioned accountant. Very much like Mr Grady and Mr Stimpson, he was. Looked at you as if he had a bad smell under his nose. I remember asking him one question. He stared at me in horror and demanded I get on with my work and mind my own business. I never dared ask another after that. Just did as I was told and kept my head down. I learned the hard way, I'm afraid. It took years.' She shook her head. 'I feel it shouldn't be like that. I feel you youngsters should be taught everything you need to know to make your work interesting, but it doesn't happen like that, does it?'

Evie shook her head. She suddenly felt very close to this little woman and decided she liked her very much.

Mrs Fanshaw patted Evie's arm. 'If you want to know anything, anything at all, then you come to me. If I know the answer, I will help you as much as I can. Don't bother with Mr Grady, he won't help. Although he's helped your sister,' she muttered under her breath. She smiled. 'You come to me, my dear.'

Evie grinned broadly. 'I will, Mrs Fanshaw, and thank you.'

'It's my pleasure. Now we had better get back to work.'

Evie went back to her desk and sat down just as her other office colleagues started to pour through the door. She felt quite positive that somehow an invoice she had typed had been replaced with another one. For what reason? That's what she must find out. Her nature would not let the matter lie.

That night, Evie walked slowly into the house and closed the door behind her. It was a bitterly cold evening and she shivered as the warmth of the kitchen surrounded her. She took off her coat and scarf and after hanging them up sank gratefully down on a chair at the table. She could hear voices coming from the hall and realised her mother was on the telephone. She strained her ears to hear what was being said. She heard the telephone receiver being replaced in its cradle and a moment later her mother came into the room.

'That was the hospital. Florrie is on the mend and out of intensive care. Oh, I'm so relieved.' She looked at Evie expectantly. 'We can go and see her tonight.'

Evie paled. 'But I'm already going out tonight.'

'I would have thought your sister came before a boy you have only known for five minutes,' Edith said sharply.

Evie tried to hide her annoyance. 'I'll telephone him and say I'll meet him later. What time is visiting? I'll pop to the corner shop and get her some fruit or something.'

'About seven, so we'd better get a move on.'

Edith dished up the dinner of liver and onions which was quickly eaten and, having purchased some grapes and oranges and a bottle of barley water, the two women set off for the hospital. Evie had never been inside a hospital before and wrinkled her nose as the smell of disinfectant hit her. She was amazed at the length of the corridors as they traipsed down one after the other in search of the ward that housed Florrie. They were met by a nurse who asked them to sit and wait with the other visitors until the bell sounded.

They found Florrie looking very pale and wan, propped up in a bed at the far end of the ward. A muscle twitched at the corner of her mouth as Edith and Evie approached.

'So you managed to come then?' she croaked, and gave a wheezing cough.

'How are you, Florrie dear? You certainly look better than yesterday,' Edith said.

'It's a small wonder. The nurses are like prison warders and the food is garbage. They made me eat some stew and dumplings tonight and it was disgusting,' Florrie moaned.

'She's feeling better,' Evie muttered under her breath.

'What did you say, dear?' Edith turned and addressed her.

'Oh, I said she does look better,' Evie said quickly. 'Here's some fruit for you.' She placed the brown paper bags full of produce on the cabinet at the side of Florrie's bed.

The visiting hour seemed more like three to Evie. She stifled yawn after yawn as Florrie wailed and moaned, while Edith tried her hardest to cheer her. Five minutes before the bell sounded Edith rose from the bedside.

'I just want to have a quick word with the Sister.'

Evie made to follow her mother, wanting to get away as quickly as possible.

'Don't go, Evie. Stay for a minute,' Florrie whispered.

Evie looked at her and then at her mother.

'Stay with Florrie till the bell goes. I'll meet you outside,'

Edith addressed Evie then turned to Florrie. 'I'll see you tomorrow afternoon, dear. Is there anything you would like? Books, magazines?

Florrie shook her head.

'Well, I'll bring in some clean nightwear and some more toiletries for you.' She kissed Florrie on the cheek and walked down the ward.

As soon as Edith was out of earshot, Florrie awkwardly raised herself further up the bed.

'What are things like at work?' she asked breathlessly.

'What d'you mean?' Evie frowned.

'Are you still in the Accounts Department?'

'Yes, why?'

'Is Hor . . . Mr Grady still away ill?' Florrie asked nervously.

'Yes. Why?'

'I suppose that Fanshaw woman is twittering about, causing mayhem?'

'Mrs Fanshaw is taking charge, and if you ask me she is doing a grand job,' Evie said coldly.

'I didn't ask you,' Florrie answered back, using the same tone as Evie.

She rose.

'Don't go. I need you to do something for me.'

Evie stared at Florrie, bemused. 'You need me to do something for you?'

'Yes. There's no need to be sarcastic. I can't do much for myself stuck in here with this load of heathens.'

Evie took a deep breath. 'Look, just tell me what you want. I have to go.'

Florrie took several breaths before she spoke. 'I need . . . I need to know if the bank statements have come?'

Evie grimaced. 'Bank statements! What are they?'

'Oh, God! Don't you know what bank statements are?'

'No. Should I?'

'No, I suppose not. After all, you're not much more than an office junior, are you?' she said, ignoring the indignant look that crossed Evie's face. 'Anyway, they're important company business and only Mr Grady sees them. They should have arrived last week and shouldn't be left lying around for anyone to see. Ask that Fanshaw woman tomorrow. It's really important.'

'Why are they so important?'

'Because they are. Now will you do it?' Florrie spoke very sweetly, but her eyes betrayed anger.

'But if they're that important, shouldn't the boss, Mr Dawson, have them in Mr Grady's absence?'

'Evie!' Florrie raised her voice. 'Mr Grady needs them.'

'Okay, no need to shout, I'll ask her tomorrow,' Evie relented.

'Bring them in with you tomorrow night. I'll have them for safekeeping.' Florrie sighed and relaxed against her pillows.

'I'm not coming in here tomorrow, it's my College night. I don't know when I'll be back.'

'Oh!' Florrie's mouth dropped open. She lay deep in thought for a moment. 'You'll have to lock them in my drawers at work.' She paused and tightened her lips. 'You'll find the keys under my mattress at home,' she said, looking at Evie warily.

'Why on earth do you hide your desk keys under your mattress?'

'Because I keep important company documents in my drawers and it wouldn't do for prying eyes to see them and report to our rivals. Look what happened to Florentine's. They had all their designs copied by an unscrupulous member of staff. It nearly ruined them.'

Evie thought for a moment then nodded in agreement. 'Yes, I see. Okay, I'll do it tomorrow.'

'Good.' Florrie relaxed again. 'And don't dare rake through anything. Just put in the statements and lock them up. I shall know if anything has been touched.'

'If you don't trust me, get someone else to do your dirty work for you!' Evie hissed.

Florrie looked alarmed. 'I didn't mean it.'

'Well, say sorry then.' Evie smirked.

Florrie eyed her coldly. 'Sorry,' she snapped.

Evie went to walk away. Florrie called her back.

'Just what did you mean by saying I should get someone else to do my "dirty work". What dirty work?'

'Nothing. It's just an expression. You're paranoid, you are.' Evie turned on her heel and walked down the ward towards her waiting mother.

'If Florrie carries on the way she is, she should be able to come home next week. That's good news, isn't it?' Edith said.

'Yes,' she muttered.

Evie left her mother and ran to meet Edward outside the old established department store of Lea & Son at the corner of Charles Street and Humberstone Road. They spent a pleasant evening in one of the local pubs and left each other that night having made arrangements to meet the following Saturday.

Evie felt downhearted. Edward had explained that he wouldn't be able to see her over Christmas as he was spending the holiday at his grandmother's home at Kibworth

Beauchamp several miles out of Leicester. She felt like crying. A whole two weeks without Edward. It didn't bear thinking about. She told herself to stop being silly. Christmas was still four weeks away. She would see plenty of him before and after then. She climbed into bed and snuggled under the bedclothes, falling into a deep, dream-filled sleep.

It was half-way through the next morning before Evie had a chance to carry out her promise to Florrie. Two of the girls had arrived back after their illness and Mrs Fanshaw had been kept busy instructing them on their workload. As the little woman scurried past her desk, Evie stopped her.

'Mrs Fanshaw?'

'Yes, dear?' She stopped abruptly, her arms weighed down by a pile of papers.

'I went to see Florence in hospital last night,' Evie started.

'And how is she?'

'Getting better.'

'Oh, that's good,' Mrs Fanshaw said flatly, glancing nervously over her shoulder. 'Well, I must get on.' She smiled and made to hurry away.

'Mrs Fanshaw,' Evie said quickly, 'Florrie seemed concerned about some bank statements and wondered if they had arrived yet?'

Mrs Fanshaw looked surprised. 'Oh! I don't rightly know,' she said, shaking her head. 'There's a pile of post on my desk that I haven't got round to opening yet, but now two of the girls are back I might get a chance later.'

'Florrie was most insistent that they were not to be opened but locked in her desk until Mr Grady comes back,' Evie said as politely as possible.

'I see.' Mrs Fanshaw's eyes narrowed. She put the pile of papers she was holding on to the corner of Evie's desk. 'I'd better go and look then, hadn't I?'

She turned sharply on her heel and walked towards her desk.

Evie took a deep breath. Several minutes later Mrs Fanshaw came back holding three long white envelopes. She held them out towards Evie. 'I think these are what you want,' she said brusquely. 'Why there's three I don't know, because I understood we have only two company bank accounts. Here, you had better lock them away.' She thrust the letters at Evie, picked up her papers and, holding her head in the air, stalked away.

Evie stared at the offending letters. She fumbled in her handbag and pulled out Florrie's desk keys that she had retrieved from under her mattress earlier that morning. She was about to rise from her desk when one of the accounts clerks came up to her and asked for her help in a matter Evie had been dealing with previously. She placed the letters and keys in her top drawer and attended to the girl.

The lunchtime hooter sounded. All the office staff, including Evie, grabbed their handbags and headed for the door. She was sitting in the canteen with Jenny when she suddenly remembered the letters sitting in her unlocked desk drawer.

'Blast!' she exclaimed. 'I have to get back to the office, Jenny. There's something I haven't done.'

'Can't it wait? We've another 'alf an hour to go yet,' Jenny moaned. 'I want to 'ear what else Edward said.'

'It'll have to wait, Jenny. I must go.' Evie grabbed her bag and made her way back to the Accounts Department.

The office was deserted. Evie grimaced in surprise until she remembered that Mrs Fanshaw had popped into town to do some shopping. She opened her drawer and sighed with relief. The three envelopes and set of keys were still there. Going over to Florrie's desk, she tried several of the keys on the bunch until she found the right one. She unlocked the top drawer, placed the letters inside and locked the drawer again. She stood transfixed, staring at the closed door behind Florrie's desk.

Bold black letters stood out on the glass panel on the door: CHIEF ACCOUNTANT. She juggled the keys between her hands and looked down at them. The bunch had six keys on it, far too many for just Florrie's desk drawers alone. She looked up at the clock. Still twenty minutes to go before the lunch hour finished. Something nagged at the back of her mind, something that someone had said. Now what was it?

On a sudden impulse she walked towards the glass door and tried key after key until the lock released, then quickly opened the door and entered. The office was not large. It held several filing cabinets and a desk. She walked quickly behind the desk and tried the drawers. They were locked. She tried the keys until one was successful and the drawers unlocked.

Her heart thumped noisily inside her chest. She frowned. Just what am I looking for? she thought. Three of the drawers revealed nothing unusual, just general papers and correspondence relating to business. The bottom drawer on the left was larger than the rest and Evie tugged to get it open.

Several brown folders lay inside and she pulled them out. Underneath was a large box file. She opened it. Inside was a set of bank statements clipped together. Evie picked them up and flicked through them. The top one was dated October, two months previous. The balance on the statement was £39,354 16s 11d. Phew, a small fortune! she thought. Having never seen a statement before, she did not quite understand its meaning.

Still holding the statements, she glanced again inside the box. Now why would Mr Grady have a pad and a half of unused invoices hidden inside his desk? Surely these invoices would be missing from the ledger? Without thinking she grabbed a piece of paper and noted down the invoice numbers. She stuffed the paper into her jacket pocket and put the statements back inside the box. She closed the drawer quickly, locked the desk and ran from the office.

She had arrived back at her desk before she realised she had not locked the office door. It was too late. Mrs Fanshaw had arrived back, her arms full of brown carrier bags.

'Hello, dear. I thought I'd be late,' she twittered breathlessly. 'Lewis's have a sale on and I wanted to get some new towels. They were such a bargain.' She eyed Evie in concern. 'You look flushed. Are you all right?'

'Er . . . yes, thank you. I've just run from the canteen.'

'Oh, you mustn't run, dear. It's against company rules. No running in the corridors,' she scolded as she walked over to her desk.

'Sorry,' Evie answered.

She looked nervously towards Mr Grady's office and prayed that no one tried the door before she had a chance to lock it again.

Lying in bed that night, Evie wrestled with her problem.

Firstly, there was the invoice that someone had corrected. Then there was the pad and a half of unused invoices inside Mr Grady's desk and also the fact that there was only one set of bank statements in the box file when Mrs Fanshaw had said the company had two accounts. Why had Mr Grady kept only one set and not both?

There was something else that Mrs Fanshaw had said and it annoyed her that she couldn't remember what it was. Evie turned over and switched on her bedside lamp to look at her clock: it was gone twelve, and she yawned. Her heart skipped a beat as she remembered that Mr Grady's office door was still unlocked. Still, at least she had done Florrie's precious job for her.

Something clicked inside Evie's mind. She sat bolt upright and clasped her hands together. That was it! Mrs Fanshaw had handed her three separate bank statements and had said the company only had two accounts. She took a deep breath. Something was wrong. She knew deep down something was very wrong, and it had something to do with Mr Grady and Florrie. She ran her hands through her hair and her eyes narrowed.

She switched off the light and lay down, pulling her pillows down underneath her neck. She suddenly remembered the piece of paper in her jacket pocket, the one she had written the invoice numbers on. That was it, that was where she would start. She would somehow find an excuse and make enquiries about them. Having made that decision, sleep quickly overtook her and she woke refreshed the next morning and raring to go.

'Why won't yer go to the firm's Christmas dance?' Jenny

asked, frowning fiercely. 'I thought yer said Edward'll be away?'

'He will.' Evie took another mouthful of her lunch. 'I don't want to go because all the managers crowd round the boss and his wife and suck up to them. Then it's the done thing to have a dance with your boss, and there's one thing I do know – I'm not going to dance with Mr Stimpson, not for anything.'

'Nor would I. But yer won't 'ave to. You're still in the Accounts Office.'

'Same difference. Only it would be Greedy Grady if he's back in time, and I think that would be worse.'

'Yer right!' Jenny laughed as she pushed her empty plate away.

Evie folded her arms and leaned on the table. 'Eh, can you imagine Miss Sargent and Old Stingy Stimpson trying to waltz together? Doesn't bear thinking about.'

'How d'you know about all this? You ain't bin to the staff dance before.'

'I've heard. Anyway, I'll give it a miss, thank you.'

'Well, if you ain't goin' to the staff dance, 'ow about the Palais on Christmas Eve? They 'old a smashin' dance. The place is all decorated up wi' trimmings and everyone goes. Go on, say yer will. We could 'ave a great time.'

Evie frowned. 'Oh, I don't know. Maybe Edward wouldn't like it. Anyway, I thought you had to be twenty-one?'

'Well, maybe you do.' Jenny shrugged her shoulders. 'But 'ow are they to know?' She paused. 'And what's Edward got to do wi' it? 'E'll be livin' it up at his grandma's place. Does 'e expect you to shut yerself away while 'e's havin' fun?'

'No, of course not,' Evie retorted.

'Well, then. Say you'll come.'

'I don't know.' She wavered. 'Mam likes us to be in on Christmas Eve. She might be upset if I said I was going out. Anyway, I couldn't possibly tell her I was going to the Palais, she'd have a fit.'

'Then don't tell 'er where we're goin'.' Jenny leaned towards her. 'Don't be such a mardy arse! You're gettin' right stuffy in yer old age. Come on, Evie, say you'll go.'

'I might, but I'm not making any promises.'

'Oh, good. I'll get the tickets before they sell out.' She rubbed her hands together. 'I ain't 'alf lookin' forward to it.'

'What about Arnold?' Evie asked.

'What about 'im?'

'Won't he want to see you on Christmas Eve?'

''E might, but I ain't seeing 'im. I've bin tryin' to cool it for ages but 'e won't take the hint. I don't know what I'm goin' to do, but I know I ain't seeing 'im on Christmas Eve.' Jenny smiled triumphantly.

Evie raised her eyebrows. 'I'd better get back to the office.'

'What for, it's only 'alf-past one? You're always rushin' back to the office. What you up to, that's what I want to know? You've bin actin' really strange just lately.'

'Nothing. I just want to try and catch someone, that's all. I've been trying for the last couple of days and I haven't had much luck,' Evie said carefully. 'And you needn't look like that. It's only to do with work. Something I need to know for College. We've got some exams soon and I want to make sure I pass them.'

'If you say so.' Jenny looked unconvinced.

'I do say so!' Evie said sharply. She rose from the

table. 'I'll see you at home time and don't be late, we nearly missed the bus last night.'

'Weren't my fault. I can't 'elp it if the Sergeant Major throws a fit and makes us all polish our desks.'

Evie smiled. She left Jenny, who rose and went off to join some of her other colleagues. Evie arrived back at her desk and picked up a note pad with some numbers written on it. She took a deep breath and walked out of the door and made her way to the Sales Office.

'Excuse me, Mr Green,' she spoke softly as she approached a middle-aged man sitting behind his desk munching his sandwiches. A paper lay spread out in front of him. Evie noticed it was opened at the Racing page.

'Eh? What?' Mr Green looked up at her.

'I know it's lunch time . . .' Evie began.

'Yes, it is!' Mr Green said, annoyed. 'What's the meaning of disturbing me at this time?'

'I'm sorry, it's just that I have a problem, and with being so short-staffed I thought . . .' Evie blushed.

'You thought, did yer? Young chit of a lass . . . Oh, what d'you want?' He closed his paper and stared at her.

'Mr Green,' Evie began, sighing with relief, 'these invoices don't appear to have come through to us.'

'And what invoices would they be?' he snapped.

'Numbers 601230 to 601245,' Evie quoted from the half-finished pad in Mr Grady's box file.

'Hold on.' Mr Green rose from his chair and went over to a filing cabinet. He rummaged around on top and finally picked up a wad of papers.

'These them?' he said, handing the pile to her. 'They'll be handed to your department for typing shortly, only we're short-staffed as well with all this influenza about. They should have been passed through last week, but we only finished them off this morning.'

Evie took the wad of papers and looked through them. They consisted of a handwritten copy of an invoice that was clipped behind the proper blank invoice that was to be typed. The invoice numbers corresponded with the numbers she had given Mr Green and there were more besides, at least forty invoices in all. Evie looked confused.

'Well?' Mr Green snapped again. 'Are they the ones or not? I have my lunch to finish.'

More like the betting slip, she thought.

'Er . . . yes. Thank you,' she muttered. She took a deep breath. 'Do you keep the pads of invoices in here?'

'Yes, 'course we do, how else could we enter the sales in the ledger? We have to keep a record of the invoice number so we know the customer has been billed.' He looked at her keenly. 'Who wants to know all this? Is someone saying we ain't doing our jobs right?'

'Oh, no, Mr Green. Nothing like that. I've been helping in the Accounts Office and to be honest I find it all a bit confusing. Someone told me . . . well,' she smiled sweetly, 'actually it was Jenny Jones, she said you were ever such a nice man and would help me. I've been typing the invoices and entering them in the accounts ledger and was getting a bit confused about it all.'

'Oh, I see.' Mr Green sat down, flattered by Evie's comments. 'Would you like me to explain what happens, gel?'

'Oh, please,' she breathed. 'It would be ever so helpful.'

'Right. To start with, the sales people go out and about and sell our goods. They fill in an order and give it to us.

We then enter the sale against that customer in the sales ledger, and part fill one of those internal sheets there.' He pointed to a sheet clipped on the front of one of the invoices Evie was holding. 'We then get a proper printed invoice and note the number against the order in the ledger. Follow me so far?'

Evie nodded. 'Yes, I think so.'

'Good. It's then sent into the Accounts Office and you people do the rest, which I presume you know. Simple, ain't it? 'Course, some firms do it different to us, but Dawson's has this system.'

'So the Accounts Office don't keep invoice pads, then?' Evie asked.

'No, certainly not. That's our job. If they are, I want to know why,' Mr Green said crossly.

'Oh, I didn't say they were,' Evie said quickly. 'I was just trying to get things straight in my mind, that's all.'

'Oh, I see. Have I helped you then?'

'You have, Mr Green, and I'm ever so grateful. Everything is so much clearer now.' Evie smiled broadly.

'Good. But next time, young lady, don't interrupt me at lunch time. I work hard enough as it is, without having to give up my lunch.' He turned back to his paper and reopened it at the Racing page.

'Thank you,' Evie said as she backed away.

She turned and walked out of the office, deep in thought. Her suspicions had been confirmed. Duplicate invoices were being printed and substituted for original ones. The person behind it all must be Mr Grady. He had identical numbered invoices in his drawer. But why?

She walked slowly back to her desk. She would find out. She would not be able to rest until she had done so, and she hoped Florrie was not involved as she was beginning to suspect.

That evening Evie sat before her dressing table. She stared at her reflection and rubbed her hand across her aching forehead. Why am I getting involved in all this? she thought, sighing deeply. She rose from her seat and walked over to her bed, where she flopped down and leant back against the headboard.

She went over and over in her mind what Mrs Fanshaw and Mr Green had told her. She had several pieces of a jigsaw that just wouldn't fit together.

Miss Sargent . . . would she listen? Evie shook her head and grimaced. Definitely not. She smiled as a picture of Mrs Fanshaw came to mind. If anyone would listen to her, it would be Mrs Fanshaw. She would try and speak to her in the morning. She jumped up quickly as she heard the back door click shut. It would be her mother returning from the hospital. Evie rose and went down to greet her.

'Hello, Mam. How's Florrie?'

'Much better. The doctors think she'll be able to come home on Monday or Tuesday, that's providing she doesn't have a relapse. They're making her eat anything and everything and she isn't pleased about it.' Edith frowned as she picked up the kettle, shook it and placed it on the stove. 'I do feel sorry for her, the food in there isn't exactly home cooking. I promised to make her some sandwiches and cake and I'll take them in tomorrow night.' She turned to Evie. 'Will you be coming with me tomorrow?'

Evie paled. 'Er . . . I have a stack of homework to do.'

Edith raised her eyebrows. 'No need to make excuses. If you don't want to come, say so.'

'No, honestly, Mam. I really do have loads to do and with my exams looming . . .'

'Okay, I understand. To be honest, hospital visiting bores me as well. It's funny, I think of plenty to say in advance but when I get there I dry up. I'm sure Florrie is glad to see the back of me by the time the hour is up.'

Evie smiled as she collected the cups and placed them on a tray, ready to take through to the living room.

'Have we any aspirins, Mam? I've a terrible headache.'

Edith looked concerned. 'In the bathroom cabinet. Are you all right? You look very pale.'

'It's just a headache. I think I'll have an early night.'

'Oh.' Edith started. 'Before you go, Florrie asked me to ask you if you managed that little job for her? She seemed most concerned.'

'Yes, tell her to stop panicking. I did exactly what she told me,' Evie said sullenly.

'What was that?' Edith probed.

'Oh, just something to do with work.' Evie picked up her tea. 'If you don't mind, Mam, I'll take this upstairs.'

She kissed her mother on the cheek and bade her goodnight.

Evie was wakened next morning by her mother's hand on her forehead.

'You're not going anywhere today, my girl.'

Evie groaned. 'Oh, Mam, I feel terrible.' She made to rise. 'I have to get to work.'

Edith pushed her gently back against the pillows. 'Don't you dare move, you're running a fever. I just hope to God you haven't caught our Florrie's germs. If you're no better tonight, I'm going to call the doctor. Now go back to sleep. I have to pop in to the shops but I'll be back. The girls can take care of things for one day.'

'Don't do that, Mam. I'll be fine. Just let me rest and I'll be running around tonight.' She closed her eyes and fell into a deep sleep.

Evie opened her eyes and stared round. Where was she? Oh, yes, this was her bedroom. She felt stiff and weary. I must have been asleep for ages, she thought. Was it morning or night? Her room was dark, so it was hard to tell. She turned to look at her clock: the luminous hands showed the time to be four thirty-five. Was that early morning or evening? She tried to rise and fell back against the pillows. She felt weak and so terribly tired. She tried again to rise and managed to get herself in a sitting position. She eased her legs over the side of the bed and tried to stand. Her legs buckled beneath her and she fell back. Oh God, she thought, what on earth is wrong with me? She turned her head and watched the door slowly open. Edith popped her head round and quickly came in when she saw Evie.

'Get back into bed, this minute.'

She switched on the bedside light and gently took hold of Evie's legs, sliding them back under the sheets. She pulled the covers under Evie's chin and tucked the ends firmly under the mattress. She sat on the edge of the bed and ran her hand over her daughter's forehead.

'How d'you feel?'

'A bit better, thanks. Have you just come back?'

'Back! Back from where?'

'The shop. You said you were going to the shops.'

'Evie, that was almost a week ago.'

'A week ago! Have I been here a week?'

Edith nodded. 'Just about. You've had a really bad dose of influenza. Don't you remember anything?'

Evie closed her eyes. 'Yes. Yes, I do now. That foul-tasting medicine you kept pouring down my throat. It's all so hazy though.'

'I thought you'd end up in hospital. I sat up a whole two nights, mopping your forehead. You really had me worried. The first night you were delirious, mumbling about invoices and ledgers and God knows what.'

'Was I?' Evie smiled. 'Shows how keen I am on my work.' She shifted her position. 'Oh, my bones ache.'

'Yes, they will. But at least you're on the mend. Think you can manage some soup?'

'Not at the moment, but a cup of tea wouldn't go amiss.'

'Tea it is then.' Edith disappeared from the room.

Evie closed her eyes. A week! A whole week she had been lying here. She must have dozed off because it seemed only a second before Edith reappeared with a steaming cup of tea in her hand which she placed on Evie's bedside cabinet. She helped to prop up Evie against her pillows and handed her the cup. Evie sipped slowly, her eyes opening wide as a thought hit her.

'Mam – Edward! I should have met him last Saturday.'

Edith took a deep breath. 'It's all right. He telephoned,' she said coolly.

'Did he? Did you . . .' Evie began, her eyes wide with alarm.

'Don't worry, Evie. I told him you were ill. If you look over there you will see what he sent.' Edith inclined her head in the direction of Evie's kidney-shaped dressing table.

Evie followed her gaze. Set in the centre of the dressing table was the most enormous arrangement of flowers.

'They're going off a bit now, mind. But when they arrived, they were absolutely beautiful. They must have cost a fortune this time of year. It's a pity you were too ill to notice them.' Edith turned back to Evie and frowned. 'Oh, there's a card,' she said flatly.

She rose and walked over to the table and picked up a small white envelope which she handed to Evie. She sat down on the bed again and watched as her daughter opened the flap and pulled out a card.

It read: 'Get well soon. Miss you. Edward'. At the bottom he had added, 'Telephone me.'

She hugged the card to her chest. 'Oh, Mam,' she breathed.

Edith rose. 'Get some more rest, I'll be back later to check on you.' She left her daughter still hugging the card.

Evie placed it carefully on the bedside cabinet and slipped down under the sheets. She closed her eyes and fell asleep.

It was morning when she next awoke.

'How do you feel today?' Edith asked.

Evie yawned. 'Heaps better, thanks. I think I'll get up.'

'Not yet you won't. Maybe later. The doctor said you had to take things easy. I might let you come down and watch a bit of television later tonight. But for now, you stay where you are. I have to go to the wool shops today. I've neglected things rather badly while you've been ill. Florrie will get you anything you need. I've asked her to make you a cup of tea and a slice of toast, she'll be up in a minute.'

'Florrie?'

'Yes, our Florrie is home and in fine fettle, I'm glad to say. She's going back to work tomorrow.'

Evie stared blankly at her mother. Suddenly, everything sprang back to the forefront of her mind. Would Florrie's return to work quash her own plans? She breathed deeply and realised that Edith was looking at her quizzically.

'Are you all right?' she asked.

Evie mentally shook herself. 'Yes, I was just thinking of work and some unfinished business I have to attend to.'

'Well, it can wait until you're on your feet again.' Edith leaned over and kissed her on the cheek. She turned as the bedroom door opened and Florrie came in carrying a tray of tea and toast. 'Ah . . . here's Florrie with your breakfast. Try and eat it, Evie, it will do you good. I must dash. See you later.' Edith left the room.

'Where d'you want this?' Florrie said sharply, holding out the tray.

'Here will do.' Evie indicated her lap. 'And thanks, Florrie, it was good of you to make this for me.'

Florrie put down the tray and prepared to leave the room.

'You don't have to go, Florrie. Can't you stay and talk for a minute?'

Florrie's lip curled. 'And what d'you suggest we talk about?' she asked sarcastically.

'Whatever you like. I've been out of it for a week, you could tell me what's been going on?'

'Going on? Going on where? I was in hospital until four days ago, and you tell me, what ever goes on in this house? The same as always – nothing,' Florrie snapped. 'Mother's as boring as usual. "You all right dear?" "Want a cuppa tea, dear?" "What did you do today, dear?"'she mimicked sarcastically. 'Same old boring thing all the time. The only difference was that I got some more attention 'cos you were out of the way.'

Evie's anger rose sharply. 'You're hard work, our Florrie. Why d'you have to be so nasty all the time? I only wanted to pass the time of day and you make a big deal out of it. You never change, do you? I suppose it never entered your head that Mam was nearly out of her mind when you were ill. In fact, we both were. Nearly drove us mad with worry in case you died. 'Cos you nearly did, you were that poorly. I think it would have been better if you had, it would have put us all out of our misery. Eh, Florrie, what d'you say?'

'Shut up,' she snarled.

'Shut up! Is that all? Oh, poor Florrie. Poor, hard done by Florrie. D'you know something? I don't ever remember you smiling, not properly anyway. The only time you laugh is when you're making fun and being nasty about someone, and that's usually me, isn't it, Florrie? You get a great kick out of upsetting me. Well, I tell you, it doesn't bother me any more. You can say what you like in future and I won't care. So put that in your pipe and smoke it!'

Florrie's face paled and she clenched her knuckles so tight they turned white. 'Don't worry, Evie. You won't have to put up with me much longer.' She turned on her heel and made to leave the room.

'What d'you mean?' Evie snapped.

Florrie spun round and faced her, a sarcastic smile spreading across her face. 'You'll have to wait and see, won't you? Have patience, sister. But you can count on one thing. When I go, it will be in a blaze of glory.' She turned on her heel again and flounced out of the bedroom, slamming the door behind her.

Evie lay in bed shaking with anger. She shook so much

that the cup rattled in its saucer on the tray that was resting across her legs. Her chest felt tight and she coughed long and hard.

Right, Florrie, she thought. Sister or no sister, I'm going to get even with you. She picked up her toast and took a big bite.

Evie returned to work the following Monday. She was so eager to get there that Jenny had a job keeping up with her as they trotted through the factory gates.

'So what did Edward say when you telephoned 'im?' Jenny asked breathlessly.

'Oh, not much.' Evie smiled, remembering the long conversation she had had with him on the telephone.

'Well, when yer seein' 'im again?' Jenny probed further.

They reached the bottom of the stairs that led to their offices. Evie ran up them, leaving Jenny trailing behind her.

'Saturday.' Evie stopped and shouted over the wide wooden banister, before she continued up the stairs again.

'Not till Saturday?' Jenny shouted back.

'He's going down south on business.'

'Oh!' Jenny frowned, most impressed. 'Down south on business, eh?'

As Evie passed the General Office, she heard her name being called. She stopped and peered through the open door and saw Miss Sargent beckoning her. Evie frowned slightly and made her way slowly towards Miss Sargent's desk.

'Got your sick note?' Miss Sargent barked, not taking her eyes off the piece of paper laid in front of her.

Evie frowned and opened her handbag and rummaged

through it. She found what she was looking for and held it out towards Miss Sargent.

'I have it here, Miss Sargent.'

'Hmm. It needs to go to the Personnel Department, after Mr Stimpson has seen it.' Miss Sargent raised her head and looked at Evie long and hard.

She shifted position from one foot to the other, waiting for Miss Sargent to continue. The woman obviously had something on her mind and Evie wished she would spit it out so she could get on with her work in the Accounts Office. She was desperate to catch Mrs Fanshaw on her own and that did not happen very often.

Miss Sargent finally took a deep breath. 'As from now, your secondment to the Accounts Office is over.'

'Oh.' Evie gaped in horror. 'Why, Miss Sargent?'

She turned purple. 'How many times have I told you, Miss Grayson? Junior members of staff do not ask why. That word does not exist in your vocabulary. Junior members of staff do as they are told and don't ask questions. Your forthrightness will be your undoing one day, mark my words.' She paused and regained her composure. 'As I was saying before I was rudely interrupted, you are being moved back in here, but not in your old job. Mrs Lilly is not coming back and it has been decided – not by me, I might add – that you will undertake the work for Mr Haggar and Mr Pullen. That means taking telephone calls, typing their letters, etcetera.' She clasped her large hands together and narrowed her eyes. 'Don't be under the illusion that it's a secretarial position. Your title will be "Clerk Typist". I don't want you getting above yourself, understand?'

Evie sighed. 'Yes, Miss Sargent.'

'Good. You will still be reporting to me, even though

you'll be over the other side of the room. Now get to it, and I want no complaints of any sort.' Miss Sargent picked up a pile of papers and shuffled them together. 'Well, I said – get to it.'

Evie straightened her back and raised her head. 'Yes, Miss Sargent. Thank you, Miss Sargent.'

Evie found working for Mr Haggar and Mr Pullen hard work but fun, as they both fought for her attention. Both men were middle-aged and set in their ways. Both wore identical clothes, worn brown suits and olive green hand-knitted cardigans. Both were married with four children, and both had wives who nagged. They smoked pipes filled with foul-smelling tobacco and both ate a lunch of cheese sandwiches and pieces of pork pie seated at their desk reading the *Daily Sketch*, arguing over topical issues that appeared in its pages.

This small department was responsible for customer queries and Evie thoroughly enjoyed the new challenge. Mr Haggar would give her work to type and Mr Pullen would tell her that his was more important when Mr Haggar was out of the room.

'Do this first, Miss Grayson, never mind him,' he would say, placing a large pile of letters in front of her.

Mr Haggar would do exactly the same and Evie delighted in mixing the work they gave her so that both got an equal share of her time. She also enjoyed the contact she had with irate customers on the telephone, and found handling their queries and problems over delayed orders or wrong deliveries needed a special talent and one she was mastering well. Of course, she only got to deal with these people when both her managers were unavailable and the majority of her time was spent juggling her work around between the two men, keeping them plied with coffee in the morning, tea in the afternoon, and listening or commiserating when they complained about their wives.

It was a week before she had a chance to speak to Mrs Fanshaw. She bumped into the little woman in the corridor one afternoon as she was fetching the tea.

'Why, Miss Grayson. What a pleasure it is to see you. How are you getting on? I do miss your smiling face in our office.' Mrs Fanshaw smiled warmly.

'I'm getting on fine, thank you, Mrs Fanshaw.' Evie returned the smile.

'I've heard you're working for Mr Haggar and Mr Pullen.' Mrs Fanshaw frowned and before she could stop herself, added, 'Couple of old fuddy duddies if you ask me, but harmless, I suppose.' She clapped her hand over her mouth. 'Oh, please excuse me, Miss Grayson. I should not have said that.'

Evie laughed. 'I know what you mean, but believe me it's quite fun working for them both and I have learned quite a lot.'

'I'm glad to hear that, Miss Grayson. You'll go far.' She paused thoughtfully. 'How long have you been up in the office now?'

'About a year, I started in the office last January,' Evie answered. 'Doesn't seem like a whole year though.'

'Time flies when you're enjoying yourself.' Mrs Fanshaw paused and looked keenly at her. 'You've been around several departments, haven't you? On the switchboard, doing the typing and comptometering work, a short time in Accounts, now back in the General Office handling customers' queries. I've heard your shorthand and typing skills are excellent. You'll be a real asset to the company soon, with your knowledge. Not many girls get the opportunities you have, Miss Grayson, and you seem to be taking advantage of them.'

Evie blushed. 'Thank you.'

Mrs Fanshaw looked at her watch. 'Oh, dear, I'd better get back, Mr Grady will be looking for me.' She patted Evie on the arm, turned and started to walk away.

'Mrs Fanshaw . . .' Evie began.

She stopped, turned back and looked at Evie. 'Yes, dear?'

'Mrs Fanshaw, I need to talk to you.'

'Do you?' She looked at her watch again. 'I can't just now. I've been away longer than I said I would be. What do you need to talk about, anyway?'

'Oh, just a problem I have. Could I speak to you tomorrow lunchtime? It's rather private though.' Evie spoke softly.

'Oh, is it? Well, yes, of course, dear. Come through to the office at lunchtime tomorrow then. I'll help, if I can.' Mrs Fanshaw smiled.

Evie sighed with relief. 'Thank you. I appreciate your taking the time.'

'No problem, dear. I'll see you tomorrow. Now I must dash.' Mrs Fanshaw smiled as she turned and walked swiftly down the corridor towards her office.

Evie took a deep breath, Problem one was solved – that was getting Mrs Fanshaw to listen to her. Problem two was getting her to believe it and help Evie to do something. Now I just have to hope, she thought, shrugging her shoulders.

Mrs Fanshaw sat stiffly in her chair, clasping and unclasping her hands as she listened intently to Evie's story. When it was finished, she took a deep breath and exhaled loudly.

'You are sure about all this?' she asked quietly.

Evie nodded.

Mrs Fanshaw stared at her in silence. She put her hands to her face and took a deep breath. 'The first thing I have to say is that I don't approve of your going into Mr Grady's office the way you did. You do realise that if you had been caught it would have meant instant dismissal?' She frowned as she watched a guilty expression cross Evie's face.

'I know,' she said softly, 'but I just had to. Something made me do it. I can't explain. It was impulse really, after the things I'd found out.'

Mrs Fanshaw nodded. 'I understand, Miss Grayson. But that still wouldn't have saved you from getting the sack.' She paused. 'Now let me get this straight. You're convinced that Mr Grady and possibly your own sister are up to no good. I am confused about the invoice matter. It certainly appears from what you say that there are duplicate invoices being printed and used.' She paused. 'I have a theory about that, but I want to sort it out in my own mind before I discuss it. And I certainly gave you three separate bank statements. But that could be explained easily.'

'Oh, how?' Evie asked.

'Well, Mr Grady could have requested a copy of an earlier statement that had got mislaid somehow.' She paused. 'I have to say, though, that Mr Grady is not in the habit of losing things, but nevertheless it would explain why we were sent three statements and not two. We need to find out somehow.'

'You'll help me then?' Evie asked keenly.

'This is a very serious matter,' Mrs Fanshaw said gravely. 'If we're wrong, we could be sacked. For a start, we must have solid facts. You can't just accuse people of as serious a matter as this without a great deal of proof, and that might be difficult to get. I'm not young any more, Miss Grayson. I wouldn't get another job, not at my age.' She patted Evie's arm. 'I need to think. I'm not saying your suspicions are unfounded, but I have to think about it before I make a decision as to whether I get involved or not. Do you understand?'

Evie nodded. 'Yes, I do, Mrs Fanshaw. I never thought of the implications and I hope you don't mind my coming to you with this. But there was no one else I could trust.'

'That's all right, my dear. I'm glad you did turn to me and not someone else. Let me sleep on it and come back tomorrow lunchtime.'

Evie stood up. 'Thanks, Mrs Fanshaw.'

'You're welcome.' The older woman smiled.

The next lunchtime, prompt at one o'clock, Evie sat nervously facing Mrs Fanshaw who smiled and waited until she was sure everyone had left the office and they were safely on their own before she spoke.

'Miss Grayson,' she began, 'I gave your problem a lot of thought last night and I spoke to my Ernest. You probably don't know, but he is a policeman – only a constable, but a policeman all the same. He doesn't like thieves of any description and strongly feels that if there is something going on, then the culprit or culprits should be brought to justice for whatever they are doing.' She paused and took a deep breath. 'We feel, working on what you have told me, that whoever is behind all this is somehow stealing from the company. If it is Mr Grady then he's abusing his position. He's very highly respected and no one, not even Mr Dawson himself, questions him. He's been with the company since he left school and Mr Dawson sets great store by him. So he could quite possibly get away with murder and no one would know.' She paused again. 'To be honest, I've never liked Mr Grady. He is an overbearing oaf and I shouldn't say this, but I would love to see him get his just deserts. That is, if they are just,' she added quickly.

'So you do think something is going on?' Evie asked keenly.

'Yes, I do, Evie. May I call you Evie? If we are going to be partners against crime I think we had better start calling each other by our Christian names. But not in front of our colleagues. Mine's Pearl.'

She held out her hand and Evie proffered hers. They shook hands warmly.

Evelyn Grayson and Pearl Fanshaw, Detectives Incorporated. Yes, Evie thought, it has a nice ring.

'It's not just what you've told me, it's other things as well.' Pearl twiddled her wedding ring around her finger. 'I often see Grady and your sister closeted in his office together, and they work late many nights.' She stopped abruptly. 'Of course! That could be when the duplicate invoices are being typed. That makes sense. They couldn't be typed during proper work time, not by your sister anyway. She stopped doing menial tasks like that when she became Mr Grady's assistant. And since the price of wool shot up overtime has been stopped so it would explain why they are both here long after we all go. I only know this because one of the cleaners was complaining that she couldn't clean Mr Grady's office one night, since they were both in it.' She leaned forward and whispered, 'To be honest, I thought they were having an affair.' She blushed slightly.

'But I'm seeing things rather differently now.'

'Our Florrie never tells us anything, so we never know what she is doing after work. I assumed she spent most of her spare time at the church, but I don't think she ever goes there now.'

'Well, we'll find out what they are doing all right. But as my Ernest pointed out, we have to be very careful. This is a very serious matter.' Pearl paused. 'Ernest met Grady once at one of the Christmas dances. Took an instant dislike to the man, said he couldn't look you straight in the eye.' Her own eyes twinkled. 'My Ernest has a feel for criminals, can spot one a mile away.'

Evie clasped her hands together. 'When do we start our investigations?' she asked eagerly.

'Well, that's the problem. There's only a few days left until the holidays and there's so much going on at the moment, what with the bonuses and wages and end of year balances, etcetera. So what I suggest is that we start when we come back from the Christmas holidays, because you do realise, Evie, that we are going to have to get into his office again? And I have to think of Ernest's position. It wouldn't do for me to be caught doing anything untoward. So you're going to have to do that bit by yourself. Can you get hold of your sister's keys again?'

'I should think I can manage that, as long as she still keeps them under her mattress,' Evie said eagerly.

'See, that was another thing that got me puzzled. Why did she keep them hidden if there was nothing untoward?'

'I asked her that. She said it was because she kept important documents in her drawers,' Evie answered.

'Well, we'll find out, won't we?'

'Do you know what we'll be looking for?'

Mrs Fanshaw shook her head. 'Not really. We'll just have to use our initiative the same way you did when you spotted the invoice pads and bank statement.'

'Right,' Evie said keenly.

'But we'll leave it until after Christmas, and in the meantime keep our eyes and ears open. And, Evie?'

'Yes?'

'No one must know about this. It's just between us, understood?'

'Yes, understood.' Evie's heart raced. This was getting bigger than she'd ever imagined. If they were caught they could both be sacked, and so could Ernest. 'I won't breathe a word, not even to my mother.'

'Good girl. Now for God's sake smile and fetch us a cuppa. With all this talking, I'm parched.' She handed Evie two pennies, which she refused.

'My treat.'

Pearl Fanshaw watched Evie leave the office to fetch the tea. She wrung her hands together and leaned on her desk, a worried expression crossing her face.

All Jenny's descriptions of the palais de danse did not do it justice. Evie stood transfixed, not noticing the number of shoves she got as people pushed past her in their haste to get further inside to begin their jollifications.

The highly polished wooden dance floor was the largest she had ever seen and at least a dozen times bigger than the one in the local church hall. Girls of all shapes and sizes were draped on the edge of the fountain that stood in the middle of the floor, chatting to their boyfriends or hoping to catch the eye of future ones they had spotted. Above the fountain hung a large mirrored ball that slowly spun round, reflecting coloured light in all directions. Hanging from the ceiling was a large net filled to overflowing with coloured balloons all ready to be let down over the crowds of dancers; also placed here and there were bunches of holly, mistletoe and gaily coloured streamers.

The air was electric as Johnny and his Dance Band picked up their instruments and began to play a popular jive. In a sudden movement hundreds of people dived into position and all Evie could see was a mass of bodies, heaving and gyrating to the music.

Over the other side of the room ran a large bar three deep in people trying to catch the attention of the barmen. She hoped Jenny wouldn't be long as she was one of the people in the long queue waiting to be served. Tables and chairs were set along another side of the room and Evie noticed that one table had become vacant. She moved swiftly and procured the seats just as another couple were about to sit down. She looked around again, tapping her feet to the music. She wished that Jenny would hurry as she was desperate to dance.

She felt a sudden pang as she saw a couple smooching in a dark corner and thought of Edward. Her sadness was quickly dispelled as Jenny joined her. She placed a glass in front of Evie and sat down, making sure her brand new dress sat smoothly under her bottom.

'I got yer a gin and orange,' she said, picking up her glass and sipping at the liquid, her eyes fixed on the dance floor.

'I wanted lemonade,' Evie grumbled.

'Lemonade! I ain't askin' for lemonade. We're supposed to be twenty-one. Now gerrit down yer and stop moanin'.' As Jenny talked her eyes surveyed the area. She leaned over and nudged Evie. 'Cor! Look at 'im over there, and 'is mate ain't that bad either.'

Evie looked over in the direction Jenny had indicated. 'If you think I'd fancy someone dressed in a pale blue suit and suede shoes, you've got another think coming,' she announced sharply.

'Stop picking fault, I think 'e looks rather nice meself. Oh, 'ere's Freda and Paula.' Jenny moved up to allow the other two girls from the office who had come with them to sit down. 'We thought you'd fell down the lavvy,' Jenny laughed.

'It's packed in there, I couldn't get near a mirror to fix me face,' Paula moaned as she pulled a compact out of her bag and began to apply a shocking pink lipstick to her pursed lips.

Freda spat into her block of black mascara and ran the little brush backwards and forwards along it. She poised the brush ready to apply a layer to her eyelashes and looked over at Paula. 'Your mam'd 'ave a fit if she could see that colour, and I should watch 'ow much yer 'ave to drink . . .' She turned to address Jenny and Evie. 'Did you know 'er mam's a staunch member of the Women's Temperance Society?'

'You mind yer own business,' Paula said crossly. 'And what about you in that dress. If the neckline were any lower, you'd be able to see yer knickers.'

'Are we dancin' or what?' Jenny cut in quickly.

A unanimous yes rang out, drinks were gulped down and the four girls pushed their way through the crowds of dancers, looking for a place to park their handbags and show off their steps.

Evie was in her element. She loved dancing and moved

expertly to the music. She and Jenny had spent many hours in her bedroom practising their technique and it was paying off. She proudly noticed many jealous eyes were upon them as they swung round in perfect time to the music. If Mam could see me now, thought Evie wickedly, she'd have a fit. Edith was safely at home, sitting in front of a roaring fire, wrapping last-minute presents, under the mistaken impression that her beloved daughter was sitting at Jenny's house waiting to go to the Midnight Carol Service at her local church.

Several dances later, Evie and Jenny left the floor to rest their feet for a few minutes before rejoining their friends.

'Shall we take a wander upstairs, to see what talent's lurkin'?' Jenny asked, her eyes twinkling.

'Upstairs! There's an upstairs as well?' Evie's eyes opened wide.

'Oh, yeah,' Jenny said in superior tones. 'Yer can look over the balcony and watch the dancers.'

'Come on then,' Evie enthused.

Once again they pushed their way through the crowds and walked up the stairs. They both hung over the balcony and watched the proceedings below.

'What d'you think, then?' Jenny asked.

'I think it's the most wonderful place I have ever been to,' Evie breathed ecstatically. 'And I just can't believe this dress you've made for me. It's perfect. You are clever, Jenny.'

Evie fingered the navy blue taffeta dress she was wearing. It had a large full skirt, belted waist and a large white collar, showing off her slender neck to perfection. Jenny had done her hair in a French pleat and Evie felt wonderful.

'Yeah, I am, aren't I? Amazin' what yer can do with a 'alf a yard of sacking and a reel of cotton.' Jenny grinned. 'Oh, I forgot to tell yer. I've 'ad the most wonderful news!' She had to shout above the noise of the band.

'Have you? Well, tell me then!' Evie shouted back.

'Arnold's bin called up to do 'is National Service. Ain't that just wonderful? I shall be shot of 'im at long last.'

'National Service?' Evie's face fell. 'I wonder if Edward will have to go?'

'They all 'ave to. Why should 'e be any different? I'm surprised 'e ain't 'ad to go before now.' She nudged Evie in the ribs. 'When 'e does go, you just enjoy yourself for the two years 'e's away,' Jenny giggled.

Evie's face fell as she thought of losing Edward for two long years. It was bad enough not being able to see him over the Christmas holidays. How would she cope for two whole years? Jenny noticed her mood.

'Stop draggin' yer face along the floor. Come on, it's Christmas and we're at the best place in town. Let's get back to the dance floor, 'cos I ain't goin' 'ome without a ''click''. Not on Christmas Eve, I ain't!'

Evie smiled and swiftly forgot her worries as she followed Jenny down the stairs.

The evening passed far too quickly. Before the girls knew it, it was time for them to collect their coats and make their way home. Jenny and Evie had been asked to dance umpteen times and a delighted Jenny had got her 'click'.

'I'm seein' him next Friday,' she chuckled, digging her hands further into her pockets. ''E works at Gimson's the engineerin' company. ''E's a technical somethin' or other.'

Evie hunched her shoulders against the biting wind.

'You're playing with fire. What if Arnold finds out?'

'What if 'e does? 'E'll 'ave to lump it.' Jenny grimaced. 'Oh, it's a pity the chip shop ain't still open, I could just murder a bag of chips.'

'So could I,' Evie agreed.

'Tell yer what.' Jenny nudged Evie's arm. 'While you're gettin' yer face scrubbed and changing yer clothes, I'll make us a fried egg doorstep, 'ow about that?'

'Sounds wonderful. A perfect end to a perfect evening. Come on, let's run, else I'll never get home.'

Christmas Day passed easily. Evie awoke tired out from her long night of revelry. She washed her face in cold water and tried hard to chivvy herself up so her mother would not suspect anything untoward.

Edith still filled pillowcases with Christmas presents for the girls, trying to keep up family traditions. Although Evie enjoyed this piece of frivolity, Florrie thought it juvenile and made no effort to hide her feelings. Edith had decorated the living room with gaily coloured paper trimmings and the lights twinkled on the Christmas tree as Evie sat before the blazing fire and opened her presents. She was delighted with the gold bracelet and knitted cardigan from her mother, floral headscarf from Jenny and the pair of stockings from Florrie. Mavis had also sent a parcel which contained a handmade tray cloth and letter, which she put aside to read later.

The thought of Mavis spending Christmas in hospital saddened her and she hoped she wouldn't have to spend another one in there. Evie had scoured the town for a suitable present for her friend and hoped she would be pleased with the toilet bag and three paperback romance books she had finally settled on.

The best present she left until last, a small, carefully wrapped parcel given to her by Edward at their last meeting, with the strict instruction it was not to be opened until Christmas morning. Evie opened it slowly, savouring every moment, and gasped with joy as the tissue paper inside the parcel revealed a pair of tiny gold earrings. She loved them instantly and felt a warm glow envelop her. She was glad now she had chosen for him the mother-of-pearl cuff links she had agonised over for hours, and hoped he liked them. She caught Florrie sneering and quickly placed the earrings back inside the tissue.

For Christmas dinner they feasted on capon stuffed with sage and onion, Brussels sprouts, peas and roast potatoes. The rich plum pudding was drowned in thick creamy custard. Evie groaned as she refused a mince pie; she could not manage another morsel. Dinner had to be finished and cleared away before the King's speech was broadcast and the three sat by the fire listening intently. Later that evening, Evie retired thankfully to bed, after the customary roasting of the chestnuts and a small glass of cherry brandy. Before she slept, she sat and read Mavis's letter.

Although still seriously ill, it appeared that she was managing to enjoy herself. She had made plenty of friends, going into great detail about the exploits some of them got up to. Evie sat and laughed at their antics, then gasped with delight: Mavis had met a nice man who was a student doctor, and they were getting very friendly. She was pleased for her friend and could not wait for the time when she could visit her in person. She slept peacefully that night, her problems temporarily forgotten.

The holiday passed pleasantly and before she knew it

Evie was climbing the stairs towards her office, ready to face the brand new year of 1952.

Chapter Nine

It was a week after Christmas before Evie bumped into Pearl in the corridor outside the office. The little woman grabbed her arm and was speaking very low, looking over her shoulder and up and down the corridor as she did so. Evie was concerned by her worried manner.

'Something's going on.'

'What?' asked Evie.

'I'm not sure.' Pearl shook her head. 'The pair of them,' she whispered, careful not to mention names, 'have been acting strangely, but nothing I can put my finger on. We've got to get a look inside Mr Grady's office. Can you get hold of the keys?'

'I'll try,' Evie grimaced. 'But when do you suggest?'

Pearl thought. 'It's going to have to be after work, and the sooner the better. You're going to have to wait until your sister comes home, sneak the keys and come back to the office.'

Evie thought. 'Right. But what about the security guard?'

Pearl frowned. 'I know, we'll meet at an agreed time at the telephone box on the corner. I'll telephone and keep him busy while you sneak past and up to the office. When you're ready to leave you can signal from the office window and I'll telephone again to distract him.'

'Good idea,' Evie agreed. 'Tonight, then?'

'Yes, tonight, nine o'clock,' Pearl answered. 'Quick, someone is coming.'

Both women returned to their respective workplaces.

Evie struggled through the rest of the day, excitement and apprehension filling every moment.

Edith noticed her daughter's mood as they sat in front of the television later that night.

'What on earth is wrong with you, Evie? You've really got the jitters. You've not sat still for one minute tonight.'

'Oh, I'm sorry, Mam.' She rose and stretched herself. 'I think I'll pop to Jenny's for a while.'

Edith looked up sharply. 'But it's blowing a gale outside and threatening to snow . . .'

'I'll wrap up, don't worry. I'll only be a couple of hours.'

Edith shrugged her shoulders and turned her gaze back to the television. Evie left the room and quietly made her way upstairs. She placed her ear against the bathroom door and heard the splashing of water. Quickly, she let herself into Florrie's room and ran her hand underneath the mattress. She paused as her fingers touched the cold metal. She closed her hand and pulled the bunch of keys out of their hiding place. Straightening the bed covers, she quickly left the room. She had just reached her bedroom door when Florrie came out of the bathroom. She was drying her hair on a towel and humming softly to herself. She stopped abruptly as she spotted Evie.

'Creeping round, Evie? What are you up to?'

Her heart thumped against her chest. 'Nothing. I'm just going out.'

'Oh.' Florrie started to rub her hair again. 'Well, don't wake me up when you come in. You run up the stairs like a carthorse. You've got feet like lumps of lead.'

Before Evie could answer Florrie had disappeared inside her bedroom. Evie fumed for a moment before she crept down the stairs, put on her coat and went out into the freezing night.

She reached the telephone box twenty minutes before Pearl and was shivering with cold and apprehension when her accomplice finally appeared round the corner. She walked up to Evie and placed a hand on her arm.

'Are you sure you want to go on with this, because there'll be no turning back?'

Evie thought for a moment and then nodded her head.

Pearl sighed deeply. 'Okay, thought I'd just check. I've brought you a torch, you'll need it. Now make your way to the corner and I'll make the telephone call.'

Evie heard the telephone ring and several seconds later the security guard answered it. She carefully poked her head round the corner of the Security Office and as soon as the guard turned his back to the door, she nipped past and ran up the stairs.

She felt her way down the long dark corridor and stopped in front of the Accounts Office. Her hand gripped the door handle. She gently turned it and slipped inside. The thumping of her heart echoed in her ears and she took several deep breaths in order to calm herself. The office was cast in an eerie grey light and long shadows gave a ghostly effect. Evie shuddered as she stood for a moment with her back to the closed door. She pulled herself together, crept over and unlocked Mr Grady's office.

She switched on the torch and unlocked the desk drawers.

The bottom drawer containing the box file was the one she opened first. She peered inside. The file was still there. She pulled it out and emptied the contents over the desk top. The original pad and a half of invoices were now depleted and less than half a pad remained. The bank statement had been replaced with a more recent one and the balance for the end of December now showed at over forty thousand pounds. Evie gasped. Just what did this mean?

She replaced everything inside the box file and put it back as she had found it. The other drawers revealed nothing unusual. She placed her hands on her hips and looked long and hard round the office. She was about to leave when she stopped and looked back again at the row of filing cabinets lined up against the far wall. On impulse she went across and tried several drawers. They were tightly locked. It was then that she noticed the end cabinet was slightly out of line with the rest. She frowned and shone the torch on the ground. Scuff marks on the floor covering revealed that this cabinet had been regularly moved. She stood still, a deep furrow creasing her forehead. With great difficulty she eased the heavy cabinet out from its resting place and shone the torch behind it.

She beamed in triumph. Secreted behind the cabinet was a small red book. She picked it up and stuffed it into her coat pocket. With all her might she shoved back the cabinet and left the room, remembering this time to lock the door behind her. She stopped in front of Florrie's desk and opened the drawers. Again, they revealed nothing unusual, until she tried the bottom one which was wedged tightly shut. Evie tugged until it gave way. The drawer was crammed with papers and folders. She carefully took them out. At the bottom of the drawer was a brown folder. She picked it up, opened it and nodded in satisfaction.

The folder revealed two sets of invoices, about forty in each. She compared them. They were identically numbered, addressed and typed, but the amounts shown were higher in one set than in the other. She selected several invoices from each set and, opening her coat, stuffed them up her jumper. Quickly putting everything back in its place she left the office.

She was creeping down the stairs when a sound stopped her in her tracks. She froze in horror as around the corner came a lumbering figure. She stifled a scream as a bright light shone on to her face.

'What have we here?' a deep voice asked harshly.

Evie trembled and her mind raced as the voice repeated the question.

'I . . . er . . . I forgot something.' She fumbled in her pocket and pulled out her purse. 'My purse,' she declared. 'I forgot my purse.'

'Yer purse?' The voice spoke harshly again.

Evie squinted against the light. 'Please, I work here.'

'Well, if you work here you would know that you're not supposed to come in here at night without a security guard being present. I've a good mind to make you turn all your pockets out.' He eyed her thoroughly. 'You trying to lose us our jobs or what?'

Evie quickly collected her thoughts.

'I'm sorry, really I am. But the guard at the gatehouse was on the telephone, so I just nipped up.'

The guard sighed loudly. 'Oh, get out of 'ere before I report you, me tea's getting cold.'

Without further ado, Evie shot down the stairs and out

into the night. She arrived breathlessly at the telephone box and greeted Pearl.

'What happened, child? You've been gone an age, and what about your signal?'

'I forgot, Pearl, and the security guard nearly caught me.' She paused for a moment, trying to catch her breath. 'Didn't half give me a fright. Anyway, never mind that, you should see what I found.'

'You found something then? Good! We'll go back to my house. Ernest is working so we won't be disturbed.'

Seated in Pearl's living room, Evie placed the invoices and little red book on the coffee table. Pearl came into the room with a tray of tea and biscuits. She put the tray on the table and sat down. Evie poured the tea, her hands shaking in anticipation. After careful examination of the evidence, Pearl sat back and sighed.

'I know what's going on.' She looked at Evie and smiled broadly.

'What? What?' Evie shouted in exasperation.

'Well, to put it in a nutshell, they're stealing money from the company, and it looks from this book like it's been going on for years.'

'I knew it.' Evie clasped her hands together. 'Just how are they doing it?'

Pearl scratched her chin. 'Well, for a start, Mr Grady must have paid Wadham's or someone employed by them to print two sets of invoices, just as you said.'

Evie smiled in satisfaction.

Pearl continued: 'I think he also got them to print double copies of our delivery notes.'

'Delivery notes as well. Why?' Evie queried.

'If you'll let me finish, I'll explain.'

'Sorry,' muttered Evie.

'A copy of the delivery note is attached to the back of the invoice as proof of delivery, and if anyone queried the invoice, the delivery note would have to correspond.'

'Yes, of course.' Evie nodded in understanding. 'When I get a query on deliveries I just pull out the invoice and check the delivery note and tell the customer what he's had.'

Pearl nodded. 'When we pass the invoices through for Mr Grady's verification he substitutes the original invoice for the new one, changing the amounts that were delivered. Not by much, just a dozen or so pairs of socks or briefs, but over the years it mounts up. When the customer has settled his bill, he destroys the substituted invoice and delivery note and puts back the old one, so no one will ever know. He's been very careful. It was only you who spotted something wrong.'

'Yes, and that's only because I made a mistake on an invoice with the same company name as my boyfriend's Christian name.'

'The red book is a record of all the transactions he's made. Rather silly really to keep a record like that, but that's accountants for you. If you look, he has written the original invoice amount and the amount he has altered it to. Large companies probably wouldn't even notice, they order that much stuff at a time. An extra dozen or so of socks wouldn't seem untoward. I see he didn't do it with large expensive items. Companies would certainly query being charged for, say, twenty dresses when we only delivered nineteen, but no one is going to count hundreds of boxes containing dozens of socks.'

'Yes, but in small amounts like that wouldn't it take

years to amass over forty thousand pounds?' Evie asked, not quite understanding Pearl's revelations.

'We have many, many customers. You think of all the thousands of dozens of socks and briefs we've made and sold. It wouldn't take that long.'

'No. I see now.' Evie frowned. 'It's so simple, isn't it?'

'It is for someone in his position.' Pearl paused. 'He couldn't do it on his own, though. There's your Florrie and also the printers. I feel your sister is up to her neck in this business. She must be.'

'Oh, dear.' Evie sighed. 'This will break my mother's heart.'

'Yes, I'm afraid it will.'

'I don't understand how he gets his hands on the money,' Evie said in bewilderment.

'Oh, that's easy. That's where the third bank account comes in. Mr Grady pays all the cheques and cash into the company working account which, for now, we'll call account number one. Account number two is an overflow account.'

'An overflow account?'

'Yes, one that holds spare monies for investments, etcetera. Most companies have one. Then, Mr Grady transfers all his ill-gotten gains into account number three. I am almost certain that only he and the bank, and possibly Florrie, know that the third account exists. It's well known that Mr Dawson leaves everything to Mr Grady – after all, his only interest is the total profit on the balance sheet. Mr Grady even has authority to withdraw money. It's his signature that's on all the cheques we pay out.'

'That's a bit silly, isn't it?'

'Yes, but then Mr Grady has worked for the company a long time and built up Mr Dawson's trust. It'll be an expensive lesson for Mr Dawson to learn.'

'Not if we can help it.'

'No, you're right. We must put a stop to it, and quick. Because as soon as the time's right, the money will be all drawn out of the third account and that's the last we will see of Mr Grady.'

'And Florrie.'

Pearl nodded. 'And Florrie.'

'But what about Dawson's and all the money they're losing?'

'Oh, you still don't see, Evie. Dawson's aren't losing money. The companies who buy our goods are paying for merchandise they haven't had!'

'Oh, yes, I'm sorry. It's all clear now.'

Pearl looked worried.

'What's the matter?'

'I still can't help wondering why the auditor hasn't picked it up. Surely, he must have noticed the transfer of sums from account number one to account number three.'

'Auditor? What's that?'

'Oh, someone who comes in to check we're running our business right and not cooking the books.'

'But the books are being cooked.'

'Yes, so why hasn't the auditor picked it up? It's the same man who comes in every year, and he's always seemed most efficient.' Pearl paused, deep concern showing in her face. 'Just a minute. Pass me that red book again.'

Evie passed her the book and watched in awe as Pearl studied its pages.

'Ah.' Pearl sat back sounding satisfied.

'What?'

'Every year, on the same day, Mr Grady has made a large withdrawal and it corresponds with the time the auditor comes in.'

'So, he's got him in his pay as well?'

'Certainly looks like it, and it would answer my question.'

'Seems like everyone's a crook.' Evie frowned.

'Not everyone, Evie. Just a few.' Pearl leant over and patted the girl's knee. 'But sooner or later they get found out.'

'What do we do now?'

'Well, from this book it looks as though Mr Grady updates his records on a monthly basis, when we do all the balances. We have a couple of weeks to go yet before the end of the month. I want to show this little lot to Ernest and see what he suggests. That all right with you?'

'Oh, yes, that's fine. But I'm a bit worried about the invoices. Won't Florrie notice they're missing?'

Pearl frowned. 'Yes, I forgot. She's a shrewd customer. We don't want to arouse her suspicions.' She thought for a moment. 'Leave it to me, I'll think of something to distract her while I return them. Let's just hope she doesn't notice until Ernest has seen them.'

Evie smiled ruefully. 'Thanks, Pearl.' She yawned loudly. 'Oh, pardon me. I'd better be going, it's getting late.'

Evie stood up and Pearl followed suit.

'I shan't be able to talk to Ernest properly until Saturday morning, because of his shifts down at the station. In the meantime, we get on with our jobs as though nothing has happened.'

'Okay,' Evie agreed. 'But I don't know how I'll look Florrie in the face.'

'You'll have to, Evie.'

Pearl gave her a hug and wished her a safe journey home.

Evie managed to slip the keys back undetected the next morning as Florrie was eating her breakfast. So far, so good, she thought, sighing with relief. It wouldn't do to alert Florrie or Grady, not now they had their evidence.

The week dragged by and Evie arrived home on Friday night full of apprehension. She was concerned about the outcome of Pearl's talk with Ernest and wondered what his reaction and advice would be. She walked into the kitchen and flung down her bag. Her mother was ironing. She wiped the back of her hand across her damp forehead and smiled up at Evie.

'Hello, love. I've nearly finished this little lot. Fish and chips tonight. Fancy going to get them for me?'

'Yes, I'll easy do that. Only I told you to leave the ironing to me. You go to work as well, you know.' Evie frowned at her mother, pretending to be annoyed.

'Oh, away with you. You hate ironing as much as I do. Anyway, I finished early tonight. It's no good being a boss if you can't play truant now and again.'

'What, play truant to do the ironing? Mother, I could think of better things to do.'

Edith shook out a sheet and began folding it. 'Yes, so could I. Only the ironing needed doing, and if I left it to you it would never get done.'

'All right, you win.' Evie smiled. 'What d'you want from the chippy?'

'Er . . . a piece of cod and some mushy peas, please. What are you having?'

'The lot, I'm starving,' Evie answered.

She arrived back armed with newspaper parcels of fish, chips, mushy peas and pickled onions. Edith had set out the bread and butter, salt and pepper and vinegar. They both sat down and tucked in. Evie finally sat back and patted her stomach.

'That was grand. I could murder a cup of tea.' She rose and picked up the boiling kettle and tipped it over the tea leaves already waiting in the pot. 'Our Florrie doesn't know what she's missed tonight. The chippy excelled himself. Those Greeks sure know how to cook chips. I suppose she's working late?'

'Well, no, actually she's not.' Edith grimaced. 'She popped her head round the door about ten minutes before you came home. Announced she didn't want anything to eat, ran up and down stairs and went straight out again.'

'Gone! Where to?'

'She didn't say.'

Evie frowned. 'Does she still help the Vicar, Mam?'

'Funny you should ask that.' Edith raised her eyebrows. 'The Reverend Blackthorne was only asking the other day why Florrie didn't come to church any more. I must remember to have a word with her. If she doesn't want to help at the church, then she should at least have the decency to tell the Vicar.'

'Oh, well, at least it's peaceful. I must admit, though, she's been pretty amenable this week. She's probably had a message from the Archangel, telling her to mend her ways or else.'

'Evie, that was uncalled for!'

'Yes, but funny,' she answered, giving a loud belly laugh. 'I can just imagine our Florrie quivering in her bed with the Archangel looming over her.' She lowered her

240

voice as deep as it would go. 'Be good or you'll go to hell.' She waved her arms around as though they were wings.

Edith placed her hand across her mouth, but was unable to stifle her laughter.

'Oh, Evie, stop it, stop it!'

She slopped tea into the saucer as she passed her mother a cup. 'I'd better get a move on, else I'll be late.'

Edith wiped tears of mirth away on her apron. 'Going anywhere nice?'

Evie looked at her mother in silence and Edith pressed her lips together in understanding.

'Oh, I see. Well, don't be late.'

Evie half smiled, sorry that the relaxed atmosphere had been broken.

'No, I won't,' she answered quietly.

'When you go upstairs, can you take Florrie's ironing and put it on her bed?' Edith asked, trying to keep her voice light and unconcerned.

'Is this all there is?' Evie queried, pointing to a small pile of neatly folded underwear.

'Yes, I don't know what's happened to her washing this week. I hope she hasn't forgotten to put it out.'

Evie picked up the pile and trotted up the stairs. She entered Florrie's bedroom and placed the clothes on the edge of the bed. She turned to leave and groaned as the pile of ironing fell on to the floor. She sighed and walked over to pick it up. Her foot hit something solid under the bed and she winced.

She bent down to rub her foot and looked at the offending object. It was a suitcase. Evie pulled it out and was surprised to find that it was quite heavy, and there wasn't just one suitcase but two. Evie tried the clasps. They were locked. Probably full of books, she thought, pushing them back. She finished folding the clothes and hurriedly left the room to get ready for her date.

Evie glanced up again at the clock tower. Ten minutes past eight, only two minutes later than the last time she had looked. She turned and scanned the window of Timothy White's the chemist and stamped her feet in frustration. Edward was ten minutes late and she hated being kept waiting. After another ten minutes her temper got the better of her. Clutching her handbag, she stalked down Belgrave Road towards her bus stop. He'd better have a good excuse for standing me up, she fumed. Something caught her eye and she stopped abruptly. Across the road she spotted Edward deep in conversation with a young woman who was petite and dressed very expensively.

Without taking her eyes off the scene, Evie backed up and slunk into a shop doorway. She watched intently as Edward placed his hands on the woman's shoulders, leaned over and kissed her on the cheek. He turned and hailed a passing taxi, ushered the woman in and waved her off. Then he straightened his suit, raised his head, and headed towards the clock tower. Evie's heart thumped wildly. What exactly did it mean?

She stood for a moment, unsure what to do. Quickly collecting her thoughts, she straightened her shoulders and marched after Edward. She arrived at their appointed destination slightly breathless. He smiled as she came up to him.

'Hello,' she said lightly. 'Sorry I'm late, the bus got held up.' She looked straight into his eyes. 'Have you been waiting long?' she asked coolly.

Edward looked at his watch. 'About ten minutes. I was late myself.'

'Oh. Why?'

He looked at her and frowned. 'As you were late, does it matter?'

Evie squared her shoulders. 'No, I suppose not.' She placed her arm through his as they made their way towards the Crown and Thistle in Loseby Lane.

'Something wrong with your drink?' he asked her later.

'What? Oh, no, it's fine. Why?'

'Well, I might as well be sitting here on my own for all the conversation you've made.'

'Oh, come on, Edward. I've been chatting all night.'

'I suppose yes and no counts as chatting, does it? I gave up a night out with the lads to be here with you, Evie, and you've virtually ignored me. Is there someone else, is that it?'

She placed her glass down on the table and stared straight at him. 'I've not got anyone else, Edward. How about you?' she challenged.

He stared back at her blankly. 'No. You're more than a match for me.'

'And I'm supposed to believe that?' she fumed.

'What's got into you, Evie?'

She folded her arms and raised her head. 'I saw you, Edward.'

'Saw me?' he repeated, confused. 'Saw me what?'

'With that woman, so don't deny it.'

Edward frowned, then grinned. 'Oh, *that* woman. That was Sophie.'

'Oh, Sophie is it? Nice of you to tell me.'

'Shut up, Evie, and listen . . .'

'Don't you tell me to shut up, Edward Bradshaw! You've been seeing us both all this time. Does she know about me? No, I suppose not. She doesn't look the type who would suffer being two timed.'

'Evie! . . .' Edward's eyes blazed. 'Will you shut up and listen? Sophie is just a family friend.'

'Seemed more than a friend to me. She was gazing adoringly into your eyes,' Evie said, through clenched teeth. 'Must be quite an art, balancing your time between the two of us.'

Edward glared at her. 'I've known that woman since we were babies, and she wanted to see a film so I offered to take her, that's all.'

'You took her to the pictures!' Evie hissed.

'Why not? I can assure you that we didn't sit in the back row.'

'I should hope not, but I suppose it never bothered you that you left me waiting?'

Edward tilted his head back. 'Yes, it did actually, but there wasn't much I could do about it. Sophie has had a bad time lately and I wasn't about to walk out of the pictures and leave her.'

'Oh, no, Edward, that wouldn't do, would it?' Evie said sarcastically. 'But you can leave me standing waiting like an idiot!'

'For God's sake! So I was twenty minutes late . . .' he fumed.

Evie pressed her lips together angrily. She grabbed her bag and stood up.

'Where are you going?' Edward demanded.

'Home.'

'Evie, I've explained about Sophie. If you don't believe me, then that's your prerogative.'

'I don't believe you.'

He shrugged his shoulders. 'Okay.'

'Okay? Is that all you can say?'

'What do you want me to say? I could have told you a pack of lies – instead I told you the truth. Sophie is a friend, that's all.'

'Huh!' Evie began pulling on her coat.

Edward's eyes narrowed. 'If you leave, Evie, we're finished.'

She stared at him open-mouthed. 'Oh, are we? Well, that's fine with me,' she blurted angrily. She manoeuvred around the table and headed for the door.

'Evie!' he shouted after her.

She ignored his call and continued walking. She had crossed the road and walked halfway down the street before the tears welled up and cascaded down her cheeks.

Evie spent a restless night and woke early feeling drained and void of any emotion. She groped her way down the stairs and was met by her mother.

'My God, Evie, you look awful.'

'Thanks,' she answered. 'That's all I need.'

'Well, you do. It's no lie. I'll make you a cuppa.'

Evie followed her mother into the kitchen and sat in silence at the table, afraid she would burst into tears at any moment.

Edith meanwhile made the tea and popped a slice of bread under the grill, secretly hoping that her prayers had been answered and that Evie and Edward had broken up. She placed the tea and toast in front of her daughter and sat down, resting her arms on the table.

'Want to talk about it?'

'No,' came the curt reply.

Edith bit her lip and felt guilty for the relief that rose up in her.

'What are your plans for today, then?' she tried again.

'Nothing. I think I'll go back to bed.'

'Back to bed! Are you not going up the town with Jenny then, like you usually do on a Saturday?'

'No. I don't feel like it.'

'Oh, I see. Well, you'd better tell her, won't she be waiting for you?'

'Mam, please!'

'I was only trying to make conversation. You can be hurtful, Evie.'

'I really don't feel like talking, Mam, not at the moment. Can't you go and do something and leave me alone!'

'That's enough, Evie Grayson. I don't know what's ailing you, but there's no need to be rude.' Edith stood and picked up the dishes.

Evie groaned. 'I'm sorry, Mam.' She placed her head in her hands. 'I should really clean my bedroom but I'll wake Florrie and that wouldn't do, would it? You'd have two of us having a mardy.'

Edith half smiled. 'Florrie went out before I was up this morning, so you can clean your bedroom and make as much noise as you like. If it will help,' she added quietly.

'Where's she gone to this early?'

'No idea, but she was as quiet as a mouse. You know how lightly I sleep and she didn't wake me.'

Evie stared at her mother blankly for a moment as something was triggered in her brain.

'Excuse me.'

She hurriedly pushed back her chair and bounded out of the room and up the stairs. She entered Florrie's bedroom and knelt and looked under the bed. The cases had gone. She jumped up and flung open the wardrobe door. It was completely empty. So was the tallboy, and all of Florrie's bits and pieces had disappeared too.

Evie froze on the spot, her mind a jumble of thoughts which she tried desperately to put together.

She moved quickly, pulling on a pair of trousers and a jumper. She grabbed some loose change and ran down the stairs and out of the door before her mother could utter a word.

Evie had never run so fast in all her life. She arrived at Pearl's house, over two miles away, out of breath and perspiring freely. She hammered on the door, praying that Pearl was at home.

'Evie!' Pearl looked at her in astonishment. 'Whatever is the matter? Come in.'

'No! No! There's not time,' Evie panted between gasps for air. 'They're going.' She grabbed Pearl's shoulders, shaking her violently. 'They're going today. Florrie has left home. I must get to the office before it's too late.'

She turned and fled, leaving Pearl standing open-mouthed, staring after her.

Once again Evie raced down the road, turning her head now and again in search of a bus. As luck would have it, a number fourteen trundled around the corner and she just reached the bus stop in time to catch it. She sat on the long seat just inside the door, willing the driver to go faster. The bus stopped at every halt collecting passengers. It finally arrived at the bus station and Evie pushed her way past all the others and jumped off first.

She inched her head round the corner of the building and was relieved to see the security guard with his head in the morning paper munching on a sandwich. She deftly slipped by and stole up the stairs towards the Accounts Office. She paused just before the door and heard the low mumble of voices.

She took several deep breaths before she slowly turned the handle of the door and opened it just enough to see inside. Florrie was bending over her desk. She had a large stack of papers in front of her which she was quickly ripping up and throwing into a big bag. Mr Grady was in his office and was also cleaning out his desk.

Grady lumbered out and laid his large fat fingers tenderly on Florrie's shoulder. 'How's it going?' he said, wiping the beads of perspiration off his forehead with the back of his other hand.

Florrie stopped what she was doing and gazed adoringly into Grady's eyes. 'Not much to do now. Then we must have a good look to make sure all the evidence is gone.'

'Well, when I've finished in my office, I'll come and give you a hand.'

He turned to walk back into his office. Florrie caught his arm.

'Oh, Horace. I can't believe I've got you, after all the years of feeling so alone and unwanted.'

Grady turned towards her, bent his balding head and kissed her cheek. 'You're not on your own now, my darling. We make a great team, you and I, and the quicker we get out of this wretched hole, the sooner we can begin our lives together. You'll never have to see them again.' A look of hatred crossed his face and he clenched his fists tightly. 'I just wish I could see that woman! Just once would be enough. I'd tell her exactly what I thought of her. When I'd finished, she'd wish to God she'd let you go to your grandmother's instead of treating you like a slave all these years.'

'Oh, Horace,' Florrie said softly. 'This way is better, believe me. She'll never hold her head up again after all this breaks. That's vengeance enough for me.' She turned her attention to the window. 'I don't like doing this. You do believe me, don't you, Horace? Only there's no other way . . .'

'Don't! Don't reproach yourself, my love.' He caught hold of Florrie and pulled her towards him. 'You've suffered enough. We'll be married as soon as we can and put the past behind us. I'll help you forget.'

He gave Florrie a long lingering kiss, pulled away and smiled fondly at her. Then he turned and walked back into his office.

Florrie stood for a moment, a look of blissful happiness sweeping over her face. Then she shook herself and continued with her work.

Evie stared unblinkingly through the crack in the door. She was witnessing another side to her sister, one that transformed her from the spiteful, sharp-faced woman she knew into a soft caring person – a woman who was loved and needed. And the feelings were so obviously returned. But what lies she had told Grady! The man was obviously under a hideous delusion about Florrie's family life.

Evie slowly shut the door and flattened herself against the wall. Her nerves were jangling and her legs in danger of collapse. What do I do? she asked herself. She wrung her hands together and shut her eyes tightly, forcing the last picture of Florrie out of her mind. I can't let them get away with this, I just can't. She took several deep breaths and forced herself to stop shaking. Then she pulled herself away from the wall, walked slowly to the door and entered the office.

Florrie glanced up in alarm. She looked stunned for a moment before a wicked smile spread across her face.

'Hello, Evie.' She shouted to Grady, 'Horace, look who's come to wish us goodbye,' then turned back to Evie. 'You have come to wish us goodbye, I take it?'

'You bitch, Florrie! I know what you're up to. And you needn't think you're getting away with it.'

Horace Grady walked slowly out of his office, wiping his dusty hands on a towel.

'Oh, yes, young lady, and just what is it you're accusing us of?' His voice was low and toneless, but his eyes blazed with hatred.

Evie straightened her back, and held her head high. 'You've been stealing from the company.'

Horace laughed. 'That's slander, Miss Grayson. I would watch what you say, if I were you, unless you have the money to be sued.'

'Sued?' Evie shouted. 'You'll be banged up in jail for what you've done . . .'

'Oh? And what exactly have we done?' Florrie interrupted, turning to Horace and giving him a reassuring smile.

'You needn't look like that, Florrie. I know every detail,' Evie said smugly.

Florrie burst into laughter. 'All right, tell me if you know so much.'

Evie clenched her fists. 'You've been charging companies for stuff they haven't had and pocketing the money.' Her face was grim as she spoke.

Horace lunged forward, but was restrained by Florrie. Her own face was a mask of anger as she walked menacingly towards Evie.

'It was you! I might have known. You've been poking and prying into something that's none of your business. Well, it's too late.' She swung her arm back as far as it would go and brought it rapidly forward, smacking her sister across the face with all the force she could muster.

Evie fell back against a desk. Her hand touched her cheek and she felt the stickiness of blood oozing down her face. She pulled herself together and grabbed hold of Florrie's shoulders, shaking her violently.

'I warned you never to hit me again,' she said coldly, then swung her own arm and smacked Florrie back across the face.

Horace rushed over and grabbed Florrie, pushing Evie against the desk. His eyes blazed with fury.

'Get finished up here, and quick!' he addressed Florrie. 'I'll deal with her.' He grabbed Evie's arm and pulled her across the room.

'Now, young lady, it seems to me you've poked your nose in just a little too far this time. You and that mother of yours have been treating Florrie like dirt all her life and it's stopping right now.' He pushed her down on to a chair and stood menacingly over her. 'I've worked for this tinpot company for years, given it everything. Now I'm taking what I deserve, and neither you nor anybody else is going to stop me.'

'What, over forty thousand pounds' worth?' Evie uttered.

'Oh, my, you have done your homework. No, not forty thousand – nearer sixty. Shocked, are you?' He grinned slyly. 'Me and Florrie are going abroad where no one will

251

find us, and for all I care the company and Richard Dawson can go to hell! Now you sit there like a good girl and don't dare move a muscle or you'll regret it.'

Evie stared after him as he moved back to his office and continued filling a bag with papers. Florrie sauntered over and stared at her coldly.

'Silly thing to do, wasn't it?'

'What was?' Evie answered defiantly.

'To come and confront me. You know you never win, Evie.' Florrie grinned wickedly.

She made to rise, shaking.

'I wouldn't if I were you,' her sister hissed. 'Horace is more than a match. He'd flatten you with one blow.'

'How could you, Florrie? How could you do this? It will break Mother's heart.'

Florrie collapsed into laughter.

'You're still under that delusion? She's no mother of mine! My mother was a decent woman.'

Evie looked bewildered. 'What d'you mean?'

'Exactly what I said. She's no mother of mine and you're no sister, thank goodness.' She leaned forward and poked Evie in the shoulder. 'Ask her. Just you ask her . . .'

'You ready, Florrie? Let's get out of this Godforsaken place,' Horace interrupted.

'Coming, dear,' she answered, and turned again to Evie. 'Going to wish me well, then?'

'Go to hell,' Evie seethed.

Florrie laughed. 'I probably will, Evie. But I won't half enjoy the journey! I've got everything I've worked for: Horace, loads of money – more than we know what to do with – *and* I've blackened the family name. You and your mother won't ever live this down. They'll sack you for a start, and people won't go into the wool shops and buy her goods. Yes, I know. I've known for years she owned those shops. She must think I'm bloody stupid. The neighbours . . . Oh, the neighbours! You won't be able to hold your head up for years.'

'Florrie!' Horace called again.

'Well, goodbye, sister dear.' She put her hand into her pocket and pulled out half a crown. 'Here, buy yourself something as a keepsake from me.' She turned and walked over to Horace and pecked him on the cheek. Then she picked up a bag and walked with him towards the door.

Evie jumped up from her chair and rushed over, grabbing Florrie by the arm. 'No, you don't!' she shouted.

Horace grabbed her arm and pushed her violently to the floor. She hit it forcefully, knocking her head on the hard surface. The room swam and faded into darkness.

Chapter Ten

Evie's eyes flickered open and tried to focus. All she could see was a white glare. It hurt her eyes and made her headache even worse. She groaned loudly and tried to sit up, and felt a hand push her gently back against the pillows. Her ears tried to sort out the confusion of voices coming from somewhere above her. I've died, she thought. Oh, God, I've died and gone to heaven.

'Evie? Evie?'

A voice spoke soft and soothingly, calling her from somewhere in the distance. It was familiar and somehow comforting. She forced open her eyes and tried to get her bearings.

'Oh, Evie. Don't worry, you're going to be fine.'

The white glare receded as she focused her eyes. Her mother's outline appeared, hazily at first then clearer. She was smiling and holding a wet cloth.

'Where am I?' Evie asked croakily. 'God, my head hurts.' She tried to raise her body.

'Lie still. You're in hospital. You've had a nasty crack on the head.'

Evie sank back against the rock hard pillows.

'How long have I been here?'

'A couple of hours,' Edith answered, wiping her forehead

again with the cold flannel. 'I'd better tell the doctor you've come round.' She pressed a buzzer next to the bed and a nurse appeared through the door.

'How are we feeling?' the nurse asked, sticking a thermometer into Evie's mouth.

'Terrible,' she grumbled.

'Well, you've been lucky. There'll be no lasting damage, just a sore head for a couple of days. We'll keep you in overnight just for observation.' She pulled out the thermometer and checked the reading. 'Like a cup of tea?'

'Yes, please.'

The nurse bustled out of the room.

'What happened, Mam?'

'Don't you remember?

Evie closed her eyes. Suddenly the events of the morning came flooding back.

'Florrie! Oh, Mam, our Florrie . . .'

'Shh,' Edith soothed. 'It's all right . . .'

'It's not all right, Mam. Our Florrie and that Grady man have gone off with all the money!' Evie's voice rose hysterically.

'No, they haven't.' Edith sat on the bed and took her hand. 'They're both at the police station. I have to go down there soon and see what's going on. I just wanted to make sure you were all right first.'

'How . . .'

'Just rest, Evie. When I know what's going on I'll explain.' Edith rose. 'Mr Dawson is down there now talking to the police.' She looked at Evie, distress written all over her face. 'I can't understand why you never said anything to me.'

256

'I couldn't, Mam. I wasn't sure how far Florrie was involved.'

Edith held up her hand. 'Okay, don't worry about that now. We'll talk later. I must go down to the police station. If you need anything, press that buzzer and a nurse will come.' She leaned over and kissed Evie on the cheek. 'Try and rest.'

She departed, leaving Evie feeling bewildered and confused; desperate to find out what had happened after Horace had attacked her.

Edith placed the tray down on the coffee table and looked over at Evie wrapped up snugly on the settee. 'I must admit you look better than yesterday,' she said.

'My head still hurts, and I never slept a wink all night.'

Edith smiled. 'Well, you certainly were asleep when I came back from the police station. You were snoring your head off.'

'I wasn't!' Evie retorted. 'Well, now I'm home, will you please explain what happened?'

Edith poured out the tea and handed her a cup. She went over and raked the fire. The flames roared into life, crackling and spitting, sending heat to every corner of the room. She replaced the poker and sat down, holding her cup between her hands.

'Well, Mam? What happened after Grady attacked me?'

Edith took a sip of tea. 'We have Pearl to thank.'

'Pearl?'

'Yes. When you left her house raving like a banshee, she realised something was dreadfully wrong, got her husband out of bed and came after you. They were both listening outside the office door. When Ernest Fanshaw had heard enough he alerted his colleagues down at the station. When Florrie and Grady came out they were arrested and you were carted off to hospital. The hospital called me and Pearl met me there to explain as best as she could what had gone on.'

'Good old Pearl,' Evie smiled.

Edith groaned. 'You could have been killed, Evie. Why on earth did you go and confront them on your own?'

Evie shrugged her shoulders. 'I don't know. I just felt I couldn't let them get away with it. I acted on impulse.'

Edith stared into the fire. 'I still can't believe it. I still can't believe our Florrie was in on all this.'

Evie looked at her mother for a moment. 'She told Grady the most awful lies about you, Mam.'

Edith sighed deeply and nodded her head. 'Yes, I can imagine.'

'What will happen to her?'

Edith turned her head and looked at Evie. 'Nothing.'

'Nothing!' she shouted. 'What d'you mean, nothing?'

'Mr Dawson is not pressing charges.'

Evie's jaw dropped. 'You're joking! I don't believe it.'

Edith bent her head. 'He doesn't want the company name dragged down. After all, it's his fault really.'

'His fault? I don't understand?'

'Look, Evie. Mr Dawson put his trust in Grady. He let him handle all the financial side of the business. He never questioned anything Grady did. It was a big mistake and he knows it. If this all came out he wouldn't be able to hold his head up.' She lowered her voice. 'We have to thank him really, it means that Florrie will not be put into prison. I'm sure Grady hoodwinked her, got her under his spell.'

'You mean they're going to get away with it?' asked Evie, aghast.

'Yes.' Her mother nodded her head.

'But that's not fair!' she shouted. 'Grady attacked me and I want him prosecuted.'

'No, Evie, you'll not press charges,' Edith said sternly. 'If you do, the newspapers will get hold of the story and it will all come out.' She clasped her hands together. 'The police are coming later to interview you. I've already told them you slipped on the floor and banged your head, and I want you to confirm that.'

'But, Mam . . .'

'Evie, you'll do this for me! I want this matter dropped. All the money has been recovered and Grady and Florrie have been sent packing. The young lad at Wadham's who was in Grady's pay has been dealt with, and so has the auditor. That was Grady's cousin, would you believe?' Edith sighed. 'I wanted Florrie to come back here and begin again.'

'Mother, how could you?'

'She's my daughter, Evie.'

Something stirred in her mind. 'No, she's not. She told me.'

'Oh!' Edith uttered. 'Well, now you know.'

'Why didn't you tell me?' Evie whispered.

'I didn't feel it was important,' Edith said sternly. 'Florrie was only a toddler when I married her father, and as far as you're concerned there's never been a time when she wasn't around.' She frowned. 'Knowing she wasn't your real sister wouldn't have made you get on any better, would it?'

Evie bent her head. 'No, I suppose not.'

259

'Well, anyway, they've both left Leicester altogether. I don't know where for, or what they'll do with no money and no job prospects, and at the moment, I don't want to. I begged her to come back and she spat in my face. So as far as I'm concerned, she might as well be dead. I cared for that girl more than a real mother would have done, and she did this to me.' Edith raised her head proudly. 'You and I will carry on with our lives and try to forget.'

'How can we?' Evie groaned. 'It's like a nightmare.'

'Think how I feel, Evie. It nearly broke me up, finding out about all this. At least you knew something was wrong and were prepared.'

'Sorry, Mam,' she said, downcast.

'It's all right, I'll survive. And to begin with we're going away for a couple of weeks, courtesy of Mr Dawson.'

'What?'

'It's a way of saying thank you. You're to have the next week off to recover and we'll go on Saturday. That's just enough time to organise things at the shops and make the travel arrangements. Where would you like to go?'

Evie thought. 'Somewhere hot and expensive, if Mr Dawson is paying.'

'My sentiments exactly. How about the South of France?'

'The South of France! Oh, Mam, that's really exotic. A whole two weeks in France.'

Edith smiled warmly. 'And I'll buy you some new clothes to go with.'

'Wow!' Evie's eyes lit up. 'I'll get a new bathing costume – no, two, I'll get two.' She clasped her hands in delight, then frowned. 'What about Pearl? She deserves something after all she did. It was her who really worked all this out.'

'Mr Dawson knows. Although Pearl tried to put all the

praise on you, she's being rewarded with a holiday, same as you, and a promotion.'

'Oh, good. And I have to keep my mouth shut about this whole business?'

'That's the general idea. Mr Dawson wants all this hushed up, and you can't blame him. Now you lie back. You've had enough excitement to last a lifetime. I'll go and get you something to eat.'

Evie lay back against her pillow. She stared into the fire, going over and over recent events. It all seemed like a dream, as though it had never happened, and she half expected Florrie to poke her head round the door at any moment and make a nasty comment. She closed her eyes and shuddered as a momentary fear assailed her. Florrie was still free . . . free to cross their paths at any time. The moment passed. Not even Florrie would dare to show her face here again!

Edith came back into the room bringing a light meal of a boiled egg and toast. Evie sat up.

'Mam?'

'Yes, dear.'

'Did . . . er . . . did Edward telephone or anything?'

Edith looked at her daughter. 'No.'

'Oh.' She picked up her spoon and hammered the top of the egg.

Chapter Eleven

Evie bent her head against the April shower. Shower! she thought in disgust. It was more like a torrent. The wind caught her umbrella and blew it inside out. 'Blast!' she grunted as she tried to retrieve what was left of her cover against the appalling weather.

Over three months had passed since her encounter with Florrie and Horace Grady and nothing had been heard of them since that fateful day. Evie could tell that her mother was still hurting badly over the incident and marvelled at the way that she held her head up and carried on as normal, but she wondered in the dark hours of the night whether her mother would ever heal completely. Rumours surrounding the sudden departure of Horace and Florrie ran rife throughout the company. Evie heard them all and kept her silence. Life quickly returned to normal and a new accountant had been installed. He was a younger man and much more liberal in his views. Pearl Fanshaw had been promoted to become his assistant and was thoroughly enjoying her new role.

Evie's trip to the South of France had been wonderful. From the moment they departed, Evie's relationship with her mother took a new turn. They had got to know each other better as they lazed by the swimming pool, took strolls through the ancient town and sipped drinks late into the night. On their return, Evie had taken to helping occasionally in the wool shops. She had even dared to suggest to her mother new lines to stock and different ways to display the merchandise. Much to her delight Edith had responded readily, and over the months the pair became closer than they had ever been.

The only dark side to the whole business was Edward. He had never contacted her and she wondered if her heart would ever heal. She missed him dreadfully and did not believe she would ever fall in love again.

Evie braced herself as she turned the corner of the factory into the wind. She held her umbrella down, covering her face, and bent forward as she beat her way towards the bus station. She halted her steps for a moment, thinking she had heard her name being called, then continued as the wind whistled through the buildings.

'Evie! Evie!'

This time the voice was much louder. She stopped and struggled to turn as the wind whipped round her legs. Her umbrella blew inside out again and she silently blasphemed as she wrestled with it. A hand touched her arm. She looked up, startled for a moment, then regained her composure and frowned.

'What d'you want?' she said coldly.

'We need to talk.'

'There's nothing to say.' She made to walk off.

'I'm going away, Evie. I came to say goodbye.'

She froze for a moment, then took a deep breath. 'Well, have a good journey, and goodbye.'

'Stop being stubborn, Evie Grayson. That damned temper

of yours will be your undoing one day. I want to talk to you!'

'Oh, you want to talk? You don't contact me for months and then you expect me to jump as soon as you decide to make a move. Well, you've got another think coming, Edward Bradshaw! Now excuse me, I have a bus to catch.'

He grabbed her arm. 'You'll hear me out first.' He gripped her arm more tightly and dragged her across the road to a small coffee shop. There he unceremoniously plonked her down at a vacant table and summoned the waitress.

'Two coffees, please.'

'I don't want coffee,' Evie retorted angrily.

'Well, I'll drink the bloody thing then. Two coffees please,' he addressed the waitress sharply. She slouched off and Edward turned back to Evie. 'I heard about what happened at Dawson's, and about your involvement.'

Her mouth fell open. 'How? That was hushed up.'

'You can't hush things like that up. The whole trade knows about it.'

'Oh.' She lowered her head.

'I thought you were very brave, and I'm proud of you.'

'Proud?' Evie's head jerked up. 'Proud enough not to contact me for three months.'

'It was you who walked out on me, remember?'

'Yes, I remember. You were two timing me as I recall.' She paused and stared at him. 'What's the matter? Has Sophie given you the elbow?'

'Don't be sarcastic, Evie! I explained about Sophie, but you chose not to believe me.'

'Okay. I admit I was out of order there. I apologise,' she answered sulkily. 'Are you and Sophie still friends?'

'Yes, Evie, but that's all we are. How many times do I have to tell you? Now, look, if we're going to sit here arguing, I'll leave now.' Edward stared coldly at her. 'And I won't contact you again, Evie.'

She sat stunned for a moment. She knew he meant what he said and the thought frightened her. She bit her bottom lip and looked up at him shyly. 'I'm sorry, Edward. I'm afraid my temper got the better of me. I've suffered for it, believe me.'

The waitress brought over their coffee and Edward, pulling his cup before him, shovelled in two spoons of sugar from the container on the table. He stirred it and took a sip.

'Why didn't you contact me?' he asked softly.

'Why should I?' she retorted, her apologies of a few seconds ago forgotten. 'It was you who said we were finished. Anyway, what brings you here now? I vowed after the last time that I wouldn't lose sleep over you, and I haven't,' she lied.

'That's not what Mavis says,' he responded before he could stop himself.

'Mavis! What's she got to do with this?' Evie's voice rose sharply.

Edward took a deep breath. 'I've had a letter from her.'

'A letter! I don't believe it.'

'Calm down. She wrote to try and make me see what an idiot I've been – and I have, Evie. I'm stubborn like you. I didn't want to be the first to make a move. But when Mavis told me how upset you were . . .'

'She had no right,' Evie retorted. 'What I wrote to her was in confidence . . .'

'Stop it, Evie. Get off your high horse for once and face

266

facts. We've both missed each other and it's taken your friend Mavis to do something about it.' He lowered his voice. 'You have missed me, haven't you?'

She stared at him for a moment then nodded. 'Yes,' she whispered.

He reached for her hand across the table.

'D'you want anythin' else?' a thin voice asked.

They turned to see the waitress standing with pad and pen poised at the side of them. They both looked at each other and burst into laughter.

'Well, would the lady like anything?' Edward asked her.

'I'd like another coffee, this one's cold.'

'Two coffees please,' he addressed the waitress.

She sniffed and departed.

'Are you really going away?'

'Yes, I am.' Edward looked at her for a moment before he continued: 'I'm going to do my National Service.'

'Oh.' Evie looked dejected.

'It's only for two years. We can write, and I'll see you every leave I get.' He moved his hand as the waitress plonked the two coffees down on the table, spilling half the contents into the saucers.

Evie watched the waitress intently as her heart sank like a lead weight.

'My father's fuming,' continued Edward. 'He tried his best to get me out of it, but I was adamant. Why should his money buy me out when all the other lads have to go?' He lowered his voice. 'Anyway, it was a chance to get away and forget about you.'

'Is that what you wanted to do, Edward, forget about me?'

'It was until Mavis's letter arrived. I thought you didn't care. It wouldn't have made any difference to my doing National Service, though, that's a matter of principle.'

Evie smiled. 'Yes, I understand that and admire you for it.' She hesitated. 'When do you have to go?'

'Saturday.'

'Saturday! Only two days. Oh, Edward.'

'You will write, won't you, Evie?'

'You try and stop me!'

He grinned. 'And don't forget to write and thank Mavis. Tell her I'll take her for a drink when she gets out of hospital.

Evie frowned fiercely 'That you won't, Edward Bradshaw.'

'You can come as well,' he laughed.

'I should think so.'

'Will you meet me tomorrow night?'

'Of course.'

He rose and went to pay the bill. They walked silently, arm in arm, to the bus station.

'Sure you won't let me drive you home?' he asked.

'No, thanks. I like to sit on the bus and think.'

They settled themselves on the wooden benches in the concrete shelter and shivered as the wind whipped through the entrance. Edward pulled her up into the darkened corner and put his arm around her. They nestled close together and kissed passionately.

Reluctantly they parted as the red double decker pulled into its spot. Evie stood hesitantly on the step, clinging to the pole.

'Edward, will your parents be seeing you off on Saturday?'

'No, I've asked them not to,' he answered.

'Can I?'

His beaming face gave her the answer.

She boarded the bus and watched his figure grow small and indistinct as the bus took her home.

Saturday came round in a flash. Evie felt the tears flow unashamedly down her cheeks as Edward's train disappeared in a cloud of smoke out of the station. She slowly walked down the platform amongst the crowds, calculating how long it would take him to reach his destination, get settled and put pen to paper.

Much to her delight, Edward wrote regularly. His letters were full of news. He wrote a bit each day in diary form and Evie felt she was living each moment with him. She shared his triumphs and his failures, got to know his friends and his brute of a sergeant like the back of her hand. The army had cleverly placed him into a trade he thoroughly enjoyed: maintenance of vehicles, it couldn't have suited him better and Edward was in his element.

He came home as often as possible, which was not enough for Evie, and had great difficulty balancing his time between her and his family. But it was always a tearful Evie who saw him off at the station on a Sunday night. Edward's first year in the army passed slowly and the only joyful occasion was Mavis's departure from hospital in the early spring of 1953 after being given the all clear. She was welcomed home like royalty and given a large party.

Evie hugged her friend until her arms ached and Mavis's ribs were sore.

'Oh, you don't know how much I've missed you!'

'Me too,' Mavis answered. 'But you've had Jenny.'

She tried to keep the jealousy out of her voice.

'Jenny is a good friend, a smashing friend, but she's not you.'

Mavis beamed. 'Oh, Evie, I'm sorry for sounding envious. I've made other friends too, but they'll never take the place of you.'

'We'll have each other crying soon,' Evie sniffed. 'Come on, let's change the subject. Tell me about Phil?' she asked eagerly.

'He's wonderful. So kind and caring.' Mavis paused. 'He's asked me to marry him.'

Evie clasped her hands in delight. 'When?'

'Not yet. I want to be sure this time.' Mavis looked sad for a moment. 'Paul has signed all rights to Rosie over to me. He doesn't want to see her or me again.'

'Bastard,' Evie muttered under her breath. 'You're well rid of him, Mavis. Put him behind you.'

'I have,' she answered. She paused and eyed Evie mischievously. 'What about a double wedding?'

Evie blushed. 'Double wedding?'

'Don't be coy with me. You know damned well what I'm talking about.'

'He hasn't asked me.'

'Not yet, but he will,' Mavis said with conviction.

Evie laughed. 'I'm not so sure. Our relationship is very turbulent.'

'That's only because you've got such a temper – and anyway, would you have fallen in love with Edward if he had been one of those men who follow you around like a little lapdog, hanging on your every word?'

Evie raised her eyebrows. 'No, I wouldn't.' She frowned. 'But I'm not the only one with a temper. Edward can stand his ground all right.'

Mavis thought for a moment. 'You'll be twenty-one in a few months. Maybe he'll propose then?'

Evie sighed. 'Oh, I'm not sure. He might propose, but it might not be to me.'

'What makes you say that?'

Evie hesitated before she spoke. 'Well, there's the girl that Edward and I had the fight over. He's done his best to convince me that she's just a family friend, but I can't help but wonder.'

'Oh! Why?' Mavis questioned. 'Has he given you any reason to be worried?'

'Well, no. It's just that he's never mentioned her again. I've been afraid to ask in case he said something I didn't want to hear. I know I've never met them, but I get the feeling that the family would be delighted if they got together.'

'I shouldn't worry about that.' Mavis pursed her lips. 'I know I haven't met Edward yet, but from what you've told me, he's certainly not the type of man to be pushed into anything he didn't want, especially marriage. Family or no family!'

Evie thought for a moment. 'Yes, you're right. He's pretty strong-minded, and to be honest I don't think he's the type to two time me.' She grimaced. 'I damned well hope not, anyway!'

Mavis grinned. 'No, take it from me, he's far too fond of you, Evie.'

'D'you think so?' she asked eagerly, then paused for a moment and shook her head. 'I wish I felt as sure as you do. He's never actually told me he loves me, though I'm sure he does.'

'Blokes never tell you things like that, they take it for granted you know,' Mavis said as she waved over to her uncle. 'By the way, what are you doing for your birthday?'

Evie grimaced. 'Mam asked me that only the other day. She wants to know if I want a party. To be honest, with Edward away I don't feel much like celebrating on a grand scale. Getting leave is simple, it's not as though there's a war on, but it would be just my luck to arrange a party when he had to do a weekend training exercise. Anyway, my actual birthday is on a Thursday, so I thought it would be nice if, you, me, Mam and Jenny went for a posh meal. What d'you say?'

'Oh, I'd like that, Evie.'

'Good. Talking of food, I'm starving and it's a shame to waste all your mother's good grub.'

The friends made their way through to the spacious dining room and Evie packed a plate with food.

'Are you going to stay here with your family?' she asked.

Mavis picked up a piece of pork pie and added it to her plate. 'For the time being I am. I can't afford to live on my own just yet.' She took a deep breath. 'I'd love to do something on my own, but I'm not quite sure what. Mother and Father say I can stay with them as long as I like, and I can see that being for quite a while.' She grimaced. 'I don't fancy going back into an office, I never really got the hang of that. It was only 'cos my father was a bigwig in the business that they kept me on.' She laughed. 'I wouldn't have lasted five minutes if it hadn't been for him. Anyway, the doctor says I've still to take things easy, and to be honest it would break Mam's heart if I left just yet. She's done a grand job with Rosie. That child is the only thing that kept me going. It broke my heart to miss her first birthday. I sat and cried all day.' She paused. 'I had a picture of her on my bedside cabinet and willed myself to pull through for her sake.'

Evie felt the tears stab the back of her eyes. 'I so wanted to visit you . . .'

'That would have been stupid, Evie,' Mavis cut in. 'You might have caught the disease yourself, and think how I would have felt if that had happened. Anyway, you wouldn't have survived in there.'

'Why not? You did!'

'Yes, but I don't mind the cold as much as you. They keep all the windows and doors open, whatever the weather. Apart from the drugs, which were very unpleasant, plenty of fresh air is the only treatment there is for tuberculosis. If the disease didn't kill you, frostbite did.'

Evie laughed. 'I'm glad to see you've still got your sense of humour.'

'We built a snowman in the ward one day.' Mavis looked at her friend seriously.

'You never!' Evie gawped. 'I don't believe you.'

'Honest.' Mavis burst into laughter at Evie's expression, unable to keep up the act any longer. 'No, I'm telling fibs, but it was cold, believe me.'

Evie laughed as she looked at her friend fondly. 'Oh, I'm so glad you're home, and just in time for the Coronation celebrations. Jenny's mam has helped to organise a street party. You could come and bring Rosie.'

'Oh, that sounds good.'

'It should be. All the women are preparing mountains of food and the wooden tables will be decorated with blue, red and white striped cloths. And to top it all, some of the men have got together and formed a band.' Evie grinned. 'I tell you, Mave, they're terrible. I couldn't stop laughing when I heard them practising, and Jenny – well, she fell off her chair in hysterics. She reckons she's going to dress up as Britannia. She's already made her costume and it looks great.'

'It sounds just what I need.'

'And me,' Evie said. 'It will help keep my mind off Edward, although I'm hoping he can get home for it. Mam's shutting the shops for the day and she's asked all the staff round to our house to watch the ceremony on the television.' She grimaced. 'Guess who'll have the job of supplying everyone with tea and cakes?'

The two women looked at each other knowingly.

'Talking of food, let's find a chair and eat ours. I'm starving,' said Evie.

The pair walked over to some chairs and began to demolish their food. Evie marvelled at how much her friend had changed. She seemed more sure of herself, as though her time in hospital had made her grow up. The Mavis who had been her childhood friend, whom she had supported and carried through the years, had gone. In her place was a mature woman, a woman who had had to fight for her life so she could return to her child. Evie felt sad for a moment, wondering if their friendship would ever be the same. She turned and smiled at Mavis. Of course it would, if not stronger than before.

She tackled her food with gusto and unashamedly went over and filled her plate with a second helping.

Evie had had a particularly trying week. Mr Pullen had retired a few months previously and she had taken over his role in the office. When it had been offered to her she had accepted the challenge with gusto, until she had found out that the position was not to be that of manager as it was previously, but demoted to senior clerk. No explanation had been given, she had been expected to be grateful for the opportunity and get on with it.

Thank goodness it's Friday, she thought gratefully. For the last three evenings she had been helping her mother with the stocktaking and they had both worked long and hard into the night. Lack of sleep was now telling on her and she kept looking at the clock as its hands slowly moved round to five-thirty. Edward was on a training exercise all weekend and would not be home, so she was looking forward to a relaxing two days.

Evie tidied her desk, put the cover on her typewriter and picked up her bag. She opened her mouth to say her goodnights to Mr Haggar.

'Oh, Miss Grayson.' Hubert Haggar looked flustered as he spoke. 'Can you do me a favour before you go?'

Evie tried to hide her annoyance as she put her bag down and smiled at him. If she missed her bus the next one would not arrive for another twenty minutes.

'Mr Dawson asked me for this report this afternoon and I've just finished it.' Hubert looked at her and smiled sweetly. 'Would you be an angel and take it up to his office for me? I wouldn't ask, only I'm in a hurry to get home. I would leave it till Monday, Mr Dawson always finishes early on a Friday night but since Mr Grady's departure our Mr Dawson has been shoving his nose into everything. He wants a report on this and a report on that, and it would just be my luck for him to come in over the weekend . . .'

'Okay, okay. Give it to me,' Evie relented. 'I've never been up to the third floor before, it'll be an experience. I've heard it's quite posh.'

'Oh, it is. Very tasteful. But mind you just put the report on his secretary's desk and come straight down. It wouldn't do to be caught snooping around up there.'

'Don't worry.' Evie half smiled. 'I'm quite trustworthy, you know. Have a nice weekend.'

She grabbed the report and headed towards the stairs. Most of the staff had now gone home and the journey to the third floor reminded her of the night she stole back and ransacked Mr Grady's office.

Evie opened the door to the secretary's office and gazed round. It was plush to say the least. The walls were lined with a heavy embossed paper and brocade curtains adorned the windows. In the corner of the office was a small seating area for visitors and on the occasional table sat an assortment of trade magazines. Evie went over to the secretary's desk and put the report into the post tray.

She was about to leave when she noticed the heavy wooden door to the right of the office was ajar. She opened the door to the corridor and looked out. It was dark and empty. Moving swiftly back inside she ran over to the wooden door, switched on the light and peered into the inner office.

So this was the head man's domain. She pushed her nose further inside. Again the furnishings were plush and very tasteful, but in this office there was a luxurious cream-coloured carpet covering the whole floor. One wall of the large room was covered by a bookcase crammed with books of all descriptions and off centre sat a large mahogany desk. Evie walked over to this and ran her hand over the highly polished wood. She walked round and put her hand on the back of the leather chair, pulled it out and sat down.

Her thoughts wandered for a moment as she pictured herself as the boss of a large enterprise. She laughed at her daydream and ran her eyes across a collection of silver-framed photographs covering the far side of the desk. There was a wedding group, a picture of an older couple and a photograph of a woman. Evie's eyes lingered on the last photograph and she frowned slightly. She leaned forward and picked up the frame. She turned it towards the light for a better look – and froze. Staring up at her was the face of her mother. The photograph had been taken a few years ago, but there was no mistake. It was definitely Edith.

She threw the frame back on the desk and ran from the room. Flicking off the lights, she ran down the stairs to her own floor and barged into the toilets. She entered a cubicle and fell down on the closed seat. She was shaking from head to foot and her stomach churned. She doubled over, clutched her stomach, and rocked backwards and forwards. Suddenly the pieces of the jigsaw all slotted together.

So that was it! That was how her mother had got the money for the wool shops, where she went to on her Saturdays out, and how Evie herself had been moved through the factory to her present position. She threw her head back and gasped for air. Her mother was having an affair with Mr Dawson! She jumped up, raised the lid of the toilet and was violently sick.

Afterwards she walked slowly over to the sink and rinsed out her mouth. Raising her head, she took a long, hard look in the mirror. What on earth was she going to do? She leaned wearily against the sink, jumping as the door opened and a cleaner came sauntering in, dragging her mop and bucket behind her. Evie smiled wanly at her and slowly walked back to her office to collect her bag. She sat down in her chair and stared into space. Finally she stood up. She knew exactly what she would do: nothing. It had taken Edith a long time to recover from the business with Florrie. Evie and her mother had both worked hard to rebuild their relationship and Evie felt she could not jeopardise the bond they now had between them for anything. Her mother had her own life to live and so had she.

She picked up her bag and ran out of the factory to catch the bus home.

At last Edward's National Service came to an end. It had been the longest two years of Evie's life and she was so glad it was finally over. For the last three weekends, to her dismay, Edward had not been home. His friends had cajoled him into staying with them at their respective homes and from his letters it seemed Edward had thoroughly enjoyed himself. Evie was concerned. Did his absence mean his feelings for her had cooled? She stood on the platform and waited with trepidation for his train to arrive. Spring had finally put in an appearance, but it still wasn't the kind of day to be standing on a chilly, wind-whipped platform.

A crackling announcement over the tannoy heralded the arrival of Edward's train and Evie grimaced, wondering if she had enough time to visit the toilet. In her nervousness she had already been four times that morning and was desperately in need again. It was too late. The train drew to a halt, spewing out clouds of dense white smoke and steam, and all the doors flew open. The platform came alive with a stampede of passengers hurrying to get to their destinations.

Evie's eyes darted round in search of Edward. Suddenly he was there. She made to run towards him and stopped abruptly as she noticed with horror a young attractive woman at his side. She stared in disbelief, her mouth gaping in astonishment. How dare he? she thought angrily. She turned on her heel and marched down the platform, tears of frustration welling in her eyes. I haven't seen him for weeks and he does this to me. Well, that's it!

Edward caught up with her, his arms laden down with his belongings. 'Evie, where are you going?' he asked breathlessly.

She turned on him. 'Don't you dare speak to me. You . . . you . . . bastard! I haven't seen you for weeks, and I take time off work to meet your train, and you turn up with one of your . . . your . . . floozies!' She shook herself from his grasp and made to storm away.

'Oh, for God's sake, you stupid girl!' Edward snarled. 'I met her for the first time on the train . . .' He stopped abruptly and acknowledged the woman as she passed by them. He turned back to Evie, his face inches away from hers. 'Now look what you've done. If you ever show me up like that again, I'll, I'll . . .' He straightened up and took a deep breath. 'Damn! I feel such an idiot.'

'*You* feel an idiot! What about me? I thought you cared about me, Edward Bradshaw. Well, it just shows how wrong I was.'

He threw down his belongings and grabbed her by the shoulders, shaking her hard. Her teeth rattled together and her hat fell off.

'I do care about you, Evie Grayson. I've spent the last

couple of hours telling that woman just that.' He dropped her arms and glared at her in anger.

Evie stared at him wide-eyed and her anger subsided. 'You did?'

'Yes, I did,' he snapped. 'And she gave me her advice on how to ask you to marry me,' he blurted before he could stop himself.

'Marry you!'

'Yes, marry me!'

'Oh, Edward.' Evie blushed with embarrassment. 'I feel such a fool.'

'I should damned well think so!' He bent down to pick up his bags. 'Look, I'm not standing here while everyone gawps at us. Come on.'

He strode off in the direction of the station buffet. Evie quickly retrieved her hat and raced after him, her thoughts racing wildly. Had he really just proposed? Oh, God, her bad temper and childish actions would surely change his mind. Why, oh why, do I have to jump to conclusions? she thought in anguish. Finding a vacant seat, she waited with trepidation while Edward queued for the coffee. He strode back towards her and banged the coffee cups down on the table. He sat down and sipped, his eyes looking everywhere but at her.

Evie shifted position, feeling uncomfortable in the awkward silence.

Edward finally raised his eyes and grinned.

'Calmed down now, have you?'

She smiled wanly and nodded. 'I'm sorry, Edward. I shouldn't have jumped to conclusions. Only, after not seeing you for such a while, I thought . . . I thought. . . well, that you didn't want me any more.'

'Evie! I spent some time with my friends. Friends I might never see again. I thought you wouldn't mind.'

'I might not have if you'd written and explained. I thought you preferred their company to mine.'

'Okay.' Edward shrugged his shoulders nonchalantly. 'My fault.' He took another sip of his coffee and stared around at the crowded buffet.

There was another long, awkward silence.

Finally Evie spoke. 'Did you mean what you said?' she whispered.

Edward's eyes came to rest on her. 'What did I say?' he asked abruptly.

She shuffled nervously in her seat. 'About . . . about getting married?'

Edward stared blankly at her. 'Did I say that?' His expression softened and his eyes twinkled. 'Yes, I did, Evie. Only I wanted to ask you properly, not in a crowded station buffet!'

'Oh.' She let out a sigh of relief. 'It doesn't matter where it is, Edward. I'd still answer the same.'

He looked at her tenderly. 'And?'

'Yes! Yes, yes, yes.'

Edward beamed. 'Good, that's settled then. Phew! You're hard work, Evie Grayson, but I do love you,' he whispered shyly.

'I love you too.'

'I know you do,' he said with conviction. 'You fell in love with me the first time we met on the beach.' He raised his hands, seeing Evie's expression. 'Calm down, I'm only joking.' He frowned. 'I should really have proposed properly though. What are our grandchildren going to think when you tell them I proposed on a crowded station?'

'They'll think it romantic. Oh, Edward, it was the best proposal any girl could have had!'

'And it's the last one you'll ever get,' he answered. He half rose and leaned over the table to kiss her.

'My family is having a welcome home party for me on Saturday night. Everyone will be there. Will you come with me, so I can introduce them to my future wife?'

Evie took a deep breath and nodded slowly. 'Okay, Edward,' she said hesitantly.

'Don't worry, they're not that bad. And don't forget, we've to face your mother as well,' he said, frowning at the prospect.

'Oh, Edward, one hurdle at a time, please. I'm not sure how my mother will take this, let alone yours.'

He grimaced. 'Okay, mine first.' He looked at his watch. 'We'd better make a move.'

He stood up and picked up his case.

'Saturday morning – are you doing anything?'

'Not that I know of.'

'Good. We'll go and buy you the biggest engagement ring we can find.'

Evie beamed up at him and took his outstretched hand.

'It's really beautiful, Evie,' Mavis gasped.

She held her hand up to the light and admired the solitaire ring nestling snugly on her finger.

'Yes, it is, isn't it?' she breathed rapturously.

'What did your mam say when you showed her?'

'Nothing. I haven't told her yet.'

'You haven't told her? Blimey! There'll be hell to pay when you do.'

'Oh, don't I know it! That's why I'm waiting till Sunday

after she comes back from church.'

'It's still a pity you couldn't tell her before his parents.'

'Yes, that would have been much better. But there hasn't been time. Edward's adamant that we announce it to them tonight.'

'She does know you've been seeing him?'

Evie frowned. 'Oh, yes. I told her that quite bluntly. But after her reaction when I first met him, I thought it best to play it down. There've been moments when I would have loved to have talked to her, especially when we split up that time.' Evie smiled. 'The proposal came out of the blue and since then things have happened so quickly, I haven't had time to think straight, let alone anything else.'

'Well, it makes for more family intrigue.' Mavis grinned.

'What d'you mean?'

Mavis shrugged. 'You and Edward. Your mother and Mr Dawson.'

'Mavis! I told you about that in confidence.'

'I know, and I haven't said a word. I personally think it's rather romantic. I'm glad your mother's got somebody, even if he is married.'

'Mavis, before Paul you wouldn't have thought like that, but it still came as a hell of a shock to me.'

'No more of a shock than this will be to your mother.'

'Well, that's not my fault. Every time I've mentioned Edward's name, she's paled and changed the subject.'

'Funny about that, isn't it?' Mavis frowned.

'Yes, it is.' Evie looked thoughtful. 'But I can't worry about that now. I've Edward's parents to face tonight and that will be some ordeal, I can tell you.'

'Best of luck,' Mavis volunteered.

'Thanks. I'll need it.'

Mavis clasped her hands together. 'I thought an engagement was supposed to be a happy affair. Come on, what are you going to wear tonight?'

'Oh, I've bought a new dress,' Evie said excitedly. She went over to her wardrobe and pulled out a shimmering creation of emerald green.

'Phew! Some dress,' Mavis exhaled loudly.

'Cost me a month's wages.'

'I bet it did. Where does your mam think you're going tonight?'

'That was tricky. I told her I was going to a cricket dance. She looked at me really strangely. I know she didn't believe me.'

'A cricket dance, in that dress? I'm sure she didn't! There's one thing I do know, Evie, your mother's not stupid. In fact, when it comes down to it, she probably knows everything that's happened between you and Edward.'

'You're probably right.' Evie grinned. 'But I still couldn't tell her that I was going to meet my future in-laws, could I? I need to sit her down and explain properly about me and Edward, not as I'm passing her on the stairs. It's not as though I could tell her tonight. I'll be gone before she gets back from The Knitting Pin.'

Evie looked down once more at her ring. 'I'd better put this away before I lose it.' She pulled it gently off her finger and placed it in a little box on her dressing table. 'Edward didn't want me to have it until tonight, but I was desperate to show you and Jenny.'

'What time is she coming?' Mavis asked, looking at her watch. 'Only I'll have to be going soon, I don't like leaving Rosie too long.'

'About four,' Evie answered. 'She's going to do my hair for me.'

'She's a clever girl, is Jenny. I want to catch her and ask if she'll make a dress for me. I've seen a smashing pattern in Lewis's.'

'I'm sure she will. She's in between boyfriends at the moment, so she has some time to spare.'

Mavis laughed. 'I've never known anyone get through as many lads as she does.'

'That's our Jenny. A different one each week. She's a bit down though since she finished with Graham.'

'Graham? I thought his name was Peter?'

'Oh, no. Peter was the one before last.'

Both women looked at each other and burst out laughing.

'I'm going to have to take some lessons from her,' Mavis giggled.

Evie jumped up as she heard the front doorbell ring.

'Good, there she is now. I'll make some tea and we can really have a good gossip, before I have to make myself beautiful for Edward.'

Chapter Twelve

Edward met Evie's taxi at the gates of his house. She alighted and smiled up at him.

'You look wonderful,' he told her.

'Thanks. Just an old dress I threw on,' she answered nonchalantly, then frowned in alarm. 'I'm not overdressed, am I?'

'Evie, I said you look wonderful and I meant it.' He eyed her thoroughly. 'I could ravish you on the spot.' He grinned wickedly.

She grinned back at him, took his arm and started to walk with him up the gravel drive. Cars lined the approach and Evie grimaced.

'I thought you said just your family would be here?' she said in alarm.

'That's what I thought. But it appears Mother took it upon herself to invite half of Leicester here tonight. Still, she had the foresight to get a marquee put in the garden for all us younger lot to dance in, and there's a great band playing.'

'Oh, God!' Evie exclaimed. 'I don't think I can cope with all this.'

He laughed. 'Yes, you can, Evie Grayson. You can cope with anything.'

From the front gate, the house could not be seen for the assortment of trees and shrubs that grew in the spacious gardens. Stoneygate was a residential area on the south side of Leicester and the large gabled houses were set well back from the road, giving the residents all the privacy they could afford. As they rounded the bend in the drive the house came into view and Evie stopped and stared in awe.

'Blimey! What a house. I never for a minute thought you lived in something this big.'

Edward smiled. 'It isn't that big, Evie.'

'Well, it's not exactly a terrace in Luther Street, is it?'

'No, I suppose not,' he answered lightly.

Just then a girl of about nineteen approached them. She had long brown hair tied up in a pony tail. Her dress of pale pink seersucker was gathered in at her small waist and finished off with a broad white belt. Edward placed his arm round the girl's shoulders.

'This is Geraldine, my sister.' He looked at her fondly. 'This is Evie,' he said proudly.

Geraldine stretched out her hand and smiled. Evie accepted it graciously.

'Pleased to meet you.' Geraldine grinned. She turned to Edward. 'They're all gathered in the marquee.'

'What about Mother and Father?' he asked.

'Oh, they're in the drawing room, entertaining their old cronies. I overheard Father remark on your absence. He wasn't pleased.'

Edward shrugged his shoulders and grabbed Evie's elbow. 'Come on, I want to introduce you to the crowd.'

Geraldine pulled him aside and stretched up to whisper in his ear. 'I overheard Father and Sidney Gold talking.

They both want to speak to you, in private.' She grimaced. 'Could it be something to do with you and Sophie?'

Edward raised his eyebrows. 'Well, if it is, they're in for a bit of a shock.' He paused and took a deep breath. 'Don't you worry about anything. I'm fed up with Father trying to rule my life. It's about time he stopped.' He smiled broadly. 'I intend to enjoy myself tonight and I suggest you do the same.'

Geraldine bit her lip. 'I shouldn't take this so lightly, Edward. You know what Father's like and what he expects of us.'

'Father can manipulate as much as he wishes, but I can be as bloody minded as he is and he should know that by now. I've already crossed him once by insisting on doing my National Service. He should have learned he can't push me around any more.' Edward straightened his back and raised his head. 'Whether Father likes it or not, I have my own life to live. And so, my girl, have you.' He kissed Geraldine lightly on the cheek. 'Now let's enjoy ourselves.'

She smiled wanly and watched her brother take Evie's arm and guide her round the back of the house.

'What was all that about?' Evie asked.

'Oh, nothing. Come on.'

As they turned the corner, loud music reached their ears and Evie felt excitement rise inside her. They approached the marquee and a crowd of revellers appeared. Evie and Edward were separated as his friends pounced.

She stepped back and watched as Edward was swallowed up in the crowd. She realised that the man she loved was very popular amongst his friends and she felt a warm glow envelop her body as he turned and caught her eye. He frowned slightly and shrugged his shoulders as though to tell her he was sorry for their separation, then was lost again.

Evie turned and stared up at the house. Twilight was closing in and all the windows were ablaze with lights. The large French doors were wide open and she could see the room was packed with people. She decided to go and investigate, leaving Edward with his friends for a while.

She climbed the steps that led to the French doors, entered and looked round in awe. A maid appeared carrying a tray and Evie accepted the drink that she was offered. She took a sip and continued looking round the room. From what she could see through the throng of people, she thought it magnificent. Paintings of all sizes adorned the walls and ornaments graced the occasional tables that were placed strategically round the room. The main wall at the back of the room housed a large fireplace. Evie inched her way round the edges of the room and sat down on a red velvet-covered chair.

Several people moved aside and she had a clear view towards the fireplace. Her eyes alighted on a distinguished man standing in the centre of a group of people. He had his arm draped around the shoulders of a tall stately woman and Evie watched, fascinated, as they held court. A tremor of apprehension shot through her as she suddenly realised that this couple could well be Edward's parents. The crowds moved together once more and her view was blocked.

She felt someone by her side and turned to see that a petite blonde had sat down beside her. She was nursing a glass of champagne and took a sip as her eyes darted round the room. The woman was pale-skinned and wore an old-fashioned, heavy brocade evening dress. Its colour did nothing but accentuate her drab appearance. Her fine hair was scraped back into an unbecoming bun at the back of her head and she fingered a tendril by her ear as she turned and looked at Evie. Evie smiled and inclined her head. The woman paused for a moment before smiling back. Cold fear ran through Evie as she suddenly realised that this was the woman she had seen with Edward on the night he was late for their meeting.

'Do I know you?' Sophie said casually.

'I don't think so,' Evie answered, her mind in a turmoil. 'I've never been here before.'

Sophie looked her up and down. 'Have you come with one of Edward's friends, then? I thought I knew all the girlfriends, but obviously not.' She spoke flatly. 'I suppose they're all gathered in that marquee. I can't be doing with that sort of thing myself. This popular music does nothing for my ears at all. What about you?'

'Oh!' Evie said, taken aback. 'I quite like it myself.'

'Oh, do you? Well, I suppose upbringing comes into it,' Sophie said, raising her head and eyeing Evie coldly. 'My father doesn't allow this kind of thing, says it breeds discontent. Edward will have to change his habits drastically once we're married. Those so-called friends of his will have to go for a start. They're not the kind of people I'll want at my musical evenings or poetry readings.'

'Married!' Evie's mouth fell open. 'You and Edward are getting married?'

'Yes,' Sophie said bluntly. 'We've been promised since we were babies.' She gave a little giggle. 'I shouldn't be telling you all this, you being a stranger. But I'm hopeful it will be announced tonight, after our fathers have had a little chat with him.' She rose and placed her glass on a passing waitress's tray. 'Well, I must go and rescue the poor lamb, we have so much to talk about. It's been nice chatting to you.'

Sophie walked away towards the French doors. Evie stared after her transfixed. She jumped as she felt a hand on her shoulder.

'There you are. I've been looking all over for you.' Edward noticed her frozen expression and sat down beside her.

'Hey, what's the matter?'

She turned and looked at him blankly.

'Well, is it something I've said? Look, I'm sorry if I left you on your own, only you know what it's like when you haven't seen your friends for a while. Can I get you another drink?' he asked, taking the empty glass from her hand. Evie nodded as Edward placed the glass on a tray and collected two full ones. He handed Evie hers and took a sip from the other. 'I think there must be over a hundred people here tonight. You should hear that band, they're great!' He nudged her arm. 'We could book them for our wedding.'

'Whose wedding?' she asked coldly.

'Ours.' He frowned. 'Evie, what's got into you?'

She took a deep breath. 'I've just met your future fiancée.'

'You've just met who?' he laughed.

'I presume it was Sophie. Well, it was certainly the woman I saw you with that night you left me waiting.' She glared at him. 'And she's definitely under the impression that you and she are having your engagement announced tonight,' she said haughtily, feeling tears sting the back of her eyes.

Edward's face paled then clouded over, his eyes ablaze with anger. He grabbed the glass out of Evie's hand and placed it down with his own. He took her hand and pulled her up. 'Right, Evie, I've had enough!' he fumed.

He pulled her through the crowd of people until he reached the group in front of the fireplace. He stopped abruptly as the tall man and statuesque woman stared at him. The man looked at Edward, then at Evie, his anger apparent. Then he relaxed and smiled at his son.

'Ah, Edward. We wondered where you were. Sophie's been looking for you, she's around here somewhere.' Edward's father completely ignored the presence of Evie as his cold grey eyes stared at his son. 'Samuel's beginning to think you're neglecting his daughter.' He turned and patted a shorter man on the shoulder, then turned again to address Edward. 'Go and find her, my boy, we'd like to talk to you both.'

Edward's face turned white with fury and Evie stifled a scream of pain as his nails pressed into her hand.

'I want to talk to you, Father. In private,' he demanded.

'Not now . . .'

'Now, Father,' he said coldly, trying to control his emotions.

He pulled Evie towards the door. The room they entered was the library and she stared in amazement at the rows and rows of shelves lined with books. Her feet sank into the thick pile carpet as Edward deposited her in the centre of the room and turned to face his father. Charles Bradshaw came storming in after them and slammed the door shut.

'Just what is the meaning of this?' he shouted. 'Does it give you pleasure causing a scene in front of all our friends?' He turned to Evie. 'Do you mind? This is a private discussion.'

'Stay where you are.' Edward addressed Evie firmly.

He turned to his father. 'I've just heard you're announcing my engagement tonight?'

Charles Bradshaw eyed his son thoughtfully and walked slowly round the huge walnut desk that stood in the centre of the room. He placed his hands on the highly polished surface and leaned forward.

'Well, you heard wrong. Someone has their lines crossed. But, yes, Samuel and I would like to speak to you on that very subject.'

Evie felt Edward's body stiffen as he clenched his fists.

'Well, in that case, I'd better introduce my future wife to you.'

Charles looked at Evie and laughed. 'Stop fooling. It's always been understood you would marry Sophie.'

'Understood! Understood by whom? Not me. I don't love the woman and never will,' Edward said coldly.

'Now, look here. Sophie is a fine girl and if you don't love her now, you'll soon grow to, I'm sure.' Charles frowned. 'This marriage will be good all round – for you, Sophie and the business.'

'Ah, the business,' Edward said mockingly. 'What you mean is this marriage will be good for Bradshaw's, eh, Father? Well, I've told you before. I will not marry Sophie, for you or Bradshaw's. I'm marrying Evie. I love her and that's that.'

'Over my dead body,' Charles stormed. He looked over at Evie. 'I've already asked you, young lady, to leave us.'

'Stay, Evie,' Edward said, gripping her hand tighter. 'You had better get used to the idea, Father. Whether you like it or not, I'm marrying her.'

Charles walked round the desk and planted himself in

front of his son. He eyed Evie thoroughly.

'Who is she, this Evie? What d'you know about her or her family?' he asked, taking a cigar out of his pocket and lighting it. He blew a puff of smoke into the air and looked at her disdainfully.

Evie could control herself no longer. She took a deep breath.

'Excuse me, Mr Bradshaw,' she began.

Charles Bradshaw narrowed his eyes. 'Stay out of this,' he hissed.

Edward opened his mouth to protest at his father's words but the door opened and Adele Bradshaw glided in. She was a handsome woman dressed to the hilt in a red Chinese silk dress, her arms and neck covered in elaborate gold jewellery.

'What's going on, Charles? Our guests are waiting.'

He turned to his wife. 'Our son here is just telling me his intentions towards this woman, Adele.'

She looked at Evie and raised her eyebrows. 'Now is not the time for jokes, Edward. Now come on, Samuel and Sophie are waiting.'

'Mother!' Edward said through clenched teeth. 'Will you please listen to me? I'm not marrying Sophie.'

Adele walked over to the desk. She looked at her husband. 'I tried to tell you, Charles.'

'Shut up, Adele,' he said coldly, and took another draw from his cigar. 'I've asked you once, what d'you know about this woman?' he addressed Edward.

'And I've already told you,' Edward answered, 'I know enough. Her name is Evelyn Grayson. She lives with her mother, the woman who owns the Knitting Pin wool shops, and I love her.'

Charles Bradshaw's mouth dropped open. 'Grayson! Edith Grayson's daughter?'

'Yes,' Edward answered defiantly.

'Get her out of my house.' Charles's face turned purple. 'Now! Get her out now!'

Edward stared at him in amazement. 'Father . . .'

'Don't "Father" me. Get that woman out of my house,' Charles demanded. 'And don't ever, ever, bring her back.'

Adele ran to her husband and put her hand on his arm. 'Charles, your blood pressure . . .'

He shook his arm free and pushed his wife away.

'Why?' Edward shouted.

'Why?' Charles raged. 'Ask that mother of hers why. And I'll tell you this, Edward. If you have any more dealings with that family, you needn't darken my door again!'

'Charles!' Adele placed her hand over her mouth in anguish. 'He's our son.'

'I don't care. If he marries this woman, I want nothing more to do with him.'

Edward turned to Evie and saw the anguish in her face.

'Okay, Father. We're leaving.' He pulled her towards the door.

'I mean it,' Charles shouted.

'And so do I.' Edward let go of Evie's hand and pointed at his father. 'I'm marrying her and you can go to hell!'

'Charles, do something,' Adele cried.

'You'll regret it, take my word for it. That family is poison. I'll . . . I'll cut you off without a penny.'

'I don't need your money,' Edward hissed. He grabbed Evie's hand again and made to leave.

'Edward, Edward!' Adele shouted as she ran over. 'Don't leave, please don't leave.'

Edward dropped Evie's hand and hugged his mother to him.

'I'll be back for my things, Mother, and I'll keep in touch.'

'Oh, don't! Please, Edward, you don't understand.'

'No, I don't, and I don't want to. I love Evie, Mother. If you think I'm going to marry Sophie just to please him . . .'

'No, I've never really gone along with that. But you know what your father's like.' She sniffed. 'He thinks he's doing what's best for all of us, but this outburst is nothing to do with Sophie . . .'

'Let him go, Adele. Let the boy find out the hard way,' Charles bellowed.

Edward let go of Adele and stared defiantly at his father. He turned to Evie and smiled reassuringly at her as he took her hand and walked towards the door, his mother's quiet sobs echoing in his ears.

As they pushed their way through the crowd in the large entrance hall, Sophie appeared before them and caught hold of Edward's arm.

'Oh, there you are. I've been looking all over for you,' she smiled sweetly.

'Not now, Sophie,' he snapped, pulling his arm free.

Sophie stared at him. 'What d'you mean, not now?' She turned to Evie. 'You can leave us. I need to talk in private to my fiancé.'

Edward grabbed her by the shoulders. 'Once and for all, Sophie, I am not your fiancé.'

'But, Edward,' she said in amazement, 'it's always been understood we would marry.'

'No, it hasn't,' he said, trying to keep his voice calm.

'We've only ever been friends, that's all.'

Evie watched as the tears sprang to Sophie's eyes.

'But I love you! You can't mean it, Edward. You've always led me to believe . . .'

'I've led you to believe nothing, Sophie. What you thought we had was in your own mind, spurred on by your father and mine.'

'But everyone is expecting an announcement tonight. I've told them . . .'

'Well, you shouldn't have,' he exploded. 'Evie is the one I'm going to marry.'

Sophie looked at her coldly. 'Her! You're going to marry her?'

'Yes. Now out of my way, Sophie, I've had enough of this. If I've hurt you, I'm sorry, but it's all been in your own mind.' He grabbed hold of Evie's hand again and dragged her out of the house.

As they hurried down the driveway, a voice reached their ears.

'Edward! Edward!'

They stopped and turned as Geraldine came running towards them.

'What happened?' she asked breathlessly.

'Everything,' Edward blurted. 'Father's in a rage, Mother's upset, and Sophie is crying her eyes out. She's told everyone we're announcing our engagement tonight.'

'I did try to tell you,' Geraldine said gravely. She turned to Evie. 'I'm sorry you had to witness all this. We're not usually as hostile as this.'

'It's not your fault, Gerry. Evie knows that. It's Father, he's really gone over the top. He's even had a go at Evie.'

'But where are you going? You can't leave the party,

Edward, all your friends are here.'

'We're leaving, and, Geraldine . . . I'm never coming back. He's gone too far this time.'

'Oh, no!' she cried. 'Please, Edward. Please don't go. It was bad enough when you were away in the army. I couldn't stand it if it were for good.'

Edward placed his arm round his sister's shoulders. 'I have to go, Gerry. I've done all I could for that man. I went to university, passed all my exams, then joined the business. But it wasn't enough. He now wants me to marry Sophie and I can't.' He turned to Evie. 'I love this woman and plan to spend the rest of my life with her. You'll have to understand, Gerry.'

Geraldine sniffed. 'I do, believe me I do. It's just that I'll miss you.'

'You can come and visit.' He kissed his sister on the cheek and took Evie's hand again.

She looked at Edward then at Geraldine. 'I can't, Edward. I can't take you away from your family.'

He frowned deeply and gripped her hand tighter.

'Come on.' He smiled at Geraldine and guided Evie towards his car.

She pulled him to a halt. 'What d'you think your father meant about asking my mother? Ask my mother what? And he seemed to know her. He was in an awful rage about something.'

Edward shrugged and frowned deeply. 'I don't know. But I intend to find out. We're going to see your mother, now.'

'Oh, Edward, I'm frightened.' Evie started to shake.

'Don't be. Whatever it is we'll face it together. Anyway, it's probably something and nothing. Father's in a rage because I wouldn't marry Sophie. He can't stand anyone saying no to him, that's all. Now get in, I want to get away from here.'

Evie did as she was told and Edward started the car and headed it towards her home.

Evie hesitantly put her key in the lock. She stopped and turned to Edward who smiled reassuringly at her.

'Come on, Evie. I want to get this over with.'

Edith looked up at her daughter's anguished face as she stood framed in the living-room doorway. She opened her mouth to speak, but stopped when she noticed Edward standing behind her. She put down her book and looked at them both in bewilderment.

'What's going on?' she asked anxiously.

'That's what I'd like to know, Mother,' Evie answered coldly.

She walked over and turned off the television set and stood in front of her mother. 'This is Edward.'

'I gathered that,' Edith answered slowly, 'but what is he doing here? I thought I'd forbidden you . . .'

'Mother!' Evie took a deep breath. 'We have just come from Edward's home . . .'

'Oh! Oh, no.' Edith groaned and placed her head in her hands. 'Evie, why didn't you tell me . . .'

'Tell you! How could I tell you anything? Every time I mention Edward's name you clam up.'

Edith looked from one to the other. She wrung her hands and groaned loudly again. 'I'm sorry, Evie. I'm so sorry. I never thought it would go this far between you both.'

Edward stepped forward. 'Mrs Grayson, just what is going on?'

'Yes, Mother, we want to know. Edward's father threw a fit when he found out I was your daughter. Why? I want to know, and no more lies, please.'

Edith rubbed her hands over her face. She took a deep breath and stood up.

'Where are you going?' Evie asked.

'I need to use the telephone. I need to have somebody here for this.' She walked out of the room, leaving Edward and Evie staring at each other in bewilderment.

Evie heard the telephone click and her mother came back into the room. 'Make some tea, Evie.' She looked at Edward. 'I have something stronger if you wish. Whisky? Gin?'

'Please,' Edward answered. 'I'll have a whisky.'

'Mother . . .' Evie started.

She held up her hand to stop her daughter. 'Half an hour, Evie. He'll be here in half an hour.'

'Who will?'

'Just be patient, please, Evie. I can't handle this on my own.' Edith handed Edward a large glass of whisky and a jug of water. 'I'm sorry, I have no ginger ale.'

'This will be fine,' Edward answered, taking the whisky and pouring a drop of water into it. He sat down next to Evie on the settee and watched Edith sipping slowly at her own drink.

The room echoed to the sound of silence as the three sat patiently waiting. Finally the doorbell rang and Edith jumped up and rushed to open the front door. Evie could hear the low mumble of voices. She looked at Edward blankly.

The living-room door opened and Edith walked in followed by a tall, greying man in his late forties. Evie frowned as Edward stood up and held out his hand.

'Richard,' he addressed the man in bewilderment.

'Hello, Edward. Please, sit down.'

Evie looked from one to the other in astonishment. She turned to Edward.

'You know this man?'

'Yes.' Edward looked up at the man standing next to Edith. 'This is Richard Dawson. The man who runs the company you work for.'

'Oh!' Evie muttered. She felt her hackles rise as Richard smiled at Edith and placed his arm round her shoulder. She stared at her mother and her eyes narrowed in anger.

'What do you need your lover here for?' she shouted. 'Can't you face us on your own?'

Edith paled. 'Lover! Oh, Evie, Richard's not my lover.'

'What is he then?' she snarled.

'Richard's my brother.'

'Brother!' Evie's face turned ashen and her body sagged. 'I don't understand.' She turned to Edward. 'Did you know about this?'

'No. I'm as confused as you are,' he answered in astonishment.

Edith sank down in her armchair and Richard followed suit in the chair opposite.

Edith looked over at her daughter, love and concern written all over her face. 'There's no easy way to start this,' she began. She looked over at Richard, pleading for his help.

'Look, Evie . . .' he started.

She interrupted. 'If you don't mind, I'd sooner my mother told me.'

Richard looked at Edith and raised his eyebrows.

'Okay.' She clasped her hands together and took a sip of her drink. 'I was born into a very wealthy family. My father – our father,' she looked over at Richard and smiled wanly, 'was a tyrant. We were expected to do everything he told us, without question. The Dawsons and the Bradshaws, although rivals in business, go back a long way and right from an early age it was expected that I would marry Charles.' She looked over at Edward and nodded. 'Your father.' She paused. 'I never loved Charles. To be truthful, I let him court me to please my father. I don't think he really cared all that much for me either.' She stroked the side of her face and looked at Evie. 'I would have married him, I suppose, if I hadn't have met Freddy.' She sighed deeply, a faraway look in her eyes. 'I used to go with Richard down to the factory on a Saturday morning. I wasn't supposed to be there, so while Richard helped Father, I would wander round and talk to the workers down in the despatch department where nobody would find me.' Edith's hands started to shake.

Richard looked at her in concern.

'I'm all right,' she said quickly. 'Would anyone like another drink?' She jumped up and grabbed the bottle of whisky and tipped some into Edward's and Richard's glass. 'Can I get you anything, Evie?'

She shook her head.

Edith put the bottle back into the cocktail cabinet and sat down again.

'I was only fourteen when I met Freddy and I think I fell in love with him there and then.' She paused and gave a watery smile. 'I was a thin, gawky schoolgirl and he was eighteen – tall, dark and handsome.' Edith looked faraway as her memories came flooding back. 'I used to go to the factory as often as possible and seek him out and make him talk to me. After all, I was the boss's daughter. He didn't seem to mind. He would stop what he was doing and we'd perch on top of the cloth bales and talk non-stop about anything and everything. He made me laugh.' She looked at Evie. 'He was such a humorous man.'

She paused again and her eyes misted over. 'I remember vividly the day he told me he was getting married. I would have been about seventeen at the time and the news broke my heart. I never went near the factory for months. He told me afterwards that it cut him in two when he had to tell me. He was so taken aback by my reaction; it hadn't entered the poor dear's head that I was in love with him. Still, he'd got Edna Badcock in the family way and he had to marry her. It was about that time that my father told me of his plans to marry me off.' She looked over at Richard. 'You remember, don't you, Richard? It was about a year after you married Frances.'

He nodded. 'I do. I suppose I had a lucky escape, Frances was my own choice.' He turned to Evie and Edward. 'Edith was distraught, but our father was adamant. She was to marry Bradshaw the following spring, regardless of how she felt. It was expected, and that was that.'

Edith took up the story. 'I cried for days at the thought. Anyway, one Saturday morning I found myself in the factory looking at Freddy. He was delighted to see me. We fell into each other's arms.' She sniffed. 'His marriage was an absolute disaster. After one of their many terrible fights, Edna told him that the baby she was expecting wasn't his and that she had only married him to give the child a name. My heart cried out to him and we both ended up divulging our feelings towards each other. I knew that I could never love Charles or would ever want to marry him. But I couldn't see how I could get out of it. All the preparations had been made and the invitations sent out.'

'Oh, Mam,' Evie muttered under her breath. Edward's arm slipped round her shoulders.

'I decided not to see Freddy again, it was too painful, and I didn't go near the factory for months. I had to face my responsibilities and marry Charles and that was that.' She smiled over at Richard. 'Almost a year passed and I was just about to be married to Charles when Richard decided to take matters into his own hands. He knew how Freddy and I felt about each other and could not stand by any longer and watch us both suffer. So he took a gamble and told me that Edna had walked out on Freddy and Florrie a few months earlier. Just after that she had had an accident crossing the road and was hit by a bus. She was apparently as drunk as a lord and never felt a thing. The poor woman died instantly.' Edith shook her head. 'Oh, Evie. I'm ashamed to admit it, but I was overjoyed. Freddy was free. Even though he had Florrie to care for, he was free. Richard came with me to face Father.' She lowered her head. 'I won't go into detail about his reaction. It was dreadful. All the family were gathered together, Charles and his father were summoned and I had to face them. I stood my ground and eventually, when they knew they weren't going to win, I was thrown out. My father cut me off without a penny and Charles threatened to kill me if he ever set eyes on me again.'

'Oh, Mam,' was all Evie could utter again as she listened intently to her mother's story. Her heart bled as Edith's pain gripped her soul. She turned and looked to Edward for comfort, her eyes filling with tears.

'I know how you must have felt,' he said to Edith. 'I've just experienced the same thing.'

She nodded. 'I wish I could have spared you the pain. I tried to ignore the facts that were staring me in the face. It was like history repeating itself and I shut my eyes hoping it would go away.'

'What happened after you left, Mam?'

Edith smiled. 'I married Freddy a week later. He got a special licence, cost him seven shillings and sixpence.' She grimaced. 'I thought my father would come round then, but no. It got worse. He flatly refused to see me or Freddy, and Richard and my mother were sworn under oath not to have anything more to do with us. Freddy's life was made hell in the factory. He tried everything to get another job, but my father had seen to it that nobody would employ him. So he was tied.'

'What! You mean my grandfather made sure Dad had no option but to stay in his employment?' Evie asked, aghast.

'Yes, and he treated your father like dirt. I witnessed it,' Richard answered gravely.

Edith continued her story. 'We tried to move up north. Your father got a job in a Yorkshire mill. We had even packed our bags. Then the letter came, telling Freddy that the job was no longer available.' She turned to Edward. 'That was your father's doing. He got wind of our plans and put a stop to them.'

'My father did that?' Edward gasped.

'Yes. But it wasn't all his fault, he was egged on by my father.' Edith took a deep breath. 'Freddy started to drink. He hated going to work, but he had a wife and now two children to support.' She took a deep breath. 'The night he died we had a violent row, the first one we had ever had. We both said things we didn't mean and Freddy took off. He was found the next morning hanging from the rafters in the despatch department.' Edith wiped away the tears that rolled down her cheeks. 'I loved that man and they killed him. Yes, between them they killed him, and now they're making you both suffer.'

'Don't, Edith. Don't torture yourself,' Richard said as he rushed over and sat on the arm of her chair. He placed his arm around her shoulders and pulled her towards him for comfort.

Evie jumped up. 'I'll get her a cup of tea.' She ran to the kitchen and with shaking hands filled the kettle and placed it on the stove. She leaned against the sink and put her head in her hands. She felt strong arms encircle her body as Edward pulled her towards him.

'I can't believe it, Edward. This is awful,' she sobbed. 'My poor mother. How she must have suffered all these years! Just because she loved the wrong man.'

Edward gripped her tighter. 'I can't believe this of my father. I know he can be hard, but I never thought he could stoop to something like this. It's all incredible,' he whispered. 'I feel ashamed to be related to him.'

Evie released herself. She wiped her face on a tea towel and blew her nose. 'What about my grandfather? He's just as bad.' She sniffed loudly. 'All these years I thought I had no relatives, and now all this. Oh, Edward, what are we going to do?'

He held her at arm's length. 'Let's make that tea and take it through. I think you could do with a cup as well as your mother, and I need another drink.'

They went back into the living room and placed the

tray on the coffee table. Edith had regained her composure and smiled wanly as they entered. Richard handed Edward another whisky and sat down.

'It's a bad business all round.' Richard shook his head sadly.

'Evie, I didn't lie to you deliberately, I was only trying to shield you from the truth,' Edith said softly. 'The last thing I expected was that you would meet the son of the man I hated so much and who had threatened to kill me should our paths cross again. I couldn't believe it. Then I convinced myself that you two would just drift apart, especially when Edward went into the army for two years. I thought you would get fed up, or Edward would.'

'Never,' he said sternly. 'I love your daughter.'

'I know that now.' Edith tried to smile. 'I just wish I could have plucked up the courage to speak to you sooner, Evie. At least I could have prepared you for all this.'

'Mam, don't. It's too late for that. And, believe me, I do understand,' Evie said gently.

'Oh, Evie. Do you?'

She nodded. Edith rose to meet her and they both hugged each other tightly.

Richard looked at Edward. 'Well, lad, what are we going to do with you?'

Edward grimaced. 'I don't know. I can't think straight at the moment. All I know is that I won't give Evie up, not for my father or anyone.' He puckered his lips. 'But I do need a bed for the night.'

'You can come home with me,' Richard answered, looking at his watch. 'It's three o'clock. Best try and get some sleep. You and Evie can talk in the morning.' He smiled. 'Or should I say later today.' He turned to face his sister.

'I'll come round as well, Edith, and help sort things out.'

She nodded. They walked to the door, leaving Edward and Evie alone in the living room. Edith kissed Richard on the cheek.

'Thanks. I couldn't have faced this without you.'

He sighed loudly. 'I'm glad it's all out in the open, Edith. Evie had to know about her past.'

'Yes, I am too. It's like a weight's been lifted.'

'Maybe things would have been different if I had stood up to the old so and so years ago.'

'How could you? Be honest, Richard. You were just a young lad yourself and no match for Father. You'd just married Frances and then she lost the baby. At least you were there to look after Mother. And in your way, you've looked after Evie.'

Richard sighed again. 'I'm tired, Edith, and Frances will be worried. Let's sleep on things and cast a fresh eye on them tomorrow.'

Edith nodded. 'Richard, please bring Frances round for dinner. We don't have to hide quite so much now, do we? And between us maybe we can try and sort out something for those two in there.'

'I'd love to, and I'm sure Frances will come.' He kissed her on the cheek. 'Edward,' he called.

Edward released Evie from a long, lingering kiss and smiled at her. 'Try to sleep, and I'll see you in the morning.'

She nodded slowly. 'I'm still having a job to take all this in, Edward.'

'Me too.' He heard Richard's call and turned his head to answer. 'Just coming,' he shouted. He turned back to Evie and smiled. 'It's good of your uncle to offer me a bed.'

She stared at him. 'Uncle?' she said slowly. 'Yes, he is, isn't he?'

Evie watched as Edward walked towards the door, then paused. 'Oh.' He turned and put his hand into his pocket, pulling out a little black box. 'I believe this is yours.' He walked back over and took her hand and placed the solitaire ring on her finger.

Evie looked at the ring adorning her finger as it glinted in the electric lamplight. 'Are you sure you still want me to have this?'

'More than ever,' he answered, kissing her lightly on the lips.

Evie quietly opened the bedroom door and peered in. 'Mam?' she called softly.

Edith half raised herself. 'Yes?'

'Can I sleep with you, please?'

Edith smiled in the darkness. 'I'd like that.' She pulled back the covers and helped Evie to snuggle down beside her.

'Are you all right, Mam?'

'It's me that should be asking you that.'

'I'm fine. Bewildered, confused, but fine,' Evie said, placing her arm around her mother. 'This reminds me of when I was a little girl,' she said, snuggling up closer.

'Mm,' Edith mumbled. 'We used to do this a lot. Florrie even used to at one time.'

Evie felt her mother's sadness and hugged her tighter. 'I don't blame you for anything, Mam,' she said softly. 'It must have been a terrible life for you.'

'Oh, not so terrible.' Edith sighed deeply. 'It took me a long time to get over Freddy's death and I knew that I would never love anyone else, so I made my life around you two.'

They both lay in silence for a moment.

'Mam?'

'Yes?'

'How did you come by the wool shops?'

Edith gave a little laugh. 'Oh, that was your Uncle Richard and Auntie Frances. I was working in the shop part-time when it was a little haberdasher's. The old lady who owned it wanted to sell up and I was concerned about losing my job. Frances tried to persuade Richard to buy it and install me as the manageress. Instead he bought the shop for me under a fictitious name, handed me the keys and told me to make a go of it. I changed it into a wool shop and business boomed. How on earth Father never found out is beyond me, but a relief. He would have disinherited Richard for what he had done. The rest is history. I worked my heart out and found myself in a position to expand. I had to keep my ownership a secret in case it got back to Father's ears, for Richard's sake.'

'Oh, Mother.' Evie sighed. 'I thought it was because you didn't trust me.'

'Evie, you can't realise how many times I've wanted to tell you and take you into my confidence, but it was too risky. Your grandfather is not a man to meddle with. I suppose I'm glad in a way that he lost his chance to get his hands on you.'

'Is he really that bad?'

'Yes, Well, he was anyway. I don't know if he's mellowed at all with age. Richard and I don't talk about him.'

'What about my grandmother?'

The silence that invaded the room was deafening, until

Edith finally took a deep breath.

'Your grandmother, bless her heart, was a wonderful lady, kind, caring and the soul of discretion, until my father made her a nervous wreck. He criticised everything she did until eventually she didn't dare change her underwear unless he gave her the go ahead.' Evie felt Edith's body stiffen. 'It broke her when my father disowned me. She thought I should follow my heart and be damned with the rest. She used to come round to Tudor Road, that's where we lived then, and see us. My father found out and just about committed murder. She never dared come again after that and it was the end of her. Her health quickly deteriorated and she died.' Edith sighed deeply. 'My father caused the death of the two people who were most dear to me and for that I'll never forgive him.'

Evie felt tears trickle down her cheeks.

'You know it all now, Evie. There's nothing else I've kept from you. We must try and put it all behind us.' Edith kissed her. 'I know this has all been a great shock, and it will take some getting used to, but you and Edward have to build your lives and get on with the future. The past is gone, dead and buried, and it must stay like that if you're to have any chance of making a life for yourself. I just hope for Edward's sake that Charles will let things lie, because if he doesn't he'll lose his son.'

'D'you think he will, Mam?'

Edith frowned deeply in the darkness. 'No,' she answered with conviction.

Evie closed her eyes. 'The past has a funny way of catching up with you,' she whispered under her breath.

'Sorry, what did you say?'

'Nothing, Mam.'

Edith lay still for a moment. 'Evie, why did you think that Richard was my lover?'

Evie gulped and took a breath. She described the night she found the photograph in her uncle's office.

'Oh, Evie! Your inquisitiveness will be the death of you.'

'Yes, but at least it has answered two questions that have been bothering me for ages.'

'What are those?'

'Well, now I understand why I've been moved through the factory and up into the office. That must have been you and Uncle Richard's doing.'

'Ah, but wait a minute, Evie. We might have had a hand in it, but you were given opportunities because of your own hard work. Richard has been keeping an eye on you, I admit, but he felt very strongly that you were wasted in the factory. You proved that by picking up the ropes so quickly and applying yourself. If you hadn't been worthy, you would still be on the factory floor, packing boxes.'

Evie smiled in the darkness at her mother's words.

'What was the other question?' Edith asked.

'Where you go to on your Saturday nights out?'

Edith laughed. 'Not to meet my lover, I can assure you. I go and visit Richard and Frances.'

'Mavis and I were right then.'

'Oh, yes. About what?'

'That you were too old to have a lover.'

'You cheeky thing.'

'Oh, Mam, I do love you.' Evie hugged her mother tightly.

Edith felt a warm glow creep slowly through her body. 'I love you too, Evie,' she whispered.

* * *

Richard sat back and patted his stomach. 'That was grand, gel.'

Edith beamed. 'So glad you enjoyed it, sir. Pity Frances couldn't come. I hope her mother gets better soon. Now, would anyone like some more apple pie?'

Everyone groaned in protest.

'Oh, well.' Edith looked down at the half-eaten pie. 'Your supper tomorrow night, Evie.' She laughed at her daughter's expression. 'Shall we all retire into the living room for coffee? We'll tackle these dishes later. Now that the meal is over we can get down to business.'

'That was a most enjoyable meal, Mrs Grayson, thank you,' Edward told her.

Edith smiled. 'You're more than welcome.'

Richard led the way through and they all sat down and made themselves comfortable. Edith poured the coffee and passed the cups round.

Edward gave a small cough and perched himself on the edge of the settee. 'I went to see my father this morning and tried to talk to him.' He paused, aware that three pairs of eyes were resting on him anxiously. 'I'm afraid my visit was useless.' He shook his head in sorrow. 'He wants nothing more to do with me unless I give up Evie.' He bent his head and rubbed his fingers over his forehead. 'I must admit, his reaction has upset me badly.' He looked across at Edith. 'I do love my father even though he's being stubborn over this matter. I really did try to reason with him.'

Evie placed her hand on his and gently squeezed it. Richard took out a cigarette and lit it and leaned forward to accept the ashtray that Edith offered him.

'As I said last night,' Edward continued, 'I won't give up Evie, so I packed all my belongings and I don't intend going back. My father made his feelings pretty clear and I left him in no doubt about mine.'

Richard blew a cloud of smoke into the air. 'Edward and I have already discussed this matter at length. I'm quite happy the lad knows what he's doing.'

'Yes, and thanks for the offer to put me up. But I think it better I stay with a friend, while I find a job and get a flat or something sorted out.'

'Job?' Evie queried.

'I can't continue working for my father, can I?'

'No, I suppose not.'

Edward took a sip of his coffee. 'I've given matters a lot of thought and spoken to Richard. There is one thing I would like to do.'

'What's that?' Evie asked.

'I'd like us to get married as soon as possible.' He turned to Evie. 'That's if you have no objections? Or you, Mrs Grayson?'

Evie gasped. 'I haven't! Mother?'

Edith shook her head and smiled. 'I think, if you have decided, I see no point in waiting.'

Evie grabbed Edward's hand. 'Don't worry, Edward. I can support us while you're looking for work.'

A slow smile formed on his lips. 'I don't think there'll be any need for that.'

'Why?' She looked hurt. 'Lots of wives support their husbands.'

'You don't understand, Evie. Money is no problem. My grandfather left me over ten thousand pounds when he died and I haven't touched it yet. So we'll survive.'

Evie looked at her mother.

'I'd like a few days to decide just what road I'm going to take. I'd like to go into business for myself,' Edward continued, smiling over at Richard. 'I have asked your uncle's advice and he thinks my plans are sound enough. I would like to add that I have been thinking for a while of going it alone.'

'Well, my job will keep us going until you get on your feet.'

Richard told her, 'We both think it would be best if you left Dawson's now this has all come out. It's surprising how news like this gets round and things could get difficult for all of us if my father gets wind of it.' He grimaced. 'If he and I become estranged, it would be a catastrophe. He's far too crippled with arthritis to run the business, and I have over four thousand employees to worry about.'

'Yes, I see.' Evie thought for a moment. 'I'll start looking for a new job tomorrow.'

'You won't need to do that, Evie,' Edward told her. 'We'll be married soon, so you needn't bother about working.'

Evie raised her head sharply. 'Oh, needn't I? What am I expected to do then?'

'Well, er . . .'

'Edward Bradshaw, if you think I'm staying at home, you'd better think again.'

'Evie!' Edith warned.

'Mam!' Evie turned to face her mother. 'You made me go to College to better myself and if you think I am going to waste all my experience and vegetate at home, then you can *all* think again. Edward will need me if he's going it alone. I'm quite capable of running the office side of any business!'

'Evie, no wife of mine is going to work,' Edward snapped. 'What will people think?'

'Sod what people think! Is that what you really want, Edward, for me to waste all my talents? I really thought you'd changed. You're still as narrow-minded as when we first met.' She stared straight into his eyes. 'If we are going to make a success of this, you're going to have to treat me as an equal partner.'

'She's right, you know.' Richard spoke slowly. 'It's a big venture you're undertaking, Edward, and Evie could be a help. You need to be together in this.'

'I agree,' Edith said, looking at them both. 'Lots of women go out to work now and it would be a shame to waste all Evie's hard efforts.'

Evie smiled at her mother. 'Thanks, Mam.'

'Yes, well. We'll see how things go.' Edward turned to Evie and placed his hand on her arm. 'Although it would be nice for us to work together, I really like the idea. Only it seems strange . . .'

'Oh, you'll soon get used to me bossing you about, Edward.'

'I thought you said equal?'

Evie smiled. 'Yes, I did.'

He rubbed his hands together. 'Yes, it's going to be a lot of hard work and fun. I should think between us we know all there is to know about the hosiery trade. Yes, I like the idea,' he said with enthusiasm.

'And I'll help all I can,' Richard volunteered. He looked across at Evie and grinned. 'Although I doubt you'll need any help with the way you handled the Grady business.

You saved my skin, Evie, in more ways than one. I was a fool to put all my trust into that man and I nearly paid dearly for it.'

She smiled. 'It taught me a lot too.'

'Well, let's hope we all learned a lesson,' he said grimly.

Edith leant over the side of the chair and picked up her handbag. She opened it and rummaged about until she found what she was looking for. She pulled out a red book and gave it to Evie.

'I think you should have this.'

Evie frowned as she bent over and took the book from her mother. It was a bank book and Evie gingerly opened it. She gasped.

'Mother!'

Edith smiled. 'It's all yours. Every penny you gave me to save, plus your board money and some I've added myself.'

Evie looked down at the book again. 'But there's over three thousand pounds here!'

'I know,' Edith answered. 'I did the same for Florrie. I kept adding to it so you would both have something when you married. Florrie's book is in the bureau,' she added softly.

'Oh, Mam.' Evie bit her lip as a tear fell down her cheek.

'I suggest you give it to Edward,' Edith said sternly. 'Else it will all go on clothes if I know you, our Evie.'

'It won't,' she retorted, then smiled. 'She's right. Here, you'd better have it.' She handed the book to Edward.

He refused it. 'Oh, no. If you insist on working with me, you can start by helping with the finances.' He rubbed his hands together. 'Now, our wedding. Where would you like to get married, Evie, and when?'

She was silent for a moment. 'I'd just like a quiet wedding in the Register Office, please.' She looked at her mother. 'D'you mind, Mam?'

'Not if that's what you want.'

'It is.'

'It makes no difference to me,' Edward said, 'as long as Evie is happy.' He turned and looked at her, love in his eyes. 'As we are both unemployed, we could go and set a date tomorrow. Okay?'

'Okay.' Evie breathed ecstatically. She turned to her Uncle Richard. 'Will you give me away, please?'

Richard's chest swelled with pride. 'I'd be delighted, absolutely delighted.'

Evie clasped her hands together. 'A dress. I must have a new dress.'

'What did I tell you, Edward? You'd better change your mind about that bank book and quick,' Edith said, trying her best to sound stern and formidable.

They all laughed in unison and spent the next few hours making plans for the wedding and their future, until it was way past the time for Richard and Edward to leave.

The next morning, Edith rose early. She had a mission to accomplish and felt very nervous about the prospect. She bathed and dressed very carefully in a smart navy blue, A-line suit and matching pill box hat. She looked hard and long into the mirror, nodded in satisfaction and let herself out of the house.

When she arrived at her destination, she walked briskly through the tall iron gates, pushed open the door to reception and entered. Edith took a quick look round and walked over to the receptionist's desk. She looked up.

'Yes?' she asked brusquely.

'I want to see Charles Bradshaw, please.'

'Do you have an appointment?'

'No.'

'Well, he won't be able to see you then. I suggest you ring up and make an appointment with his secretary.' The receptionist dismissed Edith by returning to her typing.

She stood transfixed for a moment, staring stonily at the young girl who looked up again and glowered at her.

Edith glowered back. 'I suggest you ring his secretary and tell her I would like to see Charles Bradshaw,' she quietly demanded.

The receptionist gave a deep, uninterested sigh and picked up the telephone. 'Who shall I say is here?' she asked nonchalantly.

'Edith Grayson.'

The receptionist mumbled something into the telephone and waited. She nodded twice and put down the receiver.

'I'm sorry, he's busy,' she said, smiling sweetly.

Edith straightened her back, turned and headed towards the stairs. She stopped and turned back towards the receptionist. 'I suggest you telephone and say I'm on my way up.'

'Oh!' The receptionist rose from her seat. 'You can't do that,' she said in alarm.

'Can't I?' Edith said crossly. 'Watch me.' She turned back and walked quickly up the three flights of stairs until she came to a door marked PRIVATE. She pushed it open and was met by an irate woman.

'You can't come in here. Mr Bradshaw is busy,' she bristled.

320

Edith pushed past the woman and made her way to a heavy wooden door marked C. BRADSHAW in large black letters. The woman grabbed her arm.

'I told you, you can't go in there.'

Edith shook her arm free and stared at the woman angrily. 'Listen, I have come halfway across town to see Charles Bradshaw and I'm not going away until I have.' She rapped on the door loudly and turned the handle.

Charles looked up at her as she walked into the large, lavishly furnished office. His mouth gaped as he realised who it was and he jumped up in astonishment. 'You!' he exclaimed, his face dark with anger. He turned to his quivering secretary, hovering behind Edith. 'What's the meaning of letting this woman in here? Show her the door immediately.'

Before the secretary could take action, Edith calmly walked up to Charles's desk and sat down in a comfortable leather chair placed before it. She pulled off her gloves and placed them over her handbag.

'I'm not leaving, Charles, until you hear what I have to say,' she said serenely.

He stared at her, his mouth opening and closing in protest. Finally he looked over at his secretary. 'Get out of here,' he bellowed.

The secretary hurriedly left and closed the door firmly behind her.

Edith looked up at Charles. 'Still playing the ogre, I see.'

His eyes bulged. 'Well, what d'you want?' he demanded savagely.

Edith slowly tilted her head to the side. 'Let's cut the polite chat, Charles. We both know why I'm here.'

'Do we?' he answered sarcastically, slowly sinking into his chair.

'Yes, we do.' Edith spoke firmly, looking him straight in the eye. 'Your son and my daughter.'

Charles stared stonily at her as he leaned forward, clasped his hands together and rested them on the desk. 'My son is no concern of yours, and I thought I told you I never wanted to see you again?' he snarled. 'I don't know how you've got the nerve . . .'

'Oh, cut the dramatics, Charles. What happened between us was over twenty-five years ago.' Edith crossed her legs and relaxed back in her chair. 'Let's face it, you didn't give two hoots for me. It was your pride that was hurt. You were only marrying me to please your father and mine. If you're honest, you'll admit you had a lucky escape. You and I weren't right for each other and you know it. Christ, we couldn't even agree on what picture to see at the cinema.'

Charles grimaced. 'That's beside the point. You jilted me on the eve of our wedding . . .'

'Yes, I admit I did that, but I paid for it, didn't I?' She narrowed her eyes and her voice was icy. 'You lost Freddy the job in the mill.'

Charles lowered his head. 'It's only what he deserved.'

'No. It's not what he deserved, and you know it. Freddy did nothing to you. It was me who wouldn't marry you. Your action contributed to his death and I'll never forgive you for that.' She paused. 'So, Charles Bradshaw, I think we're even, don't you?'

She watched as Charles sat back in his chair and raised his eyes to meet hers. His face was still with anger.

'My son is nothing to do with you.'

'He is, when he's going to marry my daughter,' she snapped. 'And he is, you know. Your threats to cut him off will make no difference.' She paused for a moment. 'Tell me, Charles, do you really want to lose him? He's a fine boy and worthy of better treatment than this. If you don't give a damn about him, think of your wife. Don't let her suffer because of your selfishness. It's not fair, Charles. What happened in the past between you and me is nothing to do with Edward, Evie or your wife, and it's not fair that they are being made to pay because of your stubbornness and pride.' She paused and eyed him thoughtfully. 'Think of the future, Charles, and what it would be like without your son. Never seeing him again. Never seeing any children he might have. Don't forget, they'll be your grandchildren.' She stopped and stared intently at him.

Charles stared back at her as the impact of her words hit home. Finally he sat back in his chair again and sighed. 'You're right, Edith. I've harboured a grievance against you for years, an unwarranted grievance, so I just hit the roof when Edward sprang his announcement.' He shrugged his shoulders. 'I was hoping, you see, that he would settle for a friend's daughter. It was bad enough him wanting to marry someone else, but when I realised who Evie was, I just saw red.'

'Oh, Charles, history repeating itself.' She shook her head. 'You didn't really think a man like Edward would marry someone just to please his father? Kids these days won't be dictated to. And shouldn't love come into it somewhere? She paused and took a breath. 'I know she's my daughter, but Evie's a fine girl and will make Edward a good wife.'

'Yes, I'm sure she will, and she's attractive too, just

like her mother.' He smiled wanly. 'I've been a stupid man, Edith. I've ruled my family with a rod of iron and I know they're all frightened of me.' He met her eyes. 'I do love them all, you know. I just find it very difficult to show it.' He put his face in his hands and groaned, 'Oh, what a mess.'

Suddenly, Edith felt sorry for the man facing her, the one she had hated all these years.

'It's not too late, Charles.'

'Isn't it?'

She shook her head. 'No, it isn't. You have to learn to let up a bit. For a start, you could contact Edward and make things up with him. I know that's what he really wants.'

'Is it?'

'Of course. Do you really think he's happy about this situation? Oh, Charles, come on. You're the lad's father, he loves you.'

'I haven't slept since the argument, but I just could not bring myself to do anything about it. Adele and Geraldine are barely speaking to me. It's been a nightmare.'

'Well, put matters right, before it's too late.'

'I will, Edith, and thank you. It must have taken a lot for you to come here,' he said. 'I'm not the easiest man to approach.'

She laughed. 'No, you're not. But I was angry, very angry over what you were doing to Edward.'

'You always did have a temper.'

'You remember, then?'

'Oh, yes.' Charles nodded his head. He paused and looked at her fondly. 'I did love you, you know. And you hurt me terribly.'

She shook her head. 'No, you never loved me, Charles. You believed you loved me for your father's sake. It was he and my father who pushed us together, just like you tried to do with Edward and your friend's daughter. And it's wrong.'

'Yes, I know, and I've paid for it.'

'You will come to the wedding, won't you?' she asked tentatively.

He took a deep breath. 'If Edward wishes me to.'

'Oh, I'm sure he'll be delighted, and so will Evie.'

'And you?'

'Of course. We must try and be friends for the children's sake. Let's put the past behind us and start again.'

'I'd like that, Edith, and I'm sure Adele will. I want you to know, I've always regretted what I did to Freddy about that job. If I'd have known the consequences . . .'

'It wasn't all your fault,' she interrupted. 'My father was the real culprit, you just put the lid on the matter.'

'Yes, but if I hadn't lost him that job maybe he wouldn't have . . .'

'We'll never know,' she cut in sharply. 'And, as I said before, we have to let the past lie. Nothing will bring Freddy back to me. We have to think of our children now, they're the ones who matter, and I'm sure if I'm willing to forgive . . .'

Charles sighed loudly and clasped his hands together. 'You're a fine woman, Edith. A fine woman, and I have a lot to thank you for.'

'Just make it up with Edward, that will be thanks enough for me. I just want to see those two kids happy.' She picked up her bag and smiled at him. 'I must be going. I have a wedding to arrange. It's just a family affair at the

Register Office with a small reception at the Saracen's Head Hotel. That's what the children want.' She pulled on her gloves and stood up. 'Edward will tell you the arrangements.'

He stood up and walked round the desk to her. He put his hands on her shoulders and kissed her lightly on the cheek, and watched thoughtfully as she walked out of his office.

Edith made her way quickly down the stairs, stopped and leaned briefly against the wall. She sighed deeply with relief, straightened herself up and continued on her way.

'I can't believe it.' Edward addressed Evie across the kitchen table. 'My father's a different person.' He looked over at Edith who was drying the dishes. 'He's completely changed his mind about everything. He seems delighted about the wedding and has even offered to make me a full partner in the business.' He shook his head in bewilderment. 'I can't take all this in. It's like a miracle. When I told Mother and Geraldine, they just cried.'

Edith smiled as she bent her head over the sink.

'I'm so glad, Edward,' she said softly. 'You must feel so relieved about his change of heart.'

'Oh, yes, I do. The argument with him broke me up. I know I tried not to show it, but it did.'

'They're all coming to the wedding,' Evie said delightedly. 'How do you feel about that, Mam?'

'I'll be fine. I'm just so pleased everything has worked out.'

Later that night, Evie popped her head round her mother's

bedroom door. She walked over to the bed and sat down.

'It was you, Mam, wasn't it?'

Edith put down the book she was reading and looked at her daughter. 'What was?'

'Getting Edward's father to change his mind. I know you're behind it and I just wanted to thank you. It must have taken a lot of courage.'

Edith smiled and took her daughter's hand. 'Go to bed, Evie. You have a lot to do before the wedding.'

She bent over and kissed her mother on the cheek. 'Thanks, Mam. I do love you.'

'So you keep saying. Now get out of here, I've just got to a good part in my book.'

Evie stood up and smiled fondly at her. She left the room, closing the door gently behind her.

Chapter Thirteen

Edith crept down the stairs and tiptoed into the living room where she walked over to the windows and threw open the curtains. It was far too dark to tell what kind of day it would be. She shivered. It was certainly cold. She knelt down in front of the fire and gently raked out the grate. Pulling out the ash tray, she picked it up and made her way quietly to the kitchen. She stopped abruptly and frowned as she spotted a shaft of light under the kitchen door.

'Evie, what on earth are you doing up at this time in the morning? It's only half past six. You should still be in bed.'

Evie smiled. 'Like you, I couldn't sleep.'

Edith looked hard at her daughter. 'How long have you been up? This room's quite warm.'

'Half an hour or so.' Evie smiled. 'I can't believe that in a few hours' time I'll be Mrs Edward Bradshaw.'

'Neither can I,' Edith sighed. 'I shall miss you.'

'Miss me!' Evie giggled. 'We're going to be living with you until we find a house.'

Edith shrugged. 'I know. But you'll leave eventually and I'll miss you then.'

'Oh, Mam.' Evie smiled warmly at her mother. She

looked at her intently for a moment. 'Are you upset we're not getting married in church?'

Edith smiled. 'I suppose a little bit of me is. I would have liked to see you walk up the aisle dressed all in your finery, but to be honest, I've realised over the years, Evie, that it's not where you marry but whom, and I've no doubts about Edward. He'll make you a fine husband.'

Evie's face lit up in delight. 'Yes, he will, and I'll do my best to make him a good wife.' She rose from the table. 'Come on, I'll make us some toast. I suddenly feel very hungry.'

She placed a plate of hot buttered toast on the table along with a pot of tea. Edith picked up a piece of toast and took a large bite.

'Evie?'

'Mm?'

'I've been thinking.' Edith spoke slowly. 'How about coming to help me in the shops on a full-time basis, whilst Edward looks for premises and secures the equipment for your new business? There's not much you can do at the moment on that side. I'll pay you, of course.'

Evie looked at her mother with interest. 'I think I'd like that. What would you want me to do?'

'I thought you could help me with the books – the end of the tax year is coming, it'll be good experience for you – and maybe you'd like to do a bit of serving to cover for sickness or holidays.' Edith noticed Evie's eyes light up. 'I'd also like your thoughts on some new ideas I have. Those other ones you suggested went down a treat.'

'Sounds great. Thanks, Mam.'

'My pleasure.' Edith smiled. 'It'll be nice having you

on board. I enjoyed it when we did all the stocktaking together.'

'So did I,' Evie answered. She looked up at the clock on the wall. 'It's only seven-thirty and Mavis and Jenny aren't coming until nine. I could just as easily have gone to the hairdresser's, but Jenny insisted on doing my hair and Mavis wants to make sure I'm dressed properly.'

'Jenny's as good as any hairdresser I know,' Edith said. 'I've asked her to have a go at mine as well.'

'Wise choice, Mam. She'll make you look a treat. But watch her with the sugar and water spray – she's lethal.'

Mother and daughter both laughed, then a serious look crossed Evie's face.

'What's the matter, dear? Not second thoughts, I hope?'

Evie looked up sharply. 'What? Oh, no. Definitely not. I was just thinking, that's all.'

'What about?' Edith asked in concern.

Evie sighed deeply. 'Florrie. I was just thinking about Florrie.'

Edith placed her elbow on the table and rested her cheek in her hand. 'What about her, dear?'

Evie sighed again. 'It sounds stupid really after all she's done and the way she treated us, but I miss her, especially today.'

Edith smiled wanly. 'I understand perfectly what you mean. Whether we like it or not she's part of our lives, and I suppose always will be.'

'I hope she's all right,' Evie said sincerely.

'She's fine, Evie,' Edith answered.

Evie stared at her for a moment. 'How d'you know?'

'I made it my business to find out.' Edith paused for a second. 'I went to see her.'

'You went to see her?' Evie repeated in bewilderment.

'Yes. I know what I said before, but I still couldn't stop myself from feeling I had failed her somehow.' She sighed deeply. 'They came back to Leicester. She's living with Grady in a terrace in Braunstone Gate.' She lowered her head. 'The walls are running with water and they share a toilet with four other families.'

'Oh, God,' Evie muttered.

'Grady is working as a pot man in the pub next door, and as far as I know Florrie hasn't got a job.' Edith shook her head sadly. 'I was appalled at how low she has sunk for the sake of that man and begged her to come home. I even told her all about your wedding and asked her to come. I know I should have asked you first,' she said apologetically, 'but it doesn't matter anyhow because she spat in my face and said she would sooner dance on my grave than go to your wedding.'

'Oh, Mother.' Evie's shoulders sagged. She exhaled loudly and sat upright in her chair. 'Her downfall was her own doing.'

'No, it wasn't, Evie. It was her grandmother that turned her. If only I had explained to her about her mother and father, maybe things would have been different.' Edith took a deep breath. 'I shudder when I think how long she must have known just who I was.'

'What d'you mean, Mam?'

'Well, she must have found out that I was a Dawson. How she did is beyond me, I was so careful, but why else would she wreak her vengeance in that way? She started to work at Dawson's right from leaving school. I never steered her in that direction like I did you. She applied for the job voluntarily, wouldn't try anywhere else. She must have been plotting for years and I never had the slightest suspicion. Oh, Evie, I brought that girl up from a baby and it breaks my heart to see what she's come down to. I even tried to give her the bank book, so at least they would have some money. After all, it is hers. But she threw it back at me. The venom that came out of her mouth was disgusting. I just had to leave. I couldn't stand it any more.' Edith sighed deeply. 'I tried. Believe me, I tried.' She bowed her head. 'I've changed my will, Evie. I can't take any more. I've cut her out completely. Whatever Florrie's share of my estate would have been, I have donated to the Westcoates Maternity Home, so they can buy equipment for sick babies.'

Evie's eyes filled with tears. 'Mother, I think that's a good idea, and as far as I'm concerned you did more than most people would have.'

Edith looked at her for a moment, the pain she felt showing in her face. 'No, Evie. I didn't do enough. But no more of this. Today is your wedding day and it's going to be the happiest day of your life. So, come on, my girl. I want you to go and have a nice long soak in the bath while I make the fire.' She stood up and looked fondly at her daughter.

'Yes, I will, Mam. It'll give me time to gear myself up for the onslaught of Jenny and Mavis.' Evie laughed as she stood up, pulled her dressing gown belt tighter and headed for the door.

Four hours later, Edith, Mavis and Jenny clasped their hands in delight as Evie stood before them dressed in her wedding attire. Edith walked forward and kissed her daughter on the cheek, love and pride shining out of her eyes.

'You look beautiful,' she breathed. 'Edward will be so proud.'

Evie took one more look in the mirror. She took a deep breath of satisfaction and turned back, a delighted smile on her face. 'You've all done a grand job,' she said, gently patting her hair. She ran her hand down the ivory satin costume. The fitted jacket was edged around the collar and cuffs with matching Nottingham, handmade lace. The skirt was straight and finished just below her knees, flattering her long, slender legs. Her copper hair was dressed loose and cascaded down to her shoulders. On the back of her head sat a garland of tiny yellow roses cleverly sewn on to a net veil which covered her eyes. 'Mother, this suit was a perfect choice, and you've done a great job of taking up the hem, Jenny.'

'My pleasure. I'll send yer the bill later.'

Edith smiled at her quip as she headed for the door. 'I'd better go and check the fire.' She departed, leaving the three friends together.

'Not long now,' Mavis said, looking at her watch.

'No.' Evie's face lit up as she clasped her hands together. 'Oh, I feel like I'm in a dream.'

'Well, you'll soon wake up when yer 'ave to wash Edward's dirty underpants and cook for him morning and night,' Jenny grimaced.

'Trust you!' Mavis frowned. 'Let the girl get married first, then we'll tell her the hard facts of life. By the way, Evie, do you need any advice about tonight?'

'Tonight! Oh, Mavis, don't you start. I've had enough of my mother trying to tell me the facts of life. I can cope by myself, thank you.'

'Oh. She knows it all, Mavis. She doesn't need our

'elp,' Jenny chided. 'Just make sure yer don't act too eager. Edward might think 'e's married a wanton woman.'

'Jenny! Stop it. You're making me embarrassed.' Evie spoke sharply, going red in the face. 'And stop putting more lipstick on. It's an inch thick already.'

Jenny pursed her lips as she looked in the mirror. 'Just making sure I look nice and provocative.'

'Who for?' Mavis asked. 'I thought you said Kevin couldn't come to the wedding because he was working.'

Jenny turned and looked at Mavis. 'I never asked Kevin.'

'Why not?' Evie piped up. 'The invitation was for both of you.'

'I know it wa', but Edward's mates will be there won't they? I wouldn't 'ave gone to all this trouble over me new dress and coat for Kevin.'

Evie and Mavis looked knowingly at each other.

'Jenny, I give up on you.' Evie smiled.

'Well, you 'ave to keep your options open,' she said seriously, grabbing her bag from under the bed. 'Come on, let's go downstairs and gerra drink. I certainly need one. It's fair wore me out gettin' you three all tarted up. Anyone would think we were going to a wedding or somethin'.'

Evie looked up into Edward's eyes and paused for a second before she whispered, 'I do.'

He took her hand and held it firmly between his strong fingers as they both heard the Registrar pronounce them man and wife. Then Edward took Evie in his arms and kissed her deeply. They drew back and looked at each other.

'I love you so much,' he whispered.

'I love you too,' Evie responded softly.

They both turned to face the small congregation of family and friends, gathered in the plainly furnished, oak-panelled room. Evie turned to kiss her mother and Edward to shake his father's hand. Edward spotted his mother out of the corner of his eye, wiping a tear from her cheek. He winked at her and smiled reassuringly. Evie placed her arm through his and they walked slowly out into the April sunshine.

The room upstairs in the Saracen's Head was not over large and housed the small wedding party comfortably. The landlord had prepared a sumptuous buffet and was now presiding over the private bar. Edward's friends were taking it in turns to select the music that played continuously on the gramophone, making sure their choices reflected the ages of all the guests gathered.

'How do you feel, Mrs Bradshaw?' Edward asked his new wife as they waltzed together around the room.

Evie gazed lovingly up into his eyes. 'I'm the happiest woman alive, Edward. I will never forget this day, never.'

'Well, you won't have another wedding day, I shall see to that,' he said firmly before a grin spread across his face. 'The ball and chain is all ready. I'll make sure it's just long enough for you to reach from the sink to the stove and back to the table.'

'Edward! If I thought for a minute you were serious . . .'

'You'd what?'

'Nothing. I love you too much to do anything.'

They danced past a trestle table groaning under the weight of the many presents given to them by their respective families, friends and well wishers. Evie's eyes scanned the crystal glasses, dinner services, and all manner of articles that filled the table. Her heart warmed to think that they were both so well thought of.

Her eyes alighted next on a group of people talking near the bar. She smiled. A warm glow enveloped her body as she took in the figures of her mother, Uncle Richard, his wife Frances and Edward's father and mother. They were laughing and chatting together, and she saw Edward's father place his hand on Richard's shoulder as he addressed him.

'I'm so glad your mother and father are here,' she said.

Edward followed her gaze. 'So am I.' He paused. 'By the way, Father has had the papers drawn up by the solicitors. I have to sign them on Wednesday, then I shall be a full partner.'

Before Evie could answer, Jenny glided up and gently pushed her out of the way. 'Excuse me,' she said sweetly, 'I want to borrow your 'usband for a minute.' She turned to Edward. 'I want you to introduce me to 'im over there.' She nodded in the direction of a tall, good-looking man standing in the corner of the room drinking a pint of bitter.

Edward looked at Evie, who grinned slightly as she shrugged her shoulders in amazement.

'Be my guest,' she laughed.

Evie walked away and went to join her mother.

'All right, Mam?'

'Fine,' Edith answered. 'Thank you for the bouquet of flowers, they were a lovely thought. Adele was delighted with hers too. They must have cost a fortune.'

'That was Edward's idea,' Evie said quietly, 'but they're not enough to thank you for all you have done for me over the years, or Mrs Bradshaw for Edward.'

'Your happiness is payment enough,' Edith said, smiling.

Then she frowned slightly. 'What's Jenny up to with Edward?'

'Oh, she's taken a fancy to one of Edward's friends and he's making the introduction.'

Edith shook her head. 'She doesn't waste any time, does our Jenny.' She scanned the room again and her eyes settled on Mavis sitting quietly in a corner, deep in conversation with a fair-haired man. 'I must say, Mavis's young man seems nice enough.'

'Yes, he does. But I don't think she will get married again in a hurry. She wants to be really sure this time.'

Edith nodded. 'I hope young Geraldine's as sensible. That girl has danced with all of Edward's friends, and she's going round them all over again now.'

'Good for her!' Evie laughed. 'She's such a nice girl, and if it's all right with you, I'd like to ask her to dinner one night.'

'That's fine with me, but why don't we ask them all and make a do of it?'

'That would be great, Mam, and I'll do all the cooking.'

Edith grimaced. 'We'll see.'

They were both suddenly interrupted by Richard.

'Come on, little sister, let's have a dance.' He pulled Edith's arm and guided her on to the dance floor.

Evie watched as they attempted to rock and roll, the brand new craze hitting the ballrooms. Edward came up and sat beside her.

'Did you make the introductions, then?'

'I didn't need to. Jenny did all the talking. Anyway, Mrs Bradshaw, we'll have to be going soon.'

'Going!'

'Yes, going. I've booked us into a hotel for the night.

Somewhere where no one will find us. Just me and you.'

'Oh, Edward,' she cried. 'Where? Tell me or I won't go!'

He frowned. 'Looks like I'll be spending the night by myself then.'

She nudged him with her elbow. 'A surprise. I love surprises. I hope it's somewhere nice and expensive.'

'It certainly is.' He took out his wallet and checked his cash. 'Hope you've got your purse handy.'

Evie nudged him again and grinned. 'Edward Bradshaw, there's one thing I do know, and that's that I'm not paying for my own honeymoon.'

He leaned over and kissed her on the lips. 'It's all booked and paid for and I've ordered breakfast in bed,' he told her in a low voice. 'Now, I'm not telling you any more, except to say that it's a pity it's only for one night. But I promise you, as soon as possible we will go away for two whole weeks. Anywhere you wish.'

'Oh, Edward.' Evie clasped her hands together. 'I'll have to go home first and pack.'

'That's all taken care of. Our overnight cases are behind the bar, courtesy of your mother and mine. They're the only ones who know. We'll slip away when no one is looking.'

'You are wonderful, Edward,' she laughed, kissing him on the cheek.

'I know. You got a bargain when you landed me.' He stood up and pulled her to her feet. 'Come on, let's go and have a drink with our families.'

He guided her over to the bar. Evie noticed Frances's anxious expression.

'Anything wrong?'

'Yes, there is.' She turned to Evie. 'Richard has just had a telephone call. My mother has been taken ill and we'll have to go home, I'm afraid. I'm just trying to convince Richard that there's no need for us both to go. I can drive myself there and he can come home later in a taxi.'

'We'll drop Richard home,' chipped in Charles. 'Edith, you can go with Edward and Evie.'

Edith and Adele looked at each other. Edith gulped. 'Er . . . no. I'll get a taxi. Edward and Evie won't be coming home tonight.'

Charles slapped his son on the back. 'I understand, lad, no need to say any more.' He looked at Edward knowingly, and much to his annoyance Edward blushed. Geraldine bounced up and placed her arm through her father's.

'What's going on?'

'Oh, Frances has to go home because her mother's ill and we're just making arrangements for the rest of us.'

'Well, don't worry about me. I'll cadge a lift with one of Edward's friends.' Geraldine frowned. 'Don't look like that, Father. I'm twenty-one and old enough to find my own way home.'

Charles nodded reluctantly and turned back to the others. 'That's settled then. Edith and Richard can come home with us and Edward and Evie can get their own taxi to wherever it is they're going.' He paused and pursed his lips together. 'I hate to tell you this, folks, but we'll be in Edward's car. He insisted on driving us all here this morning. I did offer the Daimler, but it was declined.'

'There's nothing wrong with my car, Father. You know I only wanted to use it so I could concentrate on something other than the wedding.'

'Yes, we noticed!' Adele laughed. 'We nearly ended up

at the cemetery, he was so nervous.'

Edward blushed again as he handed his father his car keys.

'Well, now that's all settled, maybe we can get on and enjoy the wedding,' Charles said. 'Sorry about your mother, Frances, but we'll get together soon. When these two love birds have settled we'll have a dinner party, eh, Adele?'

'Yes. I'll telephone you to make the arrangements.'

They all said their goodbyes to Frances. Evie kissed her on the cheek.

'Thanks for coming, and we'll see you soon.'

Frances hugged her newfound niece. 'You don't know what a difference this has made to Richard and me. I just feel sad for all the years we've lost out on.'

'Me too, but we've plenty of time in the future to get to know each other.' Evie smiled. She hugged Frances again and watched as Richard escorted her to the door. He kissed her on the cheek and made his way back towards the others.

Edward pulled Evie aside. 'We'll slip away too.'

She nodded in agreement. 'I'll just say cheerio to my mother.'

'No, don't. You'll see her tomorrow. Let's just go, while no one is looking.' He signalled to the landlord who discreetly brought over their cases. Evie took Edward's hand and they stole down the stairs.

Evie stood at the bottom of the bed and stared at her husband. He was sitting with his back propped against the snow white pillows in the four-poster bed. He put his arms behind his head and watched her intently, a smile playing on his lips. Evie let her new silk négligée slip slowly to the ground. A slight smile formed around the corners of her mouth. Edward looked at her hungrily. He took in her slim body, her firm breasts pressing against the silk nightdress and the outline of her slender thighs. Slowly he pulled back the covers, inviting her to join him. She accepted, slipping her long legs as gracefully as possible between the cool sheets. Her feet touched his bare leg and she withdrew them quickly. Edward smiled at her reassuringly. He drew her towards him and their lips met. Evie pulled away slightly.

'Thank you for bringing me here,' she whispered. 'The Bridal Suite of the Grand Hotel. It must have cost a fortune.'

'It did,' he said softly, 'but you're worth every penny.' He drew her towards him again and his hand slipped down the thin straps of her nightdress. He found her breast and Evie sighed in ecstasy.

Edward groaned and turned over as a loud banging noise reached his ears. The banging stopped and he snuggled closer to Evie and placed his arm around her, pulling her against him. The banging started again and he forced open his eyes. It was still pitch black and he fumbled for the bedside lamp. He blinked several times as the light blinded him. His watch showed the time to be just after three-thirty. He realised the banging was coming from the outer door and frowned as he looked quickly at Evie. She was peacefully asleep, a look of blissful contentment on her face, and he smiled as he remembered their uninhibited lovemaking of a few hours earlier.

He slid out of bed, grabbed his dressing gown and padded towards the door. He opened it hesitantly and looked startled as the ashen face of the night porter was revealed. Edward stepped into the corridor, half closing the door behind him.

'What's the matter, man? It's three-thirty in the morning.'

Evie sighed contentedly as she slowly opened her eyes. She reached out her hand and frowned as she realised she was in bed alone. She rubbed her eyes and sat up.

'Edward?' she said softly, spotting her husband sitting in a chair, staring out of the window. 'Edward?'

Getting no response she climbed out of the bed and tiptoed towards him. She quickly realised by the look on his face that something was dreadfully wrong. She knelt before him.

'Edward!' she said in alarm. 'Whatever's the matter?'

He slowly turned his face towards her. Fear gripped her heart as she took in the marks of tears. Slowly he lifted his hand and ran his finger tips down her cheek.

'Evie . . . oh, Evie,' he muttered.

'Edward! For God's sake, what's wrong?'

He gulped. Tears welled up in his eyes as he leaned forward and grabbed both of her hands.

'There's been an accident. A terrible accident.'

She caught her breath. Her chest tightened as suddenly she shivered with impending doom.

'Accident?'

Edward nodded. 'The car. My car. It crashed.'

'Crashed!'

'Yes.'

'My mother!' Evie pulled her hand free and clasped it over her mouth. 'Edward, my mother . . .'

He slid to the floor and grabbed hold of her, hugging her tightly.

'She's dead, Evie, and so is your Uncle Richard.'

Her screams could be heard echoing round the hotel as she and Edward rocked backwards and forwards, locked together in overwhelming grief.

Chapter Fourteen

Evie slowly opened her eyes and focused them. Her face was drawn and ashen from lack of sleep. She stared at her husband who was standing forlornly by her bed.

'How's your father?' she whispered.

He hung his head. 'Not good, Evie. I get the impression the doctors don't expect him to pull through.'

Her body sagged. 'We can only hope for a miracle.'

'Yes.' He nodded slowly. 'That's all we can do at the moment.' He looked at his wife enquiringly. 'Did you get any sleep?' he asked as he sat down gently on the bed and took her hand.

'Sleep? Is that what it's called?' She looked at Edward for a moment and her face softened. 'I'm sorry, I didn't mean to snap at you. It's just that I keep thinking I'll wake up from this nightmare.' She sniffed loudly. 'I can't believe that only four days ago we were all dancing at our wedding, and now Mam and Uncle Richard are . . . are dead. Oh, Edward, it's just too awful. When will the pain go away?' she looked to him for comfort.

He shrugged his shoulders sadly. 'I don't know, my love. But people do say that once the funeral is over . . .'

'Funeral!' Evie looked at him in alarm. 'Oh, Edward, I'm dreading the funeral. I can't bear the thought of them putting my mother's body into the ground. I can't bear the thought that I'll never see her again.' Tears flowed like a river down her cheeks. Edward pulled her towards him and she buried her head in his chest.

The last four days had been torture for both of them. The police were still uncertain how the crash had happened but what they did know was that Edward's car, being driven by Richard, had ploughed into a wall at the bottom of a hill as they had taken a short cut towards the Bradshaws' home. Edith and Richard had been killed outright. Charles had been thrown out of the back seat with the force of the smash and had sustained terrible head injuries as he hit the stone pavement. Adele was lucky. She had only a few bruises and a small cut on her forehead. But the horror of that night would live with her forever.

Evie pulled herself away from Edward and wiped her eyes on the sheet.

'I heard a knock earlier on. Who was it?'

'The police,' he answered quietly.

Evie looked at him in concern.

'They say the crash happened because the brakes were faulty,' he said gravely.

Evie clasped her hand to her mouth. 'I don't understand. What do you mean, the brakes were faulty?' she asked in shock. 'You had the car in the garage last week because it had been standing so long while you were away in the army. You said it had been checked all over.'

'I know. That's what I can't understand. But the police are adamant that they failed. They say the brakes had no fluid in them.'

'What does that mean?'

'It means, Evie, that somehow all the brake fluid had

leaked out. I'm as confused as you are. The police are going round to the garage to check over the service report.' He gave a deep sigh and shook his head sadly. 'Whatever is found won't bring them back.' He slowly stood up. 'Come on, you have a bath. They'll all be arriving in a couple of hours and I have to collect my mother and Geraldine.'

Evie smiled wanly as tears filled her eyes again.

'Don't worry, Evie. I know it's going to be terrible but I'll be with you.' Edward bent over and kissed her lightly on the cheek before he left the room.

The two funerals were being held a day apart. Edith's was being held first and it had been agreed that Evie and Edward would not attend Richard's funeral because of the trouble it would cause with her grandfather. The procession was to leave Edith's house at eleven o'clock and Frances had insisted the mourners come back to her house after the service. Evie had organised the caterers.

The kitchen door slowly opened and Evie ran forward and embraced her aunt warmly. 'Oh, Auntie Frances, how are you?' she asked, pulling back from the embrace and taking in her aunt's gaunt face.

Frances had aged over the last few days and it was obvious that she hadn't slept since the accident happened.

'Bearing up, I suppose,' she answered, trying to smile. 'How about you?'

Evie shrugged her shoulders. 'How do you explain how you feel at a time like this? There's no words strong enough.' She sighed deeply. 'I feel in limbo, as though the world is moving round me. I want to stop everyone and shout at them: "Hey, you, I've lost my mother. How dare you carry on as though nothing has happened?'''

Frances nodded in understanding as she pulled off her black gloves and sat at the kitchen table.

'I'd like to thank you again for having us all back to your house after the service, although I'm sure it's more of an ordeal than you're making out. You still have tomorrow to get through as well,' Evie said with a lump in her throat.

'It's the least I can do, Evie, and I think that's what Richard would have wanted. He loved his sister,' Francis said softly. 'Anyway, it's given me something to occupy my mind.'

Evie leaned over and kissed her aunt again. 'Everyone is in the living room, Auntie Frances.'

Frances shook her head. 'I'll stay here, if it's all right with you. I can't face anyone at the moment.' She opened her handbag and pulled out a handkerchief. 'It's the nights that are the worst. It's so lonely in that bed.' She blew her nose loudly and looked at Evie pitifully. 'It was such a senseless accident. It wasn't as though Richard was drunk or anything. He's never been a drinker and had only had a couple of shandies. That's why he insisted on driving. Charles had had quite a few, you see.'

Evie walked over and placed her arm around her aunt's shoulders.

'It wasn't his fault,' she said softly. 'The brakes failed. The police are still looking into it.'

'Oh!' Frances said, her face full of confusion.

'I'll make you a cup of tea. The hearse won't be here for a few minutes yet,' Evie said without emotion. She suddenly felt old and tired and prayed that she could make it through the next few hours.

* * *

Evie felt Edward's hand tighten its grip on hers as they watched the pall bearers lift the coffin and proceed slowly down the aisle of the church. She vaguely remembered hearing the Vicar drone his way through the service. As the hymns were being sung, her throat had dried and she was obliged to mouth the words. She turned as the coffin passed her. Mavis and Jenny were weeping uncontrollably in the pew behind, hanging on to each other for comfort. Evie gripped Edward's arm as she felt her legs buckle beneath her. He turned and looked at her, his ashen face twisted in pain. They sidled out of the pew and down the aisle, supporting each other as they slowly followed the coffin.

Evie stopped abruptly. To the side of the large wooden church doors sat a man in a wheelchair. His legs were covered by a black woollen blanket. The top half of his body was bent over and although Evie was standing quite a distance away from him, she could still make out the gnarled hands, with their enlarged knuckles, clutching the blanket. He spotted Evie and stared at her stonily. He motioned to the nurse standing at his side. She took hold of the wheelchair handles and pushed him outside.

Evie's eyes narrowed and her mouth set grimly. She knew the man was her grandfather. She felt a tremendous rage surge through her body and struggled to catch her breath.

'Evie?' Edward's eyes bored into hers, concern and worry written all over his face. He had not seen the figure in the wheelchair and wondered why his wife had stopped so abruptly.

Evie stared at him for a moment. With a great effort

she managed to force her lips into a brief smile. She clutched his arm tighter as they continued their long journey out of the church.

Two hours later Evie stood in the doorway, nursing a large glass of sherry, and looked round the room. Her late Uncle Richard's house was large and comfortably furnished with a lived-in charm about it. At any other time Evie would have been able to sit down in one of the inviting armchairs and tuck her feet underneath her as she relaxed against the large soft, chintz-covered cushions. But today she felt anything but relaxed and wandered round the house in a daze.

Edward sat huddled between his mother and sister and she could see the look of anguish written on their faces as they tried desperately to gain comfort from each other. Edward sensed she was looking at him and glanced across at her. He shrugged his shoulders slightly in apology at leaving her on her own. She smiled wanly back and turned and walked into the dining room. Standing before the French windows she stared out into the large landscaped garden that was just coming into bloom, and tightly clenched her fists.

She wanted to scream – long, loud, bloodcurdling screams that would shake everyone and make them listen to her. She wanted to talk about her mother. Instead she had endured polite conversations on all sorts of subjects bar the one she wanted to talk about. She could stand it no longer. The anguish and pain of the senseless accident built up to fever pitch inside her. Clutching her handbag, she ran up to the bedroom, grabbed her coat and raced out of the house.

Evie bent her head against the wind and walked and

walked until her legs felt like lead. She stopped abruptly. Before her were the gates to the cemetery. Dusk was falling now and she pulled up the collar on her coat. The cemetery looked cold and forbidding and a mist was beginning to form between the trees. She took a deep breath and walked inside, dragging her feet along the path leading to her mother's grave. She stood before the heaped mound. Evie had demanded that her mother's body should not be laid to rest in the Dawson vault, she could not bear the thought that eventually her grandfather would join her, and Edward and Frances had agreed.

Her mother's grave was beneath an old oak tree and she could hear the wind whistle eerily through its leaves. She shivered and dug her hands further inside her pockets. The grave was now devoid of the wreaths and bouquets of flowers that only a few hours ago had covered the large mound. Many of the tributes had been sent from people she had never heard of, and it warmed her for a brief moment to think that her mother had been so well respected. Now the hospital would benefit from their generosity.

She hitched up her skirt and knelt on the damp grass by the side of the grave. She picked up a handful of earth and clutched it in her fingers. Grief overcame her and she doubled over, clutching her stomach as the tears rolled down her cheeks.

'Oh, Mam,' she sobbed. 'I miss you.'

She finally straightened up and wiped her face on her handkerchief, took a deep breath and stood up. She froze as she heard someone cough behind her. Turning abruptly, she peered into the darkness. Sitting on the bench on the other side of the path was Florrie. She had her arms folded and her face set grimly.

351

'Florrie!' Evie said the name in astonishment. She slowly walked over and sat down next to her. She looked at her sister for a moment before she spoke.

'It's good to see you, Florrie.' She took a deep breath and sighed deeply. 'It's awful about Mam, isn't it? But it's comforting for me to see you paying your last respects, although you should have been with us this morning.' She paused for a moment and looked hard at Florrie. Her face softened. 'You look terrible. Mam's death has hit us both badly, hasn't it?' She placed her arm round Florrie's shoulders. 'Let's forget about the past. Mam wanted that more than anything. Let's try, Florrie, please, for her sake?' she pleaded.

With a sudden jerk Florrie shook Evie's arm free and started to laugh – a low menacing laugh which quickly rose to an hysterical pitch.

Evie stared at her in bewilderment. 'What's the matter with you?' she asked, frowning deeply.

Florrie stood up and walked over to the grave. She turned and stared at Evie, a sly smile playing on her lips. Evie stood up and followed her.

'Florrie, just what are you doing here?' she asked.

Her sister stared at her.

'I asked what you are doing here,' Evie said again in the same tone.

'Well, it's not paying my last respects,' Florrie said coldly. 'More like gloating.'

'Gloating!' Evie repeated in disgust. Her mouth set grimly as the truth dawned on her. 'I might have known. Nothing has changed with you, has it, Florrie? You're still the same nasty, spiteful woman you ever were. In fact, I think you've got worse if that's possible.'

'You've no idea what levels I can sink to to get what I want,' Florrie said icily.

'Well, you've had your fun. Now get out of here. You're not fit to be near my mother,' Evie shouted.

'Oh, I'm not leaving until I've accomplished what I set out to do,' Florrie hissed. 'I followed you from the house. I knew you'd come here.' She raised her hand and struck Evie on the shoulder. She stumbled back, her face wreathed in astonishment as Florrie continued: 'You should have been in that car as well as her – then I would have got you both. Instead, that excuse for a man you married had other ideas. You've always been a lucky beggar, Evie, but we're on our own now. There'll be no one to save you this time.'

Evie steadied herself. 'Florrie, what on earth has got into you?' Her voice was uneven as fear stole over her.

Florrie took a step forward and pushed her again. This time Evie's heels stuck in the wet mud and she fell back with a thud against a mound of earth. Florrie's hysterical laughter echoed around the deserted cemetery.

'You really don't know, do you?' she said, a menacing smile on her lips. 'It was me.' She raised her head defiantly. 'I killed her,' she announced proudly.

'You killed her?' Evie whispered disbelievingly.

'Yes. And you should have died with her. Then I would have got everything.' Florrie prowled backwards and forwards in front of Evie. She held her head high and clenched and unclenched her fists. 'I fixed the car while you were all cavorting at the Saracen's. It was easy. It's surprising what you can find out from people who are out of work and have no money. I drained all the brake fluid out.' She stopped her pacing abruptly and stared at Evie, her eyes wide in triumph. 'I thought it was rather clever myself.'

Evie felt all her breath leave her body and gasped for air as the impact of Florrie's words sank in.

'It was you!' she shouted, as she clawed at the earth and pulled herself awkwardly up. 'You murdered my mother and Uncle Richard. But why, Florrie? Why?'

'Why!' she shouted angrily. 'The Dawson family killed my father. The money we stole was his blood money.' She stopped, her eyes blazing in fury.

Evie's anger mounted to fever pitch. 'Freddy Grayson was not your father,' she spat. 'Your mother lied to him. Nobody knows who your father was.'

'You liar!' Florrie screamed. 'How dare you blacken my mother's name? He was my father! He was! Stop lying!' Florrie shook uncontrollably as she gasped for breath. 'You've always had everything. Edith showered everything on you. As long as little Evie was all right, then life was fine. But what about me, eh? Nobody cared about me, least of all Edith. She put up with me on sufferance.'

'How dare you! My mother treated us both the same and you know it,' Evie shouted. 'She promised Dad she would look after you, and she did – even though you belonged to neither of them. She could have put you in a home, but she didn't. She kept you and brought you up as her own daughter, and for that you killed her.'

'Stop it,' Florrie snarled menacingly. 'I won't listen to you. I won't!' She put her hands to her ears. 'She had to die. You put a stop to our plans, didn't you, little sister? You ruined everything. Just like Edith did when she married my father. You've nearly killed Horace. We were going to live in luxury in Spain. Instead, he's on the verge of a nervous breakdown, and I can't have that, can I? I can't have the person I love ending up in a mental home because of you and her.' She inclined her head towards the grave. 'Edith signed her own death warrant by inviting me to your wedding. She even told me the time and place, the stupid woman. The rest was simple. And once I get rid of you and get her money, me and Horace can carry on with our original plans. I'm in the will, you see,' she said smugly. 'Edith took great pains to tell me that.'

Evie's body shook as uncontrollable rage filled her. 'My mother cut you out of her will. You'll get nothing. Nothing!' she shouted. 'You killed her for nothing!' Her voice rose in hysteria as she stepped forward and pushed Florrie hard with the flat of her hand. 'My mother loved you. You repaid her by being nasty and spiteful. You treated us both like dirt and now you're telling me you murdered her for your own greed. You bitch!'

Evie lunged forward and grabbed Florrie by the hair. She swung back her other arm and smacked her across the face with all the force she could muster. Florrie reeled backwards. She fingered the side of her face where Evie had struck her, and laughed. She quickly put her hand in her coat pocket and pulled out a flick knife.

'Try that again,' she snarled, brandishing the knife backwards and forwards in front of Evie, who paled at the sight.

'You really are mad. Do you honestly think you'll get away with this?'

'Why not? I've got away with the others. Why not you?' Florrie lunged forward and the knife caught Evie's hand.

She stared at the blood as it oozed out of the deep cut the knife had caused. She raised her head, and the women's eyes locked. Florrie inched forward, the knife stained with Evie's blood glinting in the moonlight. Evie stepped back and stumbled on the mound of earth that she had previously fallen over. She regained her balance and stepped to the side.

'Don't do this, Florrie,' she pleaded.

Florrie continued to step slowly forward, her face twisted in hatred. Evie's back came up against a solid object; she was trapped against the oak tree and Florrie was upon her. Evie froze as she heard rustling behind her.

'What was that? Someone's behind the tree.'

Florrie grinned. 'Don't try that one, Evie. Think I'm stupid or something? There's no one around for miles. You can scream as much as you like. No one will hear you.'

Suddenly, the trauma and pain of the last few days overtook Evie and she felt all the fight drain out of her body. Her life flashed before her as she closed her eyes and waited.

Suddenly, there was a loud wail of protest followed by a thud. Evie, shaking in fear, felt a strong hand grab her wrist and she was pulled forward. Gingerly she opened her eyes. Her legs buckled as Edward caught her in his strong arms.

'It's all right, Evie.' He pulled her towards him and held her tightly. 'I've got you. Nobody will ever hurt you again.'

She shook uncontrollably. 'Oh, Edward, she killed my mother,' she sobbed.

'I know,' he whispered.

Evie raised her head and looked round. Florrie was being manhandled away by two policemen. Evie looked at

Edward enquiringly. He put his arm around her and guided her towards the path.

'Come on. Let's get you home and I'll explain everything.'

Evie shivered in the armchair. The thick blanket and hot cup of tea could not quell her fear and anger after the ordeal she had just faced.

Edward looked at her, his face white with concern. 'How's the hand?'

She gave a watery smile. 'It's okay,' she said as she fingered the bandage. 'It could have been a lot worse. But how did you know where I was?'

He smiled. 'Frances saw you run out of the house and thought you might need me. I caught sight of you at the bottom of Groby Road. I noticed someone following you and saw it was Florrie. She was acting very strangely and it worried me. So I hung back and followed you both.'

He grinned. 'God, Evie, you walked for miles. Then I realised you were heading towards the cemetery. As you stopped in front of the gates, Florrie slunk behind a tree. It was then that I realised something was wrong. Luckily, there's a police box just outside the gates, so when you had both gone inside, I rang them. They told me not to do anything but wait. God, it seemed like a lifetime before they arrived, and I was worried sick about you. I knew you'd be at your mother's grave, so the police and I crept up there. We heard most of her confession, but the policemen wouldn't let me move until they caught her fully in the act.'

He paused and wrung his hands together. 'I was frantic, I felt sure Florrie would hear us.' He smiled wanly. 'You did. I went to make a move when you came up against the tree we were hiding behind, but one of the policemen stopped me.'

'That was you! The rustle I heard was you? Oh, Edward, if only I'd known you were there. I thought I was going to die.'

He sighed. 'I'm just glad Frances saw you leave, else I dread to think what would have happened.' He paused and looked at her. 'Florrie's mad, you know?'

She nodded sadly, then started to shake while tears ran down her cheeks. 'I can't understand it, Edward. I can't understand how she deliberately planned to kill my mother . . . and me. It's not as though it was done on the spur of the moment. To actually plan it . . .' She wiped the tears away on the back of her hand and took a deep breath. She shook as she spoke, her voice low and icy. 'I want to kill her, Edward. I want to put my hands round her throat and see the life drain out of her.' She raised her head and her eyes blazed in anger. 'I hate her, and I hope she rots in hell for what she's done,' she said savagely.

'She will, Evie. Be assured of that.' His eyes hardened. 'All I can say is that it was a good job the police were with me or I dread to think what I would have done.'

Evie took a long drink of her tea. She jumped as the telephone let out its loud shrill ring. Edward dragged himself out of the chair to answer it. After a few moments he appeared in the doorway. His body sagged and he leaned on the doorknob for support as he looked across at Evie.

'That was the hospital,' he said as his eyes filled with tears. 'My father died a few minutes ago.'

Chapter Fifteen

It was four weeks after the death of Edward's father, four weeks in which the newlyweds had tried to come to terms with their grief and put the pieces of their lives back together. Edward walked slowly down the side of his late mother-in-law's house and threw open the back door.

'Well, that's it,' he groaned as he pulled off his overcoat and threw it on the back of the chair. Evie replaced the lid on the pan of potatoes she was holding and put them down. She walked over to where Edward was sitting and stood before him. He looked up at her and frowned. 'The company is almost bankrupt and the creditors are moving in.'

She pulled out a chair and sat down. 'It's really that bad, eh?' She sighed. 'What are we going to do?'

'There's not much we can do. I can't believe it myself. Apparently, there hasn't been a substantial order for any of our garments for over two years. Father just got deeper and deeper into debt with the bank, and now he's gone they want their money.' He paused and sighed deeply. 'They don't think I'm up to running the company. Too young and inexperienced, they said.'

'Oh, Edward.' Evie sighed loudly. She thought for a

moment. 'What about the money we have? What if we put all that in?'

He shook his head. 'No good, I'm afraid. What we have is just a fraction of the overall total.'

Evie rested her elbows on the table. 'What if we sold the shops?' she said softly. 'I wouldn't mind, honestly, if it saved the business . . .'

He smiled at her. 'No, Evie. We can't do that. Besides, they want the money now.'

'What! They won't wait while we try and raise it?'

'We can't raise over a hundred thousand pounds, Evie. We have no chance, and the bank knows it.'

'A hundred thousand pounds? Phew!' she said in astonishment. 'That's an absolute fortune. How come your father owed that much?'

'Easy,' Edward sighed. 'He had wages to pay, maintenance on the machines, raw materials and other overheads. And with hardly any money coming in, he borrowed heavily from the bank. He also owes quite a lot to his suppliers. He put up the business as collateral, thinking things would work out. A couple of big orders would have set him on the right road. Instead he died, and now the bank wants the business.' Edward folded his arms. 'No wonder he got so crotchety and bad-tempered with all this hanging over him, and he never said a word. He let us all carry on thinking we were comfortable and the business thriving.' He banged his fist on the table. 'Now I know why he was so desperate for me to marry Sophie Gold. Put Gold's and Bradshaw's together and the company would have been saved. Gold's would have carried us until we picked up.'

'But Bradshaw's have been established for years. What happened?'

'Father turned all production over to supplying the Military with uniforms during the war, and afterwards for the men doing National Service.' He gave a brief smile. 'He said it was his bit for King and Country. Of course, our old customers went elsewhere for their goods and when the Military contracts started to dry up we had no other products to offer. Father apparently brought in a whole new team of design experts, but the larger outlets were quite happy with their new suppliers and wouldn't give us a chance. We had let them down once and could do it again.' He shrugged his shoulders. 'Dawson's did very well out of us. They picked up a lot of our old customers.' He scratched his chin and grimaced. 'I suppose there's always someone willing to jump in. If it hadn't been Dawson's, it would have been another company.'

Evie looked downcast and sighed deeply. 'Oh, I wish my mother was here. She'd know what to do.'

'Well, she's not and nor is my father. We have to sort this one out ourselves. But how? That's the problem.'

'I'm worried about all the people who will lose their jobs.'

'So am I. Some workers have been with the company all their lives and in some cases the whole family works for us, but I'm afraid there's nothing I can do about it,' he said, shaking his head sadly.

'No, I suppose not. You've done your best.' Evie looked startled for a moment. 'What about your mother? Will she lose the house?'

'No, thank goodness. Father put it in her name about four years ago and she's some money of her own. I just hope there'll be some left over for her after the business has been sold. The bank is planning to auction all the machinery and equipment and then sell the buildings separately.'

'How is your mother, did you have a chance to pop in today?' Evie asked.

'Yes. I went before my appointment with the bank manager.' Edward sighed. 'She's bearing up. It's hit her badly though, you can tell she's still not sleeping properly. Your Auntie Frances was with her. It's good to see them becoming friends, they'll be a comfort for each other.' He shook his head. 'It's such a shame about the circumstances.' He gave a quick smile. 'I've asked both them and Geraldine to come for tea on Saturday night, is that okay?'

'Yes, of course.' Evie smiled. 'They're all welcome any time, you know that.'

She stood up and went over to the stove. She picked up the pan of potatoes, added a knob of butter and started to mash them with a fork. She turned to Edward.

'Have you any ideas on what we could do?'

'Ideas? Yes, I've a few.'

'Good.' She sighed with relief. 'Let's have our dinner before it gets cold then we'll go into the living room and talk.'

He stood up and walked over to her, putting his arms round her waist and pulling her close.

'Good idea. Whatever it is, it smells wonderful.'

'It should do. I've spent ages making it from the recipe book Jenny gave us as a wedding present.' Evie lifted a saucepan lid and peered inside. 'It's supposed to be Coq-au-Vin, but it looks more like chicken stew to me.' She laughed. 'Anyway, whatever it is will be ruined if you don't get out of my way.'

They ate their meal, which surprisingly turned out to be

quite palatable, and retired to the living room.

'Do you want a glass of beer or a shandy? We've no lemonade, but I can pop to the off licence for some,' Edward asked.

Evie finished drawing the curtains and smiled over at him. 'No, thanks.' She walked over and settled herself in her mother's old armchair and drew her legs up underneath her. 'Well, Edward Bradshaw. Tell me about these ideas?'

He stretched out his own legs and leaned back against the cushions. 'I think we should pool our resources and go it alone. I know a little factory for rent on Tudor Road.' He paused. 'What are you smiling at?'

'Oh, nothing. Just the mention of Tudor Road. We used to live there many years ago. It seems like a good omen.'

'Did you?' Edward looked interested. 'Well, anyway, I might be able to purchase one or two machines from the auction and other bits we need. Between us we have the expertise to run the business. All we really need is some good designs and first-class garments to sell.' He cradled his glass between his hands. 'I want to build up an unbeatable reputation for quality. If we promise to deliver on a certain date, then we will. And our garments will be perfect. No loose threads hanging, no seams coming apart, no buttons missing. I want us to be the best, Evie. I want people to be begging us to supply them.'

'You're right, Edward. When I worked in Customer Queries, most of the complaints were about late deliveries – and I mean late. Sometimes we were weeks and weeks overdue, and we had no end of stuff returned because of poor finishing.'

Edward nodded. 'Bradshaw's was just as bad.' He paused. 'Of course, we'll be a small company to start with, but as soon as we have established ourselves we can expand.'

Evie clasped her hands together. 'Oh, Edward, I feel so excited. This is going to be an exciting venture.'

'And a lot of hard work.'

'I don't mind that. I'm used to hard work. But promise me something?'

'What's that?'

'Just don't bung me down in the cellar to sort out all the files. That was my worst experience ever.'

Edward laughed. 'I promise. Besides, we'll have office juniors to do jobs like that.'

'No, we won't,' she retorted. 'We'll treat all our staff like human beings.'

'When we get some. For a start, it will be you and me and a couple of machinists, and of course a first-class designer.' Edward stared down into his glass. 'Now where on earth are we going to get one of those, for hardly any pay?' He frowned, deep in thought.

Evie let a slow smile spread across her face. 'I know,' she said smugly.

'You do?' He looked up in astonishment. 'Who?'

'I'm not telling you. Just leave it with me. I'll talk to her tomorrow.'

'You never cease to amaze me, Evie Bradshaw. How on earth do you know a designer?'

'I'm not telling you, you'll have to wait and see.' She eased herself up and walked over to the cocktail cabinet. 'Another beer?'

'Please.'

Evie's face clouded over.

Edward looked at her in concern. 'What's the matter?'

'With all this, I forgot to tell you,' she began as she

handed him his beer and walked over to the fireplace. She picked up an envelope. 'I had a letter this morning.' She handed the envelope to him.

Edward took it and pulled out the contents. He studied the piece of paper, folded it and placed it back inside the envelope. He looked at her closely.

'Are you going?'

'No,' she answered sharply, 'and if you ask me, he has a damned nerve asking – no, demanding – that I go and see him.'

'He is your grandfather,' Edward said gravely.

'He's no grandfather of mine, not now or ever,' she said through clenched teeth. She looked hard at Edward for a moment. 'Are you saying I should go?'

'That's up to you, Evie. But it wouldn't hurt to go and see what he wants. It must be something important or why bother?' Edward paused for moment. 'It could be that he wants to make things up. After all, you're the only family he has left.'

Evie sank slowly down on to her chair. 'I don't feel I can face him, not after what he did to my mother and father. He's an evil monster, he must be, to cut off his family like that, and I can't for the life of me think what he wants.'

'Well, as I said, Evie, the decision is yours and I'll stand by you, whatever you decide. You have a day or so to think about it.'

'Oh, of all the cheek,' she said angrily. 'He even had the gall to make a precise appointment. You think he would have the decency to ask me to drop in at my own convenience, wouldn't you?'

Edward shrugged his shoulders. 'Just think on it, Evie.

You don't have to go.' He held out his arms and yawned. 'How about an early night?'

She forgot her immediate problem and smiled at her husband. 'After you do the dishes.'

'Oh, Evie!' he responded. 'Okay, you wash, I'll dry, and then I'll scrub your back in the bath.'

'Just what are you doing?' Evie asked Jenny as she sat on her bed the following evening.

Jenny was sitting at her sewing machine, which was wedged between the bed and the wall. She peered intently at her sewing as she chatted to her friend.

'I'm sewin',' she said sharply.

'I can see that, but what are you sewing? Whatever it is, it looks most peculiar.'

Jenny finished the seam she was working on and cut the thread. She held up the beige material and smiled. 'Oh, these are for me granny. She's always complainin' of the wind whistlin' round the tops of 'er legs. So I've made these for 'er.' She held up the shapeless material and saw Evie grimace. 'I know they look funny but they don't when they're on. 'Ere, I'll show yer.'

Jenny pulled up her skirt, revealing her slim legs which were encased in a laddered pair of stockings and suspenders that had seen better days. One suspender had popped and the back half of Jenny's stocking was hanging down her leg. Evie hid a smile as she watched her friend pull on the strange-looking garment.

'See.' Jenny looked at Evie in triumph as she wriggled her backside from side to side. 'They're drawers, but not the old-fashioned baggy kind. They're ones that'll cling to yer legs and keep out the draughts. Good, ain't they?' she said as she smoothed down the legs of the drawers to hide her stocking tops.

'Amazing!' Evie responded. 'I wouldn't mind a pair myself for winter.'

'I'll make yer some. But not in this awful colour, somethin' more bright and cheerful, and I'll put some lace round the edge to make 'em more sexy.' Jenny giggled. 'I'm makin' a sort of vest top to make a set.'

'You are clever. Whatever made you think of an idea like that?'

'I told yer, me granny.' Jenny pulled off the drawers and pulled down her skirt. 'Now, Evie Bradshaw, you ain't come 'ere to look at me granny's new drawers.'

'No, I haven't. I came to see how you are, and . . . to ask you something.'

'Oh. If it's money, I ain't got none!'

'That'll be the day, when I ask you for money!' Evie laughed. 'No, I came here to bounce an idea off you.'

Evie spent the next twenty minutes going through Edward's plans. Then she sat back and looked hard at Jenny.

'Well, what d'you say? 'Course, we couldn't pay you much to start. I wondered if you'd do the designs after work? Then, when we really get going, we could hopefully offer you a full-time job.' She leaned forward and clasped her hands together. 'Say you will, Jenny. You're the most talented person I know and this will be a wonderful opportunity for you to see your designs come alive.'

Jenny sat back and pursed her lips. Her eyes twinkled and she smiled. ''Ow can I refuse, eh? 'Ere.' She bent down and pulled out a large folder from under her bed and threw it at Evie. 'Take a gander at them and tell me what yer think. If yer like any of 'em, I could make up a sample. 'Course, you'd 'ave to buy me the material and cottons, 'cos I'm broke at the moment.'

Evie leafed through the book, gasping in delight at every page she studied.

'Jenny, these are wonderful,' she breathed.

'Not bad, I suppose.' Jenny smiled, hiding her pleasure at her friend's compliment.

'Can I show them to Edward, please?'

'Be my guest.' Jenny shrugged her shoulders nonchalantly.

Evie shut the folder and placed it next to her handbag so she wouldn't forget it when she left.

'How are things going with Nigel?' she asked. 'Did you see him again after the wedding?'

Jenny's eyes took on a glazed look and she exhaled loudly. 'Nigel . . . oh, Nigel!' She looked at Evie and smiled dreamily. 'I'm in love, Evie. I'm in love for the first time. Nigel is all I've ever dreamed of. I'm so glad you got married, else I might never 'ave met 'im.'

Evie hid a smile. 'You're always falling in love.'

'Oh, but Evie, it's the real thing this time.' Jenny clasped her hands together. 'Honest, I ain't never looked at another man since I met 'im.' She looked at her bedside clock. 'You'll 'ave to go soon, I'm meeting 'im tonight.'

'Oh, chucking me out, eh?' Evie chided.

'Yes, if yer put it like that. Even me greatest friend wouldn't stop me from seein' Nigel.'

Both women smiled fondly at each other. Jenny looked closely at Evie and frowned.

'Anything up, me duck? You ain't really yerself yet, are yer?'

'I'm all right, thanks. I still keep thinking Mam will

walk through the door, but Edward assures me that will pass. He's been wonderful, even though he's lost his own father.'

'I 'ope that Florrie is committed good and proper,' Jenny said angrily. 'She don't deserve to walk wi' decent people.'

'She's committed all right. Carlton Hayes. The biggest and most secure mental home for miles around.' Evie bent her head. 'I had to sign the papers myself. D'you know, I felt nothing when I signed them? Just relief that she wouldn't be able to harm us again.'

'Not that you should 'ave felt anythin' – the bitch deserves 'anging if you ask me.' Jenny looked closely at Evie again. 'That's not all, though, is it? There's somethin' else botherin' yer. Come on, tell yer Auntie Jenny?'

Evie smiled wanly. 'You always were astute.'

'A' what?'

'Astute. Crafty,' Evie answered. 'You always know when something's not quite right. And you're right this time.' She paused and lowered her voice. 'I had a letter from my grandfather.'

Jenny's mouth dropped open. 'What, the old geezer that owns Dawson's?'

'Yes. He wants to see me.'

Jenny laughed. 'Phew! Cheeky buggar. I 'ope you told 'im where to get off?'

'I haven't told him anything yet. I haven't made up my mind whether to go or not, although I get the impression Edward thinks I should, just to see what he wants.'

Jenny blew out her cheeks and raised her eyebrows. ''E could be right. 'Ave you realised, there might be money in it?'

'Oh, Jenny,' Evie scolded. 'I haven't given that a thought.'

'It's the first thing I thought of,' her friend laughed. 'Still, if yer do go, you'll have to watch that temper of yours.'

'I know. I can't promise to sit still and behave myself.' Evie rose and buttoned up her coat. 'I've still a day to think about it. The old so and so made an appointment for Thursday, would you believe, at two o'clock.'

'Besta luck,' Jenny offered.

'Thanks. If I go, I'll need it.' Evie frowned. 'How's Dawson's, Jenny?' she asked casually.

'Dawson's! Don't mention Dawson's to me. The place is in chaos at the moment. Nobody's sure what the old man's gonna do about replacin' yer uncle. All the managers 'ave the idea that they're in the runnin'. It ain't 'alf a laugh, 'cos not one of 'em is up to the job.'

'Sounds fun.' Evie smiled.

'It is. You don't know what yer missin'.'

'Mm. I think I do,' Evie said thoughtfully. She picked up her handbag and Jenny's folder. 'I'll let you know about these designs and what samples we'll need. I know Edward is going to love them.' She smiled broadly. 'It's going to be great, Jenny. Think of all the money we'll make.'

'That's the only reason I'm considerin' it. Now get off, I'm gonna be late for Nigel.'

Evie laughed as she closed the bedroom door and shouted her goodbyes to Jenny's parents.

'These are great, Evie. Are you sure Jenny's responsible?' Edward asked as he sat at the kitchen table studying the designs.

'She sure is,' Evie answered proudly as she leaned over his shoulder.

He took a deep breath. 'We're on to a winner then. She's certainly talented. I can't believe no one's spotted her before.' He looked hard at Evie. 'Do you think she'll make a sample of all of these?'

'That's some tall order, Edward. She'd be up all night for the next six months tackling that little lot. Don't forget she still has her job at Dawson's to hold down until we can offer her something better.'

He frowned. 'Mm. You're right. I'll try and pick out the best ones, although they're all marvellous.' He sighed in contentment. 'This is wonderful, Evie. With these designs we're on our way. How long d'you think it will take her to make the samples up?'

'By the time you've the factory sorted out and made loads of appointments, we should have something put together. Stop panicking, Edward. I'll give her a hand.' Evie smiled in triumph and kissed his forehead. 'I told you I knew a great designer. If I'd told you before that it was Jenny, you'd have scoffed.' She placed her arms around his neck and rested her head on his shoulder.

Edward turned and kissed her lightly on the cheek. 'Yes, I would have,' he said apologetically. He rubbed his hands together. 'I sorted out the lease on the factory. All we need to do now is get the solicitor to go over it. I also went to Bradshaw's to have a good look at some machinery. I'm off to the bank tomorrow to see what I can sort out with them. They might give me first refusal.' A broad grin crossed his face. 'We're on our way, Evie.' He looked at her gleefully. 'We're definitely on our way.' He paused.

'I'm sorry, I haven't asked how your day went? Did you manage to get round all the shops?'

'Yes.' She withdrew her arms and sat down opposite him. 'It was a bit daunting. I could still feel Mother's presence.' She paused as memories came flooding back, then mentally shook herself and smiled at Edward. 'I talked to all the staff and things are in hand. I've a couple of ideas I want to bounce off you.'

'Oh?' He looked at her with interest. 'Fire away.'

'Well, at the moment the shops are our only source of income. The money we have will soon be eaten up by all our overheads, and we have to eat.'

'Yes,' he said, nodding in agreement.

'You need me to work with you and we'll be working long hours, right?'

He nodded again.

'Well, I won't be able to spend as much time in the shops as I would like. So I got all the senior assistants together and put a proposition to them. I told them that every year end they would get five per cent of the profits, and I also made them up to manageresses. I thought with that in mind they would work harder to sell more goods, and I also asked them to think about new lines we could sell. They're in a good position to know what will move and what won't.' She paused. 'Of course, they would have to okay anything with me first. I don't want to lose control. I couldn't let the shops go down the pan, not after all Mother's hard work.' She paused, noting Edward's serious expression. 'Are you mad with me?'

'Mad! I think it's a great idea. I'm really proud of you. This means we'll be able to put all our efforts into the new business. Well done, Evie.' He leaned forward and folded his arms. 'Have you given any more thought to your other little problem?'

'I wouldn't call it little, Edward, but yes I have and I haven't made a final decision yet.'

'Well, there's not much time left. The appointment's tomorrow afternoon.'

'I know that. I'm going to sleep on it. Stop pressurising me.'

'I'm not, Evie. I'm just concerned. I told you before, whatever you decide is all right with me.' He looked at his wife fondly. Then he raised his head and looked around the kitchen, mystified. 'Hey, woman, where's my dinner?'

'At the chippy. Sorry, I haven't had the time to cook.' Evie smiled. 'I'll pay, if you fetch it.'

'Oh, you strike a hard bargain.' Edward laughed and stood up. 'One of these days I might surprise you myself with a meal.'

'Oh, yes! Since when have you been able to cook?'

'I'm a man of many talents, Evie Bradshaw. I'm a dab hand at welsh rarebit.'

She pushed him away. 'Welsh rarebit is only glorified cheese on toast. Anyone can do that,' she chided.

'Not the way I do it, Evie. You have to be an expert to burn the edges just right and when you've really got the knack, the cheese slips over the side and into the grill pan.'

She laughed loudly. 'Get up the chippy, Edward, before he sells out.'

'Yes, dear.'

Evie smiled to herself as she got out two plates and put them into the oven to warm. When Edward returned, they settled themselves into the living room, turned on the television set and demolished their supper as though they hadn't eaten for weeks.

After he had eaten, Edward realised something. 'Evie, there's one very important matter we haven't discussed yet.'

She poked a chip into her mouth and looked at him. 'Oh, what's that?'

'A name. We haven't got a name for our new company.'

She chewed on another chip, deep in thought. 'That's a real problem. A name can make or break a company. We need something that has a ring to it.' She paused and gave the matter serious consideration. 'What about Evie's Fashions? No,' she grimaced.

For the next hour the pair concocted various names until they were exhausted. Suddenly she clapped her hands together.

'I have it!' she shouted.

'Well, let's hear this great revelation then.'

'Grayshaw.' She smiled. 'Just plain and simple Grayshaw. It's a mixture of Grayson and Bradshaw, in memory of our parents. When people hear the Grayshaw name they will immediately think of our excellent designs and quality garments.'

'Grayshaw.' Edward nodded in approval. 'Well done, Evie. I like it. I like it very much. Now for God's sake let's go to bed. I don't know about you but I'm finished for today.'

They retired to bed and fell into a deep, dream-filled sleep.

Chapter Sixteen

The next morning Evie was raring to go. She had made up her mind: she would go and see her grandfather and at least hear what he had to say. She dressed very carefully in a dark blue suit with matching shoes and handbag. She bent down to straighten the seams in her stockings and stood back to admire herself in her dressing-table mirror. She nodded in approval. 'That'll do,' she said aloud. She applied a smidgen of lipstick and a touch of face powder.

At precisely one o'clock and with a sick feeling in her stomach she let herself out of the house in order to catch the ten minutes past one bus for Knighton, a select residential area on the south side of Leicester.

Alighting from the bus she searched for the address printed in gold leaf on the top of the letter. She soon found it and stood before the iron gates. The house was very imposing and at least twice the size of Edward's parents'. She took several large deep breaths, checked her face in her compact mirror, pushed open the gates and walked sedately up the long gravel drive.

The doorbell clanged loudly and Evie jumped at the sound it made. The large, highly polished wooden door was opened by a butler who frowned at her.

'Yes?' he said coldly.

Evie held her head high. 'I've an appointment with Mr Dawson,' she said, trying to control her body which was shaking violently in anticipation.

'Name?' the butler asked haughtily.

Evie narrowed her eyes at the man's attitude. 'Evelyn Gray . . . Evelyn Bradshaw,' she answered firmly.

He nodded and moved aside to allow her to enter. He pointed her in the direction of the library and asked her to wait. Before Evie had time to take in the lavishness of her surroundings, the butler had returned.

'This way,' he commanded. Without waiting for her, he disappeared.

Evie rushed from the room and found him crossing the enormous tiled entrance hall towards another door. He knocked, waited, then opened the door and stood aside, allowing her to enter. Evie paused on the threshold. Raising her head high, she walked through the door and heard it click shut behind her. Her eyes stared unblinkingly ahead. On the other side of the large room, half hidden by a large desk, sat a shrivelled old man, the same man that Evie had seen in the church on the day of her mother's funeral.

She halted in the centre of the room and waited. The old man's eyes locked on to hers and they stared at each other for a moment. Finally he spoke, his voice low and rasping.

'Sit down,' he commanded, slowly raising his gnarled hand to indicate a chair to the left of his desk.

Evie continued to stare as she took a breath.

'I'd sooner stand, thank you,' she said firmly.

'I said sit, girl,' her grandfather commanded again. His eyes narrowed and his lips formed into a thin line.

Evie's hackles rose. She stood defiantly for a moment,

then did as she was bade. She was sure she noted a slight smile playing on the old man's lips and her hackles rose even more. She eyed her grandfather closely and did not like what she saw.

'So.' He clasped his hands awkwardly together. 'You're Edith's daughter?'

'Yes,' she said icily. 'And proud of it.'

'So you should be. She was a Dawson,' Jerod Dawson snarled.

Evie clenched her hands together. 'What did you wish to see me about?' she asked. 'I'm afraid I haven't much time.'

'Oh!' Jerod gave a rasping laugh. 'Impatient – just like your mother. But I'm sure now you've taken the time and trouble to come here, you'll do me the courtesy of hearing me out.'

Evie nodded slowly.

'Fine. Then I'll get straight to the point. I've never been a man to mince my words.' Jerod unclenched his hands and sat painfully back in his chair. 'I want you and Edward Bradshaw to take over the running of the factory.' He paused for a moment. 'I'll tell you what to do and you will carry out my wishes. You'll be handsomely rewarded.' He eyed her thoroughly. 'Well?'

Evie tightened her lips as his words echoed in her ears.

'Well?' Jerod repeated impatiently.

She clenched her hands even tighter. 'You want Edward and me to take over the running of Dawson's?' she repeated to clarify his words.

'Yes, and I want you to start as soon as possible.'

'Oh, you do?' Evie said sharply, eyeing the old man angrily. 'You're really serious about this, aren't you?'

Jerod's eyebrows knitted together as he frowned. 'Why shouldn't I be? There's no one else to take over.' He scratched his chin. 'Richard was good enough, but he was too soft. He hadn't the gumption to kill a spider let alone sack a slack worker. Look how he let Grady and that supposed sister of yours walk all over him.' He grinned. 'Your quick thinking saved the day, and me a fortune. Admirable. Really admirable.' He paused and looked hard at Evie. 'I need someone in the factory who'll do exactly as I tell them.'

'And you think Edward and I fit the bill?' she cut in.

'Yes, very much so. You could do a lot worse than work for me, and of course you're family,' he said flatly.

Evie jumped up from her chair, her face white with anger. 'I've heard enough.' She turned and headed for the door, hoping her legs had enough strength in them to carry her away from this evil old man.

'Where are you going?' Jerod demanded. 'Come back here!'

Evie halted abruptly and swung round, her eyes blazing with fury.

'How dare you!' she shouted. She walked slowly back towards the desk and stood before him. 'How dare you assume that at the snap of your fingers I will jump to your commands? You're the most contemptible man I have ever met, and you're no grandfather of mine.' She clutched her handbag tightly. 'I came here in the hope that we could salvage something out of the past. I'm the only family you have left. But you don't care about that. The word "family" has no meaning to you, has it? You threw my mother aside because she dared to defy you, and you speak of Uncle Richard as though he was a piece of dirt, not your own

378

flesh and blood.' She gasped for breath. 'You use people for your own ends, then throw them away when they're no longer of any use to you.' She paused and lowered her voice. 'Well, you can go to hell, because, believe me, that's where you belong.' She gasped for breath again and desperately tried to control her temper.

A slow smile spread on Jerod's lips. 'You've got guts, girl, I'll say that for you. The last person who stood up to me like that was your mother.' He gave a gravelly laugh. 'I quite enjoyed it.' He nodded towards the chair. 'Now sit down and let's get down to some serious business.' He looked at the ornate clock on his desk. 'I've an appointment in an hour and we've a lot to discuss.'

Evie's mouth dropped open. 'You haven't heard a word I've said, have you?' she said coldly.

'Oh, I heard,' Jerod answered tonelessly. 'I'd be very careful if I were you, Evelyn. I accepted that outburst because of your bereavement, but I won't stand another,' he said menacingly. 'Now, I know you're a sensible girl, and as such I suggest you accept my proposition, because if you don't I'll see that you live to regret it.'

Evie froze as she listened in disbelief to his words.

'The one good thing that Richard did was to teach you the ropes.' Jerod quickly noticed Evie's puzzled look. 'Yes, I knew all about that. I may be crippled, but there's nothing wrong with my brain. I know exactly what goes on in the factory, right down to the number of bars of soap we use.' He cackled. 'Pity that Charles Bradshaw wasn't so astute – the man deserved to go bankrupt. I made a killing out of him, picked up some lucrative contracts while he turned everything he had over to the war effort.' He paused. 'I'm glad to see his son isn't quite so gullible. That lad's bright and has a future. I've had his background checked out and I'm pleased to say there are no skeletons in his cupboard.'

'You did what?' Evie uttered in disbelief.

'Can't be too careful, girl. Not when my business is at stake. He was away for two years in the army and at university before that. Could have got up to anything. But he's sound, and so are you. If she didn't do much else, Edith did a good job on you.'

Evie clenched her fists tightly, her knuckles straining dangerously against her skin.

'You're a monster,' she whispered. 'I wouldn't work for you if I was starving.'

Jerod looked at her in disbelief. 'You're turning me down?' He paused and eyed her coldly. 'I warn you again, girl, I'd be very careful about crossing me. If you turn down my offer, I'll make sure you suffer. I'm a very powerful man . . .'

'You don't scare me,' she said icily. 'The best thing my mother did was to get away from you, and I'm not listening to you any more.'

She turned and fled from the room, leaving Jerod staring after her. Hatred filled his face as he sat back in his chair, an evil smile playing on his lips.

'It was awful, Edward. Awful!' Evie sobbed later that night. Edward held her tightly as she buried her head in his chest. 'I've never met such a horrible person in all my life. He and Florrie could be twins. He's got no regard for human life whatsoever, and just took it for granted that you and I would jump at the chance of being his servants. I can't believe it. I can't!'

'Shh, Evie. Calm down,' he soothed. 'I wish to God I'd

been with you. The man wants shooting,' he said coldly. 'But don't you worry, we'll show that bastard that we aren't frightened of him. We'll build up our business and be bigger and better than he ever imagined, and make him eat his words.'

'Oh, Edward, I'm frightened. I'm sure his threats weren't idle. He's got a lot of clout . . .'

'Evie, he's a crippled old man. What can he do? Look, stop worrying. At least you know what he's like, and you now know what you've missed – nothing.' He held her away from him and looked at her, the love he felt for her shining out of his eyes. 'He doesn't sound the type that would have bounced you on his knee and read you fairy stories, so he's no loss, is he?'

Evie managed to smile. 'No,' she sniffed. She looked up at Edward pitifully. 'I'm sorry. It's just been a terrible shock. I never expected to meet anyone so callous, especially my own grandfather. My mam was far too kind when she described him to me. I really thought the meeting between us was to put things right.'

Edward frowned. 'I must admit those were exactly my thoughts. Still, try to forget it and concentrate on us.'

Evie smiled. 'Yes, let's. Sod the old bugger!'

'That's better. Now I want you to come and see the factory with me tomorrow and . . . guess what?'

'What?' she asked.

'I've persuaded the bank to sell me three industrial sewing machines and two overlockers plus some other bits and pieces, for a good price. They're the best ones in the factory,' he announced triumphantly.

Evie bit her bottom lip. 'Oh, Edward, I am proud of you.'

He grinned. 'And so you should be. It took a lot of cunning on my part. Now you sit down while I make you a nice cup of tea.'

He guided her towards the settee and left the room to carry out his promise. Evie, exhausted from her unexpected ordeal, sat back, pulled her handkerchief from out of her cardigan sleeve and blew her nose.

'Oh, Mam,' she whispered, feeling the tears well up in her eyes again. 'How on earth could a lovely person like you have been fathered by a monster like that? But, I showed him, Mam. I stood up to him just like you did all those years ago.' She held her head in her hands and quietly sobbed.

Chapter Seventeen

Evie slumped down in her seat, yawned loudly and stretched out her arms.

'Oh, God, Jenny, I'm absolutely shattered. What time is it?'

Jenny squinted over at the small alarm clock perched on the shelf amid an array of bobbins, zips and numerous other items that over the last few weeks had been placed ready for use when needed. The lease on the factory had gone through without a hitch and it had been decided to move into the office space to complete the samples instead of commuting between Jenny's and Evie's houses. The move had proved successful, and instead of a small selection from Jenny's portfolio, they had completed them all.

'It's just comin' up for two.' Jenny looked at Evie and her eyes twinkled. 'Is it still 1955? I feel I've aged years since we started this lot.' She winked at Evie as she picked up her scissors and clipped at a thread. 'There. We've finished.' She sat back in satisfaction and looked over at the assortment of clothes they had painstakingly made up. She nodded and sighed deeply. 'You were right, Evie. It's a wonderful sight seein' me designs come alive.' She grimaced. 'I just 'ope the buyers like 'em.'

Evie leaned forward and rested her tired arms on the sewing table. 'They will, believe me. They'd be fools not to. It's a pity Mavis couldn't come tonight. It would have been nice to have the four of us seeing our hard work come to an end.'

'Yeah,' Jenny agreed. 'She can't sew a straight stitch to save 'er life, but she sure kept us goin' with 'er tea and sandwiches.'

'And the clearing up.'

Jenny laughed. 'Yeah, that's the bit I enjoyed the most. I could make as much mess as I liked and Mavis would be behind me wi' 'er brush and shovel. She's sure bin a godsend.'

'So have you,' Evie said firmly. 'None of this would have been possible without you.'

'Ah, get off. You'd 'ave got someone else.'

Evie sniffed and hid a smile. 'Not so cheaply, Jenny, I can assure you.'

'Not so cheaply?' she repeated. 'Yer mean for free, don't yer?'

Evie laughed loudly. 'Just send us your invoice, although I can't promise it'll be paid just yet.'

'Bloody right, I will, and I'll add on the cost of me cut fingers and the matches I needed to keep me eyes propped open.' She yawned loudly. 'I just 'ope yer right about those buyers, I couldn't bear the thought that we'd done this all for nothin'.' She placed her elbows on the table and rested her chin in her hands, looking fondly at her friend. 'I'm glad we've finally finished. I might get to see Nigel. 'E's beginnin' to think I've another man.'

'And have you?' Evie asked seriously.

'What? Wi' all the long hours I've been doin' for you –

you must be joking.' She frowned. 'Oh, but I'm just glad it's Sunday tomorrow. I'm gonna stay in bed all day, then 'ave a leisurely bath and meet Nigel tomorrow night – or should I say today?'

Evie smiled. 'I'd love to stay in bed tomorrow, but we have to get the van packed ready for Edward's departure first thing Monday morning.' She yawned again. 'Then it's a case of waiting and praying, 'cos if he comes back without any orders, we're done for.'

Jenny grimaced. 'That bad?'

'Yes. We're just about skint. Edward's inheritance from his grandfather has gone completely and I have about two hundred pounds left from the money my mother left me.' She shrugged. 'Of course there's still the shops, but the money they bring in wouldn't keep a venture like this going.'

Jenny stood up, walked over to the rack and fingered the sample garments lovingly. 'I can see us doin' a lot of prayin' during the next week. I'd better do a block bookin' at the church.'

'Oh, you are a card, Jenny,' Evie giggled, looking over towards the door. 'Where's Edward got to with that damned tea? I'm parched.'

Just then he walked through the door and placed three steaming half pint mugs of tea on the table.

'We thought you'd gone 'ome,' Jenny chided.

'What!' he smiled. 'And leave my two favourite ladies alone and defenceless?'

'Jenny will never be defenceless. One of her dirty looks could kill at a hundred paces.'

Jenny grinned as she continued to straighten the garments on the rack. She stopped and stared at one particular coat hanger. 'What's this?' She unhooked the offending garment and held it aloft.

Evie looked sheepish. 'That's the underwear you made me.'

'I can see that,' Jenny said sharply. 'But what's it doin' 'ere?'

Evie scraped back her chair and walked over to her, snatching the coat hanger and putting it back into place.

'Edward is going to take them as a sample with the rest of the clothes.'

'What!' Jenny laughed. 'Me granny's underwear? Yer not serious?'

'Perfectly,' Evie said. 'Anyway, they're not your granny's. You made this set for me, remember? And I happen to think they're great.'

'Edward will be laughed out of the showrooms.' Jenny shrugged her shoulders. 'I think you're mad.'

'Mad or not, trust me,' Evie said firmly.

'She could be right, Evie,' Edward chipped in. 'I could take them on my next rounds.'

'You'll take them with you this time, Edward Bradshaw. We might as well show the buyers all we have to offer.'

'Okay, okay, boss!' Edward shrugged his shoulders and winked over at Jenny. 'We won't say "we told you so" when I return.' He drained his mug and stood up. 'Right, I'm going to start packing the van.'

Jenny and Evie looked at each other and groaned.

'Oh, no, Edward. Not tonight. Let's do it tomorrow, please. We're shattered.'

He gave a yawn. 'So am I, Evie, but it'll only take us about half an hour and then we can have the whole day off tomorrow, the first for weeks.'

Her body sagged and she gave a deep sigh. 'Oh, okay.' She dragged herself towards the table and started to clear up. She stopped and looked at Jenny, standing forlornly by the clothes racks. 'D'you want to go, Jenny? Edward can run you home in the van.'

She sighed. 'No. I might as well stay and 'elp. You'd only call me blind if I abandoned you to go 'ome. Anyway, what's the point? I've forgotten what me bed looks like.'

Evie laughed loudly as she walked over and put her arm around her friend. 'Good on you, Jenny. We'll make it up to you.'

'Bloody right you will! Come on then, let's get cracking.'

For the next hour, they worked hard to put the racks of clothes carefully in the van and strap them so they would not sway dangerously about on the long drive to London. Edward placed his new order book and all the other paperwork he needed in the front of the van and went to join the girls. He stood in the doorway of the office and frowned. Evie looked across at him.

'What's up?'

'Oh, nothing. I was just thinking that we could move the other three sewing machines back in here now. We only put them across the other side of the factory in order to give you more room in here.'

Jenny and Evie looked at each other. They both advanced towards Edward and grabbed his arms.

'No, you don't. That can wait,' Evie said firmly. 'You're all set for London and me and Jenny are going home to our beds. And so, my dear, are you.'

Edward shrugged his shoulders and laughed as he was herded outside by Evie and Jenny. He locked up the premises and climbed gratefully into the van. Resting his arms over the steering wheel, he turned to face the girls who were sitting beside him.

'Well, you've been marvellous, I couldn't have wished for a better team. Now it's all up to me,' he said as he turned the key in the ignition. The van purred into life and Edward headed it out of the factory premises towards their respective homes.

Once home he parked the van and grimaced, not liking the thought of leaving it on the street loaded with its precious cargo. He walked round it and nodded. It was as securely locked as it would ever be. He stood back, smiled, and went into the house to join his wife.

'What the hell's that?' Evie sat up and peered at the clock. It read five minutes to six and they had been in bed for precisely two hours.

'What's what?' Edward mumbled as he turned over and gave a loud snore.

'Edward, there's somebody banging on the door,' she said sharply.

He prised open his eyes. 'Eh? Oh, God, so there is.' He crawled out of bed and grabbed his dressing gown. 'You stay here,' he ordered Evie as he headed towards the bedroom door.

She heard him open the front door and the low mumble of voices. Frowning deeply, she threw back the covers and walked to the landing, where she hung over the banister and strained her eyes and ears. She saw Edward clasp his hand to his forehead and heard him groan. He said something and turned and headed towards the stairs. He was halfway up when he spotted her.

'What's wrong?' she asked in alarm.

He stopped. 'There's been a fire at the factory.' He continued up the stairs and headed for the bedroom where he threw on some clothes.

'A fire!' She sank to her knees and groaned loudly. 'Oh, God, Edward. How bad?'

'Dunno. It's the police at the door. I'm going to have to go down with them to the factory and inspect the damage.'

She jumped up. 'I'll come with you.'

He came out of the bedroom, tucking his pyjama top into his trousers. 'No! You'll stay here. There's nothing you can do. I'll try not to be too long.' He raised his eyebrows. 'Just pray the damage is light.'

He rushed past her and down the stairs, banging the front door behind him.

Evie went back into the bedroom, picked up her dressing gown and headed down the stairs towards the kitchen. She lit the paraffin stove and put on the kettle. She sat downing cup after cup of tea whilst watching the clock slowly move its hands. It was half-past seven before Edward returned. He slouched into the kitchen and sat down, resting his head in his hands. Evie stared at him, afraid to ask any questions. She poured him a cup of tea and pushed it towards him. He grabbed the cup and drank the contents greedily.

'Thanks, love. I needed that.' He paused and looked at her.

'How bad is it?' she asked quietly.

He ran his hand across his mouth. 'Bad enough, although we've been very lucky – it could have been a lot worse. If it hadn't been for a man whose bedroom window overlooks the yard, the whole factory would have been lost. He saw the flames and called the fire brigade.' He paused and sighed deeply. 'The office we used as the sewing room is practically gutted. As you know, the room was cluttered with ends of rolls of material and other stuff and it just went up in flames. The rest of the factory is okay, but we've lost the two machines you and Jenny were using, they're beyond repair. Oh, Evie, I'm just glad we didn't move those other three machines back. And thank God I insisted we packed the van, or I dread to think of the consequences.'

She clasped her hands together. 'How the hell did it happen? The place was perfectly all right when we left.'

Edward looked at her, his lips forming a thin line. 'The police aren't sure, they seem to think it was a cigarette end.'

'What! But none of us was smoking.'

'I know, that's what I can't understand, but there's nothing else that it could have been. The heaters were all switched off and so was the small camping stove that we boiled the kettle on. The only thing that was a bit funny was that the office window had been smashed and the police reckon the fire couldn't possibly have caused it.'

She shook her head in disbelief. 'I can't believe all this, just when we were getting on so well.'

'Well, we have another problem,' he groaned.

'What?'

'We're not insured. In all the confusion of getting the business started, I forgot.'

'Oh, Edward. How the hell are we going to pay for all the damage?' Evie said angrily.

He shrugged his shoulders. 'The gutted room will have to wait until we have enough money to fix it up. We can easily manage in the rest of the factory.' He gave her a smile. 'We have to look on the bright side, gel. Matters could have been a whole lot worse.' He paused. 'I'll have to see about employing a night watchman.'

Evie looked at him anxiously. 'But we can't afford it.'

'We can't afford not to.' Edward yawned long and loud. 'Right now all I want is my bed. I have to be down at the police station at twelve to make a statement. Then I need to go back to the factory and board up the windows. While I'm away in London, Evie, you could get a couple of estimates then we'll know how much it's going to cost us.'

She smiled wanly. 'Yes, I'll do that, and I'll start cleaning up the mess on Monday. It will give me something to occupy me while you're away.'

'I wish I could put off my trip for a couple of days and give you a hand but I've got all those appointments.'

'Oh, no, Edward. That will never do. We need whatever orders you get to stay in business. We can't let a little thing like this set us back.'

He grinned at his wife. 'That's my girl, forever the optimist.' He stood up and grabbed her hand. 'Come on, let's try and get some sleep.'

For the second time that morning, they walked slowly up the stairs and climbed gratefully into bed.

'Any news from Edward yet?' Jenny asked as she entered Evie's kitchen.

She had invited her two friends round for a meal in appreciation of all their hard work. It was now the following Thursday night and Evie was getting anxious.

'No. He telephoned me on Tuesday. He's made a few sales but not on the scale we need.' She checked the steak under the grill and turned to her friend. 'I'm getting a bit worried. Edward tried to sound really confident on the telephone, but I could tell he was feeling dejected. Still, we'll have to keep our fingers crossed. He had quite a few people to see.' She looked at the clock. 'I hope Mavis hurries. This steak cost me a fortune and I don't want it ruined.'

'Give 'er another five minutes. If she ain't 'ere by then, I'll 'ave 'er piece and she can 'ave bread and drippin',' Jenny quipped. She moved towards her friend and put an arm around her shoulders. 'Stop worryin', Evie. Everythin' will be fine, you'll see.'

'I'm trying,' she said. 'But so much hinges on Edward's sales technique.'

'Oh, is that all?' Jenny chided. 'I certainly wouldn't be worried then. Our Edward could sell Buckingham Palace to the Queen wi' 'is patter.'

Evie laughed and relaxed. 'Yes, you're right. He'll have no problems, not with those fabulous samples you made up.'

Just then a knock sounded on the door and Mavis came in.

'Hi, sorry I'm late,' she apologised.

'Mavis, you'd be late for your own funeral,' Evie said, trying to sound annoyed but really pleased to see her friend. 'Take off your coat, I'm all ready to dish up.'

The two girls sat down at the table and stared in appreciation at the meal Evie placed before them.

Afterwards Jenny pushed her plate away and groaned. 'Not bad for a woman who only a few months ago couldn't boil an egg.'

'You cheeky devil!' Evie laughed, putting down her own knife and fork. 'I'd like to see you cook a meal like that. And if you've got any designs on Nigel, you'd better start practising.' She picked up the bottle of wine to replenish their glasses.

'Nigel!' Jenny said. 'Oh, I've finished wi' him. Wanted us to go away on 'oliday – wi' 'is parents would yer believe? Anyway, I've got my eye on a new lad . . .'

Evie and Mavis looked at each other and groaned.

'Jenny!' Evie said firmly. 'Shut up and drink your wine.'

The three girls had picked up their glasses when the back door suddenly opened and Edward walked in. He looked extremely tired and dishevelled from his long journey.

'Oh, I see. I'm away slogging myself to death while you three live it up. Any of that wine left?'

Evie looked at him in astonishment. 'Edward,' she breathed. 'Oh, Edward, you're home.' She jumped up and threw her arms around him, hugging him tightly. 'Sit down,' she commanded. 'Tell us all your news whilst I get you something to eat.'

'This wine will do.' He smiled. 'I grabbed something at a transport café.'

'See. He prefers Greasy Lil's cooking to yours,' Jenny jeered.

'Shut up, Jenny,' Evie said for the second time that night, pretending to look hurt. She joined the other three at the table and waited for Edward to begin.

'Before I start, what's the state of the factory? Did you manage to get it cleaned up?'

'Yes,' Evie nodded. 'And it's not as bad as we first thought. The two machines are definitely ruined. But after I washed all the walls and swept up the mess, it just wants decorating and the window replaced, along with all the odds and ends.'

'Thank God for that,' he sighed. 'I was worried that it might be worse.'

'Right then,' Evie said impatiently. 'Now tell us your news before I burst.'

'Well,' he began, 'there's not much to tell.' He took another sip of his wine. 'London's a terrible place to get round. I kept getting lost. I've been many times before, as you know, but with a van loaded with samples parking was a terrible problem . . .'

'Edward,' Evie said sternly, 'get to the point. Are we in business or not?'

A slow smile formed on his lips as he shook his head. 'What an impatient wife I've got.' He looked in turn at Jenny and Mavis. 'I've been away all week, tramping round the streets of London, sleeping in cold draughty lodgings with only my memories to keep me warm . . .'

'Edward.' Evie laughed and slapped him playfully on the arm. 'Did you sell anything or not? Our future depends on this.'

'Yes, I sold a few,' he said slowly.

'A few? A few what? And how many's a few?' Evie asked, leaning across the table and glaring at him.

'A few dozen,' he said cagily.

'A few dozen what?' Evie raised her voice, feeling her temper rise.

'No, Evie.' He grinned cheekily. 'Not a few dozen. A few *thousand* dozen.'

The room went silent as the three women stared at him.

'A few thousand dozen!' Evie uttered, her eyes fixed on him. 'What of?'

He scraped back his chair, stood up and looked across at Jenny.

'Her granny's underwear,' he said with a grin.

'What?' the three girls cried in unison. 'You sold granny's drawers!'

'Yes. Well, not just her drawers but the matching vest as well. They went down a bomb. You'll never guess who placed the order?'

The three girls shook their heads in disbelief.

'Mains and Russell,' he announced.

'Mains and Russell!' Evie shouted as she jumped up from her chair. 'But they're the biggest retailers in Great Britain, with outlets in Europe as well.' She stopped abruptly and frowned at her husband. 'You're joking, Edward, aren't you?'

He shook his head. 'No, I'm perfectly serious. They want three thousand dozen in assorted colours and sizes for the end of August, ready to put into the shops at the beginning of September, and if they sell well, they'll want more. I have the written order in the van. They think the design is absolutely wonderful, especially for the teenage market. They feel it will get the youngsters wearing warm winter underwear again.'

Evie sank down into her chair and looked in turn at the dumbstruck Jenny and Mavis. 'I told you, Jenny, didn't I? But I never expected this.' She sat still for a moment as a broad smile spread itself across her face. She suddenly jumped up out of her chair and threw her arms in the air.

'Yippee!' she shrieked at the top of her voice. 'We've done it! We've really done it!' She bounded over to Edward and grabbed hold of him in delight. 'Oh, Edward, I really can't believe it. This is wonderful news.'

Her face suddenly fell as a thought struck her. She pulled away from him and sat back down at the table.

'We'll never do it, Edward. We've only got two sewing machines and an overlocker.'

He grinned. 'I gave that very problem a lot of thought on the drive home and I've come up with two answers.'

'Oh, yes?'

'On the strength of the order I've received, I can get a bank loan to buy some more machines and hire some experienced girls, but a better option would be to get some out-workers. There's plenty about and we can vet them beforehand to see that they come up to standard. That option would be better for us just now. The out-workers have their own machines so we wouldn't have the initial outlay until we get paid for the order.'

'What about their wages? They won't wait until we've been paid from Mains and Russell.'

'That's what we would use the bank loan for,' he answered. 'We could pay it all back once we were paid for our work.'

Evie nodded. 'Mm, I see.' She paused and thought for a moment. 'We'd still have to go at a hell of a pace.'

Edward shrugged his shoulders and held out his hands. 'We'll do it, Evie. This order can make or break us.'

'Phew! I still can't believe it. It's wonderful news, Edward.'

'We'll all help.' Jenny spoke at last, finding her voice. 'And I happen to know a good out-worker. She lives around the corner from us and she's bound to know some more.'

'Oh, good. That's a start.' Edward smiled, rubbing his hands together.

'What about Jenny's other designs? Wasn't anyone interested in those?'

'You must be kidding! Mains and Russell are definitely

interested, but they want to see how we handle this order first before they make a firm order for anything else. Once all this happened I played down my other appointments and came home. I knew we couldn't handle anything else at the moment. The first few buyers I saw were interested, but were too concerned about the fact that we were just starting up. They told me to come back when we were more established as a company. Luckily, Mains and Russell were willing to give us a try.'

'Some try,' Mavis quipped.

'Oh, the order they gave us is quite small compared to some. Don't forget, they have at least one store in every town and city in Great Britain, plus their stores abroad.'

'Oh, Edward, stop frightening me. I dread to think what would have happened if the order had been any bigger.' Evie frowned.

'We'd have coped with it, like we will with this one.' He couldn't help yawning. 'Now, ladies, if you don't mind, I'm going to have a long soak in the bath. I have to be up early in the morning to get the hired van back.' He looked at Evie. 'We'll have to get our own transport as soon as possible. Hiring vans willy nilly is costing a fortune and I can't really do errands around Leicester on a push bike.'

She frowned, her eyebrows nearly meeting. 'Go and have your bath, Edward, I've had enough excitement for one day. The last thing I want to do is have a row with you about money or the lack of it. Transport can wait.'

His face clouded. 'I need a car or a van, Evie. We'll discuss it tomorrow.' He acknowledged Mavis and Jenny, turned on his heel and left the room.

'Oh, masterful!!' Jenny spoke in admiration. 'I love masterful men.'

'Shut up, Jenny!' Evie scolded.

'Well!' Mavis said. 'Mains and Russell. You couldn't have done better than that.'

'No,' Evie agreed. 'We're definitely on our way. And it's all due to Edward and Jenny's granny's drawers.' She laughed. 'I suppose the least I can do is let him have a van.'

'Or a butcher's bike! Make 'im do wi' one of them for a while.'

'Shut up, Jenny!'

All the girls laughed together as Evie shared what was left of the wine between the three of them.

For the next few weeks, Evie and Edward practically spent their lives in the factory, amid piles of off-cuts, reels of cotton, and frayed tempers. Jenny and Mavis were as good as their word and spent all their spare time helping out. Jenny's neighbour had proved to be worth her weight in gold. She was an expert machinist who turned out a completed set of granny's underwear quickly and neatly, and was nearly as good as Jenny and Evie.

Mavis proved her worth as an inspector, examining each garment before she passed it as perfect, with no hesitation in returning one that was the slightest bit faulty. Edward's latest brainwave had caused Evie a big headache. He suddenly decided that all the sets of underwear should be individually boxed with their size and colour displayed for easy viewing by the buying public. He said it would enhance Grayshaw's reputation and give their product class. Evie argued about the cost until she was blue in the face then shrugged her shoulders in defeat as she waved him off on his visit to the box manufacturer's.

He arrived back triumphantly, having struck an amazing deal for the supply of enough boxes to fill their order at a quarter of the price they should have been. Evie congratulated her husband over and over again. Even she had to admit that the sample box he had been sent really gave the final polish to the garments. She knew her husband had been right and that Mains and Russell would be suitably impressed. Evie found out later that the person who owned the box company was an old university chum of Edward's who had been promised all their future business. Her words to him on that subject were very sharp and choice.

The only incident of any note that happened during that hectic time concerned Jenny. She arrived at the factory one morning out of breath and deeply distraught.

Evie made her a cup of tea and tried to calm her down.

'Whatever's the matter?' she asked.

'You may well ask,' Jenny said coldly as she cradled the cup between her hands. 'I've been sacked,' she announced.

'Sacked! They can't do that,' Evie said disbelievingly. 'Whatever did they sack you for?'

'I don't bloody know!' Jenny shouted as she slammed down her cup, jumped up from her chair and started to pace the floor. 'I arrived for work and hadn't even put down me bag when old Stimpson calls me into the office and tells me to clear my desk. Said me work wa' sloppy and they were not puttin' up wi' it any longer. Sloppy work, I ask you! Cheeky sod. I've worked for that company for seven years and my work is as good as the next person's.' She stopped abruptly. 'Well, sod 'em! I 'ope the place goes bankrupt. I'll gerra 'nother job and work wi' decent people.'

Evie placed her arm round her friend. 'I am sorry, Jenny, they don't deserve you. Let's hope we can offer you something permanent soon.'

'Yeah,' she agreed. 'In the meantime I'm gonna' sign on wi' one of those temporary places. I've always fancied movin' about.'

'What about your mother?'

'What about 'er? I ain't tellin' 'er I've got the sack. As long as she gets 'er board money, she'll be none the wiser. Anyway, I've 'ad enough of this conversation. I'm gonna go and register wi' an agency and see what work's goin' about.'

Without saying goodbye, Jenny flounced out of the room. She was found work the following day and made a great point of telling Evie that Dawson's had done her the biggest favour ever.

Two days before the completed order was to be delivered to the Mains and Russell warehouse, Evie packed the final box of underwear into a large container and closed the lid. She sighed deeply and sank back in her chair. She looked around the large expanse of floor space and let her mind wander. Hopefully the factory would soon be filled with machines and machinists, sewing away to their hearts' content in order to complete the mountain of orders they had on their books.

Jenny would be beavering away in an office across the corridor, dreaming up wonderful new designs, and hopefully Mavis would be here too. Doing what? Evie frowned. They could surely find something for her to do. Her friend was a great worker but not actually adept in anything except inspecting, and she couldn't see Mavis doing that on a permanent basis.

Evie felt suddenly lonely. Edward had gone home for a couple of hours' sleep, having worked through the night making up the last of the boxes. Jenny was at her job and Mavis at home with her daughter. The out-workers had been paid off courtesy of the bank loan and with the promise of more work as soon as possible.

Evie's eyes lit up at the sight of the mountain of large containers piled high in the corner, ready to be loaded into the hired van which Edward had ordered for that afternoon. She smiled as a warm feeling enveloped her body. This was the start of their dream. By sheer hard work, they had landed the order and were now about to complete their end of the bargain by delivering on time.

She jumped as the door opened behind her and the postman appeared wearing his usual grin.

'There you go, me duck. Only two letters this morning. One's the electricity bill, I'm afraid, and I don't know about the other.'

Evie took the letters and slapped the postman playfully on the arm with them. 'I'll keep the white envelope and you can take the electricity bill back with you.'

The postman laughed as he tipped his cap and jauntily left the room to continue his round.

Evie turned the white envelope over and withdrew the letter. Her mouth dropped open in horror as the words leaped out at her.

Dear Mr Bradshaw
Due to information received by us concerning the

rightful ownership and authenticity of the designs you offered us, we are sorry to inform you that until the dispute has been settled, we are withdrawing our order. We do hope the outcome of the dispute will be satisfactorily concluded and until then we wish you every success for the future.

Yours sincerely,

Raymond Heard

Chief Buyer

Mains and Russell Ltd

Evie froze. Her heart pounded dangerously inside her chest and her legs trembled. She rushed over to the telephone and dialled the number on the letterhead.

'Mains and Russell,' a polite voice answered.

'I'd like to speak to Mr Heard, please,' Evie asked, trying to stop her voice from shaking.

'Who may I say is calling?'

'Evelyn Bradshaw of Grayshaw's.'

'One moment, please.'

Evie waited with bated breath. Finally the operator came back on the line.

'I'm sorry, Mr Heard is not available to speak to you,' she said apologetically.

Evie put down the receiver and groaned. She frowned as her mind raced. What on earth was she going to do? Suddenly an idea came to her. If Mr Heard would not speak to her, then she would go to see him. Their future was hanging in the balance and there was no time to lose.

She telephoned the railway station and found out the time of the next train to London. She had an hour to change and get to the platform. Luckily, she had taken to keeping one of her smartest suits and a change of underwear in a locker at the factory in case of emergencies.

She quickly changed, brushed her hair, applied a small amount of lipstick and mascara, grabbed her handbag and headed for the door. She stopped abruptly as a thought struck her. The letter had mentioned the authenticity of Jenny's designs. She would need them to show Mr Heard. She ran back and rummaged around the cluttered room for Jenny's folder. She sighed with relief as she found it beneath a pile of odds and ends of material and thought of the night of the fire. Thank goodness Jenny had taken her folder home a few nights previous, or what on earth would they have done? She placed the precious folder under her arm and once again headed for the door.

The train journey was slow and painful for Evie. Her mind was full of what she would say to Mr Heard, if she managed to have an audience with him. To her dismay, she found her temper getting the better of her. The letter was a damned cheek. Whatever Mr Heard was playing at, she didn't like it. They had put everything they owned into getting that order completed and now he had decided to cancel it.

'Well, we'll see about that,' Evie said aloud, then blushed as several eyes stared at her. She crossed her slender legs and stared sedately out of the window.

She walked out of St Pancras station and into the bright sunlight. The city bustled and heaved as the pounding of feet and the drone of heavy traffic drowned out all other sounds. For a moment she felt lost and alone. Pulling herself together, she hailed a taxi and instructed it to take her to the headquarters of Mains and Russell. Walking through the entrance doors, she became suddenly unnerved at the plushness of the building. Across the far side of the pillared entrance hall sat a large sweeping counter. Evie could see several smart women seated behind, dealing adeptly with telephone calls and visitors.

Clutching her handbag and Jenny's folder, Evie walked swiftly across the foyer towards the reception desk. She stood and waited her turn in the queue, then froze in horror as she heard the receptionist ask a man who his appointment was with and checked in a book to clarify the time. She sidled out of the queue and hovered several feet away, wondering what to do next. To the side of the desk was a small corridor and Evie quickly realised that this was where the lifts were housed.

She moved swiftly towards the corridor and waited in front of the iron grid gates. She could see by the indicator that the lift was on its way down and tapped her feet impatiently, praying that one of the receptionists would not spot her and ask awkward questions.

She held her breath as the lift arrived and the doors slowly opened. A swarm of people alighted. Evie waited then moved quickly inside. Her mind raced. What would she say when the lift attendant asked for her destination? Just as the attendant was closing the doors a man squeezed himself through. He was carrying a large brown envelope.

'Phew! Just in time.' He smiled at Evie.

The attendant asked, 'Where to, sir?'

'Third floor. Mr Heard's office, please.'

Evie turned her eyes towards the ceiling and mouthed a thank you.

'Where to, madam?'

'Third Floor, please.'

The lift rose, juddering slightly as it passed each floor. It arrived at its destination and they alighted.

The man smiled at Evie and skipped ahead of her. She walked slowly down the corridor. She watched which room the man entered and stopped to gather her thoughts and calm her nerves. He came out and smiled as he passed her minus the envelope. Evie reached the door, took a deep breath and entered.

She stood before Mr Heard's secretary and coughed. The secretary looked up at her and smiled warmly.

'Yes, what can I do for you?' she said politely.

'I'd like to see Mr Heard, please,' Evie requested.

The woman reached for a large blue book and opened it. She looked at Evie.

'I'm sorry, have you an appointment? Only there's nothing in the diary for today.'

Evie took a breath. 'No, I haven't,' she answered, shaking her head, 'but it's very important I see him.'

'Well, I'm sorry, but Mr Heard is not seeing anyone else today. I'll have to have a word with the reception desk. They should never had allowed you up.' The secretary sighed. 'Still, I can make you an appointment.' She flicked through the diary. 'It won't be for another two weeks. He's a very busy man.'

Evie raised her head. 'That won't do. I need to see him now,' she said, trying to keep her voice light as panic rose inside her.

'Well, I'm sorry that's not possible,' the woman said firmly. 'Now I can make you an appointment, but that's all.'

Evie felt her body sag. All that gruelling work, plus their future hopes, for nothing. She made a decision. She turned her head and saw to the left of her a large door with Mr Heard's name printed on it in large black letters. She moved swiftly towards it and turned the handle.

Before the secretary could rise and run round her desk, Evie had pushed open the door and entered Mr Heard's office.

A man sat at his desk, immersed in paperwork. He looked in astonishment at the woman standing before him, biting her bottom lip with nervousness. Raymond Heard was in his late fifties. His once black hair was greying round the temples and large kindly brown eyes twinkled at Evie behind spectacles as he stared at her.

'Look, I'm sorry to barge in here, but it's very important that I speak to you. It's a matter of life and death,' she blurted as a loud buzzing noise erupted from the intercom on Mr Heard's desk.

He looked down at it and pressed a button.

The secretary's voice boomed out, 'I'm sorry, Mr Heard. That woman barged in before I could stop her.'

He released the buzzer and looked at the agitated Evie.

'Please, Mr Heard. Please give me five minutes of your time.'

He paused, and pressed the buzzer again.

'It's all right, Agnes. Please finish those letters for me, I need to get them in the post tonight.' He released the button and turned his full attention to Evie. He indicated a chair to the left of his desk.

'Please, sit down and tell me what's so important?'

She inched forward and sat down, still clutching her handbag and Jenny's folder.

'My name is Evelyn Bradshaw of Grayshaw's, Mr Heard, and it's about the letter you sent us.'

'Oh.' He sat back in his chair and ran his fingers through his hair.

Evie unclipped her handbag and fished inside for the letter he had sent her. She found it and held it out towards him.

'I don't understand this letter at all. What d'you mean about a dispute over the authenticity of the designs? My friend did all the designs. There's no dispute. She did them for us of her own free will. Why are you questioning them?'

Mr Heard twined his fingers together as he looked at her. 'I'm sorry, Mrs Bradshaw. I'm really not at liberty to discuss this matter. Mains and Russell is a reputable company and cannot be involved in any underhand dealings.'

Evie frowned deeply. 'What underhand dealings?' she said in bewilderment.'

Mr Heard sighed. 'I'm sorry. As I've already said, I'm not at liberty to discuss this matter. When you get it sorted out, providing it is in your favour, I would be willing to see your future designs. I was very impressed with the last ones and I'm sorry, very sorry indeed, that all this has come to light.'

The panic in Evie's stomach rose to fever pitch and she began to feel sick.

'Mr Heard, please, I assure you there's been no underhand dealings. I can't stress that enough.' She paused and gasped for breath. 'We've put everything we own and more into this order, and we've kept our side of the bargain.' Evie felt the tears spring to her eyes. 'We've all worked day and night. The garments are perfect, all boxed ready to despatch to you. I can't leave without an explanation. It wouldn't be fair to all the people who have helped us.'

Much to her dismay the tears started to roll down her cheeks. She fumbled in her handbag for her handkerchief and wiped her eyes.

'I'm sorry,' she said apologetically. 'I didn't mean this to happen, only I can't leave until I understand why you've withdrawn your order.'

Mr Heard sighed and leaned across his desk. He pressed the buzzer on the intercom and ordered Agnes to bring in a tray of tea.

Evie controlled her emotion and looked at him hopefully.

He eyed her. She didn't seem the type of girl who was corrupt or dishonest. He felt deeply concerned. Had the information he had received not been genuine after all?

'Look, Mrs Bradshaw, I only acted on information received.' He paused as Agnes entered with a tray of tea, thanked her and waited until she had left.

'I was told that you and your designer once worked for Dawson's, and while you were there stole some important designs that were to be included in their next collection. The theft was not discovered until some time after. By then it was too late, you had both resigned. It wasn't until this person heard that you had gone into business and we had placed an order with you that two and two were put together. Neither of you had had designing experience before, you see, so how could you possibly put a collection together?'

Evie slumped back in her chair and raised her eyes to the ceiling as her brain ticked over.

'Is there anything the matter?' Mr Heard asked.

Evie lowered her gaze and looked at him for a second. 'I'd like to ask you a question. Was the person who informed you of all this Jerod Dawson by any chance?'

Mr Heard's mouth dropped open. 'Why, yes,' he answered before he could stop himself.

'I thought so.' Evie pursed her lips.

'How did you know?' he asked.

'It's a long story, Mr Heard, and I would like you to listen to it before you finally abandon us as a supplier.'

He thought for a moment. 'It's most unethical, but I've a terrible feeling I've made a mistake here. Please go ahead. But first let me pour some tea. I've a feeling I'll need it.'

For the next three-quarters of an hour, Evie poured out her story. Raymond Heard sat back in his chair, his face not moving a muscle as he listened intently to the young girl who sat before him. When she had finished, Evie sat back and waited for his response.

'Well!' he said in amazement. He shifted position in his chair and looked at Evie, his mouth set grimly. 'So you're Jerod Dawson's granddaughter? Mmm . . .' He scratched his chin thoughtfully.

'I'm sorry I had to go into such detail but I felt you wouldn't understand unless you heard the full story of the relationship between my mother and grandfather.'

'You're right there, my girl. Jerod Dawson is a much respected man in the trade and he's got a lot of clout.' Raymond Heard paused. 'I've heard stories about him before, but I never for a moment thought they were true. I'm beginning to wonder now.' He looked sad. 'I've two daughters myself, and whatever they did I couldn't banish them from the family or stop loving them. No, it takes a hell of a hard man to do that.'

'My grandfather *is* hard. He only cares about the business and will do anything to make sure it doesn't suffer.'

'It certainly seems like it.'

'You can check out what I've been saying,' she said quickly.

'Oh, I will, Mrs Bradshaw. It appears I've made one mistake. I'm not about to make another.' Raymond Heard smiled warmly. 'No offence, but a few discreet enquiries will soon put my mind at rest on this matter. It's not that I doubt your story,' he added quickly.

'I understand,' she answered, 'and, as I said before, I have birth certificates that will prove who my mother was.' She paused for a moment as a thought struck her. 'There's something I've forgotten.'

'Oh?'

'My friend Jenny did not resign. She was sacked, and it was well after we got our order from you. I don't know if it means much, but it does show that my grandfather lied about that matter, as well as the designs being stolen – although I can't prove that point myself. The folder I've shown you of Jenny's designs could have been done at any time. I can only give you my word that they were done by her and had nothing at all to do with Dawson's.'

Raymond Heard sat back in his chair and clasped his hands together. 'I've been dealing with Jerod Dawson for years and it worries me greatly to think that he can stoop to these depths to get his own way. His family life is nothing to do with me, or the fact that you are his grand-daughter. Lots of companies fight dirty to secure orders. To be honest it's not really my problem as long as the deal between my company and theirs is honest and above board. But on this occasion Jerod has actually involved the good name of Mains and Russell, and if all this is true – and I think it must be or you wouldn't be sitting here, young lady – I can assure you, I won't be dealing with him again.'

Evie's eyes opened wide as she stared at him. 'Oh, I didn't mean that to happen! I'm only trying to clear our name . . .'

'Yes, I know,' he cut in. 'But I have to think of our shareholders and customers. If this story got out, it could be very detrimental to the company.' He looked at his watch. 'Leave it with me, Mrs Bradshaw. Try not to worry too much and I'll get back to you in a day or so.' He shook his head. 'I'm sorry I cannot say any more than that at the moment. I feel very bad that I took Jerod's word for all this in the first place. I should have checked it out before I wrote to you. For that I'm sorry, and can only ask you to be patient.'

Evie tried to smile. 'I understand, and I want to thank you for at least listening to me.'

'I'm glad I did, and I just hope everything works out.' Raymond Heard stood up and held out his hand. 'Have a good journey home and I'll be in touch, either way, very shortly.'

Evie took his hand and shook it. She gathered up her belongings and left the office.

Evie arrived home exhausted from her ordeal. The train she caught back to Leicester stopped at every station on the way, and by the time she reached the house her patience and temper were frayed and she had a blinding headache. She opened the back door and was greeted by a distraught Edward.

'My God, Evie! Where the hell have you been?' he demanded angrily as he rushed up to her and grabbed her

by the shoulders. 'I was just about to have the canal dragged
. . .' He stopped abruptly as he saw her eyes harden.
'What's happened? Whatever's the matter?'

She looked up at her husband, unable to control her
emotions.

'I've had a long day, I'm tired and hungry, and shouting
at me won't make things any better,' she snapped.

'Well, what do you expect when you just disappear like
that? You left no message or anything,' he shouted. 'I've
been worried sick. I've called all the hospitals and the
police station.' He stopped abruptly. 'Just where have you
been?'

She pulled herself away from his grasp. 'I've been to
London . . .'

'London!' Edward cut in. 'How can you go gallivanting
at a time like this, Evie? You know we've hardly any
money, and you knew I wanted to get away this afternoon
and deliver the order early, and you go to London for the
day!' His eyes bored into hers. 'Well, I hope you had a
jolly good time . . . '

Evie's temper snapped. 'Oh, I did,' she said sarcastically.
'I went sightseeing and had lunch at Lyons Corner House.
Oxford Street was packed with shoppers . . . I had a simply
wonderful time!'

They glared at each other for several seconds. Edward
suddenly pushed past her and grabbed his jacket from the
back of the chair.

'Where are you going?' she demanded.

'Out!' he shouted back.

Evie rushed over and grabbed him by the arm. 'Look,
I'm sorry, Edward. I haven't really been gallivanting. Sit
down and let me explain . . .'

'Not likely, I'm off for a pint! If you'd had any regard for me at all, you wouldn't have gone off in the first place without telling me.' He spoke sharply as he pulled on his jacket.

'There wasn't time . . .'

'Wasn't time! How long does it take to write a note, or better still to wait until we could go together? He turned and grabbed her by the shoulders again and shook her. 'How d'you think I felt when I arrived back at the factory ready to start my journey, and you were gone? The factory doors were wide open and our precious stock just sitting there ready for anyone to take.'

Evie's mouth dropped open. 'Oh! I forgot to lock up . . .'

'Yes. In your haste to go out for the day you put our whole project in jeopardy.' He gripped her tighter and shook her. 'Now I'm going out before I really lose my temper.' He turned and strode towards the back door.

'Edward, please . . .' she pleaded, but it was too late. Edward had left and slammed the door behind him.

She leaned against the sink and burst into tears.

Evie sat huddled in the armchair. The room was cold and she shivered. The clock above the fireplace showed the time to be two-thirty in the morning and her face was drawn and streaked with dried tears. She cradled a mug of lukewarm coffee and took a slow sip. Her heart leapt as she heard a key turn in the front door. She jumped up and ran to the hall where she found Edward and Geraldine. He was being propped up by his sister. A silly grin spread across his face as he looked at his wife with blurred gaze.

'This is yours, I believe,' Geraldine smiled. 'I found

him sitting on our front doorstep when I came home. He was so drunk he could hardly stand, so I poured gallons of black coffee down him and brought him back where he belongs.'

Evie's shoulders sagged as she looked at Edward. She walked over and took his arm.

'Thanks, Geraldine. I'm afraid we've had a little misunderstanding.'

'No need to explain to me, just be thankful Mother was in bed or you would have had the Spanish Inquisition on your hands.' She turned to Edward. ''Bye brother dear. And next time please don't make it on a night I've got a hot date.' Geraldine grimaced at Evie. 'My big brother frightened my date to death. He thought Edward was waiting to thump him for keeping me out late. I had a hell of a job convincing him otherwise.'

Evie frowned. 'Oh, I'm sorry, Geraldine.'

She laughed. 'It's all right. He's promised to telephone me tomorrow, and if he doesn't Edward here will be in the doghouse. Anyway, I'm off. The taxi will be running up a fortune.'

Edward put his hand in his pocket. 'Here, let me pay,' he slurred as he pulled out a ten shilling note and handed it to Geraldine who pushed his hand away.

'You keep your money, have this one on me.' She laughed as she winked at Evie and disappeared through the door.

Edward turned to Evie and wobbled dangerously as he placed his arms around her and pulled her closely to him.

'I'm sorry.'

'No, Edward, I'm sorry. I shouldn't have just gone off like that.'

'No. It's me that's at fault. You deserved a day out and I've neglected you lately. All I've thought about is that damned business.'

He started to hiccup and Evie laughed.

'Come on up to bed and I'll get you a glass of water.'

She placed her arm around his waist and they started to climb the stairs. Edward twice missed a step and fell flat on his face. Evie was glad when he finally gave up trying to walk and crawled the rest of the way instead. She went into the bathroom and poured him a glass of water. On entering the bedroom, she smiled at the sight that met her. Edward was slumped in the middle of the bed, fully dressed and snoring his head off. Evie carefully removed his clothes and covered him up. She collected some spare blankets from the airing cupboard and quickly made up the bed in her mother's old room.

She sighed deeply as she climbed into bed and pulled the bedclothes up around her ears.

'Oh, Evie, my head hurts!' Edward groaned the next morning as he looked in alarm at a plate of bacon and eggs she had placed before him. 'I don't think I can eat this,' he said, a feeling of nausea settling in his stomach.

'You'll eat it while you listen to what I have to say, Edward Bradshaw.'

He was not in the mood for another fight and slowly picked up his knife and fork and pierced his egg. He watched in silence as the yolk spilled its contents all over the plate, looked up at Evie and gave her a boyish grin.

'I've already said I'm sorry,' he said, 'and I'd better get a move on and deliver that order to Mains and Russell.'

She pulled out a chair at the table and sat down opposite her husband.

'Edward,' she said gravely, 'you have to listen to me. You can't deliver that order today. That's why I went to London.'

He looked at her in confusion, his knife and fork poised in mid air. 'What? I don't understand. Why can't I deliver the order?'

Evie sighed and took a deep breath. 'We had a letter yesterday from Mr Heard of Mains and Russell cancelling the order. I was so angry, I just upped and went to London and demanded to see him.' She paused for a moment. 'It appears my grandfather is accusing us of stealing his designs.'

'He's what?' Edward shouted, and grimaced as pain throbbed through his head. He lowered his voice. 'The old bastard accused us of what?'

'Calm down,' she tried to soothe him. 'Hopefully I've sorted it out. But we have to wait while Raymond Heard makes his investigations.'

'Like hell we'll wait!' Edward snapped as he stood up. 'I'll go and see that grandfather of yours . . .'

'No, Edward!' She jumped up and grabbed her husband's arm. 'We'll wait. It won't do for Jerod to know we're on to him. We have to let him think he's lost us that order.'

'I can't, Evie. I can't let our hard work go down the drain because of that callous old man.'

'It won't, Edward. Once Raymond Heard finds out we're telling the truth, he'll reinstate the order and we'll have got our own back on Jerod.'

'Yes, and what will he do next?' Edward said angrily. 'He won't stop, Evie, not until he's buried us good and proper. And all because we wouldn't run his damned

416

company for him.' He narrowed his eyes. 'It wouldn't surprise me if he was behind that fire we had.'

'You could be right. I never thought of that.' She paused, deep in thought. 'We still have to wait until Raymond Heard comes back to us. It'll be all right, Edward, you'll see. I don't want us to stoop to my grandfather's level. Raymond promised it would only take a day or so. Please, Edward. My grandfather will get his just deserts at the end of the day.'

'Will he, I wonder?'

'He will, believe me. Raymond Heard told me he wouldn't be buying any more of Dawson's garments, and you know that Dawson's rely heavily on that account. It's more than half of their business.'

Edward looked at her and nodded. 'Yes, you're right. But I'm so damned angry!'

'Yes, so am I, but please, just sit down and eat your breakfast. There's plenty we can do while we wait for news.'

His shoulders sagged. 'Okay, I'll play it your way. But if Heard hasn't contacted us by Thursday, I'll take matters into my own hands. I can play mean and dirty as well.'

Evie folded her arms and set her mouth grimly. 'No, you won't. I won't let my grandfather get the better of us, Edward. My mother went through too much and he never beat her. She rose above him and made a life for herself, and we'll do the same. We've done everything by the rules and we'll continue to do that. I won't play dirty. It doesn't pay in the long run.'

'I don't know about that, Evie. Your grandfather has done pretty well for himself.'

'Money-wise, yes, I agree.' Evie nodded. 'But what

else has he got? Nothing. He's a crippled, lonely old man, who spends his days plotting ways to make people miserable, just for his own ends. Think of the way he summoned me and demanded we run his business. It takes a man with no morals to do that, and you have morals, Edward. It's not in your nature to lie and cheat your way to the top. No, we'll get there by sheer hard work or not at all.'

He rested his elbows on the table. 'What a woman.' He looked at her lovingly. 'You're right. I could no more walk over someone for my own ends than you could. But,' he said firmly, 'neither could I sit by and let my family suffer at someone else's hands, grandfather or no grandfather.'

'No, I know you couldn't and that's what I love about you.' She got up from the table, walked around the back of his chair and put her arms round his neck. 'We'll see this through together. I know Raymond Heard is on our side and it won't take much checking to see we're honest and reliable.'

He turned and kissed her on the cheek. 'I'm sorry for last night. I shouldn't have jumped to conclusions.'

'That's all right. I was just as bad as you. I was so tired and worried that I just retaliated when I realised you thought I had been gallivanting for the day.'

'That temper of yours will land us both in trouble one day,' Edward laughed. 'Now, have you got any aspirins? My head feels as though a train is running through it.'

'Good!' Evie laughed. 'It's what you deserve, and I just hope that lad of Geraldine's telephones her or you'll really know what it is to suffer.'

He frowned forlornly as he put a piece of bacon into his mouth and began to chew.

* * *

Edward paced backwards and forwards across the office floor. He stopped abruptly and stared at Evie helplessly.

'I can't stand it any more. This waiting is driving me mad.'

She looked up from the accounts book and sighed. 'You'll have to be patient, Edward. Christ, it's only been two days! I feel just as bad as you. The only way I'm coping is by keeping myself busy.'

'Busy! God, woman, I've just about worn myself out keeping busy. The factory looks like a new pin. I've tidied the yard and painted the fence. There's nothing left to do.'

'Well, make a cup of tea then,' she snapped. She looked up and smiled gratefully as Jenny walked through the door.

'Any news yet?' she asked, trying to sound casual.

'Don't you start.' Evie frowned. 'I've enough with him asking me that every two minutes.'

'Sorry,' Jenny said apologetically as she sat down opposite Evie. She looked over at Edward. 'Well, if yer not busy yer could mash a cuppa.'

'I could!' Edward said dryly. 'It's about all I'm fit for at the moment.' He walked out of the door towards the small alcove they used as a makeshift kitchen.

Evie put down her pen and looked hard at her friend. 'What are you doing here at this time in the morning? Shouldn't you be at work?'

'I should, but I walked out,' Jenny said coldly. 'Honestly, Evie, the old bat of a supervisor 'ad a face like a sour lemon and a personality to match. I couldn't stand it any more so I left.' She folded her arms and leaned on the desk. 'I've made a decision,' she announced.

'Oh!' Evie looked at her with interest.

'I'm comin' to work for you permanently.'

'But we can't pay you and . . .' Evie sighed and lowered her voice . . . 'it doesn't look like we have got that order, does it?'

'Oh, Evie, it's not like you to let a little setback like this get yer down.'

'A little setback!' Evie repeated.

'Yes, 'cos that's all it is.' Jenny paused as Edward returned to the room carrying three mugs of tea. 'Look, Mains and Russell wouldn't 'ave given you that order if they 'adn't bin impressed wi' our work. And if they do decide not to reinstate it, well, there's plenty more firms about that will.'

Edward sighed. 'I wish I had your optimism, because at the moment losing that order seems like the end of the world.'

'Rubbish! Maybe Mains and Russell are the biggest retailers around, but not everyone shops there.' Jenny paused and looked at Edward. 'If you 'aven't 'eard from 'em by this time tomorrow, I think yer should get off yer arse and go and get some more bloody orders. In the meantime, I'm goin' to take up residency in this office and design some new clothes. I'm fed up wi' workin' for tinpot companies that pay me a pittance. I'd sooner work for you for nothin'.'

Evie let a slow smile spread across her face. 'She's right, Edward. We've let ourselves think that everything depends on Mains and Russell. Jerod Dawson can't have influence with everyone, can he?'

Edward grinned and spread his arms wide. 'Okay, girls. If there's no contact by this time tomorrow, I'll pack my case and head out.' He frowned thoughtfully. 'I think I'll go up north this time. Leeds and York have some fine stores . . .' He stopped as the loud ringing of the telephone echoed around the office.

All three looked at each other. Evie took a deep breath and picked up the receiver. Several minutes later, she replaced it and looked at Edward and Jenny who were staring intently at her.

'That was Mr Heard,' she said calmly. 'Edward, you have to deliver that order by no later than tomorrow lunchtime. Mr Heard is desperate to have the garments on the shelves as soon as possible.' She paused as she heard his intake of breath and slowly turned to Jenny. 'Mr Heard wants to see some more of your designs so that they can plan the winter collection.' She turned back to Edward. 'He's also very interested in several of the samples that you showed him, so you have to go and see him again. He's made an appointment for four o'clock tomorrow afternoon. That should give you plenty of time to deliver the order and get tidied up for your meeting. In the meantime, I'll place an advertisement for experienced workers in the *Leicester Mercury*.' She smiled. 'I think we're going to need them.'

Evie stopped her speech and sat back, watching their expressions as the good news began to sink in. She opened a drawer in her desk, pulled out a bottle of champagne that she had bought just in case, and placed it on the desk.

'I think this is in order.'

She laughed loudly as cheers of delight echoed round the room. Edward grabbed the bottle out of her hand and quickly popped the cork. He filled three fresh mugs and proposed a toast.

'To Grayshaw's,' he shouted excitedly.

'To Grayshaw's,' they all sang out in unison.

'And Raymond Heard,' Evie added.

'Raymond Heard,' Edward and Jenny repeated, clinking their mugs together.

Jenny drained hers and sat back in her chair. 'Well, Evie, I 'ope you're goin' to see that old bugger of a grandfather of yours and tell 'im what's what?'

Evie shook her head. 'No. He'll find out soon enough that he's lost. I don't think rubbing salt into his wounds will solve anything, do you?' She looked at Edward and waited for his response.

He looked at her with a wicked gleam in his eye. 'I'd love to rub salt into his wounds. But you're right, Evie. It wouldn't solve anything.' He rubbed his hands together. 'I think this calls for a celebration. I'll take the lot of you out for a slap-up meal at the Grand Hotel.'

'Wow!' Jenny screamed in delight. 'The Grand Hotel, I ain't never bin there.'

'Hang on, Edward. We can't afford it.'

'To hell with the expense, Evie.' He paused and nodded his head towards the desk. 'Am I right in thinking that's a bottle of champagne? If that's not extravagance . . .'

Evie looked at him sheepishly and grinned.

'You just telephone my mother, Geraldine and Mavis. I'll make the reservation for eight o'clock.'

'Excuse me,' Jenny said quietly. 'Would this be a good time to discuss me wages?'

Evie looked at her seriously. 'But you said you'd be prepared to work for us for nothing!'

'Oh, you tease!' Jenny laughed as she watched Evie's face crease into a smile.

'Jenny, we'll pay you the best wages we can afford, and you'll get a share of our profits,' Edward said warmly.

Her mouth fell open. 'D'you mean it?'

Evie reached across the desk and placed her hand on her friend's arm. 'We mean it, Jenny. Edward and I have already discussed the matter, and the same goes for Mavis.'

'Wow!' Jenny said for the second time that morning. She jumped up out of her chair. 'I'm off 'ome to get ready.'

Evie looked at her watch. 'But it's only eleven-thirty.'

Jenny looked sheepishly at Evie. 'I'm goin' to buy meself a new dress. I feel like splashin' out.'

'Buy a dress?' Edward piped up. 'You've enough time to make one, for you and Evie!'

Once again the room echoed to the sound of laughter and before Jenny finally managed to get away, Edward insisted they finish the bottle of champagne.

Chapter Eighteen

Evie slammed the large red book shut, leaned back in her seat and stared up at the ceiling. Thank goodness that's finished, she thought with relief. She detested doing the accounts, but on Edward's insistence kept them up to date, even if she did have to steel herself for days before she attempted them. Still, the job was done for another month and she could get back to what she enjoyed doing most – helping him with the day to day running of the factory.

A tiny money spider spun a long silver thread and landed on her hand. She smiled at it before she blew softly, sending the spider on its journey. A good omen. Yes, definitely a good omen. Not that they needed it at the moment. Since Raymond Heard had given his approval to their order, word had spread and the work had flooded in. The small factory on the Tudor Road had soon been outgrown and new and bigger premises had been sought.

Had they really been here nine months? Time had flown by. Evie laughed to herself as she remembered the arguments she and Edward had had as they had scoured the town and outskirts in search of the right place to house their flourishing business. Many painful inspections found them just the place on the new industrial site off the Blackbird

Road, two miles out of town. It was perfect for their needs and they had moved in full of enthusiasm, ready to service the ever growing demand for their exclusive garments.

Edward had just returned from a three-day sales trip, and by the size of the orders he had secured it seemed very much like they would have to add to their five hundred workforce. Not that getting labour was a problem. They had files full of names of people desperate to join their company and enjoy the good conditions and above average wages.

She heard the telephone ring in Edward's office which adjoined hers and hoped it was not another customer wanting to place an order. It was so good to have Edward home. Three nights in a lonely bed without him was almost more than she could bear. She would have to talk to him about employing a sales manager. Time spent together was getting very limited and if business carried on the way it was, then they would see even less of each other. And that wouldn't do, not with the news she had to tell him.

A temporary feeling of sadness enveloped her as she thought of her mother and wished with all her heart that she was still here to share in their success. And, she thought with a little selfishness, because she missed and needed her. Evie had learned, in moments like these, quickly to switch her thoughts, and this she did to Jenny and Mavis.

What wonderful friends she had! Not only had they both seen her through the dark days that followed her mother's and Edward's father's deaths, but they were both doing more than their fair share to see that the business thrived.

Mavis, to the complete amazement of all who knew her, was employed as the canteen supervisor. She had a natural talent for cooking and was enjoying every minute of her day, sifting through recipes and preparing them in the large purpose-built kitchen. The workers gladly handed over their hard-earned coppers in exchange for one of her delicious creations.

Evie smiled broadly. What was she going to do about Jenny? She seemed totally unaffected by the transition into the glamorous world of fashion. Her talent as a designer was renowned throughout the trade. Had she not been approached on several occasions with tempting offers to leave Grayshaw's and work for much larger and more established companies? On those occasions Jenny's language had been choice and to the point. Grayshaw's was where she worked and that's where she would stay.

She still spent every penny she earned. She promised to save but by the end of the week was desperate for her generous remuneration. She still lived at home, giving her mother a large slice of her wages for her board, and the rest went on . . . what did she spend it on? Evie shrugged her shoulders. Edward's idea of opening a bank account in Jenny's name and putting money aside for her was a good one. Jenny would never know about it until the right time. If something wasn't done, the girl would have nothing for her old age, as it still didn't look as if she had any intention of settling down.

Evie gave a sigh of contentment and clasped her hands together. Life was grand. Hard work, exasperating, fun . . . but oh so grand. And Edward, her Edward, was everything she had hoped and dreamed of. They worked together, discussed problems, fought ferociously until they completely forgot what the argument was about, then made up with a fierce passion that only two people so obviously suited could experience. With his help, she was fulfilling her aims, making her mark on the world, and the results far exceeded those she had ever hoped for.

A noise outside her door jolted her out of her thoughts and her face lit up in delight as Edward came in. She stared at him for a moment as he stood with his back against the door and quickly became worried by his grave expression.

'What's the matter?' she asked.

He moved towards her and placed his arm around her shoulders.

'I've just had some news, my love.'

'Oh? It's obviously not good news by the look on your face.'

He sighed. 'No, it's not. It's your grandfather, Evie. He had a heart attack last night and has died.' He felt her stiffen and looked at her with concern.

'Oh,' she muttered as she placed her hand over her mouth. 'Well, I hope he's at peace.' She looked up at Edward blankly. 'I'm sorry, I feel nothing. Does that sound awful?'

'No. Not really. I'd have been surprised if you had after what he did to us and your mother.'

Evie smiled wanly, raised herself from her chair and walked towards the window, staring out over the yard. She watched a lorry backing into the loading bay and ran her hand over her forehead.

'What d'you think will happen to Dawson's?'

Edward grimaced. 'I suppose it will either be shut down or sold. What's left of it, that is. When Mains and Russell withdrew their account, others followed suit and the firm is practically bankrupt. From what I gather, your grandfather ploughed in his own money to keep it going and to save face. But it's well known that nearly all the orders dried up practically overnight. I heard that the old man was virtually penniless.'

'D'you think that's what caused his heart attack?'

'More than likely. Your grandfather was no longer a force to be reckoned with, and he knew it.'

Evie walked over to the desk and sat down. She sighed loudly. 'Oh, Edward, I feel it's the end of an era. Dawson's has been in this town for over a hundred years and there's many people who will be sorry to see it go.'

'And you? Will you be sorry?' he asked.

'No, I won't. I feel a weight has been lifted from my shoulders. I feel that my mother can finally rest.' She shuddered. 'I always felt he was behind us, waiting to pounce. Maybe now I can relax and put the past firmly behind me.' She paused thoughtfully. 'I wonder what will happen to Miss Sargent and Mr Stimpson?'

Edward tilted his head to one side. 'Are you really concerned about them, after the way they both treated you?'

Evie took a deep breath. 'Yes. Funnily enough, I am.'

'I suppose they'll get other jobs. We could always ask them to come and work here.'

'No. I don't think so somehow. I don't see them fitting in, do you?'

He shook his head in agreement.

'But there is one person who would.'

'Who?' Edward asked.

'Pearl Fanshaw. I'd like to ask her to come and work

for us. Funnily enough, I've been thinking about it for a while and this clinches it. She could come and take care of both Grayshaw's and the wool shops' accounts plus help me out with other things in the office.'

Edward nodded and smiled. 'Okay. I know how much you hate doing the accounts. Sound her out and see what she says.'

'I will. Thanks, Edward.'

'I've some other news, Evie,' he said.

'Oh, what? Not more bad news. Not today,' she groaned.

'Well, I don't think it's that bad.' He smiled warmly. 'I've had a call from the Lord Mayor's office. They want us to be present at the luncheon they're giving in honour of Princess Margaret's visit to Leicester in July, and there's a possibility that we might be presented to her.'

'Oh, Edward! That's wonderful news,' she breathed.

'Yes, it is. Only we have to keep it under our hats for the time being.'

'What will I wear? Edward, I've nothing that's fit for a princess to see me in!'

He laughed loudly. 'Good God, woman! You have the best designer in the business working for you and you're worried about a little thing like that.'

She grinned. 'Well, I want to look nice.'

'You always look nice.'

'Thank you, kind sir.' She looked at her husband. 'Come on, we've a business to run. There's five hundred workers all relying on us now.'

Edward grinned at her. 'I've got to go outside and supervise the fixing of the new sign. Will you join me?'

'In a minute. There's something I want to tell you, but I have to check on Jenny's latest design first. One of the girls is making the sample up and apparently the neckline is a bit of a devil to sew.'

After Evie had checked on the sample, she walked down the long line of machinists, stopping here and there to chat to a worker or to examine a garment. She knew all her employees by name and took a great deal of trouble to listen to their problems and take an interest in their lives. As she walked to the end of the line she turned and looked back down the long room. Row upon row of machines were working away, 'Workers' Playtime' was blasting out over the tannoy, and Evie watched as the women and men went happily about their work.

She turned and headed for the canteen where she found Mavis covered in flour, beating away at a peculiar-looking mixture in a large metal bowl. She beamed as she spotted Evie and put down the bowl.

'Just the woman I wanted to see. What d'you think of this?' she said, placing a rough sketch of the canteen in front of Evie. 'With a few alterations, it could work,' she said enthusiastically.

Evie studied the piece of paper and smiled. 'I like it, Mavis. A snack bar is a great idea. What d'you propose to sell?'

'Well, I thought I could make cakes, different ones every day, and we could sell chocolate, crisps and an assortment of filled cobs. It would stop the workers having to send out their long lists to the shops every morning.'

Evie nodded. 'Yes, it would. I've always felt sorry for the poor young 'uns. They have to traipse round to the cob shop in all weathers and invariably get the order wrong. Yes, it's a grand idea. I'll talk it over with Edward.' She paused and smiled. 'Half the profits could be placed in a separate fund to be put towards the annual outing.'

'Oh, Evie. That would be great. What a nice gesture.'

She smiled. 'Well, don't say anything yet, not until I get Edward's approval as well.' She made to walk away, then stopped and turned back to Mavis. 'By the way, how are the wedding plans coming along?'

'Oh, don't mention it, Evie. Phil is adamant he wants us to get married in church and has even found a vicar willing to marry us, and to top it all he insists on having our Rosie as bridesmaid.' She pursed her lips. 'The child can't stand still for five minutes, let alone while we take our vows. I've a good mind to call the whole thing off.'

'That's the last thing you'll do, Mavis Humphreys, you can't wait to marry Phil. Anyway, you're not going to do me and Edward out of a good do, we're both looking forward to it. And I shouldn't tell you this but . . .' she bent her head over and whispered in Mavis's ear, 'Jenny's new boyfriend is Scottish and she's managed to persuade him to wear his kilt.' She watched as Mavis's eyes opened wide in astonishment. 'Jenny told me she wants to find out what they wear underneath.'

Evie left Mavis rocking with laughter as she made her way towards the offices.

She found Jenny sitting on the floor amid a pile of fabrics and patterns. Jenny raised her head as her friend entered.

'Your new design is coming along fine,' Evie smiled. 'Only I think the sample would be better in that new blue crepe that you picked up in London on your last trip. I think it would let the collar sit better. Why don't you pop down and see what you think? I gave the sample to Pauline.'

'Yeah, I think yer could be right,' said Jenny. 'Tell yer

what, I'll 'ave both materials made up, then we can judge which is the better one.'

'Great. See you at lunch.' Evie raised her eyebrows. 'I've an appointment with Edward. He's supervising the putting up of the new sign.'

Jenny grinned. 'I'll have to skip lunch, I've an appointment with a sales rep, and 'e's rather dishy . . .'

Evie smiled and shook her head as she left the office and closed the door.

She walked across the road and joined her husband. It was a warm sunny day and Evie shielded her eyes as she looked across at the workmen putting the finishing touches to their new sign. Edward placed his arm around her shoulders and sighed happily.

'Well, what d'you think?' he asked. 'At long last, after months of humming and ha-ing on your part, the sign's ready.'

'Mm,' Evie muttered. 'It's fine. Only . . .'

'Only what?' He turned and looked at her sharply.

'Well . . . it's not quite right,' she said casually.

'Not quite right!' he repeated. 'Evie Bradshaw, you take months to choose the design and wording. Now you're saying it's not quite right?'

'Well, it's not,' she said sharply. 'And it will have to be changed.'

'Oh, God!' Edward groaned. 'I give up with you, woman. You decided that a plain and simple GRAYSHAW was what you wanted and I agreed.' He turned and faced her, his voice exasperated. 'Just what is it you want to add now?'

'Well,' she said slowly, tilting her head to one side, 'GRAYSHAW AND SON would be nice. Or GRAYSHAW

AND DAUGHTER.' She let a slow smile spread over her face as Edward's brain ticked over.

'You're not! Evie, you're not, are you?'

She nodded slowly. 'I am,' she said proudly. 'The doctor confirmed it this morning.'

He picked her up and swung her round, then put her down slowly and eyed her wonderingly. 'Oh, my God, Evie, I'm going to be a father! I can't believe it.'

'Well, you better had, and it won't be the last. I want a whole load of little overlockers to look after us in our old age.' She grinned broadly. 'Well, maybe not. Maybe we should see how we get on with this one first.'

Edward laughed as he took her in his arms and hugged her tightly. Their lips met and they kissed long and passionately.

'I love you, Mrs Bradshaw,' he said huskily.

'And, I love you, Mr Bradshaw,' she answered sincerely.

Evie looked across the road and her face reddened. 'The workmen are watching us.'

'Let them.' Edward turned towards the men and shouted, 'Hey, my wife's having a baby. I'm going to be a father.' He smiled broadly and gave a little skip as the workmen gave a loud cheer. He turned back to his embarrassed wife. 'Do Jenny and Mavis know about this yet?'

She shook her head.

'Right, come on. Let's go and break the news. Then I'll telephone my mother and we'll book you into the maternity home. And we need to buy some baby clothes and . . . oh, d'you think the house is big enough? And what about a Nanny or an au pair?' Edward's eyes twinkled. 'I've always fancied an au pair . . .'

'Edward!'

'Sorry.' He grinned as he grabbed hold of her hand and they raced together across the road and into their future.

POLLY OF PENN'S PLACE

Dee Williams

Polly Perkins and her older brother Sid have never really liked each other and when, in a fit of spite, he flicks a fishbone at her and accidentally blinds her in one eye, it seems to Polly that he has blighted her entire future. But life carries on in 1930s Rotherhithe and Polly, like the other tenants of Penn's Place, is soon caught up in its daily struggles: battling to keep treasured possessions from being sold at the pawn shop, to hold her own in the rows which rage through her warring family, and to find herself a job. In the latter she succeeds and, having started as a tea girl at Blooms Fashions, to her delight is offered a job in the office. There her friendship with the prosperous Bloom family grows, in particular with Sarah and her handsome brother David, whose lifestyle in Putney is so different from her own.

Meanwhile in Rotherhithe Polly finds herself being courted ever more insistently by Ron, Sid's best friend and, Polly sometimes suspects, his partner in crime. When in frustration he points out that, disfigured by her accident, Polly is lucky to get any suitors at all, she decides, reluctantly, to accept his proposal of marriage. But, as the country finds itself in the grip of war, it becomes clear that Sid – and her husband Ron – have jeopardized Polly's future once more.

FICTION / SAGA 0 7472 3845 6

More Enchanting Fiction from Headline

PEGGIE

ONE WOMAN'S STRUGGLE TO
FULFIL HER DREAMS

Lynda Page

An unexpected windfall gives Peggie Cartwright the
lucky break she deserves. At last she can save her
family from financial ruin. Ever since Cyrus Crabbe
stole her father Septimus's brake and claimed it as his
own vehicle, Sep has dreamed of the day when he
would run a bus service for the villagers of
Leicestershire to put the Crabbes out of business once
and for all. It now looks as if that day is in sight.

But Cyrus Crabbe is a dangerous man, determined to
stop the Cartwrights from succeeding. A wicked
remark from his acid tongue forces Septimus to
abandon his beloved brood, and as Sep's absence
stretches from weeks to months, Peggie watches her
mother sink into a deep decline. Peggie's brothers and
sisters are used to heartache but when Billy is beaten
black and blue and Cyrus's son Reginald turns his
attentions to young Letty it seems that none of the
family is to be spared . . .

Peggie knows it is up to her to keep the business afloat
and spirits raised. For no matter what obstacles are
thrown her way she is determined to fulfil her father's
dream.

FICTION / SAGA 0 7472 4798 6

JOSIE

Lynda Page

Josie Rawlings is a saint!

Well, she *must* be to care for her cantankerous old grandmother and tolerate her conceited cousin Marilyn, who attracts all the boys, having fun when she should be helping Josie run their vegetable stall in Leicester's market square. And when Marilyn's ex-sweetheart Stephen – whom Josie has secretly worshipped since childhood – drunkenly finds comfort in Josie's arms, it seems that her goodwill has been stretched to the limit. Surely, one day her virtues will be rewarded?

Things don't look too bright, though, when Josie's inheritance is stolen and her grandmother's death brings eviction from the only home she has ever known. Determined to rise above these bitter blows, Josie struggles to support herself, and, desperate for affection, stumbles into an ill-fated love affair.

But there are those who *do* recognise Josie's worth; genuine friends who rally round and see her on the road to success. And, although she is unaware of it, one man, in particular, is keeping a close eye on her progress . . .

FICTION / SAGA 0 7472 4511 8

BORN TO SERVE

Josephine Cox

'*I can take him away from you any time I want.*'

Her mistress's cruel taunt is deeply disturbing to Jenny. But why should Claudia be interested in a servant's sweetheart? All the same, Jenny reckons without Claudia's vicious nature; using a wily trick, she eventually seduces Frank, who, overcome with shame, leaves the household for a new life in Blackburn.

Losing her sweetheart is just the first of many disasters that leave Jenny struggling to cope alone. When Claudia gives birth to a baby girl – Frank's child – she cruelly disowns the helpless infant and relies on Jenny to care for little Katie and love her as her own.

Despite luring a kindly man into a marriage that offers comfort and security to them all, Claudia secretly indulges her corrupt desires.

Always afraid for the beloved child who has come to depend on her, Jenny is constantly called upon to show courage and fortitude to fight for all she holds dear. In her heart she yearns for Frank, believing that one day they must be reunited. When Fate takes a hand, it seems as though Jenny may see her dreams come true.

'Driven and passionate, she stirs a pot spiced with incest, wife beating . . . and murder' *The Sunday Times*

'Pulls at the heartstrings' *Today*

'Not to be missed' *Bolton Evening News*

FICTION / SAGA 0 7472 4415 4

Now you can buy any of these other bestselling books from your bookshop or *direct from the publisher*.

FREE P&P AND UK DELIVERY
(Overseas and Ireland £3.50 per book)

My Sister's Child	Lyn Andrews	£5.99
Liverpool Lies	Anne Baker	£5.99
The Whispering Years	Harry Bowling	£5.99
Ragamuffin Angel	Rita Bradshaw	£5.99
The Stationmaster's Daughter	Maggie Craig	£5.99
Our Kid	Billy Hopkins	£6.99
Dream a Little Dream	Joan Jonker	£5.99
For Love and Glory	Janet MacLeod Trotter	£5.99
In for a Penny	Lynda Page	£5.99
Goodnight Amy	Victor Pemberton	£5.99
My Dark-Eyed Girl	Wendy Robertson	£5.99
For the Love of a Soldier	June Tate	£5.99
Sorrows and Smiles	Dee Williams	£5.99

TO ORDER SIMPLY CALL THIS NUMBER

01235 400 414

or e-mail <u>orders@bookpoint.co.uk</u>

Prices and availability subject to change without notice.